Bedford (

REBECCA HARDING

Life in the Iron-Mills

EDITED BY

Cecelia Tichi

Vanderbilt University

BEDFORD/ST. MARTIN'S   BOSTON ♦ NEW YORK

For Bedford/St. Martin's

President and Publisher: Charles H. Christensen
General Manager and Associate Publisher: Joan E. Feinberg
Managing Editor: Elizabeth M. Schaaf
Developmental Editor: Katherine A. Retan
Editorial Assistants: Joanne Diaz and Aron Keesbury
Production Editor: Maureen Murray
Production Assistant: Deborah Baker
Copyeditor: Carolyn Ingalls
Cover Design: Terry Govan
Cover Art: Detail from *The Manufacture of Iron, Harper's Weekly,* November 1, 1873.
Composition: Pine Tree Composition, Inc.
Printing and Binding: Haddon Craftsmen, Inc.

Library of Congress Catalog Card Number: 96–86795

Manufactured in the United States of America.

2
f   e   d

For information, write: Bedford/St. Martin's, 75 Arlington Street, Boston, MA 02116 (617–399–4000)

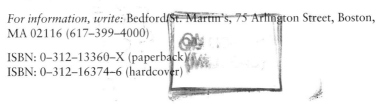

ISBN: 0–312–13360–X (paperback)
ISBN: 0–312–16374–6 (hardcover)

Published and distributed outside North America by:
MACMILLAN PRESS, LTD.
Houndmills, Basingstoke, Hampshire RG21 2XS and London
Companies and representatives throughout the world.
ISBN: 0–333–69093–1

Acknowledgments

About the Series

The need to "historicize" literary texts — and even more to analyze the historical and cultural issues all texts embody — is now embraced by almost all teachers, scholars, critics, and theoreticians. But the question of how to teach such issues in the undergraduate classroom is still a difficult one. Teachers do not always have the historical information they need for a given text, and contextual documents and sources are not always readily available in the library — even if the teacher has the expertise (and students have the energy) to ferret them out. The Bedford Cultural Editions represent an effort to make available for the classroom the kinds of facts and documents that will enable teachers to use the latest historical approaches to textual analysis and cultural criticism. The best scholarly and theoretical work has for many years gone well beyond the "new critical" practices of formalist analysis and close reading, and we offer here a practical classroom model of the ways that many different kinds of issues can be engaged when texts are not thought of as islands unto themselves.

The impetus for the recent cultural and historical emphasis has come from many directions: the so-called new historicism of the late 1980s, the dominant historical versions of both feminism and Marxism, the cultural studies movement, and a sharply changed focus in older movements such as reader response, structuralism, deconstruction, and psychoanalytic theory. Emphases differ, of course, among schools and individuals, but what these movements and approaches have in common is a commitment to explore — and to have students in the classroom study interactively — texts in their full historical and cultural dimensions. The aim is to discover how older texts (and those from other traditions) differ from our own assumptions and expectations, and thus the focus in teaching falls on cultural and historical difference rather than on similarity or continuity.

The most striking feature of the Bedford Cultural Editions — and the one most likely to promote creative classroom discussion — is the inclusion of a generous selection of historical documents that contextualize the main text in a variety of ways. Each volume contains works (or passages from works) that are contemporary with the main text: legal and social documents, journalistic and autobiographical accounts, histories, sections from conduct books, travel books, poems, novels, and other historical sources. These materials have several uses. Often they provide information beyond what the main text offers. They provide, too, different perspectives on a particular theme, issue, or event central to the text, suggesting the range of opinions contemporary readers would have brought to their reading and allowing students to experience for themselves the details of cultural disagreement and debate. The documents are organized in thematic units — each with an introduction by the volume editor that historicizes a particular issue and suggests the ways in which individual selections work to contextualize the main text.

Each volume also contains a general introduction that provides students with information concerning the political, social, and intellectual context for the work as well as information concerning the material aspects of the text's creation, production, and distribution. There are also relevant illustrations, a chronology of important events, and, when helpful, an account of the reception history of the text. Finally, both the main work and its accompanying documents are carefully annotated in order to enable students to grasp the significance of historical references, literary allusions, and unfamiliar terms. Everywhere we have tried to keep the special needs of the modern student — especially the culturally conscious student of the turn of the millennium — in mind.

For each title, the volume editor has chosen the best teaching text of the main work and explained his or her choice. Old spellings and capitalizations have been preserved (except that the long "s" has been regularized to the modern "s") — the overwhelming preference of the two hundred teacher-scholars we surveyed in preparing the series.

Original habits of punctuation have also been kept, except for occasional places where the unusual usage would obscure the syntax for modern readers. Whenever possible, the supplementary texts and documents are reprinted from the first edition or the one most relevant to the issue at hand. We have thus meant to preserve — rather than counter — for modern students the sense of "strangeness" in older texts, expecting that the oddness will help students to see where older texts are *not* like modern ones, and expecting too that today's historically informed teachers will find their own creative ways to make something of such historical and cultural differences.

In developing this series, our goal has been to foreground the kinds of issues that typically engage teachers and students of literature and history now. We have not tried to move readers toward a particular ideological, political, or social position or to be exhaustive in our choice of contextual materials. Rather, our aim has been to be provocative — to enable teachers and students of literature to raise the most pressing political, economic, social, religious, intellectual, and artistic issues on a larger field than any single text can offer.

J. Paul Hunter, University of Chicago
William E. Cain, Wellesley College
Series Editors

About This Volume

Life in the Iron-Mills entered the canon of American literature in the later twentieth century as a direct result of the 1960s' women's movement in the United States. In particular, Rebecca Harding Davis's novella came to light through the efforts of the Feminist Press and Tillie Olsen, who rescued the text from decades of oblivion with their 1972 edition. In her introduction to the Feminist Press edition, Olsen provides a wide-ranging biographical profile of Davis, inviting readers to grasp the extent to which the fictional Hugh Wolfe and his sculpture of the korl woman can be seen as representations of the suppressed and thwarted nineteenth-century woman writer desperately trying to speak publicly through her art. Olsen draws on many of Davis's novels and stories to construct a moving psychological portrait of the author. An entire generation of readers, including this editor, have read and taught *Life in the Iron-Mills* as presented through Olsen's sympathetic and subtle interpretation.

This cultural edition of *Life in the Iron-Mills* moves outward from the reading of the novella as a parable of the difficult life of a woman writer to include a variety of historical and cultural documents that open up the text to the consideration of a range of social and cultural issues vital to Rebecca Harding Davis's nineteenth century. At a time when such scholarly areas as new historicism and cultural studies have refocused literary study, making race, class, and gender central concerns of classroom work, it is appropriate that *Life in the*

Iron-Mills should be made available in a format that enables the consideration of these matters. The documents included in this edition are intended to encourage students to read Davis's text in relation to nineteenth-century American discussions of work and social class, moral and social reform, the conditions of women writers, and the development of American art. It is my hope that this edition of *Life in the Iron-Mills* will widen the parameters of the discussion that has been so vigorously conducted in classrooms, in scholarship, and in professional meetings over the past quarter of a century.

ACKNOWLEDGMENTS

Everyone involved in this project has been extraordinarily helpful. I am very thankful to Chuck Christensen and Joan Feinberg of Bedford Books for suggesting this project and encouraging my interest in it. Kathy Retan has been a first-rate editor all along — encouraging, tactful, careful, scrupulous. Maureen Murray expertly guided the book through production, and Aron Keesbury and Joanne Diaz assisted with numerous details. In addition, I appreciate the focused and imaginative attention I have received from an excellent group of scholarly advisors, including Dale Bauer, Nancy Bentley, John Kasson, Joy Kasson, William Vance, and Bill Cain, who is the series editor for American titles in the Bedford Cultural Editions series. These advisors made invaluable suggestions for the documents included in Part Two of this edition and guided revisions of the introductory material. Their collective knowledge has gone very far to shape this project.

Colleagues and staff at Vanderbilt University have been most generous. Nancy Walker suggested texts and from the outset encouraged this project in a most positive light. Peggy Earhart, the librarian at the University Library Annex, arranged for me to work there for several weeks in the summer of 1995, and Jamie Adams, a staff photographer for Vanderbilt's Learning Resource Center, responded with good cheer to my request to photograph numerous images.

Two graduate students in the doctoral program of the Department of English at Vanderbilt University have contributed tremendously to my work on this edition. It has moved along on schedule largely because of Rory Dicker, who helped with research and made crucial textual suggestions for the section on women writers. This project has also benefited from my numerous discussions with Rory of

Davis's work. In addition, Alison Piepmeier has worked tirelessly on the tasks of annotation and research, as well as handling textual permissions. The annotations and bibliography include a depth of information on nineteenth-century sources that is attributable to her efforts. It has been a pleasure to work with such competent young scholars-in-training, who instill confidence about the future of the profession.

Finally, I am grateful for the many informal conversations I have had over the years with Amy Schrager Lang. Those talks both frame and inform this project in its entirety. Any shortcomings herein are solely my responsibility.

Cecelia Tichi
Vanderbilt University

Contents

2. Social Reform and the Promise of the Dawn   203

3. Art and Artists 293

4. Women and Writing: The Public Platform 357

Part One

Life in the Iron-Mills
The Complete Text

Introduction:
Cultural and
Historical Background

In December 1860, Miss Rebecca Harding of the western Virginia city of Wheeling summoned the courage to submit the manuscript of her new story to the editor of *The Atlantic Monthly*, the prestigious Boston-based magazine of "Literature, Art, and Politics." The submission was at once sensible and bold. Miss Harding was a self-styled backwoods author audaciously bidding for publication in the nation's center of literary prestige, and yet her decision was sensible because of the *Atlantic*'s reputation for publishing fiction by women and its recent trend toward the new mode of fictional realism.

Life in the Iron-Mills — the tale of an artistic but chronically ill young immigrant iron worker, Hugh Wolfe, and his female cousin, both toiling in poverty in a hilly inland industrial river city bearing marked resemblance to the author's own Wheeling — certainly fit the category of realism. In addition, Harding's narrative developed themes of unrequited love and the aesthetic price of thwarted artistic talent in a new nation whose well-educated affluent class was eager to encourage the development of the arts. The author's bleak narrative worldview was relieved only in part by a concluding message of spiritual hopefulness — "the promise of the dawn" — which was doubtless somewhat reassuring to readers of sentimental fiction.

Mainly, however, *Life in the Iron-Mills* was meant to jolt its middle-class readers into a head-on recognition of the wretched conditions of immigrant laborers, who worked in obscurity to produce the plentiful textiles and iron products that made comfortable middle-class living conditions possible. Harding's novella diverged from such positions as those of the nineteenth-century American travel writer Willard Glazier, who glorified the iron-mill city in terms of Greek mythology ("This is the domain of Vulcan"), and of the West Virginia promotional writers who boasted of Wheeling's large iron industry that was made possible by cheap fuel and rail or water access to markets (see Part Two, Chapter 1). Instead, Harding sought to make her readers aware that their material comfort was enabled neither by palliative classical gods nor by cheap coal and river barges but by real human beings, who ate, slept, and toiled in unspeakable conditions.

REBECCA HARDING DAVIS IN CONTEXT

In some ways it seems odd that Rebecca Harding, herself a daughter of gentility and comfort, would write a novella such as *Life in the Iron-Mills* some ten years before her fellow American realist writers represented the lives of those laboring at a subsistence level in American industrial and agricultural production. In contrast, the British author Charles Dickens seems autobiographically compatible with his industrial novel *Hard Times* (1854) because he worked for a time in a blacking factory, while members of his family served time in debtors' prison.

Rebecca Harding Davis was, by her own description, born into an "easy-going generation" (*Bits* 6) of children treated to taffy and cakes, to outdoor fantasy in which garden hillocks became glacial Alps, and to visits to houses with family portraits on the walls, silver flatware on the table, and winter warmth from ample coal fires like those burning in her own family's parlor grates. There were also a few slaves in some households in this Mason-Dixon border town, possibly in her own. In her memoir, *Bits of Gossip* (1904), Davis notes the presence of slaves as if they existed only at the edge of her vision — which may be why, in *Life in the Iron-Mills*, she recognized and yet removed slaves by providing a mere passing glimpse of a mulatto and by turning a key term of slavery into one of geography in her image of a "negro-like river slavishly bearing its burden day after day." Late in life, she recalled the slaves of Wheeling as having been "too comfortable and satisfied to run away" (*Bits* 170); moreover, she recorded contempt for the firebrand abolitionists heedlessly ready to plunge the nation into a war to be conducted on the Southern soil where her family and friends lived. She later came to explore the plight of the newly freed African Americans in the ambitious novel *Waiting for the Verdict* (1868).

Given Davis's security in the upper echelon of her society, it is all the more remarkable that on the eve of the Civil War, she produced her closely observed novella on the virtual enslavement of one class by another in the United States, a novella that blames her own class for destructive hypocrisy and charts the faultlines of social divisions that are certain to stunt or ruin those at the bottom.

Born Rebecca Blaine Harding in 1831 in Washington, Pennsylvania, Davis was the eldest of five children. Her mother, Rachel Leet Wilson, was a genteel western Pennsylvanian whose father had served at Valley Forge and whose mother had danced with Lafayette and gossiped firsthand about George and Martha Washington. Davis's father, Richard Harding, was an Englishman who had immigrated to the United States to make his fortune in what is now Huntsville, Alabama, where the family lived for the first five years of Rebecca's life, moving to Wheeling in 1836. Until age fourteen, Rebecca, along with her brothers and sisters, was schooled at home by tutors and by her mother, whom she dubbed "our good Angel" and "the most accurate historian and grammarian I have ever known." Davis remembered her businessman father, a onetime Wheeling city treasurer, as "a man of stern integrity" and an avid reader of Shakespeare. From this home, Rebecca went forth in her fifteenth year to attend the Washington Female Seminary in Pennsylvania, where she studied French, English literature, philosophy, geometry, music, drawing, and religion, and where she heard Oliver Wendell Holmes, a laureate of the day, give a reading of his poetry. In addition, she attended abolitionist lectures given by the New York newspaper editor Horace Greeley and by Francis LeMoyne.

Rebecca graduated from the seminary as class valedictorian in June 1848, a momentous year of revolution throughout continental Europe and a momentous year for U. S. women's history. In the summer following Davis's graduation, leading American feminists met in Seneca Falls, New York, to draft a document calling for the implementation of constitutional rights for women. The new graduate of the Washington Female Seminary, however, took no part in this feminist movement and probably knew nothing of it at the time. After graduation, she returned to Wheeling to the family hearth, as was customary for unmarried, educated young ladies of upper middle-class families. She remained at home for the next twelve years. In "Song of Myself," the poet Walt Whitman offered a mid-nineteenth-century profile of such a maiden lady at the age of twenty-eight, sequestered behind the household window blinds, yearning in vain for a life of personal freedom foreclosed to her by the norms of respectability. Though there is no direct evidence that Davis fit Whitman's representation, her comments on "thwarted, wasted lives" and "unawakened power" may refer to women like herself as well as to the Hugh Wolfes of the world. A half-century after the publication of *Life in the Iron-Mills,* Jane Addams, in *Democracy and Education,* called for families like the Hardings to encourage their educated, energetic daughters to seek careers in a wider world that desperately needed their talents rather than keeping them at home as ornaments.

The family fellowship, however, was evidently Rebecca's de facto fellowship in creative writing over the next dozen years. She not only helped her parents and siblings with household management but also read avidly and began to write regularly, sometimes from whim, sometimes from inner necessity. The growing city of Wheeling fostered a certain intellectual activity. Although it was not Boston or Philadelphia, its proximity to Pittsburgh and its accessibility by rail brought leading writers and lecturers through on Lyceum tours. In her memoir, Davis recalls hearing and meeting the abolitionist Frances Harper, the poet-critic James Russell Lowell, and the poet John Greenleaf Whittier.

This author-to-be did not confine herself to the library, drawing room, church, and lecture hall. As a close observer of society, Davis gained much from the long outdoor walks that she later, in *Bits of Gossip,* termed "vagabond tramps." A young lady might be expected to exercise her limbs and refresh her mind with rural walks or rambles, but the apprentice writer gained tremendously from her pedestrian excursions in industrial Wheeling — a world from which her upbringing was largely designed to insulate her. Davis encountered firsthand what the late-nineteenth-century documentary photographer Jacob Riis called "how the other half lives": a world of industrial capitalism that was foreseen even in the 1830s by Alexis de Tocqueville to be degrading to the worker who toiled day after day in repetitive tasks (see Part Two, Chapter 1). She did not envision the trade union movement that would bring a measure of personal and social power to workers such as William Weihe, an iron puddler who testified before a U. S. Senate Committee on Education and Labor in 1883 to urge the passage of labor laws and to defend the collective bargaining practices of his union, the Amalgamated Association of

Iron and Steel Workers (see Part Two, Chapter 1). Instead, Davis adopted the viewpoint of Orestes Brownson, whose 1840 essay "The Laboring Classes" castigated the "*nouveau riches* . . . upstarts" and self-styled "better sort" who exploited the proletarian laboring classes (see Part Two, p. 210). In *Life in the Iron-Mills*, Davis represents the world of industrial work as dreary, demeaning, and toilsome, with "smoke on the wharves, smoke on the dingy boats, on the yellow river" and "mules dragging masses of pig-iron through the narrow street . . . a foul vapor hanging to their reeking sides."

Davis's "vagabond tramps" undoubtedly also gave her the opportunity to observe the immigrant laborers on whom she based Hugh and Deborah in *Life in the Iron-Mills*. The plentiful land and the job opportunities in an urbanizing, industrializing United States brought 1.7 million immigrants into the nation in the 1840s and another 2.6 million in the 1850s. By 1860, the nation's population had reached 31 million, with one out of eight people foreign born. Most of the newcomers were Irish (1.6 million) who had been displaced by economic collapse and a blight that had rotted their dietary staple, potatoes. Just over half a million were British, like the Welsh Wolfe family. Irish women worked in domestic service and, like Deborah, in the textile mills, while the men joined construction gangs and labored in the iron industry. (German immigrants, many of them escapees from the revolutions of 1830 and 1848, included skilled workers, educated professionals, and farmers. The Scandinavians and Chinese, who made up other visible groups, were centered respectively in the upper Midwest and in California.)

Davis's portrayal of Hugh and Deborah as immigrants is significant in light of a sociopolitical nativism — hostility to immigrants and fear of their conspiratorial power — that gained particular force in the 1850s through the so-called Know-Nothing Party. In 1854 this party elected over forty congressmen on a platform demanding the exclusion of immigrants and Catholics from public office and the extension of the period of naturalization from five to twenty-five years. Had Davis chosen to make her characters Irish, her readers would have presumed them to be Catholics, who were denounced by nativists as subversives controlled by the Vatican and Catholic clergy. An Irish version of Hugh and Deborah would have brought religious-political controversy to the novella, diverting attention from its clear theme of class conflict.

Davis, nonetheless, may have decided to exploit the immigrant status of her characters in order to deepen the cultural gulf between them and the affluent Protestant Americans whom they encounter in the mill-visit scene and in the judicial system. In the United States, anti-immigrant sentiment was often coupled with exaltation of the Anglo-Saxons as comprising the "highest Christian civilization," in Josiah Strong's terms (see Part Two, Chapter 2). Though nativist politics was strongest in New England, New York, and Maryland, Davis's decision to portray her protagonist and his cousin as Welsh immigrants would have served for most readers to underscore the separation between Hugh and Deborah and the party of educated visitors to the mill. In a story involving the U. S. criminal justice system, Davis's portrayal of recent immigrants served to heighten awareness that justice and compassion were not available to newcomers like Hugh and Deborah.

THE SCHOOLING OF A WRITER
IN THE LITERARY MARKETPLACE

Rebecca Harding's first publications, like those of numerous other American writers, were occasional local newspaper pieces — reviews, verses, stories, and editorials that appeared in the *Wheeling Intelligencer* in the late 1850s. Though she later dismissed these efforts as ephemera, American journalism, from the publications of Benjamin Franklin onward, has provided a pathway for the development of ambitious writers. The process of working with an editor and the experience of seeing her work in print doubtless enabled Davis to hone the writing skills that are evident in *Life in the Iron-Mills*. The manuscript dispatched to the *Atlantic* in December 1860, was the product of an educated, literate, well-practiced writer. Its author was then twenty-nine years of age.

The swift acceptance and publication of *Life in the Iron-Mills* gave Rebecca Harding a position in the public sphere and even led to her 1863 marriage to Lemuel Clarke Davis, a Philadelphia newspaper editor. The new author first had to learn a lesson in marketplace realities, however. Davis had waited only a month for the favorable reply from editor James T. Fields accepting *Life in the Iron-Mills* with a fifty-dollar check and offering her one hundred dollars for another manuscript. Her literary future could not have seemed brighter, although the ground was literally shifting under her; April 1861 brought not only the publication of *Life in the Iron-Mills* but also the Confederate attack on Fort Sumter, which marked the onset of the Civil War. Harding's own Wheeling became part of the western section that seceded from the Confederacy and became the pro-Union state of New Virginia, then West Virginia.

Still, Rebecca had every reason to anticipate a flourishing literary future, particularly among the cohort of *Atlantic* women writers whose significant presence in the magazine's pages was due in large part to the influence of James Fields's wife, Annie Adams Fields, who had persuaded her husband to open his magazine to such figures as Harriet Beecher Stowe, Celia Thaxter, Louisa May Alcott, Rose Terry Cooke, Lucy Larcom, and Elizabeth Stuart Phelps. James Fields, whom Phelps commended for his feminist advocacy of "the political advancement of our sex, coeducation, and kindred movements," also had good reason to publish the work of women: they comprised more than half the readership for American fiction in the 1860s.

In the spring of 1861, *Life in the Iron-Mills* was creating a literary sensation as readers clamored to know more about the new "genius" who so shocked them with her grim but moral vision. Davis even received a note of admiration from Nathaniel Hawthorne. The second manuscript Fields had solicited from Davis was taking shape as well, but the *Atlantic* editor hesitated when he saw it. He said that the new story played out its pathos in a relentlessly minor key, and he thought that the working title, "The Deaf and the Dumb," was overly negative. The title referred not to impaired speech and hearing but to the disastrous impasse in communication that occurs when the members of one class (identified as the "deaf") fail to hear those trying desperately to send them urgent messages. Because their messages are as garbled as Hugh Wolfe's speech, the workers are categorized as inarticulate or "dumb." The former group, the deaf, is callous, the latter fatally ill-equipped to voice its plight.

In this new work, Davis was expanding the situation of the inarticulate Hugh Wolfe, who in *Life in the Iron-Mills* is desperate to express his state of physical and spiritual starvation (his "foreign thoughts and longings") when he encounters the affluent and educated though unfeeling and hypocritical group of visitors to the iron mill. Representing a different social order, the overseer, the mill owner's son, the doctor, the newspaper reporter, and the gentleman — "this mysterious class that shone down on [him] perpetually with the glamor of another order of being" — are essentially deaf to the workers' plight.

Davis saw this tragic impasse — this widening gulf between the classes — as a product of the new industrial capitalist order. "A man may make himself anything he chooses," proclaims the physician to the iron worker, but Davis's novella portrays Hugh Wolfe as being trapped in wretched conditions dictated by a system of manufacturing that benefits investors, stockholders, and managers rather than laborers. For Davis, this was not merely an individual or local matter but one nationally momentous in a democracy in which the "underlife of America . . . where all men are born free and equal . . . [is] a bit of hell." It is significant that as blocs of states warred over the principle of national union in geographic terms, Davis perceived the democratic union as being imperiled by the class divisions of the new capitalist economic order.

"The Deaf and the Dumb" grew to novel length, and Fields published it in serial form in the *Atlantic* after substantial editorial intervention and authorial revision. Fields was doubtless worried that the bleak vision of *Life in the Iron-Mills,* if continued into a second project, might adversely affect reader response and possibly subscriptions. At his request, Davis changed the title to the more sanguine "A Story of To-day" and wrote a marriage into the ending to make it happier and more socially conventional. Retitled yet again at Fields's urging, as *Margret Howth: A Story of To-day,* it became her first novel.

Those who study Rebecca Harding Davis's career view the title change from "The Deaf and the Dumb" to "A Story of To-day" and the rewritten ending as a serious capitulation to public taste, a weakness that was to undermine the integrity of her hard-hitting fiction throughout her career. Furthermore, it has been argued that Rebecca's marriage to L. Clarke Davis perpetuated the problem of debilitating compromises in her work. In the spring of 1862, L. Clarke Davis, a *Philadelphia Inquirer* newspaper editor and an admirer of Rebecca Harding's fiction, traveled to Wheeling to meet her. That summer, following a trip of her own to the Fields home in Boston and the Hawthorne family in Concord, Rebecca spent "a happy week in Philadelphia" with Davis, after which they became engaged, marrying in the spring of 1863 and then settling in Philadelphia.

The thirty-one-year marriage of Clarke and Rebecca Harding Davis was by most accounts a satisfying one; the two were temperamentally well suited. Clarke, however, exerted an influence on his wife's fiction that critics have found reason to regret. He read from the vantage point of a newspaper journalist committed to working quickly against deadlines and to stating his reformist positions with forceful directness, and he counseled his wife as if she were a reporter moonlighting in fiction. In addition, at certain points Davis took it upon herself as a wifely duty to hasten her writing into print because her income was needed to help support the growing Davis family, which included two sons — Richard Harding, born in 1864, and Charles Belmont, born in 1866 — and a daughter, Nora, born in 1872.

It remains a matter of speculation whether Davis's fiction would have been different if she had withstood the pressures of gatekeepers like Fields and advisers like her husband. The painful literary career of her near-contemporary Herman Melville, who struggled to please magazine editors, book publishers, and the consumerist public while still sheltering and nurturing his private fictional vision, provides a cautionary tale. In spite of his early success with such works as *Typee* (1846), Melville spent most of his career laboring in literary obscurity and dire financial straits. His novel *Moby-Dick* (1851) was not appreciated until he had been years in his grave. The public backlash that Kate Chopin suffered when she published *The Awakening* (1899), a story of sexual liberation, at the end of the nineteenth century serves as another cautionary tale. Chopin saw copies of her book burned and was ostracized by friends and associates in her own city of St. Louis. This public outrage in effect ended Chopin's literary career. The price of independence and integrity for an author who marched to a different drummer could be exorbitant.

At the same time, the financial opportunities for authors expanded tremendously in the later nineteenth century. Between 1860 and 1880, a literary journalist's financial compensation tripled in the United States, and it became possible to earn a living entirely through authorship. The southern abolitionist writer Angelina Grimké noted that truth is propagated through "the tongue, the pen, and the press" (17) and in fact women authors found success in these media. Augusta Evans Wilson's novel *St. Elmo* (1867) defines a woman intellectual, or "blue-stocking," as "a woman whose fingers are more frequently adorned with ink-spots than thimble"; and indeed numerous women found greater power in ink than in thimble and thread (see Part Two, p. 374). Harriet Beecher Stowe's *Uncle Tom's Cabin* (1852) — a scene from which is included in this volume — was an unprecedented bestseller, and writers like Fanny Fern and E. D. E. N. Southworth earned substantial sums in the 1850s, which the literary historian Fred Lewis Pattee has called "The Feminine Fifties" (see Part Two, Chapter 4).

Nathaniel Hawthorne jealously belittled these writers as a "mob of scribbling women" (see Part Two, p. 364) but the women themselves were in earnest. The realization that she might become a journalist ("Yes, write for the papers — why not?") constitutes an epiphany for Fern's character Ruth Hall (see Part Two, p. 394). Similarly, Lucy Larcom recalls her serious reflection on life's purpose ("What was I here for? What could I make of myself?") and her discovery of the firm literary resolution: "I knew I should write; I could not help doing that, for my hand seemed instinctively to move towards pen and paper" (see Part Two, p. 398–99). In her pathbreaking feminist treatise, *The Great Lawsuit* (1843), Margaret Fuller, whom Davis respected and often quoted, issues a strong plea for women writers and public speakers to secure a legitimate platform or place from which to voice their views (see Part Two, Chapter 4). By midcentury, the printed page had become that platform.

Given the opportunity to join one of the few new professions open to women — authorship — Davis would have been hard-pressed to reject such a lucrative and prestigious identity. She maintained her position by tailoring her work to popular taste, as did countless of her peers, both men and women.

Writers like Davis competed in a marketplace of entertainments and amusements that extended beyond books and magazines. The earlier agricultural and preindustrial America of towns and villages had featured social life based on neighborliness and tasks, such as husking bees, barn raisings, and the gathering of women in groups for quilting and sewing. The urban industrial society of the nineteenth century, however, produced quite a different structure of social or leisure activities. Formal and informal organizations developed for individuals interested in sports, music, reading, or plays. A young lady like Davis might eagerly join a book-discussion club, and Harriet Beecher Stowe participated in the literary Semi-Colon Club in Cincinnati. The stories and novels that Davis and her cohorts were producing thus competed with several other forms of popular entertainment.

The commercial and manufacturing schedules of industrial America led to a more distinct separation between hours of work and hours of leisure. Workers used their off-hours to seek diversion and pleasure in the new baseball parks, music halls, commercial theaters, and circuses. For the price of a ticket to P. T. Barnum's American Museum, visitors could see such exotica as bearded ladies, Feegee mermaids, wax figures, and dwarfs. The theater was also extremely popular; plays were noisy affairs, with audience members loudly expressing appreciation or disapproval, often drowning out the actors' voices. Shakespeare was tremendously popular for his melodramatic value, and audiences flocked to plays with clear moral messages and unambiguous heroes and villains. Plays such as *The Drunkard, or the Fallen Saved* were very well received.

At the same time, popular fiction flourished, not only the sentimental novels by writers such as Louisa May Alcott and E. D. E. N. Southworth but the genre became known as the dime novel, which featured lurid action plots. Writers like Ned Buntline (E. Z. C. Judson) and George Lippard exploited American class divisions in stories portraying the destitution of the poor and the scheming of the corrupt rich, the latter often lawyers or bankers. Novels with titles like *The Black Avenger* (1847) and *The Monks of Monk Hall* (1844) cast the working-class "b'hoys" (boys) as heroic figures of great physical courage, and featured plots that included numerous melodramatic twists and turns. Today they are read chiefly by students of nineteenth-century American popular culture and social history.

The genteel Rebecca Harding doubtless wrote *Life in the Iron-Mills* unaware of dime novels and other working-class forms of recreation. Over the course of her career, however, Davis published in a wide range of magazines, including several catering to popular taste. Those seeking to discover why more of her work has not continued to attract readers must bear in mind that the qualitative integrity of her novels and stories was protected neither by the advice of her journalist husband nor by her own tendency to cater to the vagaries of popular taste.

Davis's energies very much served the interest of productivity per se in a literary career that included 9 novels, 292 stories and serials, and 124 juvenile pieces. The publications in which Davis's work appeared form a galaxy of leading magazines of the late nineteenth and early twentieth centuries: *The Atlantic Monthly, Harper's Bazaar, North American Review, Independent, Outlook, Youth's Companion, St. Nicholas,* and *Saturday Evening Post.* She wrote for the selective, elite readership of the *Atlantic, Century,* and *Harper's,* as well as for the mass market readership of *Knickerbocker, Continental,* and *Peterson's.* She contributed also to women's magazines such as *Ladies Home Journal* and *Good Housekeeping.* Davis's novels engage issues of the Civil War (*Waiting for the Verdict,* 1868), political corruption (*John Andross,* 1874), female independence (*A Law unto Herself,* 1878), and manners and mores (*Natasqua,* 1886; *Doctor Warrick's Daughters,* 1896; *Frances Waldeaux,* 1898). By the end of the twentieth century, she would remain best known for her earliest works, *Life in the Iron-Mills* and *Margret Howth.*

REALISM

Life in the Iron-Mills has been identified as a precocious text in the movement known as literary realism, which flourished in the United States between 1870 and 1900. Among the leading American realists were William Dean Howells, Mary E. Wilkins Freeman, Henry James, Sarah Orne Jewett, and Mark Twain, whose literary contributions ranged from the vivid representations of regional identity in the rural New England of Freeman and Jewett, to the vernacular dialect of Twain, to the psychologically focused narrative devices of James. The realist movement was based in part on the work of such British and European writers as William Makepeace Thackery, Honoré de Balzac, Gustave Flaubert, George Eliot, and Charles Dickens. The philosophical premise of the movement was its position, based on the work of the positivist philosopher, Auguste Comte (1798–1857), that the objective world exists independently of any subjective viewer. The movement's leading American exponent, the novelist and editor William Dean Howells, said, "Realism is nothing more and nothing less than the truthful treatment of material" (*Criticism* 38).

Other American voices concurred. In 1892, the prominent attorney Clarence Darrow wrote that "the world . . . to-day . . . asks for facts. It has grown tired of fairies and angels, and asks for flesh and blood. . . . It wishes to see all; not only the prince and the millionaire, but the laborer and the begger, the master and the slave." Certainly Davis's *Life in the Iron-Mills* anticipates this position. The very flesh of her inarticulate laborer-protagonist and his cohorts is vividly described, and their gutteral speech is faithfully represented. In *Life in the Iron-Mills*, the narrator's promise to lift the curtain and penetrate the smoke voices the realist commitment to disclose truths that are otherwise hidden, in part by material conditions such as the barriers of residential zoning, and also by middle-class evasion and the escapist flights of rhetoric which the realists identified with romanticism.

The realists understood writing to be a moral act and rejected abstract absolutes such as Truth and Justice as evasive and normative. They scorned romanticism as self-deception and the deception of readers. Recent students of realism point out, however, that the line between realist and romanticist is not so clear-cut, that nineteenth-century realists strove to delineate a social world that ultimately eluded their representational grasp. The realists tended, like Davis, to be middle class in social position and outlook; and within the United States, growing class division, urbanization, and numerous productions of popular culture were creating competing realities that challenged such a bourgeois vision. It might be said, nonetheless, that the realist writer sought to capture the extraordinary in the seemingly commonplace. What was more common than the life of an inarticulate, immigrant laborer — and what more extraordinary than the revelation of his singular native talent and the momentary but ruinous impulse of his devoted friend, Deborah?

Davis's novella probes the terms on which a talented but ignorant young American artist might succeed or fail, an issue that is also explored by such nineteenth-century American writers as Nathaniel Hawthorne and Henry James. Hawthorne's *The Marble Faun* (1860) and James's *Roderick Hudson* (1876) portray promising American sculptors who are privileged to learn their art in European, chiefly Italian, studios (see Part Two, Chapter 3). Hawthorne's student-sculptors know that they must work from Old World masters, whereas James's Roderick Hudson, initially self-taught like Hugh Wolfe, is given the opportunity by a wealthy patron to study abroad, as were many accomplished American sculptors and artists. Davis, like James, focuses on the self-taught sculptor, but her working-class Hugh inspires no wealthy patron to sweep him away from the iron mill to an Italian atelier or marble quarry.

Hugh's rough-hewn korl woman signifies Davis's own effort to reject the romantic and idealistic in art, for "there was not one line of beauty or grace in it." Davis rejects the smooth contours of white Italian Carrera marble, the graceful lines preferred by nineteenth-century artists such as Hiram Powers and their patrons, in favor of the korl woman's "muscular" form with "clutching hands," "tense, rigid muscles" coarsened by labor, and "a wild eager face, like that of a starving wolf's." Only a few American artists, notably the second-generation German-American William Rimmer, executed the human form in sculpture whose rough planes and sinewed lines conveyed meanings in accord with literary realism and naturalism. Howells remarked that the realist feels the universal human condition "in every nerve" (Kaplan 23), and Davis sought to present that condition in extremis in the korl woman's sculptural physicality.

Although *Life in the Iron-Mills* predates the major works of nineteenth-century American realism, Davis did have an American model in the work of Nathaniel Hawthorne, three of whose stories she encountered (and virtually memorized) in childhood in a miscellany of *Moral Tales* (1840). Hawthorne's fiction appealed to Rebecca's childhood predilection for "the magic world of knights and pilgrims and fiends" (*Bits* 30). The author of *The Scarlet Letter* (1850) evidently attracted Davis in adulthood: Hawthorne's fictional preoccupation with psychological barriers between people provided Davis the incentive to develop her own themes of social exposé. Hawthorne's *The Blithedale Romance* (1852), with its veiled lady, together with a story like "The Minister's Black Veil" (1836), ratified Davis's sense of a world in which truth was veiled, concealed in webs of secrecy, fantasy, hypocrisy and ignorance by those whose daily routines confined them to the upholstered parlor, bed-chamber, carriage, office, drygoods mercantile establishment, clubroom, or garden path. Eventually even the formal education of her time seemed to Davis to obscure the realities of contemporary life behind the veil of the ancient world. Davis's classical education in the pantheon of Greek and Roman myth made her feel that "the rest of the world as yet were behind the curtain" (*Bits* 7). It is fitting that the conclusion of *Life in the Iron-Mills* includes the image of a curtain drawn back to reveal Hugh Wolfe's korl woman, a reminder to the reader of what lies behind the world of middle-class domesticity. Hawthorne brought the veil into visibility to explore psychological issues, but Davis committed herself, as a realist writer, to lifting it to convey sociocultural messages.

TECHNOLOGY AND THE IRON MILLS

The fact that the post–Civil War period is sometimes called the Age of Iron and Steel, or the Age of Industrialism, is an indication of Davis's precocity in identifying the iron mill as the central site of her 1860 social drama. A growing market for iron and iron-based products (such as support columns, armaments, axles, and building facades) together with the machine and structural component parts kept iron milling at the forefront of U. S. industry. Though the production of iron predates the Roman Empire, certain developments in the eighteenth and nineteenth centuries enabled unprecedented levels of production. Pig iron production in the United States grew 17 percent from 1855 to 1860, a mere 1 percent during the Civil War years, and an astounding 100 percent from 1865 to 1870. The greatest stimulus to production in the later nineteenth century was the explosive growth of the railroads (in *Life in the Iron-Mills,* Hugh Wolfe works for a mill that is filling a large order for the Lower Virginia railroads).

Iron was a recurring motif in Davis's life. She grew up to stories about her maternal great grandfather, who had fought at Valley Forge, a site named for the numerous iron works in the surrounding eastern Pennsylvania valley. Davis also recalled a forge in the Alabama village of her young childhood, where a local village blacksmith like the one eulogized by the poet Henry Wadsworth Longfellow in "The Village Blacksmith" (see Part Two, Chapter 1) fashioned and repaired tools. However, nothing would so absorb Rebecca as the iron mills of Wheeling, which represented a new stage of industrialization in the United States.

Explorers in the Americas sought precious metals, but of equal economic importance was the iron discovered in North Carolina in 1585. The Virginia Colony sent its ore to England as early as 1608, and Thomas Jefferson's Revolutionary-era *Notes on the State of Virginia* (1785) boasts of the lightweight and durable iron kettles and pans produced in ironworks in his native state. Jefferson's chapter or "Query" on "the mines and other subterraneous riches" includes impressive annual tonnage of bar iron and pig iron produced at several Virginia forges and furnaces.

The Virginia of Rebecca Harding Davis's era, however, produced its iron as an extension of the iron industry of the Northeast and Middle Atlantic states. The discovery and exploitation of iron in Lynn and other parts of Massachusetts from the 1640s to the mid-1700s not only enabled the production of cookware and agricultural tools but also became crucial to shipping and shipbuilding from the mid-seventeenth to the mid-nineteenth centuries. Forges and furnaces produced iron for anchors, bolts, chain, cannon, shot, barrel hoops, and stoves. Production moved westward into the Hudson River Valley and into New Jersey, Pennsylvania, Maryland, and the Champlain district of New York as the market for tools and utensils grew. The first furnace west of the Allegheny Mountains was built in 1790, but the mills of most significance to Rebecca Harding Davis's *Life in the Iron-Mills* were constructed in the river valleys of Ohio, Pennsylvania, and West Virginia, which continued to be crucial iron and steel centers until the early 1970s. An 1876 promotional text on the "Iron Interests of Wheeling" boasted that "Wheeling is chiefly known as the centre of a large iron industry," and lists the city's products — nails, hinges, agricultural machines, rails, and stoves (see Part Two, p. 89).

A mill of the kind in which Davis's Hugh Wolfe works operated according to centuries of metallurgical practices. The ore would be smelted, or melted, in a blast furnace and then charged with a blast of air or oxygen to drive off impurities, called slag. The metal product at this point was called pig iron, named from a method of casting in which the liquid iron was run through a main channel connected at right angles with several shorter channels. Because the design resembled a sow suckling a litter, the solid iron pieces from the shorter channels were termed *pigs*. Cast iron was formed by pouring the remelted, liquified metal into molds made of sand mixed with clay; this part of the process was known as founding (thus the term *foundry*). At the end of the eighteenth century, a "puddling" furnace was patented when it was discovered that by agitating a puddle of molten pig iron the carbon was removed by oxidation, producing a purer and stronger iron. Hugh's work as a puddler was to stir molten iron — in Davis's term, "the fiery pools of metal" — in order to expel carbon. Such work was hot, filthy, and dangerous to the body's respiratory system. Davis takes fictional liberties in burdening her puddler with physical weakness and a disabling disease (the often-fatal consumption, or tuberculosis), since puddling required physical strength and stamina, and a worker in Hugh's condition would not have been able to do the work. Readers might suspect, in fact, that Davis's knowledge of iron milling was sketchy. Testimony by the puddler, William Weihe, in 1883 before the U. S. Senate Committee on Education and Labor defines iron puddling as semiskilled labor and indicates that a Hugh Wolfe would have had a hired helper working alongside him (see Part Two, Chapter 1).

Davis's description of Hugh's sculptural medium, however, is true to the process of iron manufacture. While trained sculptors might work in marble or bronze, korl, the material from which Hugh carves his sculptures, is a waste product in the smelting process. The term is colloquial speech for "scorl" or "scoria," the slag or refuse left after metal has been smelted from ore. As the text indicates, korl is a loose, lava-like cinder.

Though the iron mills dominate Davis's text, the presence of the cotton mill in which we are told Deborah toils as a picker shows the author's awareness of another major U. S. industry that had superseded handcrafts just as the iron mills had replaced the village forge. Fiber and cloth had previously been spun and woven in colonial households, which typically also made their own shoes, soap, and leather goods. Nineteenth-century American manufactures benefited from the example of Great Britain, which had moved into industrial manufacture in the eighteenth century, both in the use of coke in the iron smelting process and in the use of steam and water power to propel textile milling machinery. James Watt had invented an improved steam engine in 1765, and British textile production was further hastened by a series of inventions that brought a high degree of automation to the spinning of fibers.

Although the British protected their industrial processes with tight secrecy and security (forbidding visitors to draw or diagram the machinery and prohibiting the emigration of knowledgeable mechanics), the secrecy was broken in 1789 when Samuel Slater reached New England with a plan for a water frame — an invention of the Englishman Richard Arkwright — held intact in his memory. Slater contracted with a Rhode Island manufacturer-entrepreneur to build a mill, known as Slater's Mill, in which nine children operated the machinery to produce an acceptable cotton yarn. U. S. mills gained from President Jefferson's embargo and from the War of 1812, both of which blocked international trade and helped American manufacturing. The textile industry flourished first in New England, where wealthy Massachusetts merchants, known as the Boston Associates, founded a factory in Waltham and later, in the 1820s, in Lowell, where the falls of the Merrimack River provided ample water power.

The Lowell mills were designed by their owners to be the antithesis of the dreary and filthy English mill towns. Under a paternalistic system of chaperonage that included dormitories, boarding houses, and after-hours educational and religious organizations, the mills employed New England farm girls who would work for lower wages than men and who outnumbered the male population that had been decimated by westward migration. For many of the operatives, or "Lowell girls," the mills provided an unprecedented opportunity for independence and an earned livelihood outside the family, and they wrote of the experience with pride. Lucy Larcom and Harriet Robinson, both represented in this volume, are notable examples. Others, dismayed by the social and economic class divisions between owners and employees, recorded their observations with satiric bitterness, which was exacerbated when cotton prices fell in the 1830s. A new generation of managers, indifferent to the original Lowell ideals, precipitated strikes by cutting wages and increasing the pace of the relentless work. On the farms around the mill towns, a seventy-hour work week during planting or harvesting time would be relieved by off-season slack time; however, a factory worker had no such relief in workdays that were limited only by the amount of available light. Immigrant labor, notably Irish, exerted a further downward pressure on wages, since the newcomers were willing to work at barest subsistence wages. By midcentury, the Lowell mills seemed to visitors to be mirror images of the dank and wretched English factory towns.

It is significant that both those who were appreciative of the Lowell mill experience and those who were hostile to it were able to write their views, since by 1840, New England had achieved nearly universal literacy. Work life in the New England textile mills was extraordinarily well documented. This was not the case in Davis's native Western Virginia, and Davis underscores the consequences of working-class illiteracy by portraying Deborah as inarticulate and "dumb," unable to tell her own story. Davis's narrator functions as spokesperson for the most downtrodden of immigrant workers in the new industrial order.

NARRATIVES OF INDUSTRIAL AMERICA

In representing the problematics of class, economics, and technology, *Life in the Iron-Mills* set a precedent for the industrial narrative in American literature. In 1854, Charles Dickens had published *Hard Times,* portraying the relentlessly bleak and desperate English factory life of his fictional Coketown. Dickens's England, however, was a stratified and hierarchal society, not a republic like the United States, whose democratic values had long been considered to be in harmony with technological development. The ameliorative potential of technology had been a recurrent theme in American literature since the colonial period, when settlers understandably considered structures and machines like bridges and mills to be godly, utilitarian gifts and necessities in wilderness settings. One mid-seventeenth-century writer, Edward Johnson, extolled the "well-ordered Commonwealth" achievable largely by "the Iron mill in constant use," "the Corn mill," and the "Fulling-mill" by which one community "set upon making of Cloth . . . first . . . in this Western World" (183).

The darker side of industrialism began to make its way into American literature in the nineteenth century as writers judged material progress to be at the expense of moral and ethical concern over the condition of the industrial working class. In 1836, one writer in the *Western Messenger* observed that "to have . . . railroads and mines, and to be devoid, as a people, of the spiritual purity and spiritual strength, is to sell . . . our souls." In 1843, Henry David Thoreau attacked a proposal for a technological utopia, J. A. Etzler's *The Paradise within the Reach of All Men, without Labour, by the Powers of Nature and Machinery*. Thoreau's review-essay condemned machinery as mere "pretty toys" and urged that specious "transcendentalism in mechanics" be replaced by "reformation of the self." Herman Melville weighed in with corresponding misgivings about human labor in a new capitalist system of machine-based production. His "Try-Works" chapter of *Moby-Dick* (1851) represents the factory as an inferno, as does his "Tartarus of Maids," which not only portrays women factory operatives as numbed automatons but suggests that prosperous families like Davis's, in purchasing ordinary items like seasonal garden seeds, are culpable because of their willing ignorance of the wretched working conditions under which their paper seed packets (and by extension all consumer products) are produced (see Part Two, Chapter 1).

Life in the Iron-Mills sought to educate middle-class readers about working conditions, and established the genre of industrial fiction in the United States. Elizabeth Stuart Phelps's "The Tenth of January" (1868) and *The Silent Partner* (1871), featuring a mill worker and a female silent partner in the mill, were directly influenced by *Life in the Iron-Mills;* and such writers of the naturalist school as Hamlin Garland (*Main-Travelled Roads,* 1891) and Frank Norris (*The Octopus,* 1901) built on the tradition Davis had founded. In the early twentieth century, Upton Sinclair's *The Jungle* (1906), which exposed working conditions in the Chicago packinghouses, took its place as another landmark novel of industrialization.

Texts like Michael Gold's *Jews Without Money* (1930) and Ruth McKenney's *Industrial Valley* (1939) furthered the tradition, as did the documentary work of muckraking journalists such as Ida Tarbell and Lincoln Stephens, who exposed monopolistic business and government practices by cartels and by individuals such as John D. Rockefeller and Andrew Carnegie, whose names are historically synonymous with oil and steel. Late-twentieth-century accounts in newspapers like the *Los Angeles Times* and the *New York Times* of factory sweatshops paying near-starvation wages to immigrant workers are an indication of the perpetuation of those social conditions for which Davis urged redress in what she saw as "the promise of the dawn."

THE PROMISE OF THE DAWN

Life in the Iron-Mills identifies numerous social problems that prompted reformist action in the United States and Britain in the nineteenth century: tobacco and alcohol addiction, rampant disease, grim prison conditions, poor diet, profound poverty and ignorance and their consequent blight of body and mind. In exposing and exploring such social ills, Davis's novella takes its place in the context of nineteenth-century American reform movements. From the 1820s, U. S. industrial workers had attempted to gain power, first through the formation of political parties such as the Working Men's Party, and later through the organization of labor unions like the Knights of Labor. Women workers organized labor unions such as the United Tailoresses of New York and the Factory Girls' Association, which attempted to secure better wages and working conditions.

Numerous reform movements were organized by members of the middle classes. In 1826, a group of Boston ministers founded the American Society for the Promotion of Temperance, precursor to the American Temperance Union and the Woman's Christian Temperance Union. Such reform movements often focused on the domestic sphere. The Kitchen Garden movement, according to its spokesperson Anna Gordon, strove to bring ideas on housekeeping to "the children of the poorer classes, who are in very wretched homes, and homes often of drunkenness" (see Part Two, p. 255). Belief in the innate goodness of human beings and their capacity for improvement also led to a prison reform movement guided by the onetime Boston school teacher Dorothea Dix. The minister Henry Ward Beecher, brother of Harriet Beecher Stowe, published a series of *Lectures to Young Men* warning against the moral decay inevitably to follow from gambling, profanity, "popular amusements," and "strange" women. Beecher also advocated education for the working classes, writing that "If I see poor people that have cultivated minds, I say, 'Thank God.'"

It should be noted that the British and American reform movements were somewhat intertwined. Throughout the nineteenth century, British reformers, like their U. S. counterparts, had worked on behalf of slum-dwellers, miners, and factory hands in such causes as public health and education. Notable and influential British reformers included Jeremy Bentham, who argued for prison reform and whose utilitarian goals of the greatest good for the greatest number were satirized in Dickens's *Hard Times* as overly regimented. Robert

Owen, an Englishman, proselytized for a utopian new agriculture and for self-governing industrial communities. Some U. S. reform efforts were directly linked with those in Britain. The settlement house movement, for example, was inspired by England's Toynbee Hall, located in a poor section of London in order to improve the lives of slum-dwellers with educational and service programs. The Young Men's Christian Association came to the United States from England in the 1850s, and the Salvation Army reached the United States in 1880, four years after its founding in London.

Life in the Iron-Mills is both of this reformist milieu and distinguishable from it. Some writers of American industrial fiction proposed sociopolitical solutions to the intractable problems of inequities of wealth, living conditions, and social status, but Rebecca Harding Davis was not one of them. Whereas Upton Sinclair would envision the formation of a new socialistic order in *The Jungle*, Davis never looked to political or social reorganization to solve the problems she exposed. Thus, it could be argued that Davis, after all, drew on the romantic or sentimental school of thought for her hopeful visions of potential joy, both in *Life in the Iron-Mills* and in other novels such as *Margret Howth* and *Kitty's Choice* (1873).

The very sunbeams that symbolize the "promise of the dawn" in *Life in the Iron-Mills* can be seen as constituting a reversion to the romantic tradition, for Davis consistently identifies a romantic and evangelistic transcendence as the only valid source of personal and social salvation. Reformism in *Life in the Iron-Mills* is associated with the character of the Quaker woman, whom Davis represents as a kind of spiritual social worker who will undertake Deborah's individual regeneration.

Quakerism is a crucial context for the uplifting conclusion to Davis's story. Nineteenth-century America was fertile ground for numerous social reform movements in which the Quakers, or Society of Friends, played major roles. Historically, Quakers had been prominent in the Atlantic saga of colonial American history, with William Penn, the Quaker founder of Pennsylvania, fostering the idea of harmonious European, British, and Native American relations in the religiously tolerant colony of "Penn's Woods."

The Quakers also had a long history of martyrdom in American culture, beginning with their banishment and persecution by the Massachusetts Bay Puritans in the seventeenth century. Several nineteenth-century novelists developed characters and situations based on the abuse, banishment, or execution of seventeenth-century

Quakers — such as Mary Dyer — whom the novelists represented as courageous pacifists embodying ideas of wisdom, simplicity, and equality. In their incorporation of Quaker characters, John Neal's *Rachel Dyer: A North American Story* (1828), Eliza Buckminster Lee's *Naomi: Or Boston Two Hundred Years Ago* (1848), and Harriet Beecher Stowe's *Uncle Tom's Cabin* (1852) can be seen as literary precursors of *Life in the Iron-Mills* (see Part Two, Chapter 2). In addition, the prominent Quakers in Rebecca Beach's *The Puritan and the Quaker: A Story of Colonial Times* (1879) and Louisa May Alcott's *Work* (1873) show the continued attraction of a figure who might be said to embody traditional American values that predated capitalist marketplace economics.

For Davis and other nineteenth-century authors, Quakers were not solely historical figures but dynamic contemporaries. Throughout the nineteenth century, Quakers worked for the abolition of slavery, prison and housing reform, women's suffrage, Native American rights, and labor reform. Rebecca Harding Davis recalled the Quaker poet John Greenleaf Whittier (see Part Two, Chapter 2) lecturing in Wheeling and speaking with a "gentle, unwearied obstinacy" on behalf of the abolition of slavery (*Bits* 189). But she also recalled "many Quaker women, honest of heart, sweet of face, soft of speech, and narrow in their beliefs as only your gentle, soft woman can be" (*Bits* 191).

Davis identified this kind of focused, intense conviction in the Quaker feminist leader Lucretia Mott, whose "power came from the fact that she was the most womanly of women. . . . She had pity and tenderness enough in her heart for the mother of mankind, and that keen sense of humor without which the tenderest of women is but a dull clod." Quakerism had other significance for Davis as well. The Society of Friends supported equal education for women and, unlike mainstream Protestant denominations, rejected patriarchal forms of worship. Quakers had no rules against women speaking in meetings. Thus for Deborah's postprison education and rehabilitation, Davis chose a figure whose fullest cultural and literary identity her readers could be expected to appreciate.

Appreciation of Davis's own fictional dawning in *Life in the Iron-Mills* has varied over time. Following its powerful reception, *Life in the Iron-Mills*, like much of Davis's subsequent fiction, came to be criticized over the succeeding decades for being didactic, morbid, and grim. At mid-twentieth century, Robert Spiller's august *Literary His-*

tory of the United States, in terms typical for the time, regretted the "fault . . . of melodrama" that marred Davis's work (2: 881). (The same charge was routinely leveled against Harriet Beecher Stowe.) When the writer Tillie Olsen rediscovered the novella and wrote an introduction for her 1972 edition, she recounted her difficulty locating information about the once-prominent writer who had sunk into obscurity. In the past twenty-five years, *Life in the Iron-Mills* has gained many readers who are eager to recover the "lost" record of writing by women.

Most readers agree that *Life in the Iron-Mills* is Davis's best work. In the late twentieth century, the novella has secured its place in the established canon of American literature; it is reprinted in anthologies and taught in high school and college classrooms. The industrial era of vast iron and steel mills that Davis represented had virtually disappeared a century or so after *Life in the Iron-Mills* was published. But the issues Davis brought before the public — class conflict, work conditions, gender identity, art education and production, immigration, technological change, and spiritual values — remain compelling because they constitute some of the nation's most crucial, contemporary, and intractable concerns even at the turn of the twenty-first century. Perhaps Elizabeth Stuart Phelps best assessed the educational impact of *Life in the Iron-Mills* when she wrote of Davis's novella that "the claims of toil and suffering upon ease had assumed new form . . . [and] one could never say again that one did not understand."

Chronology of
Davis's Life and Times

1831

June 24: Rebecca Blaine Harding is born in Washington, Pennsylvania, the first of five children of Rachel Leet Wilson (1808–1884) and Richard W. Harding (1796–1864), an English immigrant.

Nat Turner's Rebellion in Virginia.

1832

January: New England Anti-Slavery Society forms in Boston.

July: The existence of the Bank of the United States is threatened by a conflict between President Andrew Jackson (1767–1845), who refuses to recharter it, and bank president Nicholas Biddle (1786–1844).

December: Nullification crisis: South Carolina declares federal tarriff null and void and threatens to secede from the Union; President Jackson responds with a proclamation.

1833

December: American Anti-Slavery Society founded in Philadelphia.

Lydia Maria Child (1802–1880), *An Appeal in Favor of That Class of Americans Called Africans.*

1834

The Southern Literary Messenger (Richmond), 1834–1864.

ca. 1836

The Harding family moves to Wheeling, Virginia, a newly chartered city, where Richard becomes a successful businessman and public official.

1836

Ralph Waldo Emerson (1803–1882), *Nature.*

1837

May: United States experiences economic panic and collapse, leading to mass unemployment, which persists until 1843.

Emerson, "The American Scholar."

1838

Beginning of the Underground Railroad, which assists slaves in escaping to the North. Trail of Tears: the U. S. Government forces Cherokee tribes to leave their native lands in Georgia for Indian Territory in Oklahoma, a journey that kills thousands.

Edgar Allan Poe (1809–1849), *Narrative of Arthur Gordon Pym.* Alexis de Tocqueville (1805–1859), first American edition of *Democracy in America* (2 vols., 1835).

1840

June: World's Anti-Slavery Convention (London) refuses to admit American women delegates.

Washington Temperance Society is formed; three years later it claims to have reformed hundreds of thousands of intemperate drinkers and alcoholics.

Poe, *Tales of the Grotesque and Arabesque.*

1841

Dorothea Dix (1802–1887) attempts to reform Massachusetts prisons and insane asylums.

Emerson, *Essays.* Henry Wadsworth Longfellow (1807–1882), *Ballads and Other Poems.*

1844

April: Texas Annexation Treaty provides for admission of Texas as a territory, but the U. S. Senate resists.

September: Previously tutored by her mother, Rebecca Harding enters Washington Female Seminary.

December: Democrat James K. Polk (1795–1849) wins presidential election, defeating Whig candidate Henry Clay (1777–1852) and abolitionist Liberty Party candidate James Birney (1792–1857).

1845

June: Andrew Jackson dies.

July: In the first use of the phrase, the *United States Magazine and Democratic Review* declares the United States' "manifest destiny to overspread the continent."

December: Texas is admitted into the Union as the twenty-eighth state.

National Reform Association, which advocated the rights of workingmen, is established. Industrial Congress of the United States, a labor organization, forms in New York City.

Frederick Douglass (1817–1895), *Narrative of the Life of Frederick Douglass*. Margaret Fuller (1810–1850), *Woman in the Nineteenth Century*.

1846

January: *De Bow's Review*, a pro-slavery journal which studies southern culture, begins publication.

May: United States declares war on Mexico (1846–1848).

August: Wilmot Proviso, which would ban slavery in land acquired from Mexico, fails to pass.

Abraham Lincoln (1809–1865) is elected to Congress from Illinois and serves from 1847 to 1849.

Herman Melville (1819–1891), *Typee*.

1847

Longfellow, *Evangeline*.

1848

January: Gold is discovered near John Sutter's (1803–1880) sawmill in California, an event that begins the Gold Rush.

February: Treaty of Guadalupe Hidalgo ends the Mexican War; Mexico relinquishes present-day California, New Mexico, and parts of Arizona and Nevada for $15 million.

June: Rebecca Harding graduates from Washington Female Seminary as valedictorian and returns home to Wheeling.

July: The first woman's rights convention is held in Seneca Falls, New York, led by Lucretia Mott (1793–1880) and Elizabeth Cady Stanton (1815–1902).

November: Boston Female Medical School, the first medical school for women, opens.

1849

Henry David Thoreau (1817-1862), *A Week on the Concord and Merrimack Rivers*, "Resistance to Civil Government" (republished in 1866 as "Civil Disobedience").

1850

September: Congress issues the Compromise of 1850, which attempts to end the conflict over slavery and includes the controversial Fugitive Slave Act.

Amelia Bloomer dons "bloomers," pantaloon trousers thought to promote women's health by freeing the body from the constraints of stiff corsets.

Susan Warner (1819–1885), *The Wide, Wide World.* Nathaniel Hawthorne (1804–1864), *The Scarlet Letter.*

1851

Young Men's Christian Association (established in England in 1844) opens chapters in Boston, Massachusetts, and Montreal, Canada. Asylum for Friendless Boys is established in New York City.

Melville, *Moby-Dick.*

1852

November: Franklin Pierce, a Democrat, is elected U. S. president.

Harriet Beecher Stowe (1811–1896), *Uncle Tom's Cabin.*

1853

The American, or Know-Nothing, Party is established, arguing that only native-born Americans should hold public office and calling for repeal of all naturalization laws. The Crystal Palace Exhibition of the Industry of All Nations in New York City demonstrates U. S. industrial and technological prowess.

Fanny Fern (Sara Payson Willis Parton, 1811–1872), *Fern Leaves from Fanny's Port-Folio.*

1854

May: Kansas-Nebraska Act repeals the Missouri Compromise and heightens the slavery crisis. Senator Stephen A. Douglas (1813–1861) of Illinois calls for letting the people decide the slavery question in the territories ("popular sovereignty").

Rebecca Harding begins submitting reviews, poems, stories, and editorials to the *Wheeling Intelligencer*.

Children's Aid Society is formed in New York City.

Thoreau, *Walden*.

1855

May: Feminist and abolitionist Lucy Stone (1818–1893) becomes the first woman officially to keep her maiden name in marriage.

Violence erupts in Kansas territory over the slavery question.

Douglass, *My Bondage and My Freedom*. Fern, *Ruth Hall*. Longfellow, *Song of Hiawatha*. Walt Whitman (1819–1892), *Leaves of Grass*.

1856

May: Senator Charles Sumner (1811–1874) of Massachusetts gives the anti-slavery "Crime Against Kansas" speech and is assaulted by Congressman Preston Brooks (1819–1857) of South Carolina.

Melville, *The Piazza Tales*. Stowe, *Dred: A Tale of the Great Dismal Swamp*.

1857

March: Supreme Court rules in *Dred Scott v. Sandford* that slaves are not citizens and that Congress cannot prohibit slavery in the territories.

August: Widespread economic panic.

Channing Home, a hospital for poor women, opens in Boston.

The Atlantic Monthly, edited by James Russell Lowell (1819–1891), begins publication.

1858

August–October: Stephen Douglas and Abraham Lincoln engage in the Lincoln-Douglas debates to win the U. S. Senate seat from Illinois. Lincoln makes his "A House Divided" speech; Douglas is re-elected.

Cooper Union, an adult-education institution for the working class, opens in New York City. Religious revivalism engulfs the United States.

1859

October: John Brown (1800–1859) leads anti-slavery forces, which attempt to seize the federal arsenal in Harpers Ferry, Virginia.

December: John Brown is executed.

Rebecca Harding serves briefly as editor of the *Wheeling Intelligencer*.

Harriet Wilson (1808?–1870), *Our Nig*, first novel by an African American in the United States.

1860

February: Strikes and labor unrest, beginning with a shoemakers' strike over wages and working conditions in Lynn, Massachusetts.

November: Lincoln elected U. S. president.

December: Rebecca Harding sends *Life in the Iron-Mills* to *The Atlantic Monthly*.

South Carolina secedes from the Union.

1861

January: Rebecca receives a letter of acceptance from *Atlantic* editor James T. Fields (1817–1881) which includes a $50 payment and the promise of $100 for another contribution.

April: *Life in the Iron-Mills* is published in the *Atlantic*. Civil War begins when Confederate forces attack Fort Sumter, Charleston Harbor, South Carolina.

May: James T. Fields rejects Rebecca Harding's story "The Deaf and the Dumb" as "gloomy," requesting that she change the title to "A Story of To-day" and rewrite the ending.

August: Northwest portion of Virginia secedes from the Confederacy, becoming first New Virginia, then West Virginia.

October: "A Story of To-day" (later published as the novel *Margret Howth*) begins serialization in the *Atlantic*. L. Clarke Davis, an editor for the *Philadelphia Enquirer* who admires her writing, writes to Rebecca Harding.

Harriet Jacobs (1813–1897), *Incidents in the Life of a Slave Girl*. Frederick Law Olmstead (1822–1903), *The Cotton Kingdom*.

1862

Spring: L. Clarke Davis visits Rebecca Harding in Wheeling, beginning their courtship.

July: Rebecca Harding visits the Fields in Boston and the Hawthornes in Concord. She then spends a week with Clarke Davis in Philadelphia, and they become engaged.

Davis's *Margret Howth: A Story of To-day* is published by Ticknor and Fields of Boston.

1863

January: Lincoln signs the Emancipation Proclamation, which frees slaves in Confederate territory.

March 5: Rebecca Harding marries L. Clarke Davis in Wheeling, and they move to his sister's home in Philadelphia.

Summer: Rebecca becomes pregnant and suffers from depression.

Louisa May Alcott (1832–1888), *Hospital Sketches.*

1864

March 20: Rebecca's father dies.

April 18: Rebecca gives birth to her first child, named Richard Harding Davis after her father.

Summer–fall: The Davises vacation at Point Pleasant, New Jersey. Rebecca's depression ends when the family moves into a home of their own in Philadelphia.

1865

April: General Lee's surrender at Appomattox ends the Civil War. John Wilkes Booth assassinates President Lincoln.

The Thirteenth Amendment, which abolished slavery, is ratified. The Ku Klux Klan begins organizing. The Molly Maguires, a powerful Irish miners' group, becomes active (1865–1867).

Whitman, *Drum Taps.* Stowe, *House and Home Papers.*

1866

January 24: Charles Belmont Davis, the Davises' second child, is born.

Davis begins publishing stories in *Galaxy* under her own name.

The first Young Women's Christian Association is formed in Boston.

1867

Alfred Nobel patents dynamite.

Augusta Jane Evans Wilson (1835–1909), *St. Elmo.*

1868

Davis's *Dallas Galbraith*, a novel, is published by Lippincott of Philadelphia. Her realistic Civil War novel, *Waiting for the Verdict*, is published by Sheldon of New York.

President Johnson is impeached, tried, and acquitted. The Fourteenth Amendment, which permitted African Americans to be citizens of the United States, is ratified.

Alcott, *Little Women*. Elizabeth Stuart Phelps (1844–1911), *The Gates Ajar*.

1869

Davis becomes a regular contributing editor to the *New York Tribune*, beginning a twenty-year affiliation. Clarke becomes managing editor of the *Philadelphia Inquirer*. Harriet Beecher Stowe asks Davis to write for her new monthly, *Hearth and Home*.

Knights of Labor organize in Philadelphia. The first transcontinental railroad is completed.

1870

The Davises buy a house at 230 South Twenty-first Street, which will remain their home for the rest of their lives.

The Fifteenth Amendment, which allowed African Americans to vote, is ratified.

1871

Davis begins writing for children's presses, work that she will continue for the rest of her life.

Phelps, *The Silent Partner*.

1872

Nora Davis, the Davises' third child, is born.

National Labor Reform Party is founded. Susan B. Anthony is arrested for leading women voters to the polls.

1873

Davis's *Kitty's Choice, or Berrytown and Other Stories*, a novella and two stories, is published by Lippincott.

The nation enters a financial panic, precipitated by the failure of Jay Cooke and Co., which triggers a nationwide depression, the worst the United States had ever known. William Marcy ("Boss") Tweed, who controlled New York City Democratic Party politics in the 1860s and early 1870s, is convicted of fraud.

Alcott, *Work*.

1874

Davis's *John Andross*, a novel about political corruption, is published by Orange Judd of New York.

Women's Christian Temperance Union is founded in Cleveland.

1875

Davis begins writing regular editorials and fiction pieces for the *New York Independent*, an association that will continue throughout her life.

Andrew Carnegie builds the first factory to produce Bessemer steel.

1876

Centennial Exposition in Philadelphia.

1877

In response to the lingering depression and continued lowering of wages, coal miners in Martinsburg, West Virginia, begin a strike that spreads across the country, finally requiring the use of federal troops.

1878

Davis's *A Law unto Herself*, a novel about female independence, is published by Lippincott.

1880

The Salvation Army is established in the United States.

1881

Susan B. Anthony (1820–1906) and others, *History of Woman Suffrage*.

1884

Bureau of Labor created. Equal Rights Party formed by suffragettes.

Mark Twain (1835–1910), *The Adventures of Huckleberry Finn*.

1886

Davis's *Natasqua*, a satirical novel of manners, is published by Cassell of New York as part of its Rainbow Series for young readers.

Labor unrest continues, especially among railroad workers. The Haymarket Square riots erupt in Chicago, and the American Federation of Labor is established.

1888

Edward Bellamy (1850–1898), *Looking Backward: 2000–1887*.

1889

Davis resigns from the *Tribune* to protest editorial censorship of her articles. She becomes a weekly contributor to the *Independent*. Clarke leaves the *Inquirer* to be the *Philadelphia Public Ledger*'s associate editor.

Jane Addams establishes Hull-House in Chicago.

Andrew Carnegie (1835–1919), *The Gospel of Wealth*.

1890

August: Richard Harding Davis's story "Gallegher" is published in *Scribner's Magazine*, which brings him fame.

Emily Dickinson (1830–1886), *Poems*.

1891

Summer: Davis and her husband and daughter vacation in England.

Mary E. Wilkins Freeman (1852–1930), *A New England Nun and Other Stories*. Hamlin Garland (1860–1940), *Main-Travelled Roads*.

1892

Davis's *Kent Hampden*, a young person's novel and *Silhouettes of American Life*, a collection of thirteen stories, are published by Scribner's of New York.

Joel Chandler Harris (1848–1908), *Uncle Remus and His Friends*.

1893

The nation experiences a financial panic. The World's Columbian Exposition is held in Chicago.

1894

The Pullman Car Company strike begins railway and mining labor unrest.

1896

Davis's *Doctor Warrick's Daughters*, a novel of manners, is published by Harper of New York.

Klondike gold is discovered, starting a stampede the following year. Beginning of Jim Crow era, in which segregation is legalized.

1898

Davis's *Frances Waldeaux*, a novel of manners, is published by Harper.

The explosion of the Battleship *Maine* in Havana harbor leads to a ten-week Spanish-American War.

1899

May 4: Richard Harding Davis marries Cecile Clark.

Fall: First mention of Nora's suffering from a recurring nervous illness.

Charles Dana Gibson sketches the "Gibson Girl."

Kate Chopin (1851–1904), *The Awakening*. Thorstein Veblen (1857–1929), *The Theory of the Leisure Class*.

1901

Socialist Party founded by Eugene V. Debs and others. J. P. Morgan founds U. S. Steel Corporation.

Frank Norris (1870–1902), *The Octopus*. Booker T. Washington (1856–1915), *Up from Slavery*.

1902

Davis becomes a regular contributor to the *Saturday Evening Post* and continues contributing for several years.

1903

Wright brothers' first successful airplane flight at Kitty Hawk, North Carolina.

W. E. B. Du Bois (1868–1963), *The Souls of Black Folk*. Jack London (1876–1916), *The Call of the Wild*.

1904

December 14: L. Clarke Davis dies at home of heart disease.

Bits of Gossip, Davis's memoir, is published by Houghton Mifflin of Boston.

St. Louis hosts the St. Louis Exposition. First Olympic Games are held in America.

1905

Industrial Workers of the World is founded in Chicago. First motion picture theater opens in Pittsburgh.

Edith Wharton (1862–1937), *The House of Mirth*.

1906

Upton Sinclair (1878–1968), *The Jungle*.

1908

Following a brief financial panic in 1907, the nation suffers rising unemployment. The first Model T Ford is manufactured. The Singer Building in New York City becomes the first U. S. skyscraper.

1910

September: Davis suffers a stroke while visiting her son Richard at his Mt. Kisco, New York, estate. She dies there on September 29 at the age of seventy-nine.

A Note on the Text

This volume reprints the text of *Life in the Iron-Mills* from the April 1861 issue of *The Atlantic Monthly*, where the novella was first published. Mid-nineteenth-century usages and peculiarities of spelling and punctuation have been preserved in an effort to be faithful to Davis's style.

Wherever possible, the text of the documents in Part Two is that of the original edition or of the most authoritative scholarly edition. Unless otherwise indicated in the headnote for a document, the text used is that of the original edition and has not been modified from the copy text. Students should expect to encounter some archaic or variant spellings and punctuation conventions.

Life in the Iron-Mills

"Is this the end?
O Life, as futile, then, as frail!
What hope of answer or redress?"[1]

A cloudy day: do you know what that is in a town of iron-works? The sky sank down before dawn, muddy, flat, immovable. The air is thick, clammy with the breath of crowded human beings. I open the window, and, looking out, can scarcely see through the rain the grocer's shop opposite, where a crowd of drunken Irishmen are puffing Lynchburg[2] tobacco in their pipes. I can detect the scent through all the foul smells ranging loose in the air.

The idiosyncracy of this town is smoke. It rolls sullenly in slow folds from the great chimneys of the iron-foundries, and settles down in black, slimy pools on the muddy streets. Smoke on the wharves, smoke on the dingy boats, on the yellow river, — clinging in a coating of greasy soot to the house-front, the two faded poplars, the faces of the passers-by. The long train of mules, dragging masses of pig-iron through the narrow street, have a foul vapor hanging to their reeking sides. Here, inside, is a little broken figure of an angel point-

---

[1] *"Is this . . . redress?":* The second and third lines of Davis's epigraph are from Alfred, Lord Tennyson's *In Memorium* 56.25–27. The first line is Davis's own. [All notes are the editor's unless identified otherwise.]

[2] *Lynchburg:* City in Virginia known for its production of tobacco.

ing upward from the mantel-shelf; but even its wings are covered with smoke, clotted and black. Smoke everywhere! A dirty canary chirps desolately in a cage beside me. Its dream of green fields and sunshine is a very old dream — almost worn out, I think.

From the back-window I can see a narrow brick-yard sloping down to the river-side, strewed with rain-butts and tubs. The river, dull and tawny-colored, (*la bella rivière!*) drags itself sluggishly along, tired of the heavy weight of boats and coal-barges. What wonder? When I was a child, I used to fancy a look of weary, dumb appeal upon the face of the negro-like river slavishly bearing its burden day after day. Something of the same idle notion comes to me to-day, when from the street-window I look on the slow stream of human life creeping past, night and morning, to the great mills. Masses of men, with dull, besotted faces bent to the ground, sharpened here and there by pain or cunning; skin and muscle and flesh begrimed with smoke and ashes; stooping all night over boiling cauldrons of metal, laired by day in dens of drunkenness and infamy; breathing from infancy to death an air saturated with fog and grease and soot, vileness for soul and body. What do you make of a case like that, amateur psychologist? You call it an altogether serious thing to be alive: to these men it is a drunken jest, a joke, — horrible to angels perhaps, to them commonplace enough. My fancy about the river was an idle one: it is no type of such a life. What if it be stagnant and slimy here? It knows that beyond there waits for it odorous sunlight, — quaint old gardens, dusky with soft, green foliage of apple-trees, and flushing crimson with roses, — air, and fields, and mountains. The future of the Welsh puddler[3] passing just now is not so pleasant. To be stowed away, after his grimy work is done, in a hole in the muddy graveyard, and after that, —— *not* air, nor green fields, nor curious roses.

Can you see how foggy the day is? As I stand here, idly tapping the window-pane, and looking out through the rain at the dirty back-yard and the coal-boats below, fragments of an old story float up before me, — a story of this old house into which I happened to come to-day. You may think it a tiresome story enough, as foggy as the day, sharpened by no sudden flashes of pain or pleasure. — I know: only the outline of a dull life, that long since, with thousands of dull lives like its own, was vainly lived and lost: thousands of them, —

---

[3] *puddler:* A worker who converts pig iron into wrought iron or steel by *puddling* — that is, by subjecting the metal to heat and stirring it in a furnace.

massed, vile, slimy lives, like those of the torpid lizards in yonder stagnant water-butt. — Lost? There is a curious point for you to settle, my friend, who study psychology in a lazy, *dilettante*[4] way. Stop a moment. I am going to be honest. This is what I want you to do. I want you to hide your disgust, take no heed to your clean clothes, and come right down with me, — here, into the thickest of the fog and mud and foul effluvia. I want you to hear this story. There is a secret down here, in this nightmare fog, that has lain dumb for centuries: I want to make it a real thing to you. You, Egoist, or Pantheist, or Arminian,[5] busy in making straight paths for your feet on the hills, do not see it clearly, — this terrible question which men here have gone mad and died trying to answer. I dare not put this secret into words. I told you it was dumb. These men, going by with drunken faces and brains full of unawakened power, do not ask it of Society or of God. Their lives ask it; their deaths ask it. There is no reply. I will tell you plainly that I have a great hope; and I bring it to you to be tested. It is this: that this terrible dumb question is its own reply; that it is not the sentence of death we think it, but, from the very extremity of its darkness, the most solemn prophecy which the world has known of the Hope to come. I dare make my meaning no clearer, but will only tell my story. It will, perhaps, seem to you as foul and dark as this thick vapor about us, and as pregnant with death; but if your eyes are free as mine are to look deeper, no perfume-tinted dawn will be so fair with promise of the day that shall surely come.

My story is very simple, — only what I remember of the life of one of these men, — a furnace-tender in one of Kirby & John's rolling-mills,[6] — Hugh Wolfe. You know the mills? They took the great order for the Lower Virginia railroads there last winter; run usually

---

[4] *dilettante:* From the Italian verb *dilettare*, which means "to take delight in," a dilettante is a person who appreciates or loves the fine arts; the term, however, is often used disparagingly, since a dilettante tends to dabble in art, usually viewing it as one pastime among many rather than as a subject for serious or rigorous analysis.

[5] *Egoist . . . Arminian:* Not to be confused with egotists, who focus on themselves and their own worth, *egoists* assert that good can be found by pursuing self-interest; that is, for an egoist, the improvement of a person's welfare will lead to an ultimate sense of perfection and happiness. An adherent of *pantheism*, a doctrine popular with the English romantics, believes that God is everything and, conversely, that everything is God. *Arminians* belonged to a religious sect that began in Holland in the seventeenth century and then made its way to England and the American colonies. Unlike Calvinism, which it broke away from, Arminianism rejected the doctrine of absolute predestination as well as beliefs about the elect and the human will.

[6] *rolling-mills:* Mills producing iron rolled into sheets.

with about a thousand men. I cannot tell why I choose the half-forgotten story of this Wolfe more than that of myriads of these furnace-hands. Perhaps because there is a secret underlying sympathy between that story and this day with its impure fog and thwarted sunshine, — or perhaps simply for the reason that this house is the one where the Wolfes lived. There were the father and son, — both hands, as I said, in one of Kirby & John's mills for making railroad-iron, — and Deborah, their cousin, a picker in some of the cotton-mills. The house was rented then to half a dozen families. The Wolfes had two of the cellar-rooms. The old man, like many of the puddlers and feeders of the mills, was Welsh, — had spent half of his life in the Cornish tin-mines.[7] You may pick the Welsh emigrants, Cornish miners, out of the throng passing the windows, any day. They are a trifle more filthy; their muscles are not so brawny; they stoop more. When they are drunk, they neither yell, nor shout, nor stagger, but skulk along like beaten hounds. A pure, unmixed blood, I fancy: shows itself in the slight angular bodies and sharply-cut facial lines. It is nearly thirty years since the Wolfes lived here. Their lives were like those of their class: incessant labor, sleeping in kennel-like rooms, eating rank pork and molasses, drinking — God and the distillers only know what; with an occasional night in jail, to atone for some drunken excess. Is that all of their lives? — of the portion given to them and these their duplicates swarming the streets to-day? — nothing beneath? — all? So many a political reformer will tell you, — and many a private reformer too, who has gone among them with a heart tender with Christ's charity, and come out outraged, hardened.

One rainy night, about eleven o'clock, a crowd of half-clothed women stopped outside of the cellar-door. They were going home from the cotton-mill.

"Good-night, Deb," said one, a mulatto, steadying herself against the gas-post. She needed the post to steady her. So did more than one of them.

"Dah's a ball to Miss Potts' to-night. Ye'd best come."

"Inteet, Deb, if hur'll[8] come, hur'll hef fun," said a shrill Welsh voice in the crowd.

Two or three dirty hands were thrust out to catch the gown of the woman, who was groping for the latch of the door.

---

[7] *Cornish tin-mines:* That is, in Cornwall, a county in southwest England where much mining was done.

[8] *hur'll:* Dialectal pronoun used instead of *she, he, her,* and *him.*

"No."

"No? Where's Kit Small, then?"

"Begorra![9] on the spools. Alleys behint, though we helped her, we dud. An wid ye! Let Deb alone! It's ondacent frettin' a quite body. Be the powers, an' we'll have a night of it! there'll be lashin's o' drink, — the Vargent[10] be blessed and praised for't!"

They went on, the mulatto inclining for a moment to show fight, and drag the woman Wolfe off with them; but, being pacified, she staggered away.

Deborah groped her way into the cellar, and, after considerable stumbling, kindled a match, and lighted a tallow dip, that sent a yellow glimmer over the room. It was low, damp, — the earthen floor covered with a green, slimy moss, — a fetid air smothering the breath. Old Wolfe lay asleep on a heap of straw, wrapped in a torn horseblanket. He was a pale, meek little man, with a white face and red rabbit-eyes. The woman Deborah was like him; only her face was even more ghastly, her lips bluer, her eyes more watery. She wore a faded cotton gown and a slouching bonnet. When she walked, one could see that she was deformed, almost a hunchback. She trod softly, so as not to waken him, and went through into the room beyond. There she found by the half-extinguished fire an iron saucepan filled with cold boiled potatoes, which she put upon a broken chair with a pint-cup of ale. Placing the old candlestick beside this dainty repast, she untied her bonnet, which hung limp and wet over her face, and prepared to eat her supper. It was the first food that had touched her lips since morning. There was enough of it, however: there is not always. She was hungry, — one could see that easily enough, — and not drunk, as most of her companions would have been found at this hour. She did not drink, this woman, — her face told that, too, — nothing stronger than ale. Perhaps the weak, flaccid wretch had some stimulant in her pale life to keep her up, — some love or hope, it might be, or urgent need. When that stimulant was gone, she would take to whiskey. Man cannot live by work alone. While she was skinning the potatoes, and munching them, a noise behind her made her stop.

"Janey!" she called, lifting the candle and peering into the darkness. "Janey, are you there?"

A heap of ragged coats was heaved up, and the face of a young girl emerged, staring sleepily at the woman.

[9] *Begorra:* Irish-English euphemism for "by God."
[10] *Vargent:* The Virgin Mary, mother of Jesus.

"Deborah," she said, at last, "I'm here the night."

"Yes, child. Hur's welcome," she said, quietly eating on.

The girl's face was haggard and sickly; her eyes were heavy with sleep and hunger real Milesian[11] eyes they were, dark, delicate blue, glooming out from black shadows with a pitiful fright.

"I was alone," said said, timidly.

"Where's the father?" asked Deborah, holding out a potato, which the girl greedily seized.

"He's beyant,[12] — wid Haley, — in the stone house." (Did you ever hear the word *jail* from an Irish mouth?) "I came here. Hugh told me never to stay me-lone."[13]

"Hugh?"

"Yes."

A vexed frown crossed her face. The girl saw it, and added quickly, —

"I have not seen Hugh the day, Deb. The old man says his watch lasts till the mornin'."

The woman sprang up, and hastily began to arrange some bread and flitch[14] in a tin pail, and to pour her own measure of ale into a bottle. Tying on her bonnet, she blew out the candle.

"Lay ye down, Janey dear," she said, gently, covering her with the old rags. "Hur can eat the potatoes, if hur's hungry."

"Where are ye goin', Deb? The rain's sharp."

"To the mill, with Hugh's supper."

"Let him bide till th' morn. Sit ye down."

"No, no," — sharply pushing her off. "The boy'll starve."

She hurried from the cellar, while the child wearily coiled herself up for sleep. The rain was falling heavily, as the woman, pail in hand, emerged from the mouth of the alley, and turned down the narrow street, that stretched out, long and black, miles before her. Here and there a flicker of gas lighted an uncertain space of muddy footwalk and gutter; the long rows of houses, except an occasional lager-bier shop, were closed; now and then she met a band of mill-hands skulking to or from their work.

---

[11] *Milesian:* A synonym for *Irish, Milesian* refers to the followers and descendants of Miledh, who, according to the mythical history of Ireland, came from the East through Spain and into Ireland around 1000 B.C.

[12] *beyant:* Beyond.

[13] *me-lone:* Alone.

[14] *flitch:* Salted, cured pork; commonly, it refers to a side of bacon.

Not many even of the inhabitants of a manufacturing town know the vast machinery of system by which the bodies of workmen are governed, that goes unceasingly from year to year. The hands of each mill are divided into watches that relieve each other as regularly as the sentinels of an army. By night and day the work goes on, the unsleeping engines groan and shriek, the fiery pools of metal boil and surge. Only for a day in the week, a half-courtesy to public censure, the fires are partially veiled; but as soon as the clock strikes midnight, the great furnaces break forth with renewed fury, the clamor begins with fresh, breathless vigor, the engines sob and shriek like "gods in pain."

As Deborah hurried down through the heavy rain, the noise of these thousand engines sounded through the sleep and shadow of the city like far-off thunder. The mill to which she was going lay on the river, a mile below the city-limits. It was far, and she was weak, aching from standing twelve hours at the spools. Yet it was her almost nightly walk to take this man his supper, though at every square she sat down to rest, and she knew she should receive small word of thanks.

Perhaps, if she had possessed an artist's eye, the picturesque oddity of the scene might have made her step stagger less, and the path seem shorter; but to her the mills were only "summat deilish to look at by night."

The road leading to the mills had been quarried from the solid rock, which rose abrupt and bare on one side of the cinder-covered road, while the river, sluggish and black, crept past on the other. The mills for rolling iron are simply immense tent-like roofs, covering acres of ground, open on every side. Beneath these roofs Deborah looked in on a city of fires, that burned hot and fiercely in the night. Fire in every horrible form: pits of flame waving in the wind; liquid metal-flames writhing in tortuous streams through the sand; wide caldrons filled with boiling fire, over which bent ghastly wretches stirring the strange brewing; and through all, crowds of half-clad men, looking like revengeful ghosts in the red light, hurried, throwing masses of glittering fire. It was like a street in Hell. Even Deborah muttered, as she crept through, "'T looks like t' Devil's place!" It did, — in more ways than one.

She found the man she was looking for, at last, heaping coal on a furnace. He had not time to eat his supper; so she went behind the furnace, and waited. Only a few men were with him, and they noticed her only by a "Hyur comes t' hunchback, Wolfe."

Deborah was stupid with sleep; her back pained her sharply; and her teeth chattered with cold, with the rain that soaked her clothes and dripped from her at every step. She stood, however, patiently holding the pail, and waiting.

"Hout,[15] woman! ye look like a drowned cat. Come near to the fire," — said one of the men, approaching to scrape away the ashes.

She shook her head. Wolfe had forgotten her. He turned, hearing the man, and came closer.

"I did no' think; gi' me my supper, woman."

She watched him eat with a painful eagerness. With a woman's quick instinct, she saw that he was not hungry, — was eating to please her. Her pale, watery eyes began to gather a strange light.

"Is't good, Hugh? T'ale was a bit sour, I feared."

"No, good enough." He hesitated a moment. "Ye're tired, poor lass! Bide here till I go. Lay down there on that heap of ash, and go to sleep."

He threw her an old coat for a pillow, and turned to his work. The heap was the refuse of the burnt iron, and was not a hard bed; the half-smothered warmth, too, penetrated her limbs, dulling their pain and cold shiver.

Miserable enough she looked, lying there on the ashes like a limp, dirty rag, — yet not an unfitting figure to crown the scene of hopeless discomfort and veiled crime: more fitting, if one looked deeper into the heart of things, — at her thwarted woman's form, her colorless life, her waking stupor that smothered pain and hunger, — even more fit to be a type of her class. Deeper yet if one could look, was there nothing worth reading in this wet, faded thing, half-covered with ashes? no story of a soul filled with groping passionate love, heroic unselfishness, fierce jealousy? of years of weary trying to please the one human being whom she loved, to gain one look of real heart-kindness from him? If anything like this were hidden beneath the pale, bleared eyes, and dull, washed-out-looking face, no one had ever taken the trouble to read its faint signs: not the half-clothed furnace-tender, Wolfe, certainly. Yet he was kind to her: it was his nature to be kind, even to the very rats that swarmed in the cellar: kind to her in just that same way. She knew that. And it might be that very knowledge had given to her face its apathy and vacancy more than her low, torpid life. One sees that dead, vacant look steal sometimes over the rarest, finest of women's faces, — in the very

---

[15] *Hout:* Exclamatory greeting.

midst, it may be, of their warmest summer's day; and then one can guess at the secret of intolerable solitude that lies hid beneath the delicate laces and brilliant smile. There was no warmth, no brilliancy, no summer for this woman; so the stupor and vacancy had time to gnaw into her face perpetually. She was young, too, though no one guessed it; so the gnawing was the fiercer.

She lay quiet in the dark corner, listening, through the monotonous din and uncertain glare of the works, to the dull plash of the rain in the far distance, — shrinking back whenever the man Wolfe happened to look towards her. She knew, in spite of all his kindness, that there was that in her face and form which made him loathe the sight of her. She felt by instinct, although she could not comprehend it, the finer nature of the man, which made him among his fellow-workmen something unique, set apart. She knew, that, down under all the vileness and coarseness of his life, there was a groping passion for whatever was beautiful and pure, — that his soul sickened with disgust at her deformity, even when his words were kindest. Through this dull consciousness, which never left her, came, like a sting, the recollection of the little Irish girl she had left in the cellar. The recollection struck through even her stupid intellect with a vivid glow of beauty and grace. Little Janey, timid, helpless, clinging to Hugh as her only friend: that was the sharp thought, the bitter thought, that drove into the glazed eyes a fierce light of pain. You laugh at it? Are pain and jealousy less savage realities down here in this place I am taking you to than in your own house or your own heart, — your heart, which they clutch at sometimes? The note is the same, I fancy, be the octave high or low.

If you could go into this mill where Deborah lay, and drag out from the hearts of these men the terrible tragedy of their lives, taking it as a symptom of the disease of their class, no ghost Horror would terrify you more. A reality of soul-starvation, of living death, that meets you every day under the besotted faces on the street, — I can paint nothing of this, only give you the outside outlines of a night, a crisis in the life of one man: whatever muddy depth of soul-history lies beneath you can read according to the eyes God has given you.

Wolfe, while Deborah watched him as a spaniel its master, bent over the furnace with his iron pole, unconscious of her scrutiny, only stopping to receive orders. Physically, Nature had promised the man but little. He had already lost the strength and instinct vigor of a man, his muscles were thin, his nerves weak, his face (a meek, woman's face) haggard, yellow with consumption. In the mill he was known as one of the girl men: "Molly Wolfe" was his *sobriquet*.[16] He was never seen in the cockpit,[17] did not own a terrier, drank but seldom; when he did, desperately. He fought sometimes, but was always thrashed, pommelled to a jelly. The man was game enough, when his blood was up: but he was no favorite in the mill; he had the taint of school-learning on him, — not to a dangerous extent, only a quarter or so in the free-school[18] in fact, but enough to ruin him as a good hand in a fight.

For other reasons, too, he was not popular. Not one of themselves, they felt that, though outwardly as filthy and ash-covered; silent, with foreign thoughts and longings breaking out through his quietness in innumerable curious ways: this one, for instance. In the neighboring furnace-buildings lay great heaps of the refuse from the ore after the pig-metal is run. *Korl* we call it here: a light, porous substance, of a delicate, waxen, flesh-colored tinge. Out of the blocks of this korl, Wolfe, in his off-hours from the furnace, had a habit of chipping and moulding figures, — hideous, fantastic enough, but sometimes strangely beautiful: even the mill-men saw that, while they jeered at him. It was a curious fancy in the man, almost a passion. The few hours for rest he spent hewing and hacking with his blunt knife, never speaking, until his watch came again, — working at one figure for months, and, when it was finished, breaking it to pieces perhaps, in a fit of disappointment. A morbid, gloomy man, untaught, unled, left to feed his soul in grossness and crime, and hard, grinding labor.

I want you to come down and look at this Wolfe, standing there among the lowest of his kind, and see him just as he is, that you may judge him justly when you hear the story of this night. I want you to look back, as he does every day, at his birth in vice, his starved infancy; to remember the heavy years he has groped through as boy and man, — the slow, heavy years of constant, hot work. So long ago he began, that he thinks sometimes he has worked there for ages. There is no hope that it will ever end. Think that God put into this man's soul a fierce thirst for beauty, — to know it, to create it; to *be* — something, he knows not what, — other than he is. There are moments when a passing cloud, the sun glinting on the purple thistles, a kindly smile, a child's face, will rouse him to a passion of pain, — when his nature starts up with a mad cry of rage against

---

[16] *sobriquet:* "Nickname" (French).
[17] *cockpit:* Area where gamecocks fought and spectators wagered on the outcome.
[18] *free-school:* Public school.

God, man, whoever it is that has forced this vile, slimy life upon him. With all this groping, this mad desire, a great blind intellect stumbling through wrong, a loving poet's heart, the man was by habit only a coarse, vulgar laborer, familiar with sights and words you would blush to name. Be just: when I tell you about this night, see him as he is. Be just, — not like man's law, which seizes on one isolated fact, but like God's judging angel, whose clear, sad eye saw all the countless cankering days of this man's life, all the countless nights, when, sick with starving, his soul fainted in him, before it judged him for this night, the saddest of all.

I called this night the crisis of his life. If it was, it stole on him unawares. These great turning-days of life cast no shadow before, slip by unconsciously. Only a trifle, a little turn of the rudder, and the ship goes to heaven or hell.

Wolfe, while Deborah watched him, dug into the furnace of melting iron with his pole, dully thinking only how many rails the lump would yield. It was late, — nearly Sunday morning; another hour, and the heavy work would be done, — only the furnaces to replenish and cover for the next day. The workmen were growing more noisy, shouting, as they had to do, to be heard over the deep clamor of the mills. Suddenly they grew less boisterous, — at the far end, entirely silent. Something unusual had happened. After a moment, the silence came nearer; the men stopped their jeers and drunken choruses. Deborah, stupidly lifting up her head, saw the cause of the quiet. A group of five or six men were slowly approaching, stopping to examine each furnace as they came. Visitors often came to see the mills after night: except by growing less noisy, the men took no notice of them. The furnace where Wolfe worked was near the bounds of the works; they halted there hot and tired: a walk over one of these great foundries is no trifling task. The woman, drawing out of sight, turned over to sleep. Wolfe, seeing them stop, suddenly roused from his indifferent stupor, and watched them keenly. He knew some of them: the overseer, Clarke, — a son of Kirby, one of the mill-owners, — and a Doctor May, one of the town-physicians. The other two were strangers. Wolfe came closer. He seized eagerly every chance that brought him into contact with this mysterious class that shone down on him perpetually with the glamour of another order of being. What made the difference between them? That was the mystery of his life. He had a vague notion that perhaps to-night he could find it out. One of the strangers sat down on a pile of bricks, and beckoned young Kirby to his side.

"This *is* hot, with a vengeance. A match, please?" — lighting his cigar. "But the walk is worth the trouble. If it were not that you must have heard it so often, Kirby, I would tell you that your works look like Dante's Inferno."[19]

Kirby laughed.

"Yes. Yonder is Farinata[20] himself in the burning tomb," — pointing to some figure in the shimmering shadows.

"Judging from some of the faces of your men," said the other, "they bid fair to try the reality of Dante's vision, some day."

Young Kirby looked curiously around, as if seeing the faces of his hands[21] for the first time.

"They're bad enough, that's true. A desperate set, I fancy. Eh, Clarke?"

The overseer did not hear him. He was talking of net profits just then, — giving, in fact, a schedule of the annual business of the firm to a sharp peering little Yankee, who jotted down notes on a paper laid on the crown of his hat: a reporter for one of the city-papers, getting up a series of reviews of the leading manufactories. The other gentlemen had accompanied them merely for amusement. They were silent until the notes were finished, drying their feet at the furnaces, and sheltering their faces from the intolerable heat. At last the overseer concluded with —

"I believe that is a pretty fair estimate, Captain."

"Here, some of you men!" said Kirby, "bring up those boards. We may as well sit down, gentlemen, until the rain is over. It cannot last much longer at this rate."

"Pig-metal," — mumbled the reporter, — "um! — coal facilities, — um! — hands employed, twelve hundred, — bitumen, — um! — all right, I believe, Mr. Clarke; — sinking-fund,[22] — what did you say was your sinking-fund?"

---

[19] *Dante's Inferno:* The Italian poet Dante Alighieri (1265–1321) is best known as the author of *The Divine Comedy*, an epic poem completed in 1321 and divided into three sections: *Inferno* ("hell"), *Purgatorio* ("purgatory"), and *Paradiso* ("paradise"). In the *Inferno*, the poet and his guide, the spirit of the classical poet Virgil, visit the nine levels of hell, which descend conically into the earth.

[20] *Farinata:* In the sixth circle of hell (canto 10), Dante meets Farinata degli Uberti, a famous Florentine patriot whose family was an enemy of Dante's people, the Guelfs. After Farinata discusses his role in Florentine politics and explains how people in hell can see the future without understanding the present, Dante leaves with a new respect for his enemy.

[21] *hands:* Common term for workers in the nineteenth century.

[22] *coal facilities . . . sinking-fund:* Mill visitors' language of capitalist control of finance and production. *Bitumen* refers to coal, *sinking-fund* to sums set aside and invested, at interest, to pay debt and meet depreciation expenses.

"Twelve hundred hands?" said the stranger, the young man who had first spoken. "Do you control their votes,[23] Kirby?"

"Control? No." The young man smiled complacently. "But my father brought seven hundred votes to the polls for his candidate last November. No force-work, you understand, — only a speech or two, a hint to form themselves into a society, and a bit of red and blue bunting to make them a flag. The Invincible Roughs, — I believe that is their name. I forget the motto: 'Our country's hope,' I think."

There was a laugh. The young man talking to Kirby sat with an amused light in his cool gray eye, surveying critically the half-clothed figures of the puddlers, and the slow swing of their brawny muscles. He was a stranger in the city, — spending a couple of months in the borders of a Slave State,[24] to study the institutions of the South, — a brother-in-law of Kirby's, — Mitchell. He was an amateur gymnast, — hence his anatomical eye; a patron, in a *blasé* way, of the prize-ring; a man who sucked the essence out of a science or philosophy in an indifferent, gentlemanly way; who took Kant, Novalis, Humboldt,[25] for what they were worth in his own scales; accepting all, despising nothing, in heaven, earth, or hell, but one-idead men; with a temper yielding and brilliant as summer water, until his Self was touched, when it was ice, though brilliant still. Such men are not rare in the States.

As he knocked the ashes from his cigar, Wolfe caught with a quick pleasure the contour of the white hand, the blood-glow of a red ring he wore. His voice, too, and that of Kirby's, touched him like music, — low, even, with chording cadences. About this man Mitchell hung the impalpable atmosphere belonging to the thorough-bred gentleman. Wolfe, scraping away the ashes beside him, was conscious of it, did obeisance to it with his artist sense, unconscious that he did so.

The rain did not cease. Clarke and the reporter left the mills; the others, comfortably seated near the furnace, lingered, smoking and talking

[23] *control their votes:* Vote control refers to efforts of business capitalists to designate political candidates favorable to their interests and, through bribes and threats, to control the outcome of elections.

[24] *borders of a Slave State:* Wheeling, once part of Virginia, a slave state, bordered the free states of Ohio and Pennsylvania.

[25] *Kant, Novalis, Humboldt:* The German philosopher Immanuel Kant (1724–1804) explored rational understanding in his *Critique of Pure Reason, Critique of Practical Reason,* and *Critique of Judgment.* Novalis, the pen name of Friedrich von Hardenberg (1762–1801), was a novelist and leading poet of early German romanticism who believed in the mystical oneness of all things. Baron Alexander von Humboldt (1769–1859), a German naturalist and explorer, traveled throughout Latin America and studied its geography and meteorology; in *Kosmos,* his principal work, he described the physical universe.

in a desultory way. Greek would not have been more unintelligible to the furnace-tenders, whose presence they soon forgot entirely. Kirby drew out a newspaper from his pocket and read aloud some article, which they discussed eagerly. At every sentence, Wolfe listened more and more like a dumb, hopeless animal, with a duller, more stolid look creeping over his face, glancing now and then at Mitchell, marking acutely every smallest sign of refinement, then back to himself, seeing as in a mirror his filthy body, his more stained soul.

Never! He had no words for such a thought, but he knew now, in all the sharpness of the bitter certainty, that between them there was a great gulf never to be passed. Never!

The bell of the mills rang for midnight. Sunday morning had dawned. Whatever hidden message lay in the tolling bells floated past these men unknown. Yet it was there. Veiled in the solemn music ushering the risen Saviour was a key-note to solve the darkest secrets of a world gone wrong, — even this social riddle which the brain of the grimy puddler grappled with madly to-night.

The men began to withdraw the metal from the caldrons. The mills were deserted on Sundays, except by the hands who fed the fires, and those who had no lodgings and slept usually on the ash-heaps. The three strangers sat still during the next hour, watching the men cover the furnaces, laughing now and then at some jest of Kirby's.

"Do you know," said Mitchell, "I like this view of the works better than when the glare was fiercest? These heavy shadows and the amphitheatre of smothered fires are ghostly, unreal. One could fancy these red smouldering lights to be the half-shut eyes of wild beasts, and the spectral figures their victims in the den."

Kirby laughed. "You are fanciful. Come, let us get out of the den. The spectral figures, as you call them, are a little too real for me to fancy a close proximity in the darkness, — unarmed, too."

The others rose, buttoning their overcoats, and lighting cigars.

"Raining, still," said Doctor May, "and hard. Where did we leave the coach, Mitchell?"

"At the other side of the works. — Kirby, what's that?"

Mitchell started back, half-frightened, as, suddenly turning a corner, the white figure of a woman faced him in the darkness, — a woman, white, of giant proportions, crouching on the ground, her arms flung out in some wild gesture of warning.

"Stop! Make that fire burn there!" cried Kirby, stopping short.

The flame burst out, flashing the gaunt figure into bold relief.

Mitchell drew a long breath.

"I thought it was alive," he said, going up curiously.

The others followed.

"Not marble, eh?" asked Kirby, touching it.

One of the lower overseers stopped.

"Korl, Sir."

"Who did it?"

"Can't say. Some of the hands; chipped it out in off-hours."

"Chipped to some purpose, I should say. What a flesh-tint the stuff has! Do you see, Mitchell?"

"I see."

He had stepped aside where the light fell boldest on the figure, looking at it in silence. There was not one line of beauty or grace in it: a nude woman's form, muscular, grown coarse with labor, the powerful limbs instinct with some one poignant longing. One idea: there it was in the tense, rigid muscles, the clutching hands, the wild, eager face, like that of a starving wolf's. Kirby and Doctor May walked around it, critical, curious. Mitchell stood aloof, silent. The figure touched him strangely.

"Not badly done," said Doctor May. "Where did the fellow learn that sweep of the muscles in the arm and hand? Look at them! They are groping, — do you see? — clutching: the peculiar action of a man dying of thirst."

"They have ample facilities for studying anatomy," sneered Kirby, glancing at the half-naked figures.

"Look," continued the Doctor, "at this bony wrist, and the strained sinews of the instep! A working-woman, — the very type of her class."

"God forbid!" muttered Mitchell.

"Why?" demanded May. "What does the fellow intend by the figure? I cannot catch the meaning."

"Ask him," said the other, dryly. "There he stands," — pointing to Wolfe, who stood with a group of men, leaning on his ash-rake.

The Doctor beckoned him with the affable smile which kind-hearted men put on, when talking to these people.

"Mr. Mitchell has picked you out as the man who did this, — I'm sure I don't know why. But what did you mean by it?"

"She be hungry."

Wolfe's eyes answered Mitchell, not the Doctor.

"Oh-h! But what a mistake you have made, my fine fellow! You have given no sign of starvation to the body. It is strong, — terribly strong. It has the mad, half-despairing gesture of drowning."

Wolfe stammered, glanced appealingly at Mitchell, who saw the soul of the thing, he knew. But the cool, probing eyes were turned on himself now, — mocking, cruel, relentless.

"Not hungry for meat," the furnace-tender said at last.

"What then? Whiskey?" jeered Kirby, with a coarse laugh.

Wolfe was silent a moment, thinking.

"I dunno," he said, with a bewildered look. "It mebbe. Summat to make her live, I think, — like you. Whiskey ull do it, in a way."

The young man laughed again. Mitchell flashed a look of disgust somewhere, — not at Wolfe.

"May," he broke out impatiently, "are you blind? Look at that woman's face! It asks questions of God, and says 'I have a right to know.' Good God, how hungry it is!"

They looked a moment; then May turned to the mill-owner: —

"Have you many such hands as this? What are you going to do with them? Keep them at puddling iron?"

Kirby shrugged his shoulders. Mitchell's look had irritated him.

"*Ce n'est pas mon affaire.*[26] I have no fancy for nursing infant geniuses. I suppose there are some stray gleams of mind and soul among these wretches. The Lord will take care of his own; or else they can work out their own salvation. I have heard you call our American system a ladder which any man can scale. Do you doubt it? Or perhaps you want to banish all social ladders, and put us all on a flat table-land, — eh, May?"

The Doctor looked vexed, puzzled. Some terrible problem lay hid in this woman's face, and troubled these men. Kirby waited for an answer, and, receiving none, went on, warming with his subject.

"I tell you, there's something wrong that no talk of '*Liberté*' or '*Egalité*'[27] will do away. If I had the making of men, these men who do the lowest part of the world's work should be machines, — nothing more, — hands. It would be kindness. God help them! What are taste, reason, to creatures who must live such lives as that?" He pointed to Deborah, sleeping on the ash-heap. "So many nerves to sting them to pain. What if God had put your brain, with all its agony of touch, into your fingers, and bid you work and strike with that?"

"You think you could govern the world better?" laughed the Doctor.

[26] *Ce n'est pas mon affaire:* "It's not my concern" or "it's none of my business" (French).

[27] '*Liberté*' or '*Egalité*': "Liberté, égalité, fraternité" ("liberty, equality, fraternity") was the motto of the French Revolution.

"I do not think at all."

"That is true philosophy. Drift with the stream, because you cannot dive deep enough to find bottom, eh?"

"Exactly," rejoined Kirby. "I do not think. I wash my hands of all social problems, — slavery, caste, white or black. My duty to my operatives has a narrow limit, — the pay-hour on Saturday night. Outside of that, if they cut korl, or cut each other's throats, (the more popular amusement of the two,) I am not responsible."

The Doctor sighed, — a good honest sigh, from the depths of his stomach.

"God help us! Who is responsible?"

"Not I, I tell you," said Kirby, testily. "What has the man who pays them money to do with their souls' concerns, more than the grocer or butcher who takes it?"

"And yet," said Mitchell's cynical voice, "look at her! How hungry she is!"

Kirby tapped his boot with his cane. No one spoke. Only the dumb face of the rough image looking into their faces with the awful question, "What shall we do to be saved?" Only Wolfe's face, with its heavy weight of brain, its weak, uncertain mouth, its desperate eyes, out of which looked the soul of his class, — only Wolfe's face turned towards Kirby's. Mitchell laughed, — a cool, musical laugh.

"Money has spoken!" he said, seating himself lightly on a stone with the air of an amused spectator at a play. "Are you answered?" — turning to Wolfe his clear, magnetic face.

Bright and deep and cold as Arctic air, the soul of the man lay tranquil beneath. He looked at the furnace-tender as he had looked at a rare mosaic in the morning; only the man was the more amusing study of the two.

"Are you answered? Why, May, look at him! *'De profundis clamavi.'*[28] Or, to quote in English, 'Hungry and thirsty, his soul faints in him.' And so Money sends back its answer into the depths through you, Kirby! Very clear the answer, too! — I think I remember reading the same words somewhere: — washing your hands in Eau de Cologne, and saying, 'I am innocent of the blood of this man. See ye to it!'"[29]

---

[28] *'De profundis clamavi'*: "We shout out of the deep" (Latin version of Psalm 130:1). Thus, a bitter, wretched cry for help.

[29] *"I am innocent . . . . See ye to it!"*: A reference to the words of Pontius Pilate, the Roman procurator of Judea (ca. 26–36 A.D.) who allowed Christ to be crucified but would not accept responsibility for his actions. See Matthew 27:24.

Kirby flushed angrily.

"You quote Scripture freely."

"Do I not quote correctly? I think I remember another line, which may amend my meaning: 'Inasmuch as ye did it unto one of the least of these, ye did it unto me.' Deist?[30] Bless you, man, I was raised on the milk of the Word. Now, Doctor, the pocket of the world having uttered its voice, what has the heart to say? You are a philanthropist, in a small way, — *n'est ce pas?*[31] Here, boy, this gentleman can show you how to cut korl better, — or your destiny. Go on, May!"

"I think a mocking devil possesses you to-night," rejoined the Doctor, seriously.

He went to Wolfe and put his hand kindly on his arm. Something of a vague idea possessed the Doctor's brain that much good was to be done here by a friendly word or two: a latent genius to be warmed into life by a waited-for sunbeam. Here it was: he had brought it. So he went on complacently: —

"Do you know, boy, you have it in you to be a great sculptor, a great man? — do you understand?" (talking down to the capacity of his hearer: it is a way people have with children, and men like Wolfe,) — "to live a better, stronger life than I, or Mr. Kirby here? A man may make himself anything he chooses. God has given you stronger powers than many men, — me, for instance."

May stopped, heated, glowing with his own magnanimity. And it was magnanimous. The puddler had drunk in every word, looking through the Doctor's flurry, and generous heat, and self-approval, into his will, with those slow, absorbing eyes of his.

"Make yourself what you will. It is your right."

"I know," quietly. "Will you help me?"

Mitchell laughed again. The Doctor turned now, in a passion, —

"You know, Mitchell, I have not the means. You know, if I had, it is in my heart to take this boy and educate him for" ——

"The glory of God, and the glory of John May."

May did not speak for a moment; then, controlled, he said, —

"Why should one be raised, when myriads are left? — I have not the money, boy," to Wolfe, shortly.

"Money?" He said it over slowly, as one repeats the guessed answer to a riddle, doubtfully. "That is it? Money?"

---

[30] *Deist:* Deists believe in a personal God and base their religion on reason, not revelation; Deism emerged as a result of the burgeoning interest in science that started in the Renaissance and lasted into the eighteenth century.

[31] *n'est ce pas?:* "Isn't it so?" (French).

"Yes, money, — that is it," said Mitchell, rising, and drawing his furred coat about him. "You've found the cure for all the world's diseases. — Come, May, find your good-humor, and come home. This damp wind chills my very bones. Come and preach your Saint-Simonian[32] doctrines to-morrow to Kirby's hands. Let them have a clear idea of the rights of the soul, and I'll venture next week they'll strike for higher wages. That will be the end of it."

"Will you send the coach-driver to this side of the mills?" asked Kirby, turning to Wolfe.

He spoke kindly: it was his habit to do so. Deborah, seeing the puddler go, crept after him. The three men waited outside. Doctor May walked up and down, chafed. Suddenly he stopped.

"Go back, Mitchell! You say the pocket and the heart of the world speak without meaning to these people. What has its head to say? Taste, culture, refinement? Go!"

Mitchell was leaning against a brick wall. He turned his head indolently, and looked into the mills. There hung about the place a thick, unclean odor. The slightest motion of his hand marked that he perceived it, and his insufferable disgust. That was all. May said nothing, only quickened his angry tramp.

"Besides," added Mitchell, giving a corollary to his answer, "it would be of no use. I am not one of them."

"You do not mean" —— said May, facing him.

"Yes, I mean just that. Reform is born of need, not pity. No vital movement of the people's has worked down, for good or evil; fermented, instead, carried up the heaving, cloggy mass. Think back through history, and you will know it. What will this lowest deep — thieves, Magdalens,[33] negroes — do with the light filtered through ponderous Church creeds, Baconian theories, Goethe schemes?[34]

---

[32] *Saint-Simonian:* The Saint-Simonians based their protosocialist movement on the writings of the French social philosopher Claude Henry de Rouvroy, comte de Saint-Simon (1760–1825). In a series of lectures published from 1828 to 1830, the Saint-Simonians called for public control of the means of production and an end to individual inheritance.

[33] *Magdalens:* Prostitutes or reformed prostitutes; the name refers to Mary Magdalene, a follower of Christ who may have been a prostitute.

[34] *Baconian theories, Goethe schemes:* Sir Francis Bacon (1561–1626), English philosopher, statesman, and essayist who stressed the importance of developing a systemic way of amassing empirical knowledge about the natural world; Johann Wolfgang von Goethe (1749–1832), German poet, playwright, and novelist who was perhaps the greatest figure of the German romantic period.

Some day, out of their bitter need will be thrown up their own light-bringer, — their Jean Paul, their Cromwell,[35] their Messiah."

"Bah!" was the Doctor's inward criticism. However, in practice, he adopted the theory; for, when, night and morning, afterwards, he prayed that power might be given these degraded souls to rise, he glowed at heart, recognizing an accomplished duty.

Wolfe and the woman had stood in the shadow of the works as the coach drove off. The Doctor had held out his hand in a frank, generous way, telling him to "take care of himself, and to remember it was his right to rise." Mitchell had simply touched his hat, as to an equal, with a quiet look of thorough recognition. Kirby had thrown Deborah some money, which she found, and clutched eagerly enough. They were gone now, all of them. The man sat down on the cinder-road, looking up into the murky sky.

"'T be late, Hugh. Wunnot hur come?"

He shook his head doggedly, and the woman crouched out of his sight against the wall. Do you remember rare moments when a sudden light flashed over yourself, your world, God? when you stood on a mountain-peak, seeing your life as it might have been, as it is? one quick instant, when custom lost its force and every-day usage? when your friend, wife, brother, stood in a new light? your soul was bared, and the grave, — a fore-taste of the nakedness of the Judgment-Day? So it came before him, his life, that night. The slow tides of pain he had borne gathered themselves up and surged against his soul. His squalid daily life, the brutal coarseness eating into his brain, as the ashes into his skin: before, these things had been a dull aching into his consciousness; to-night, they were reality. He griped[36] the filthy red shirt that clung, stiff with soot, about him, and tore it savagely from his arm. The flesh beneath was muddy with grease and ashes, — and the heart beneath that! And the soul? God knows.

Then flashed before his vivid poetic sense the man who had left him, — the pure face, the delicate, sinewy limbs, in harmony with all he knew of beauty or truth. In his cloudy fancy he had pictured a Something like this. He had found it in this Mitchell, even when he

---

[35] *their Jean Paul, their Cromwell:* Jean Paul Marat (1743–1793), Swiss-born French politician and physician who participated in the French Revolution, first by publishing the paper *L'Ami du peuple* (*The Friend of the People*) and later by helping Danton and Robespierre overthrow the Girondists, a middle-class political party; Oliver Cromwell (1599–1658), English Puritan leader who dissolved Parliament in 1653 and became lord protector of England (1653–1658).

[36] *griped:* Gripped.

idly scoffed at his pain: a Man all-knowing, all-seeing, crowned by Nature, reigning, — the keen glance of his eye falling like a sceptre on other men. And yet his instinct taught him that he too —— He! He looked at himself with sudden loathing, sick, wrung his hands with a cry, and then was silent. With all the phantoms of his heated, ignorant fancy, Wolfe had not been vague in his ambitions. They were practical, slowly built up before him out of his knowledge of what he could do. Through years he had day by day made this hope a real thing to himself, — a clear, projected figure of himself, as he might become.

Able to speak, to know what was best, to raise these men and women working at his side up with him: sometimes he forgot this defined hope in the frantic anguish to escape, — only to escape, — out of the wet, the pain, the ashes, somewhere, anywhere, — only for one moment of free air on a hill-side, to lie down and let his sick soul throb itself out in the sunshine. But to-night he panted for life. The savage strength of his nature was roused; his cry was fierce to God for justice.

"Look at me!" he said to Deborah, with a low, bitter laugh, striking his puny chest savagely. "What am I worth, Deb? Is it my fault that I am no better? My fault? My fault?"

He stopped, stung with a sudden remorse, seeing her hunchback shape writing with sobs. For Deborah was crying thankless tears, according to the fashion of women.

"God forgi' me, woman! Things go harder wi' you nor me. It's a worse share."

He got up and helped her to rise; and they went doggedly down the muddy street, side by side.

"It's all wrong," he muttered, slowly, — "all wrong! I dunnot understan'. But it'll end some day."

"Come home, Hugh!" she said, coaxingly; for he had stopped, looking around bewildered.

"Home, — and back to the mill!" He went on saying this over to himself, as if he would mutter down every pain in this dull despair.

She followed him through the fog, her blue lips chattering with cold. They reached the cellar at last. Old Wolfe had been drinking since she went out, and had crept nearer the door. The girl Janey slept heavily in the corner. He went up to her, touching softly the worn white arm with his fingers. Some bitterer thought stung him, as he stood there. He wiped the drops from his forehead, and went into the room beyond, livid, trembling. A hope, trifling, perhaps, but very dear, had died just then out of the poor puddler's life, as he looked at the sleeping, innocent girl, — some plan for the future, in which she had borne a part. He gave it up that moment, then and forever. Only a trifle, perhaps, to us: his face grew a shade paler, — that was all. But, somehow, the man's soul, as God and the angels looked down on it, never was the same afterwards.   *— hopeless*

Deborah followed him into the inner room. She carried a candle, which she placed on the floor, closing the door after her. She had seen the look on his face, as he turned away: her own grew deadly. Yet, as she came up to him, her eyes glowed. He was seated on an old chest, quiet, holding his face in his hands.

"Hugh!" she said, softly.

He did not speak.

"Hugh, did hur hear what the man said, — him with the clear voice? Did hur hear? Money, money, — that it wud do all?"

He pushed her away, — gently, but he was worn out; her rasping tone fretted him.

"Hugh!"

The candle flared a pale yellow light over the cobwebbed brick walls, and the woman standing there. He looked at her. She was young, in deadly earnest; her faded eyes, and wet, ragged figure caught from their frantic eagerness a power akin to beauty.

"Hugh, it is true! Money ull do it! Oh, Hugh, boy, listen till me! He said it true! It is money!"

"I know. Go back! I do not want you here."

"Hugh, it is t' last time. I'll never worrit[37] hur again."

There were tears in her voice now, but she choked them back.

"Hear till me only to-night! If one of t' witch people wud come, them we heard of t' home, and gif hur all hur wants, what then? Say, Hugh!"

"What do you mean?"

"I mean money."

Her whisper shrilled through his brain.

"If one of t' witch dwarfs wud come from t' lane moors to-night, and gif hur money, to go out, — *out*, I say, — out, lad, where t' sun shines, and t' heath grows, and t' ladies walk in silken gownds, and God stays all t' time, — where t' man lives that talked to us to-night, — Hugh knows, — Hugh could walk there like a king!"

---

[37] *worrit:* Worry.

He thought the woman mad, tried to check her, but she went on, fierce in her eager haste.

"If *I* were t' witch dwarf, if I had t' money, wud hur thank me? Wud hur take me out o' this place wid hur and Janey? I wud not come into the gran' house hur wud build, to vex hur wid t' hunch, — only at night, when t' shadows were dark, stand far off to see hur."

Mad? Yes! Are many of us mad in this way?

"Poor Deb! poor Deb!" he said, soothingly.

"It is here," she said, suddenly jerking into his hand a small roll. "I took it! I did it! Me, me! — not hur! I shall be hanged, I shall be burnt in hell, if anybody knows I took it! Out of his pocket, as he leaned against t' bricks. Hur knows?"

She thrust it into his hand, and then, her errand done, began to gather chips together to make a fire, choking down hysteric sobs.

"Has it come to this?"

That was all he said. The Welsh Wolfe blood was honest. The roll was a small green pocket-book containing one or two gold pieces, and a check for an incredible amount, as it seemed to the poor puddler. He laid it down, hiding his face again in his hands.

"Hugh, don't be angry wud me! It's only poor Deb, — hur knows?"

He took the long skinny fingers kindly in his.

"Angry? God help me, no! Let me sleep. I am tired."

He threw himself heavily down on the wooden bench, stunned with pain and weariness. She brought some old rags to cover him.

It was late on Sunday evening before he awoke. I tell God's truth, when I say he had then no thought of keeping this money. Deborah had hid it in his pocket. He found it there. She watched him eagerly, as he took it out.

"I must gif it to him," he said, reading her face.

"Hur knows," she said with a bitter sigh of disappointment. "But it is hur right to keep it."

His right! The word struck him. Doctor May had used the same. He washed himself, and went out to find this man Mitchell. His right! Why did this chance word cling to him so obstinately? Do you hear the fierce devils whisper in his ear, as he went slowly down the darkening street?

The evening came on, slow and calm. He seated himself at the end of an alley leading into one of the larger streets. His brain was clear to-night, keen, intent, mastering. It would not start back, cowardly, from any hellish temptation, but meet it face to face. Therefore the great temptation of his life came to him veiled by no sophistry, but bold, defiant, owning its own vile name, trusting to one bold blow for victory.

He did not deceive himself. Theft! That was it. At first the word sickened him; then he grappled with it. Sitting there on a broken cart-wheel, the fading day, the noisy groups, the church-bells' tolling passed before him like a panorama,[38] while the sharp struggle went on within. This money! He took it out, and looked at it. If he gave it back, what then? He was going to be cool about it.

People going by to church saw only a sickly mill-boy watching them quietly at the alley's mouth. They did not know that he was mad, or they would not have gone by so quietly: mad with hunger; stretching out his hands to the world, that had given so much to them, for leave to live the life God meant him to live. His soul within him was smothering to death; he wanted so much, thought so much, and *knew* — nothing. There was nothing of which he was certain, except the mill and things there. Of God and heaven he had heard so little, that they were to him what fairy-land is to a child: something real, but not here; very far off. His brain, greedy, dwarfed, full of thwarted energy and unused powers, questioned these men and women going by, coldly, bitterly, that night. Was it not his right to live as they, — a pure life, a good, true-hearted life, full of beauty and kind words? He only wanted to know how to use the strength within him. His heart warmed, as he thought of it. He suffered himself[39] to think of it longer. If he took the money?

Then he saw himself as he might be, strong, helpful, kindly. The night crept on, as this one image slowly evolved itself from the crowd of other thoughts and stood triumphant. He looked at it. As he might be! What wonder, if it blinded him to delirium, — the madness that underlies all revolution, all progress, and all fall?

You laugh at the shallow temptation? You see the error underlying its argument so clearly, — that to him a true life was one of full development rather than self-restraint? that he was deaf to the higher tone in a cry of voluntary suffering for truth's sake than in the fullest flow of spontaneous harmony? I do not plead his cause. I only want to

---

[38] *panorama:* The extended paintings, of a landscape or other scene, that were often displayed a section at a time before nineteenth-century audiences as a form of entertainment.

[39] *suffered himself:* Allowed himself.

show you the mote in my brother's eye: then you can see clearly to take it out.[40]

The money, — there it lay on his knee, a little blotted slip of paper, nothing in itself; used to raise him out of the pit; something straight from God's hand. A thief! Well, what was it to be a thief? He met the question at last, face to face, wiping the clammy drops of sweat from his forehead. God made this money — the fresh air, too — for his children's use. He never made the difference between poor and rich. The Something who looked down on him that moment through the cool gray sky had a kindly face, he knew, — loved his children alike. Oh, he knew that!

There were times when the soft floods of color in the crimson and purple flames, or the clear depth of amber in the water below the bridge, had somehow given him a glimpse of another world than this, — of an infinite depth of beauty and of quiet somewhere, — somewhere, — a depth of quiet and rest and love. Looking up now, it became strangely real. The sun had sunk quite below the hills, but his last rays struck upward, touching the zenith. The fog had risen, and the town and river were steeped in its thick, gray, damp; but overhead, the sun-touched smoke-clouds opened like a cleft ocean, — shifting, rolling seas of crimson mist, waves of billowy silver veined with blood-scarlet, inner depths unfathomable of glancing light. Wolfe's artist-eye grew drunk with color. The gates of that other world! Fading, flashing before him now! What, in that world of Beauty, Content, and Right, were the petty laws, the mine and thine, of mill-owners and mill-hands?

A consciousness of power stirred within him. He stood up. A man, — he thought, stretching out his hands, — free to work, to live, to love! Free! His right! He folded the scrap of paper in his hand. As his nervous fingers took it in, limp and blotted, so his soul took in the mean temptation, lapped it in fancied rights, in dreams of improved existences, drifting and endless as the cloud-seas of color. Clutching it, as if the tightness of his hold would strengthen his sense of possession, he went aimlessly down the street. It was his watch at the mill.

---

[40] *I only want to show you . . . take it out:* A reference to Christ's words in the Sermon on the Mount: "And why beholdest thou the mote that is in thy brother's eye, but considerest not the beam that is in thine own eye? Or how wilt thou say to thy brother, let me pull out the mote out of thine eye, and, behold, a beam is in thine own eye?" See Matthew 7:3–4.

He need not go, need never go again, thank God! — shaking off the thought with unspeakable loathing.

Shall I go over the history of the hours of that night? how the man wandered from one to another of his old haunts, with a half-consciousness of bidding them farewell, — lanes and alleys and back-yards where the mill-hands lodged, — noting, with a new eagerness, the filth and drunkenness, the pig-pens, the ash-heaps covered with potato-skins, the bloated, pimpled women at the doors, — with a new disgust, a new sense of sudden triumph, and, under all, a new, vague dread, unknown before, smothered down, kept under, but still there? It left him but once during the night, when, for the second time in his life, he entered a church. It was a sombre Gothic pile,[41] where the stained light lost itself in far-retreating arches; built to meet the requirements and sympathies of a far other class than Wolfe's. Yet it touched, moved him uncontrollably. The distances, the shadows, the still, marble figures, the mass of silent kneeling worshippers, the mysterious music, thrilled, lifted his soul with a wonderful pain. Wolfe forgot himself, forgot the new life he was going to live, the mean terror gnawing underneath. The voice of the speaker strengthened the charm; it was clear, feeling, full, strong. An old man, who had lived much, suffered much; whose brain was keenly alive, dominant; whose heart was summer-warm with charity. He taught it to-night. He held up Humanity in its grand total; showed the great world-cancer to his people. Who could show it better? He was a Christian reformer; he had studied the age thoroughly; his outlook at man had been free, world-wide, over all time. His faith stood sublime upon the Rock of Ages; his fiery zeal guided vast schemes by which the gospel was to be preached to all nations. How did he preach it to-night? In burning, light-laden words he painted the incarnate Life, Love, the universal Man: words that became reality in the lives of these people, — that lived again in beautiful words and actions, trifling, but heroic. Sin, as he defined it, was a real foe to them; their trials, temptations, were his. His words passed far over the furnace-tender's grasp, toned to suit another class of culture; they sounded in his ears a very pleasant song in an unknown tongue. He meant to cure this world-cancer with a steady eye that had never glared with hunger, and a hand that neither poverty nor strychnine-whiskey[42] had taught to shake. In this morbid, distorted heart of the Welsh puddler he had failed.

[41] *pile:* Large building.
[42] *strychnine-whiskey:* Sickening alcoholic spirits.

Wolfe rose at last, and turned from the church down the street. He looked up; the night had come on foggy, damp; the golden mists had vanished, and the sky lay dull and ash-colored. He wandered again aimlessly down the street, idly wondering what had become of the cloud-sea of crimson and scarlet. The trial-day of this man's life was over, and he had lost the victory. What followed was mere drifting circumstance, — a quicker walking over the path, — that was all. Do you want to hear the end of it? You wish me to make a tragic story out of it? Why, in the police-reports of the morning paper you can find a dozen such tragedies: hints of shipwrecks unlike any that ever befell on the high seas; hints that here a power was lost to heaven, — that there a soul went down where no tide can ebb or flow. Commonplace enough the hints are, — jocose sometimes, done up in rhyme.

Doctor May, a month after the night I have told you of, was reading to his wife at breakfast from this fourth column of the morning-paper: an unusual thing, — these police-reports not being, in general, choice reading for ladies; but it was only one item he read.

"Oh, my dear! You remember that man I told you of, that we saw at Kirby's mill? — that was arrested for robbing Mitchell? Here he is; just listen: — 'Circuit Court. Judge Day. Hugh Wolfe, operative in Kirby & John's Loudon Mills. Charge, grand larceny. Sentence, nineteen years hard labor in penitentiary.' — Scoundrel! Serves him right! After all our kindness that night! Picking Mitchell's pocket at the very time!"

His wife said something about the ingratitude of that kind of people, and then they began to talk of something else.

Nineteen years! How easy that was to read! What a simple word for Judge Day to utter! Nineteen years! Half a lifetime!

Hugh Wolfe sat on the window-ledge of his cell, looking out. His ankles were ironed. Not usual in such cases; but he had made two desperate efforts to escape. "Well," as Haley, the jailer, said, "small blame to him! Nineteen years' imprisonment was not a pleasant thing to look forward to." Haley was very good-natured about it, though Wolfe had fought him savagely.

"When he was first caught," the jailer said afterwards, in telling the story, "before the trial, the fellow was cut down at once, — laid there on that pallet like a dead man, with his hands over his eyes. Never saw a man so cut down in my life. Time of the trial, too, came the queerest dodge of any customer I ever had. Would choose no lawyer. Judge gave him one, of course. Gibson it was. He tried to

prove the fellow crazy; but it wouldn't go. Thing was plain as daylight: money found on him. 'Twas a hard sentence, — all the law al-
lows; but it was for 'xample's sake. These mill-hands are gettin' on-
bearable. When the sentence was read, he just looked up, and said the
money was his by rights, and that all the world had gone wrong.
That night, after the trial, a gentleman came to see him here, name of
Mitchell, — him as he stole from. Talked to him for an hour.
Thought he came for curiosity, like. After he was gone, thought
Wolfe was remarkable quiet, and went into his cell. Found him very
low; bed all bloody. Doctor said he had been bleeding at the lungs.
He was as weak as a cat; yet, if ye'll b'lieve me, he tried to get a-past
me and get out. I just carried him like a baby, and threw him on the
pallet. Three days after, he tried it again: that time reached the wall.
Lord help you! he fought like a tiger, — giv' some terrible blows.
Fightin' for life, you see; for he can't live long, shut up in the stone
crib down yonder. Got a death-cough now. 'T took two of us to
bring him down that day; so I just put the irons on his feet. There he
sits, in there. Goin' to-morrow, with a batch more of 'em. That
woman, hunchback, tried with him, — you remember? — she's only
got three years. 'Complice. But *she's* a woman, you know. He's been
quiet ever since I put on irons: giv' up, I suppose. Looks white, sick-
lookin'. It acts different on 'em, bein' sentenced. Most of 'em gets
reckless, devilish-like. Some prays awful, and sings them vile songs of
the mills, all in a breath. That woman, now, she's desper't'. Been beg-
gin' to see Hugh, as she calls him, for three days. I'm a-goin' to let
her in. She don't go with him. Here she is in this next cell. I'm a-goin'
now to let her in."

He let her in. Wolfe did not see her. She crept into a corner of the
cell, and stood watching him. He was scratching the iron bars of the
window with a piece of tin which he had picked up, with an idle, uncertain, vacant stare, just as a child or idiot would do.

"Tryin' to get out, old boy?" laughed Haley. "Them irons will
need a crowbar beside your tin, before you can open 'em."

Wolfe laughed, too, in a senseless way.

"I think I'll get out," he said.

"I believe his brain's touched," said Haley, when he came out.

The puddler scraped away with the tin for half an hour. Still Deborah did not speak. At last she ventured nearer, and touched his arm.

"Blood?" she said, looking at some spots on his coat with a
shudder.

He looked up at her. "Why, Deb!" he said, smiling, — such a bright, boyish smile, that it went to poor Deborah's heart directly, and she sobbed and cried out loud.

"Oh, Hugh, lad! Hugh! dunnot look at me, when it wur my fault! To think I brought hur to it! And I loved hur so! Oh, lad, I dud!"

The confession, even in this wretch, came with the woman's blush through the sharp cry.

He did not seem to hear her, — scraping away diligently at the bars with the bit of tin.

Was he going mad? She peered closely into his face. Something she saw there made her draw suddenly back, — something which Haley had not seen, that lay beneath the pinched, vacant look it had caught since the trial, or the curious gray shadow that rested on it. That gray shadow, — yes, she knew what that meant. She had often seen it creeping over women's faces for months, who died at last of slow hunger or consumption. That meant death, distant, lingering: but this —— Whatever it was the woman saw, or thought she saw, used as she was to crime and misery, seemed to make her sick with a new horror. Forgetting her fear of him, she caught his shoulders, and looked keenly, steadily, into his eyes.

"Hugh!" she cried, in a desperate whisper, — "oh, boy, not that! for God's sake, not *that!*"

The vacant laugh went off his face, and he answered her in a muttered word or two that drove her away. Yet the words were kindly enough. Sitting there on his pallet, she cried silently a hopeless sort of tears, but did not speak again. The man looked up furtively at her now and then. Whatever his own trouble was, her distress vexed him with a momentary sting.

It was market-day. The narrow window of the jail looked down directly on the carts and wagons drawn up in a long line, where they had unloaded. He could see, too, and hear distinctly the clink of money as it changed hands, the busy crowd of whites and blacks shoving, pushing one another, and the chaffering[43] and swearing at the stalls. Somehow, the sound, more than anything else had done, wakened him up, — made the whole real to him. He was done with the world and the business of it. He let the tin fall, and looked out, pressing his face close to the rusty bars. How they crowded and pushed! And he, — he should never walk that pavement again! There

[43] *chaffering:* Teasing.

came Neff Sanders, one of the feeders at the mill, with a basket on his
arm. Sure enough, Neff was married the other week. He whistled,
hoping he would look up; but he did not. He wondered if Neff remembered he was there, — if any of the boys thought of him up
there, and thought that he never was to go down that old cinder-road
again. Never again! He had not quite understood it before; but now
he did. Not for days or years, but never! — that was it.

How clear the light fell on that stall in front of the market! and
how like a picture it was, the dark-green heaps of corn, and the crimson beets, and golden melons! There was another with game: how the
light flickered on that pheasant's breast, with the purplish blood dripping over the brown feathers! He could see the red shining of the
drops, it was so near. In one minute he could be down there. It was
just a step. So easy, as it seemed, so natural to go! Yet it could never
be — not in all the thousands of years to come — that he should put
his foot on that street again! He thought of himself with a sorrowful
pity, as of some one else. There was a dog down in the market, walking after his master with such a stately, grave look! — only a dog, yet
he could go backwards and forwards just as he pleased: he had good
luck! Why, the very vilest cur, yelping there in the gutter, had not
lived his life, had been free to act out whatever thought God had put
into his brain; while he —— No, he would not think of that! He tried
to put the thought away, and to listen to a dispute between a countryman and a woman about some meat; but it would come back. He,
what had he done to bear this?

Then came the sudden picture of what might have been, and now.
He knew what it was to be in the penitentiary, — how it went with
men there. He knew how in these long years he should slowly die, but
not until soul and body had become corrupt and rotten, — how,
when he came out, if he lived to come, even the lowest of the mill-
hands would jeer him, — how his hands would be weak, and his
brain senseless and stupid. He believed he was almost that now. He
put his hand to his head, with a puzzled, weary look. It ached, his
head, with thinking. He tried to quiet himself. It was only right, perhaps; he had done wrong. But was there right or wrong for such as
he? What was right? And who had ever taught him? He thrust the
whole matter away. A dark, cold quiet crept through his brain. It was
all wrong; but let it be! It was nothing to him more than the others.
Let it be!

The door grated, as Haley opened it.

"Come, my woman! Must lock up for t' night. Come, stir yerself!"

"Good-night, Deb," he said, carelessly.

She had not hoped he would say more; but the tired pain on her mouth just then was bitterer than death. She took his passive hand and kissed it.

"Hur'll never see Deb again!" she ventured, her lips growing colder and more bloodless.

What did she say that for? Did he not know it? Yet he would not be impatient with poor old Deb. She had trouble of her own, as well as he.

"No, never again," he said, trying to be cheerful.

She stood just a moment, looking at him. Do you laugh at her, standing there, with her hunchback, her rags, her bleared, withered face, and the great despised love tugging at her heart?

"Come, you!" called Haley, impatiently.

She did not move.

"Hugh!" she whispered.

It was to be her last word. What was it?

"Hugh, boy, not THAT!"

He did not answer. She wrung her hands, trying to be silent, looking in his face in an agony of entreaty. He smiled again, kindly.

"It is best, Deb. I cannot bear to be hurted any more."

"Hur knows," she said, humbly.

"Tell my father good-bye; and — and kiss little Janey."

She nodded, saying nothing, looked in his face again, and went out of the door. As she went, she staggered.

"Drinkin' to-day?" broke out Haley, pushing her before him. "Where the Devil did you get it? Here, in with ye!" and he shoved her into her cell, next to Wolfe's, and shut the door.

Along the wall of her cell there was a crack low down by the floor, through which she could see the light from Wolfe's. She had discovered it days before. She hurried in now, and, kneeling down by it, listened, hoping to hear some sound. Nothing but the rasping of the tin on the bars. He was at his old amusement again. Something in the noise jarred on her ear, for she shivered as she heard it. Hugh rasped away at the bars. A dull old bit of tin, not fit to cut korl with.

He looked out of the window again. People were leaving the market now. A tall mulatto girl, following her mistress, her basket on her head, crossed the street just below, and looked up. She was laughing; but, when she caught sight of the haggard face peering out through the bars, suddenly grew grave, and hurried by. A free, firm step, a clear-cut olive face, with a scarlet turban tied on one side, dark, shining eyes, and on the head the basket poised, filled with fruit and flowers, under which the scarlet turban and bright eyes looked out half-shadowed. The picture caught his eye. It was good to see a face like that. He would try to-morrow, and cut one like it. *To-morrow!* He threw down the tin, trembling, and covered his face with his hands. When he looked up again, the daylight was gone.

Deborah, crouching near by on the other side of the wall, heard no noise. He sat on the side of the low pallet, thinking. Whatever was the mystery which the woman had seen on his face, it came out now slowly, in the dark there, and became fixed, — a something never seen on his face before. The evening was darkening fast. The market had been over for an hour; the rumbling of the carts over the pavement grew more infrequent: he listened to each, as it passed, because he thought it was to be for the last time. For the same reason, it was, I suppose, that he strained his eyes to catch a glimpse of each passer-by, wondering who they were, what kind of homes they were going to, if they had children, — listening eagerly to every chance word in the street, as if — (God be merciful to the man! what strange fancy was this?) — as if he never should hear human voices again.

It was quite dark at last. The street was a lonely one. The last passenger, he thought, was gone. No, — there was a quick step: Joe Hill, lighting the lamps. Joe was a good old chap; never passed a fellow without some joke or other. He remembered once seeing the place where he lived with his wife. "Granny Hill" the boys called her. Bedridden she was; but so kind as Joe was to her! kept the room so clean! — and the old woman, when he was there, was laughing at "some of t' lad's foolishness." The step was far down the street; but he could see him place the ladder, run up, and light the gas. A longing seized him to be spoken to once more.

"Joe!" he called, out of the grating. "Good-bye, Joe!"

The old man stopped a moment, listening uncertainly; then hurried on. The prisoner thrust his hand out of the window, and called again, louder; but Joe was too far down the street. It was a little thing; but it hurt him, — this disappointment.

"Good-bye, Joe!" he called, sorrowfully enough.

"Be quiet!" said one of the jailers, passing the door, striking on it with his club.

Oh, that was the last, was it?

There was an inexpressible bitterness on his face, as he lay down on the bed, taking the bit of tin, which he had rasped to a tolerable degree of sharpness, in his hand, — to play with, it may be. He bared his arms, looking intently at their corded veins and sinews. Deborah, listening in the next cell, heard a slight clicking sound, often repeated. She shut her lips tightly, that she might not scream; the cold drops of sweat broke over her, in her dumb agony.

"Hur knows best," she muttered at last, fiercely clutching the boards where she lay.

If she could have seen Wolfe, there was nothing about him to frighten her. He lay quite still, his arms outstretched, looking at the pearly stream of moonlight coming into the window. I think in that one hour that came then he lived back over all the years that had gone before. I think that all the low, vile life, all his wrongs, all his starved hopes, came then, and stung him with a farewell poison that made him sick unto death. He made neither moan nor cry, only turned his worn face now and then to the pure light, that seemed so far off, as one that said, "How long, O Lord? how long?"

The hour was over at last. The moon, passing over her nightly path, slowly came nearer, and threw the light across his bed on his feet. He watched it steadily, as it crept up, inch by inch, slowly. It seemed to him to carry with it a great silence. He had been so hot and tired there always in the mills! The years had been so fierce and cruel! There was coming now quiet and coolness and sleep. His tense limbs relaxed, and settled in a calm languor. The blood ran fainter and slow from his heart. He did not think now with a savage anger of what might be and was not; he was conscious only of deep stillness creeping over him. At first he saw a sea of faces: the mill-men, — women he had known, drunken and bloated, — Janeys timid and pitiful, — poor old Debs: then they floated together like a mist, and faded away, leaving only the clear, pearly moonlight.

Whether, as the pure light crept up the stretched-out figure, it brought with it calm and peace, who shall say? His dumb soul was alone with God in judgment. A Voice may have spoken for it from far-off Calvary, "Father, forgive them, for they know not what they do!"[44] Who dare say? Fainter and fainter the heart rose and fell, slower and slower the moon floated from behind a cloud, until, when at last its full tide of white splendor swept over the cell, it seemed to wrap and fold into a deeper stillness the dead figure that never should move again. Silence deeper than the Night! Nothing that moved, save the black, nauseous stream of blood dripping slowly from the pallet to the floor!

[44] *"Father, forgive them, . . . what they do!"*: Christ's words on the cross in reference to his persecutors.

There was outcry and crowd enough in the cell the next day. The coroner and his jury, the local editors, Kirby himself, and boys with their hands thrust knowingly into their pockets and heads on one side, jammed into the corners. Coming and going all day. Only one woman. She came late, and outstayed them all. A Quaker, or Friend,[45] as they call themselves. I think this woman was known by that name in heaven. A homely body, coarsely dressed in gray and white. Deborah (for Haley had let her in) took notice of her. She watched them all — sitting on the end of the pallet, holding his head in her arms — with the ferocity of a watch-dog, if any of them touched the body. There was no meekness, no sorrow, in her face; the stuff out of which murderers are made, instead. All the time Haley and the woman were laying straight the limbs and cleaning the cell, Deborah sat still, keenly watching the Quaker's face. Of all the crowd there that day, this woman alone had not spoken to her, — only once or twice had put some cordial to her lips. After they all were gone, the woman, in the same still, gentle way, brought a vase of wood-leaves and berries, and placed it by the pallet, then opened the narrow window. The fresh air blew in, and swept the woody fragrance over the dead face. Deborah looked up with a quick wonder.

"Did hur know my boy wud like it? Did hur know Hugh?"

"I know Hugh now."

The white fingers passed in a slow, pitiful way over the dead, worn face. There was a heavy shadow in the quiet eyes.

"Did hur know where they'll bury Hugh?" said Deborah in a shrill tone, catching her arm.

This had been the question hanging on her lips all day.

"In t' town-yard? Under t' mud and ash? T' lad'll smother, woman! He wur born on t' lane moor, where t' air is frick[46] and strong. Take hur out, for God's sake, take hur out where t' air blows!"

The Quaker hesitated, but only for a moment. She put her strong arm around Deborah and led her to the window.

"Thee sees the hills, friend, over the river? Thee sees how the light lies warm there, and the winds of God blow all the day? I live there, — where the blue smoke is, by the trees. Look at me." She turned Deborah's face to her own, clear and earnest. "Thee will believe me? I will take Hugh and bury him there to-morrow."

---

[45] *A Quaker, or Friend:* The Society of Friends is a Christian religious sect formed in England by George Fox around 1650. Although Quakers have no precisely articulated doctrine, they believe in pacifism, the refusal to take oaths, and the guidance of an inner light.

[46] *frick:* Fresh.

Deborah did not doubt her. As the evening wore on, she leaned against the iron bars, looking at the hills that rose far off, through the thick sodden clouds, like a bright, unattainable calm. As she looked, a shadow of their solemn repose fell on her face: its fierce discontent faded into a pitiful, humble quiet. Slow, solemn tears gathered in her eyes: the poor weak eyes turned so hopelessly to the place where Hugh was to rest, the grave heights looking higher and brighter and more solemn than ever before. The Quaker watched her keenly. She came to her at last, and touched her arm.

"When thee comes back," she said, in a low, sorrowful tone, like one who speaks from a strong heart deeply moved with remorse or pity, "thee shall begin thy life again, — there on the hills. I came too late; but not for thee, — by God's help, it may be."

Not too late. Three years after, the Quaker began her work. I end my story here. At evening-time it was light. There is no need to tire you with the long years of sunshine, and fresh air, and slow, patient Christ-love, needed to make healthy and hopeful this impure body and soul. There is a homely pine house, on one of these hills, whose windows overlook broad, wooded slopes and clover-crimsoned meadows, — niched into the very place where the light is warmest, the air freest. It is the Friends' meeting-house. Once a week they sit there, in their grave, earnest way, waiting for the Spirit of Love to speak, opening their simple hearts to receive His words. There is a woman, old, deformed, who takes a humble place among them: waiting like them: in her gray dress, her worn face, pure and meek, turned now and then to the sky. A woman much loved by these silent, restful people; more silent than they, more humble, more loving. Waiting: with her eyes turned to hills higher and purer than these on which she lives, — dim and far off now, but to be reached some day. There may be in her heart some latent hope to meet there the love denied her here, — that she shall find him whom she lost, and that then she will not be all-unworthy. Who blames her? Something is lost in the passage of every soul from one eternity to the other, — something pure and beautiful, which might have been and was not: a hope, a talent, a love, over which the soul mourns, like Esau deprived of his birthright.[47] What blame to the meek Quaker, if she took her lost hope to make the hills of heaven more fair?

---

[47] *Esau deprived of his birthright:* In the Old Testament, Esau was the eldest son of Isaac and Rebekah. Upon returning from an unsuccessful hunting expedition, a hungry Esau sold his birthright to his twin brother, Jacob, for some red pottage (soup). See Genesis 25:33–34.

Nothing remains to tell that the poor Welsh puddler once lived, but this figure of the mill-woman cut in korl. I have it here in a corner of my library. I keep it hid behind a curtain, — it is such a rough, ungainly thing. Yet there are about it touches, grand sweeps of outline, that show a master's hand. Sometimes, — to-night, for instance, — the curtain is accidentally drawn back, and I see a bare arm stretched out imploringly in the darkness, and an eager, wolfish face watching mine: a wan, woful face, through which the spirit of the dead korl-cutter looks out, with its thwarted life, its mighty hunger, its unfinished work. Its pale, vague lips seem to tremble with a terrible question. "Is this the End?" they say, — "nothing beyond? — no more?" Why, you tell me you have seen that look in the eyes of dumb brutes, — horses dying under the lash. I know.

The deep of the night is passing while I write. The gas-light wakens from the shadows here and there the objects which lie scattered through the room: only faintly, though; for they belong to the open sunlight. As I glance at them, they each recall some task or pleasure of the coming day. A half-moulded child's head; Aphrodite;[48] a bough of forest-leaves; music; work; homely fragments, in which lie the secrets of all eternal truth and beauty. Prophetic all! Only this dumb, woful face seems to belong to and end with the night. I turn to look at it. Has the power of its desperate need commanded the darkness away? While the room is yet steeped in heavy shadow, a cool, gray light suddenly touches its head like a blessing, and its groping arm points through the broken cloud to the far East, where, in the flickering, nebulous crimson, God has set the promise of the Dawn.

---

[48] *Aphrodite:* Greek goddess of erotic love and marriage.

Part Two

Life in the Iron-Mills
Cultural Contexts

Figure 1. *The Manufacture of Iron* from *Harper's Weekly,* November 1, 1873. Illustration by Tavernier and Frenzeny. This image is the third in a series of three showing the steps in the process of iron manufacture. See Figure 2, page 189.

1

Work and Class

The work ethic ranks high in the value system of the United States, and the Declaration of Independence holds it to be "self-evident" that "all men are created equal." *Life in the Iron-Mills*, however, shows an America of vast socioeconomic inequality that is deeply enmeshed with problematic ideas about work. The novella continues a tradition of public discourse, dating to the colonial period, on the relation of work to social status in America. In her dramatization of this relation, Davis rejects easy slogans and enters an ongoing public debate about the connection of work to well-being, respect, self-fulfillment, social status, hope, and personal and social responsibility.

Since the colonial period, the American work ethic has been a much-vaunted part of the culture of this nation of immigrants. Captain John Smith's exploration narratives of the 1610s point out the necessity for all New World residents, whether masters or servants, to fish and hunt. The foundational concept of a resident population earning its living by working, however, is most often ascribed to the seventeenth-century New England Puritans. They identified themselves as children of Adam, who in the scriptural book of Genesis was cast from the Garden of Eden and commanded by God to earn his living by the sweat of his brow. Colonizing the New World, the Puritans felt divinely directed to convert what Edward Johnson referred to as its "wild-woody wilderness" (210) into a civilized environment of towns and farms with "goodly corn fields," a task requiring manual labor by those "having as yet no other meanes to tear up the bushy lands, but their hands and howes" (82).

The secular exponent of the American work ethic was Benjamin Franklin, who carefully cultivated his image as a hard-working printer and whose 1784 essay, "Information for Those Who Would Remove to America," proclaims, "America is the Land of Labour." Franklin separates "improper Persons" from those likely to succeed in the New World. Those expecting to indulge themselves in the socially parasitic privileges of aristocracy ought to stay away, he writes, as should those deluding themselves into the notion that the New World is an Eden or an El Dorado. Those with useful skills and the energy to employ them are encouraged to immigrate. Franklin's key word is "useful," and his essay welcomes farmers, mechanics, and tradesmen. In America, he writes, "people do not inquire concerning a Stranger, *What is he?* but, *What can he do?* If he has any useful Art, he is welcome" (977).

The message of Franklin's essay was conveyed to the public in his eighteenth-century annual calendar, *Poor Richard's Almanack*, which enjoined Americans to believe the New World to be a place that rewarded hard workers but had no room for slackers. Poor Richard dispensed advice in memorable slogans: "There are no Gains without Pains"; "He that hath a Trade hath an Estate"; "If we are industrious, we shall never starve"; "God gives all Things to Industry." In Poor Richard's scheme of things, idleness was shameful and hard work certain to be rewarded. The unfortunates, according to his proverbs, were really victims of their own sloth or their misdirected love of foolish luxury. Those who failed to prosper, in short, deserved to fail. They were entirely responsible for their condition and had only themselves to blame.

As the states ratified the new Constitution, public parades featured work groups as the centerpiece of American civic and political life. One such parade in Philadelphia on July 4, 1788, included units of artisans — carpenters, sawmakers, filemakers, boat builders, ropemakers, blacksmiths, and bricklayers — who marched under the motto, "Both Buildings and Rulers Are the Work of Our Hands." Such a sociopolitical position would have been inconceivable just a few decades earlier, and it anticipates Walt Whitman's 1855 "A Song for Occupations," which paraded every possible occupational category, from iron workers to butchers, in a psalm celebrating America as a nation built and sustained by the vitality of work (see p. 136).

Yet the nineteenth century of Rebecca Harding Davis saw social developments departing drastically from Franklin's era of handcrafts and artisanry. In Franklin's time, younger workers often served as apprentices in small shops adjacent to the master craftsman's home. That era, typified nostalgically in Longfellow's village blacksmith (see p. 83), saw men and women, masters and apprentices, adults and children performing overlapping tasks, all of which were important to the economy of the whole family and community group. In that earlier era, the totality of family life, including work and leisure, occurred in close proximity. Moreover, an apprentice would live in his master's family home, eat and perhaps worship along with the family, and know the children well.

By the time Abraham Lincoln became president in 1861, however, the sites of production were increasingly separated from the home, and the old master-apprentice system had given way to the more impersonal relationship signified by the terms employer and employee. Harriet Robinson in *Loom and Spindle* recalls the sharp transition of Lowell, Massachusetts, from "a factory village" to a "Yankee El Dorado" to which the stage coach and canal boat daily brought "an army of useful people," including mechanics, machinists, widows hoping to eke out a living with a variety store, farm girls, and single young men trying "to get money for an education or to lift the mortgage from the home-farm" (see p. 159).

In this time of rapid social shifting, men's and women's social roles underwent major changes that affected every socioeconomic group throughout the United States. The growth of cities, of commerce, and of factory technologies all increased the pace of work and led to the separation between home and place of employment. Machine manufacture replaced handcrafts, and the items produced in factories proliferated as consumer products to be bought and sold in the marketplace. The market itself, once local or regional, now extended over hundreds and thousands of miles because of the growth of railroads. Gradually the idea took hold that this new world of fast-paced economic competition — in short, a world of industry, business, and the professions — belonged properly to men. More accurately, this world belonged to men of certain social classes, especially the well-to-do, the merchants, the owners and managers of factories, and the professionals. Their activities were understood to be authoritative and worldly.

The middle-class home, meanwhile, was redefined as a soothing refuge from the harsh outside world of business and politics. Removed from any income-producing function, the home was portrayed as a shelter presided over by the wife-mother whose duty it was to maintain a calm, pleasing, smoothly operating household in which the husband-father could be morally and spiritually uplifted and rejuvenated after his day in the harsh world. Anticipating this new social order in the 1830s, Sarah Josepha Hale, the editor of *Godey's Lady's Book*, a women's magazine, advised her readers, "Our men are sufficiently money-making; let us keep our women and children free from the contagion as long as possible." Hale urged wives to be "pure, pious, domestic, and submissive," and she defined a woman's place as "eminently at the fireside."

Women's sphere included the mandate for the proper upbringing of children: boys and girls must be taught proper habits and their character developed so that they, too, would emerge in adulthood as responsible citizens in their respective, separate realms. This educational charge was the work that belonged to women. As Chapter 2 in this volume, "Social Reform and the Promise of the Dawn," shows, numerous reform movements sprung from ideas originating in the ideology of women's domestic sphere. These ideas fostered efforts to domesticate and civilize the lucrative but brutal masculine world.

The separate, rigidly gendered spheres came to define the middle class in practice and in ideology. Both realms were sustained, however, by the work of those less prosperous: the "labouring classes" who served as domestic workers, factory operatives, drovers, teamsters, and seamstresses. Young men who in Franklin's time might have been apprentices learning skilled crafts were now hourly-wage laborers in cities or manufacturing centers. The economic depressions of 1837 and 1857 subjected them to job loss, and their livelihoods were ever precarious, especially in their forced competition with new immigrants eager for subsistence work in low-wage manual labor. Robert Layton, a labor union official, testified on these matters before the Senate Committee on Education and Labor in 1883 and commented on the living conditions of Pennsylvania miners, saying the average miner earns so little that "his desire may be to economize, but his opportunities for it are so poor that he seldom is able to accumulate any savings" (see p. 124). And William Weihe, an iron puddler, told the senators, "We do not think it is right to import labor from foreign countries to supersede the American workingman" (see p. 109).

The virtual social ban on middle-class women working for wages kept them out of the labor force, but necessity forced lower-class women into domestic service, factory work, and piecework or out-work that could be carried out in the household. Middle-class women in straitened circumstances had a sort of social permission to earn a living in such sectors as journalism, education, or the operation of a boarding house. Sarah Hale, for instance, became a magazine editor after she was widowed; and Lucy Larcom, whose mother set up a boarding house after the death of her husband, entered the Lowell mills in order to help support the family, though she subsequently became a writer and educator (see Chapter 4). Working-class women found their workload doubled, since they performed both wage labor and their own housework, which was physically laborious, involving the hauling of coal, wood, and water and the hand-scrubbing of floors and laundry. Fanny Fern urged sympathy and a living wage for the "young [female operatives who] toil so unremittingly" (see p. 157). It is noteworthy that in *Life in the Iron-Mills*, Deborah provides Hugh's meals even though she, like Hugh, works long hours in a mill.

Rebecca Harding Davis's nineteenth century, then, was heir to the historical contradictions between the American democratic ideology of work and the reality of social inequality. *Life in the Iron-Mills* engages the debate about work and class by offering readers two occupational categories: "laborer" and "gentlemen." The mill visitors, who represent the latter category, are supervisors and professionals with sufficient leisure time to dabble in matters of art, sport, social theory, and philosophy. They can smoke cigars, wear jewelry, travel, and, as educated citizens, manipulate the abstractions of numbers and print. They speak the language of capitalism.

The laborers, on the other hand, are unschooled, exhausted by physical labor, and lack the necessary vocabulary to make their ideas intelligible to gentlemen. Work is important to both groups in *Life in the Iron-Mills*, but readers quickly see that *work* is a deceptively simple term, for there is little point of comparison between the respective "work" of the laborer, the overseer, and the physician. Indeed, issues of clothing, speech patterns, schooling, and ancestry divide the laborers from the others. Though their work might be expected to unite them, Davis takes great care to show that the laborers and the gentlemen are split and stratified along the lines of class.

Such class divisions preoccupied many in the nineteenth century. Franklin's ideal lingers, to be sure, in the village blacksmith of Longfellow's verse, which presents the working man as a model of sobriety, skill, industriousness, parental responsibility, piety, and independence. And devotees of the work ethic would have been pleased by the 1837 remark of a European visitor, "It is as if America were but one gigantic workshop."

Such a single-minded image, however, conceals the contemporary internal stresses over the conditions of work that were typified by the tenant strikes occurring in the Hudson River Valley and elsewhere in the 1830s and 1840s, as farmers sought redress of landowners' monopolistic practices. An owner, in the words of one strike sympathizer, could "swill his wine, loll on his cushions, fill his life with society, food, and culture," while the tenants did the actual work of farming and forestry (qtd. in Zinn 206).

When the feminist-socialist Fanny Wright was invited to Philadelphia in 1829 to address a citywide association of labor unions, she asked whether the Revolution had been fought to "crush down the sons and daughters of [the] country's industry under . . . neglect, poverty, vice, starvation, and disease" (qtd. in Zinn 216). By 1863, a New York woman worker in a hat factory found herself unable to earn a living wage despite her best efforts and wrote a letter to the *New York Sun* asking, "Are we nothing but living machines, to be driven at will for the accommodation of a set of heartless, yes, I may say souless people?" Fanny Fern argues the same point, if somewhat whimsically in her pun on women workers as "sewing machines" (see p. 156). Such terms as these resonate directly in the cleavage between the laborers and the gentlemen in *Life in the Iron-Mills*.

The growth of industrial technology gave new urgency to the problematics of work and class. Early in the nineteenth century, such critics as Alexis de Tocqueville and Orestes Brownson rejected the role of modern-day Franklins and cautioned that the new industrial technologies would create a rigid class system in America based on wealth from manufactures and the exploitation of the "laboring classes." De Tocqueville seems prophetic in pointing out this "sideroad" by which manufacturers might "bring men back to aristocracy" (see p. 85), and Brownson bluntly compares free American workers to slaves (see Chapter 2). Such voices were joined by civic and religious leaders, and also by workers speaking for the public record at United States Senate hearings and committing their personal experiences to diaries, letters, newspapers, and books. Harriet Robinson, a onetime textile mill worker, recalled that factory operatives "were not supposed to be capable of social and mental improvement" but advised the reading public (which is to say, the middle classes) to understand that workers "could be educated and developed into something more than mere work-people" (see p. 167). By the end of the century (and at the opposite end of the socioeconomic scale), the wealthy steel industrialist turned philanthropist, Andrew Carnegie, felt called upon to defend the amassing of vast fortunes by advocating the disposition of "surplus wealth" for civic benefit (see p. 154).

The various texts in this chapter by nineteenth-century workers, writers, poets, and social theorists enter into a dialogue with *Life in the Iron-Mills*. Henry Ward Beecher expresses a quandary central to these texts when he writes that "one of the things which our age and which this land has to develop is the compatibility of manual labor with real refinement and education. This is one of the great problems of the age." Perhaps Rebecca Harding Davis, whose novella asks readers to reconsider their views on work and class in America, would have agreed.

HENRY WADSWORTH LONGFELLOW

"*The Village Blacksmith*"

During his lifetime Henry Wadsworth Longfellow (1807–1882) was one of America's best-loved poets. His romantic, sentimental poetry won him great acclaim and allowed him to earn a comfortable income from writing alone. Volumes of Longfellow's poems sold tens of thousands of copies, and he became a kind of national institution, although his reputation has suffered during the twentieth century. With poems like "The Village Blacksmith" (*Ballads and Other Poems*, 1841), which made use of American settings and distinctly American characters, Longfellow helped to establish a national literature and to immortalize nineteenth-century ideals. "The Village Blacksmith" was one of his most popular and widely recited poems.

> Under a spreading chestnut tree
>   The village smithy stands;
> The smith, a mighty man is he,
>   With large and sinewy hands;
> And the muscles of his brawny arms
>   Are strong as iron bands.

His hair is crisp, and black, and long,
   His face is like the tan;
His brow is wet with honest sweat,
   He earns whate'er he can,
And looks the whole world in the face,
   For he owes not any man.

Week in, week out, from morn till night,
   You can hear his bellows blow;
You can hear him swing his heavy sledge,
   With measured beat and slow,
Like a sexton ringing the village bell,
   When the evening sun is low.

And children coming home from school
   Look in at the open door;
They love to see the flaming forge,
   And hear the bellows roar,
And catch the burning sparks that fly
   Like chaff from a threshing floor.

He goes on Sunday to the church,
   And sits among his boys;
He hears the parson pray and preach,
   He hears his daughter's voice,
Singing in the village choir,
   And it makes his heart rejoice,

It sounds to him like her mother's voice,
   Singing in Paradise!
He needs must think of her once more,
   How in the grave she lies;
And with his hard, rough hand he wipes
   A tear out of his eyes.

Toiling, — rejoicing, — sorrowing,
   Onward through life he goes;
Each morning sees some task begin,
   Each evening sees it close;
Something attempted, something done,
   Has earned a night's repose.

Thanks, thanks to thee, my worthy friend,
   For the lesson thou hast taught!
Thus at the flaming forge of life

Our fortunes must be wrought;
Thus on its sounding anvil shaped
Each burning deed and thought!

ALEXIS DE TOCQUEVILLE

"That Aristocracy May Be Engendered by Manufactures"

Alexis Henri Maurice Clerel de Tocqueville (1805–1859) was a foreign minister and author sent to the United States by the French government in 1831 to study the U. S. penitentiary system. While in the United States, he wrote travel accounts that have become crucial to the study of American democracy. His *De la democratie en Amerique* was published in England in 1835 as *Democracy in America*. In the following selection from this work, de Tocqueville examines the way in which American industry undermines the myth of American equality by establishing a class hierarchy based on industrial roles. Even in 1835, de Tocqueville could see the growing class divisions in an industrializing United States.

The text is from *Democracy in America*, trans. Henry Reeves (New York: Barnes, 1890).

I have shown that democracy is favourable to the growth of manufactures, and that it increases without limit the numbers of the manufacturing classes: we shall now see by what side-road manufactures may possibly in their turn bring men back to aristocracy.

It is acknowledged, that when a workman is engaged every day upon the same detail, the whole commodity is produced with greater ease, promptitude, and economy. It is likewise acknowledged, that the cost of the production of manufactured goods is diminished by the extent of the establishment in which they are made, and by the amount of capital employed or of credit. These truths had long been imperfectly discerned, but in our time they have been demonstrated. They have been already applied to many very important kinds of manufactures, and the humblest will gradually be governed by them. I know of nothing in politics which deserves to fix the attention of the legislator more closely than these two new axioms of the science of manufactures.

When a workman is unceasingly and exclusively engaged in the fabrication of one thing, he ultimately does his work with singular dexterity; but at the same time he loses the general faculty of applying his mind to the direction of the work. He every day becomes more adroit and less industrious; so that it may be said of him, that in proportion as the workman improves the man is degraded. What can be expected of a man who has spent twenty years of his life in making heads for pins? and to what can that mighty human intelligence, which has so often stirred the world, be applied in him, except it be to investigate the best method of making pins' heads? When a workman has spent a considerable portion of his existence in this manner, his thoughts are for ever set upon the object of his daily toil: his body has contracted certain fixed habits, which it can never shake off: in a word, he no longer belongs to himself, but to the calling which he has chosen. It is in vain that laws and manners have been at the pains to level all barriers round such a man, and to open to him on every side a thousand different paths to fortune; a theory of manufactures more powerful than manners and laws binds him to a craft, and frequently to a spot, which he cannot leave: it assigns to him a certain place in society, beyond which he cannot go: in the midst of universal movement, it has rendered him stationary.

In proportion as the principle of the division of labour is more extensively applied, the workman becomes more weak, more narrow-minded and more dependant. The art advances, the artisan recedes. On the other hand, in proportion as it becomes more manifest that the productions of manufactures are by so much the cheaper and better as the manufacture is larger and the amount of capital employed more considerable, wealthy and educated men come forward to embark in manufactures which were heretofore abandoned to poor or ignorant handicraftsmen. The magnitude of the efforts required, and the importance of the results to be obtained, attract them. Thus at the very time at which the science of manufactures lowers the class of workmen, it raises the class of masters.

Whereas the workman concentrates his faculties more and more upon the study of a single detail, the master surveys a more extensive whole, and the mind of the latter is enlarged in proportion as that of the former is narrowed. In a short time the one will require nothing but physical strength without intelligence; the other stands in need of science, and almost of genius, to ensure success. This man resembles more and more the administrator of a vast empire — that man, a brute.

The master and the workman have then here no similarity, and their differences increase every day. They are only connected as the two rings at the extremities of a long chain. Each of them fills the station which is made for him, and out of which he does not get: the one is continually, closely, and necessarily dependant upon the other, and seems as much born to obey as that other is to command. What is this but aristocracy?

As the conditions of men constituting the nation become more and more equal, the demand for manufactured commodities becomes more general and more extensive; and the cheapness which places these objects within the reach of slender fortunes becomes a great element of success. Hence there are every day more men of great opulence and education who devote their wealth and knowledge to manufactures; and who seek, by opening large establishments, and by a strict division of labour, to meet the fresh demands which are made on all sides. Thus, in proportion as the mass of the nation turns to democracy, that particular class which is engaged in manufactures becomes more aristocratic. Men grow more alike in the one — more different in the other; and inequality increases in the less numerous class, in the same ratio in which it decreases in the community.

Hence it would appear, on searching to the bottom, that aristocracy should naturally spring out of the bosom of democracy.

But this kind of aristocracy by no means resembles those kinds which preceded it. It will be observed at once, that, as it applies exclusively to manufactures and to some manufacturing callings, it is a monstrous exception in the general aspect of society. The small aristocratic societies which are formed by some manufacturers in the midst of the immense democracy of our age, contain, like the great aristocratic societies of former ages, some men who are very opulent, and a multitude who are wretchedly poor. The poor have few means of escaping from their condition and becoming rich; but the rich are constantly becoming poor, or they give up business when they have realized a fortune. Thus the elements of which the class of the poor is composed, are fixed; but the elements of which the class of the rich is composed are not so. To say the truth, though there are rich men, the class of rich men does not exist; for these rich individuals have no feelings or purposes in common, no mutual traditions or mutual hopes: there are therefore members, but no body.

Not only are the rich not compactly united among themselves, but there is no real bond between them and the poor. Their relative position is not a permanent one; they are constantly drawn together or separated by their interests. The workman is generally dependant on the master, but not on any particular master; these two men meet in the factory, but know not each other elsewhere; and while they come into contact on one point, they stand very wide apart on all others. The manufacturer asks nothing of the workman but his labour; the workman expects nothing from him but his wages. The one contracts no obligation to protect, nor the other to defend; and they are not permanently connected either by habit or by duty.

The aristocracy created by business rarely settles in the midst of the manufacturing population which it directs: the object is not to govern that population, but to use it. An aristocracy thus constituted can have no great hold upon those whom it employs; and even if it succeed in retaining them at one moment, they escape the next: it knows not how to will, and it cannot act.

The territorial aristocracy of former ages was either bound by law, or thought itself bound by usage, to come to the relief of its serving-men, and to succour their distresses. But the manufacturing aristocracy of our age first impoverishes and debases the men who serve it, and then abandons them to be supported by the charity of the public. This is a natural consequence of what has been said before. Between the workman and the master there are frequent relations, but no real partnership.

I am of opinion, upon the whole, that the manufacturing aristocracy which is growing up under our eyes, is one of the harshest which ever existed in the world; but at the same time it is one of the most confined and least dangerous. Nevertheless the friends of democracy should keep their eyes anxiously fixed in this direction; for if ever a permanent inequality of conditions and aristocracy again penetrate into the world, it may be predicted that this is the channel by which they will enter.

A. W. CAMPBELL

"Iron Interests of Wheeling"

M. F. Maury and William M. Fontaine's *Resources of West Virginia* (Wheeling: Register, 1876) is a celebration of industry. The book was written as part of the research done for a West Virginia display at the Centennial Exposition of 1876 at Philadelphia, an exhibition that glorified American industrialization. The editors' introduction makes plain their capitalistic goals and their priorities as they explain that "it was difficult to have [West Virginia's] citizens anticipate the value of the material results expected to be hereafter realized from exhibiting to the capitalists and people of the world, the wonderful natural wealth lying, and yet undeveloped, within the borders of West Virginia." The natural world is seen in terms of the money that can be made from it, and the laborers who are to work this wealth from the land are invisible. "Iron Interests of Wheeling" falls in line with the editors' goals, describing plainly the iron mills that Davis, a West Virginian, probably knew and modelled in *Life in the Iron-Mills*.

Wheeling is chiefly known as the centre of a large iron industry, particularly for Cut Nails. The city and vicinity constitute the largest Nail market in the world. The growth of this business, as indeed of all the manufactures of Wheeling, is due to the abundance of cheap fuel (stone coal) in the hills around the city, and to the facilities for reaching all the markets of the country, either by rail or water, at low rates for freight.

The iron out of which these nails is made is produced on the spot, mostly from mixtures of Missouri and Lake Superior ores, and when made is immediately in market, without cost for transportation. There are now, at Wheeling and Steubenville, nine blast furnaces for the manufacture of iron, as follows: On the Wheeling side of the river, the "Top Mill" furnace, the "Belmont," and the "Riverside." On the Ohio side, the "Bellaire" furnace, the "Benwood," the "Mingo," the two "Jefferson" furnaces, and the "Stony Hollow." These furnaces have mostly 16 feet boshes[1] and 60 feet stacks. The "Top Mill" has an 18 foot bosh, and the Benwood a 13 foot. They produce mostly "Red Short" irons, such as are used for Nails. At this time iron is made as low as $19 per ton, worth in the market say $22, on four months' time. The connection now being made, via the Hempfield Short-line, between Wheeling and Connellsville, will so reduce the price of coke as to give Wheeling a further margin in its manufacture of iron.

---

[1] *boshes:* A bosh is the section of a blast furnace between the hearth and the stack.

The Nail mills at Wheeling and vicinity are as follows: The "River-side" works, running 126 machines, including, also, a separate Bar and Rail mill belonging to the same company. Their blast furnace is three miles below their mills, with which they connect by rail and water.

The "Top Mill," running 106 machines, situated in the north part of the city, on the line of the Pittsburgh, Wheeling and Kentucky rail-road — a new road not yet completed. Their blast furnace immediately adjoins their mill, and iron can be handled at a minimum cost through all its processes.

The "Belmont Nail Works," situated in Center Wheeling, running 110 machines. This mill has turned out as high as 8,155 kegs of nails in one week, on an extraordinary run. Its blast furnace immediately adjoins the mill. It has also a large cooper shop, whereat all its kegs are made.

The La Belle Nail Works, running 85 machines, but is one of two mills owned by the same company. The other is the Jefferson, situated at Steubenville, and it also runs 85 machines, and has two blast furnaces. Together they form a large and wealthy company, which was originally started as a practical workingmen's organization.

The Benwood Nail Works, running 112 machines, four miles below the city. The company owns some 80 tenement houses, and has built up the suburb of "Benwood." The Mill has a cooper estab-lishment connected with it. Its blast furnace is on the opposite side of the river, in the suburb of Martin's Ferry.

The Bellaire Nail Works, situated immediately opposite Benwood, on the Ohio side, runs 100 machines, and has a blast furnace on its premises. Is a large and valuable property.

The Ohio City Nail Works, situated in the suburb of Martin's Ferry, a town lying opposite the north end of the city of Wheeling. This is a new mill, and only runs 50 machines. On a double turn it can produce 2,500 kegs of Nails per week.

During the years 1871, '72 and '73 the mills above named, except the Ohio City, produced 2,995,509 kegs of Nails. In those years Wheeling manufactured about one-fourth of all the Nails made in the United States.

Nails can be shipped at the following low rates of freight: To New Orleans, 20 cents per keg; to St. Louis, 10 cents; to Chicago, 22 cents; to Cincinnati, 7 cents.

The other principal iron manufactories of Wheeling and vicinity, are as follows:

The Wheeling Hinge Company, now in the 12th year of its existence, has steadily grown from a small affair to be a large concern. It owns the patent for the Dunning hinge — an article intended to supersede, to a certain extent, the old screw and strap hinge.

The Superior Machine Works, a large concern organized for the manufacture of the Superior Reaping and Mowing Machines, and where also engines and other machinery are built.

The Centripetal Power Company Works, organized for the manufacture of portable machinery for the use (principally) of farmers, whereby important advantages are claimed in overcoming friction, and in the retention of speed and momentum.

The Crescent Rail and Sheet Mills — situated on the south bank of Wheeling creek — connected by a bridge across said creek with the 4th ward of the city, and directly opposite the works of the Wheeling Hinge Co. A large concern, owned by the Whitakers, well known iron men. Is principally run now on sheet iron.

The Ætna Iron Works, situated in the suburb of Ætnaville, a new village just growing up opposite the city, midway between Bridgeport and Martin's Ferry. Manufactures bar and sheet iron, and also small rails for coal banks and light roads.

The Norway Tack Factory, situated in the 4th ward of the city; started in 1865 — owned by Jones, Heald & Phinney — manufactures all varieties of tacks and a fine three-penny nail.

The Arlington Stove Works and Foundry of Joseph Bell & Co.; the Star Stove Works and Foundry of Benjamin Fisher; the Boiler Works of Moorehead & Son; the Foundry, Machine and Repair Works of A. J. Sweeney & Son; the Foundry, Machine and Repair Works of Cecil, Hobbs & Co.; the Bellaire Implement Factory; the Stove Works and Foundry of Spence, Baggs & Co., at Martin's Ferry; the Ohio Valley Machine Works of L. Spence & Co., (same place,) whereat were built the engines of the Belmont Blast Furnace, and where also are made Threshers and Cleaners, and other machinery; the large Foundry of Culbertson, Wiley & Co., (same place,) where was cast the heavy iron work of the Ætna Mill.

The foregoing are the principal iron establishments in and around Wheeling. Quite a number of them are of recent origin, either in whole or part. Just previous to the panic of 1873, an important impetus had been given to the development of the iron business of this vicinity, growing out, as we have said, of the abundance of cheap fuel and the facilities for shipment. It is hoped that these advantages will, at an early day, re-assert themselves, and go on, as in the years '72 and '73, increasing the number of our manufactories.

CAPTAIN WILLARD GLAZIER

"Pittsburg"

Willard Glazier (1841–1905), a soldier turned author, fought for the Union in the Civil War and was taken prisoner by the Confederates. After the war, he became known for his work as a travel writer. In 1876 he ventured from Boston to San Francisco on horseback, and in 1881 he traveled the entire Mississippi River in a canoe. The following essay, "Pittsburg," forms part of Glazier's book, *Peculiarities of American Cities* (Philadelphia: Hubbard, 1883), a recounting of his adventures in the major cities of the United States. Glazier's mythic picture of the iron-mill city of Pittsburgh contrasts with Davis's gloomy, disturbing portrayal of the city in *Life in the Iron-Mills*. Note, too, that Glazier's somewhat optimistic view of class relations in the city contradicts de Tocqueville's understanding of class hierarchies constructed through industry.

By all means make your first approach to Pittsburg in the night time, and you will behold a spectacle which has not a parallel on this continent. Darkness gives the city and its surroundings a picturesqueness which they wholly lack by daylight. It lies low down in a hollow of encompassing hills, gleaming with a thousand points of light, which are reflected from the rivers, whose waters glimmer, it may be, in the faint moonlight, and catch and reflect the shadows as well. Around the city's edge, and on the sides of the hills which encircle it like a gloomy amphitheatre, their outlines rising dark against the sky, through numberless apertures, fiery lights stream forth, looking angrily and fiercely up toward the heavens, while over all these settles a heavy pall of smoke. It is as though one had reached the outer edge of the infernal regions, and saw before him the great furnace of Pandemonium[1] with all the lids lifted. The scene is so strange and weird

---

[1] *Pandemonium:* Home of all demons; represented by Milton in *Paradise Lost* as the capital of hell.

that it will live in the memory forever. One pictures, as he beholds it, the tortured spirits writhing in agony, their sinewy limbs convulsed, and the very air oppressive with pain and rage.

But the scene is illusive. This is the domain of Vulcan,[2] not of Pluto.[3] Here, in this gigantic workshop, in the midst of the materials of his labor, the god of fire, having left his ancient home on Olympus, and established himself in this newer world, stretches himself beside his forge, and sleeps the peaceful sleep which is the reward of honest industry. Right at his doorway are mountains of coal to keep a perpetual fire upon his altar; within the reach of his outstretched grasp are rivers of coal oil; and a little further away great stores of iron for him to forge and weld, and shape into a thousand forms; and at his feet is the shining river, an impetuous Mercury,[4] ever ready to do his bidding. Grecian mythology never conceived of an abode so fitting for the son of Zeus as that which he has selected for himself on this western hemisphere. And his ancient tasks were child's play compared with the mighty ones he has undertaken to-day.

Failing a night approach, the traveler should reach the Iron City on a dismal day in autumn, when the air is heavy with moisture, and the very atmosphere looks dark. All romance has disappeared. In this nineteenth century the gods of mythology find no place in daylight. There is only a very busy city shrouded in gloom. The buildings, whatever their original material and color, and the gas-lights, which are left burning at mid-day, shine out of the murkiness with a dull, reddish glare. Then is Pittsburg herself. Such days as these are her especial boast, and in their frequency and dismalness, in all the world she has no rival, save London.

In truth, Pittsburg is a smoky, dismal city, at her best. At her worst, nothing darker, dingier or more dispiriting can be imagined. The city is in the heart of the soft coal region; and the smoke from her dwellings, stores, factories, foundries and steamboats, uniting, settles in a cloud over the narrow valley in which she is built, until the very sun looks coppery through the sooty haze. According to a circular of the Pittsburg Board of Trade, about twenty per cent, or one-fifth, of all the coal used in the factories and dwellings of the city escapes into the air in the form of smoke, being the finer and lighter particles of carbon of the coal, which, set free by fire, escapes uncon-

---

[2] *Vulcan:* Roman god of fire.
[3] *Pluto:* Also known as Hades, the stern and pitiless ruler of the underworld.
[4] *Mercury:* Roman god of merchants, often associated with the Greek god Hermes, fleet-footed messenger of the gods.

sumed with the gases. The consequences of several thousand bushels of coal in the air at one and the same time may be imagined. But her inhabitants do not seem to mind it; and the doctors hold that this smoke, from the carbon, sulphur and iodine contained in it, is highly favorable to lung and cutaneous diseases, and is the sure death of malaria and its attendant fevers. And certainly, whatever the cause may be, Pittsburg is one of the healthiest cities in the United States. Her inhabitants are all too busy to reflect upon the inconvenience or uncomeliness of this smoke. Work is the object of life with them. It occupies them from morning until night, from the cradle to the grave, only on Sundays, when, for the most part, the furnaces are idle, and the forges are silent. For Pittsburg, settled by Irish-Scotch Presbyterians, is a great Sunday-keeping city. Save on this day her business men do not stop for rest or recreation, nor do they "retire" from business. They die with the harness on, and die, perhaps, all the sooner for having worn it so continuously and so long. . . .

Pittsburg is not a beautiful city. That stands to reason, with the heavy pall of smoke which constantly overhangs her. But she lacks beauty in other respects. She is substantially and compactly built, and contains some handsome edifices; but she lacks the architectural magnificence of some of her sister cities; while her suburbs present all that is unsightly and forbidding in appearance, the original beauties of nature having been ruthlessly sacrificed to utility.

Pittsburg is situated in western Pennsylvania, in a narrow valley at the confluence of the Allegheny and Monongahela Rivers, and at the head of the Ohio, and is surrounded by hills rising to the height of four or five hundred feet. These hills once possessed rounded outlines, with sufficient exceptional abruptness to lend them variety and picturesqueness. But they have been leveled down, cut into, sliced off, and ruthlessly marred and mutilated, until not a trace of their original outlines remain. Great black coal cars crawl up and down their sides, and plunge into unexpected and mysterious openings, their sudden disappearance lending, even in daylight, an air of mystery and diablerie to the region. Railroad tracks gridiron the ground everywhere, debris of all sorts lies in heaps, and is scattered over the earth, and huts and hovels are perched here and there, in every available spot. There is no verdure — nothing but mud and coal, the one yellow the other black. And on the edge of the city are the unpicturesque outlines of factories and foundries, their tall chimneys belching forth columns of inky blackness, which roll and whirl in fantastic shapes, and finally lose themselves in the general murkiness above. . . .

The Ohio River makes its beginning here, and in all but the season of low water the wharves of the city are lined with boats, barges and tugs, destined for every mentionable point on the Ohio and Mississippi rivers. The Ohio River is here, as all along its course, an uncertain and capricious stream. Sometimes, in spring, or early summer, it creeps up its banks and looks menacingly at the city. At other times it seems to become weary of bearing the boats, heavily laden with merchandise, to their destined ports, and so takes a nap, as it were. The last time we beheld this water-course its bed was lying nearly bare and dry, while a small, sluggish creek, a few feet, or at most, a few yards wide, crept along the bottom, small barges being towed down stream by horses, which waded in the water. The giant was resting. . . .

The monster iron works of Pittsburg consume large quantities of . . . coal, and it is the abundance and convenience of the latter material which have made the former possible. No other city begins to compare with Pittsburg in the number and variety of her factories. Down by the banks of the swift-flowing Allegheny most of the great foundries are to be discovered. The Fort Pitt Works are on a gigantic scale. Here are cast those monsters of artillery known as the twenty-inch gun. . . .

The American Iron Works employ two thousand five hundred hands, and cover seventeen acres. They have a coal mine at their back door, and an iron mine on Lake Superior, and they make any and every difficult iron thing the country requires. Nothing is too ponderous, nothing too delicate and exact, to be produced. The nail works of the city are well worth seeing. In them a thousand nails a minute are manufactured, each nail being headed by a blow on cold iron. The noise arising from this work can only be described as deafening. In one nail factory two hundred different kinds of nails, tacks and brads are manufactured. The productions of these different factories and foundries amount in the aggregate to an almost incredible number and value, and embrace everything made of iron which can be used by man. . . .

Pittsburg is a city of workers. From the proprietors of these extensive works, down to the youngest apprentices, all are busy; and perhaps the higher up in the scale the harder the work and the greater the worry. A man who carries upon his shoulders the responsibility of an establishment whose business amounts to millions of dollars in a year; who must oversee all departments of labor; accurately adjust the buying of the crude materials and the scale of wages on the one hand, with the price of the manufactured article on the other, so that the profit shall be on the right side; and who at the same time shall keep himself posted as to all which bears any relation to his business, has no time for leisure or social pleasures, and must even stint his hours of necessary rest.

Pittsburg illustrates more clearly than any other city in America the outcome of democratic institutions. There are no classes here except the industrious classes; and no ranks in society save those which have been created by industry. The mammoth establishments, some of them perhaps in the hands of the grandsons of their founders, have grown from small beginnings, fostered in their growth by industry and thrift. The great proprietor of to-day, it may have been, was the "boss" of yesterday, and the journeyman[5] of a few years ago, having ascended the ladder from the lowest round of apprenticeship. Industry and sobriety are the main aids to success.

The wages paid are good, for the most part, varying according to the quality of the employment, some of them being exceedingly liberal. The character of the workmen is gradually improving, though it has not yet reached the standard which it should attain. Many are intelligent, devoting their spare time to self-improvement, and especially to a comprehension of the relations of capital and labor, which so intimately concern them, and which they, more than any other class of citizens, except employers, need to understand, in order that they may not only maintain their own rights, but may avoid encroaching on the rights of others.

Too many workmen, however, have no comprehension of the dignity of their own position. They live only for present enjoyment, spend their money foolishly, not to say wickedly, and on every holiday give themselves up to that curse of the workingman — strong drink. While this class is such a considerable one, the entire ranks of working men must be the sufferers. And while ignorance as well as vice has been so prevalent among them, it is not to be wondered that they have been constantly undervalued, and almost as constantly oppressed.

The prosperity of the country depends upon the prosperity of the masses. With all the money in the hands of a few, there are only the personal wants of a few to be supplied. With wages high, work is always plentier, and everybody prospers. The gains of a large manufacturing establishment, divided, by means of fair profit and just wages,

---

[5] *journeyman:* A worker who has learned his trade.

between employers and employed, instead of being hoarded up by one man, make one hundred persons to eat where there would otherwise be but one; one hundred people to buy the productions of the looms and forges of the country, instead of only one; one hundred people, each having a little which they spend at home, instead of one man, who hoards his wealth, or takes it to Europe to dispose of it. It means all the difference between good and bad times, between a prosperous country, where all are comfortable and happy, and a country of a few millionaires and many paupers. . . .

JOHN ROACH

Senate Testimony from Iron Foundry Proprietor

The collapse of one of the country's largest investment houses in 1873 triggered the greatest depression the highly industrialized United States had ever suffered. This depression brought the economy to a halt, and for the next four years the working classes suffered tremendously, with hundreds of thousands of people unable to find work. Class tensions escalated, as did violence, until these tensions came to a head in 1877 with the Great Uprising, which began with a strike of railroad workers in Martinsburg, West Virginia. The strike quickly spread from coast to coast, enlisting the sympathy not only of many citizens of the striking states but also of the state militias who were sent to stop the strikes. Although it failed in the short run, the strike served to focus attention on class relations and class-based conflict. As a result of this emphasis, in 1883 the Senate Committee on Education and Labor began investigating the relations of labor and capital in the United States, conducting a series of interviews with laborers, labor leaders, and capitalists in order to determine how to prevent another Great Uprising.

John Roach (1813–1887) was born in Ireland and came to the United States in 1829, where he became an ironmaster and shipbuilder. In 1841 he purchased a small ironworks, and in 1860 this ironworks received a contract to construct an iron drawbridge over the Harlem River in New York. After the Civil War, Roach had one of the best iron foundries in the country, enabling him to play a large role in the development of the iron shipbuilding industry in the United States. From 1872 to 1886, Roach's ironworks built 126 iron ships. In his Senate testimony, speaking as a wealthy capitalist who was once a laborer, Roach discusses the availability and function of natural resources, the role of legislation, and the responsibility of the poor for their own poverty. Roach calls for legislation to protect American industry from foreign competitors but otherwise prefers little government interference in industry.

The following excerpt is taken from *Report of the Committee of the Senate upon the Relations between Labor and Capital, and Testimony Taken by the Committee,* vol. 1 (Washington, D.C.: Government and Printing Office, 1885).

NEW YORK, *September* 4, 1883.

I employ some 3,000 men, in Chester and New York, and these men are engaged in some twenty five different branches of mechanism. They work up materials of every kind that enter into a modern iron ship, from the ore in the mine and the timber in the forest into the forms necessary to produce the final result — the finished ship.

Being a workingman myself, and having occupied some forty-five years ago as humble a position as that of any man now in my employ, I can speak from experience on this subject. When I started out for myself I laid down a certain course of action based upon certain principles which seemed to me to be sound. I believed as a basis that *labor applied to natural resources was the foundation of all wealth.*

All our rich prairies, our boundless forests, our wealth-yielding mines, our vast coal beds, our great waterfalls — all these were here before the white man set his foot on the soil. For countless years they had remained in the undeveloped condition in which they were found; I need not say how small was the wealth of the country then. The Indian had all these natural advantages thrown open to him, yet was as though they did not exist. When he traded at all he was a free trader indeed. He would sell his valuable skins for a pouch of tobacco, a bottle of firewater, or a string of beads, giving dollars' worth for penny's worth, and he grew poor while the white trader grew rich.

The natural resources, the material of wealth, were all here. When did this country begin to accumulate wealth? When the white man began to apply labor to cultivate the soil, to fell the forests, to dig into the bowels of the earth, to make nature serve him — in a word, when he began to use the materials God had given him.

Industrial Legislation — The Duty of the Government

Taking this view of it, I held that the Government is under one supreme obligation to its citizens. It has one duty of legislation in behalf of labor. That duty is to apply legislation practically and intelligently so that it shall aid labor in the development of the natural resources of the country. To do this, the legislators must find out what the natural resources are, what the needs of the people are, and how far it is within our control to satisfy these needs from our own resources. The condition of labor at home must be compared with the condition of labor abroad. The legislation applied must be such as will make the terms of competition equal, while favoring the elevation of labor. The end to be sought is a policy that will enable our people to develop the natural resources of our own land, to develop the natural talents of the workingmen, and to supply our own wants within ourselves. This legislation should not be in the interest of any one man, sect, or section of the country, but as broad as God's law, giving an equal chance to all. The road to heaven is open to all, and the road to this great wealth buried in the soil should be as free as that, by the system of legislation instituted. We do not want class legislation, nor laws to help the profligate at the expense of the proficient man. The question is then whether our legislators have studied these things; whether they have intelligently applied legislation to labor. Where they have not, labor remains almost dead; where they have, labor rises up and becomes successful. Now, it seems to me that with one exception legislation ought to cease with this. There is legislation free to all, but then the poor have got to be taken care of, the school houses at all cost have to be kept open, and the poorest man wants such a system to exist that his child can receive as good an education as that of the man of means.

As the American legislator should, in the discharge of his duty, look with care to the future development of this great country in the interest of labor, circumstances might arise, which would call forth new legislation looking to this end, and in all nations that ever made any progress, this law I speak of has been brought into requisition and avail: Suppose that a nation older than ours, further advanced in development, with cheaper capital and cheaper labor, could produce the necessaries that our people might require cheaper than we could produce them here, and before we got up to that point where we had a fair chance for equal competition this country was flooded with the products of their labor and we let our own resources be undeveloped with the exception of developing something given us in greater abundance and with greater opportunities than others had — that would bring us down to cotton and corn. In cotton and corn we can stand up against the world; but what would this country be and what would the working people be if you drove them into that condition of things?

Unless a Government legislates for the proper protection of labor in developing the natural resources, it is a stumbling-block in the workingman's way.

Now, has that duty been performed by our Government? The wonderful development of our country in all its material resources answers the question and justifies me in saying, yes.

As to the comparative compensation of labor, I think I am pretty competent to judge of that question. Serving an apprenticeship in the city of New York, beginning at a salary of 12 shillings a week or 25 cents a day, and having to depend upon myself to pay my board by working overtime — working for that pay, and beginning work every day with the rising of the sun and ceasing only when the sun set — that was the beginning of my career here in the old Allaire Works in New York. It may be well, perhaps, at this point to compare the wages that I received and those that were paid generally then with the wages that I pay now. In those times wages were low, and very often there was no money to pay even those low wages. When I was out of my apprenticeship and a journeyman earning 12 shillings a day, it was a frequent thing for the timekeeper to come into the shop on Saturday and say, "John, how much money do you want this week?" "Well, I would like to have one-half of my wages this week." "You can't have it. What do you want to do with it?" "I want to get a suit of clothes." And if the old books are not destroyed, whoever would go down now to Brooks Brothers' store, at the corner of Catharine street, might find there an order on Brooks Brothers, given by the proprietor of the old Allaire Works, for a coat for John Roach. There were no savings banks in those days and but little to put in them. It was a common thing for the proprietor of the works to give orders to his men for clothing and different things, instead of paying them the money, and when a number of such orders had been given, so as to amount to something considerable, he would give a note for the amount. There was no coal in New York at that time, and if you wanted to know the number of occupants of an ordinary workingman's tenement, all you had to do was to pass through the hallway to the yard and count the padlocks. There were a number of little woodhouses or provision-houses fastened with padlocks — one such little house for each tenant — and matters were conducted very differently from what they are conducted now. Each workman went down to Rutgers Slip and brought his cord of wood, put it into his wood-house and sawed it up and split it himself. That was the way they lived in those days. I remember very well the first struggle that I made to get a little money ahead, and if I had thought of it I would have brought here an old memorandum book which would show you how I tried to make a little overtime so as to be able to save a little money. As I look back at those old times I see that there has been one continued progress in the elevation of the condition of the working people. When the invention and introduction of modern machinery began the workingmen thought it was going to destroy their occupation, but instead of that it only made more work for them and enabled them to have a thousand comforts and even luxuries — things that they could not afford before. The cheapness of those things produced by machinery enabled the working people to use them, thus increasing the consumption and making a greater demand for labor.

What Industry Will Do

At first I was an enthusiast on farming, and, from my observation and experience of American life, I long ago reached the conclusion that there was no man of ordinary intelligence or of ordinary industry in this country, under our system of government and our institutions, and with the great opportunities that are offered here — that there was no man, however humble he might be, who could not own his own house, his own farm, or his own workshop. It is only necessary for a man to aim at that object when he starts out in life. He should begin to think of it at least when he is eighteen, and if he strikes out in that way with a definite object in view, remembering he is probably going to have a family of children who will be as dear to him as his own life, and that old age will come on in due time — if a man strikes out with that object in view from the beginning, and pursues it in a straightforward and industrious and prudent manner, he cannot fail. I have never known such a man to fail, and I can cite thousands of instances where such men have suceeded in the highest degree.

But a new theory has been spreading among the working people. Two men start out in life together at the same time and with equal chances, both depending upon their labor for success; one of them after awhile becomes discontented, begins to think that he ought to enjoy life as he goes along, and to have more days for excursions and for enjoyments; that he ought to have more cigars and other luxuries and indulgences, and he lags and lingers on the way. The other man is thoughtful, prudent, industrious; he has a definite object in life, and he keeps that object always in view and works towards it constantly, and he succeeds. Now there is no mystery in the failure of one of these men or in the success of the other. It is all nonsense for any man to think of ever accomplishing anything in this world, no matter how trifling it may be, if he has not a definite object and motive, and is not *determined* to do it. The first of these men lagged and stumbled on the way through his own fault entirely. He took his choice. He preferred to smoke his cigars, to go on excursions, to frequent the liquor saloons, or to go gunning[1] (for I have seen men go out of my shop and spend a week at a time gunning when they had not enough to keep them out of the poorhouse for six months), and then when he finds that he is not succeeding, and that other men of more energy and industry are getting ahead of him in life, he comes out and says, "I am injured; I am suffering from injustice; I want legislation to compel this other man to divide with me that which he has acquired by his own diligence and thrift." Very often you will hear men of the character I have described taking that view and claiming that some remedy for the evils they suffer under ought to be provided by legislation, when the difficulty is all in themselves. Mark the difference in the two classes. When the man of progress has accomplished the object he worked for, he freely votes to tax his property to build schools to educate the children of the man who has no property, who lagged behind, "enjoyed" life as he went along.

Now I believe that this is

The Age of Co-operation,

and that labor and capital must co-operate in order that both shall derive the greatest advantage from their efforts; but it will never do to have labor co-operate only with itself and by itself and thus become the foe of capital. If labor does that, the worst effects of such a course will fall upon the laborer in the end. Neither, on the other hand, is it just or right or proper that capital shall combine against labor. Capital and labor should never combine against each other, because one cannot live without the other.

[1] *gunning:* Hunting with a gun or rifle.

WILLIAM WEIHE

Senate Testimony from Iron Puddler and Union Leader

A powerful union leader in the late 1800s, William Weihe (1845–1908) began working at an iron mill at the age of fifteen. Like many laborers, he joined a union, the Sons of Vulcan, and was soon elected an officer. In 1876, the Sons of Vulcan and other unions joined to form the Amalgamated Association of Iron and Steel Workers of which Weihe served as president from 1884 to 1892. As president, Weihe helped the union become one of the largest affiliates of the American Federation of Labor (AFL), and in 1890 he was elected vice president of the AFL. In the following excerpt from his testimony before the Senate Committee on Education and Labor, 1883, Weihe calls for government intervention on behalf of laborers, protection of their safety and wages, and enforcement of the laws that protect them. He suggests prohibiting child labor and providing for the welfare of children whose families cannot support them.

The following excerpt is taken from *Report of the Committee of the Senate upon the Relations between Labor and Capital, and Testimony Taken by the Committee,* vol. 2 (Washington, D.C.: Government and Printing Office, 1885).

NEW YORK, *September* 7, 1883.

WILLIAM WEIHE sworn and examined.

By Mr. CALL:

Question. What is your occupation? — Answer. I am a boiler; commonly called a puddler.[1]

Q. How long have you been in that business? — A. I have worked in the mills since 1862.

Q. That is since you were quite a boy? — A. Yes, sir.

Q. And then you have grown up in the business? — A. From that time I have been continually working in the mills.

Q. Are you connected officially with any organization or association of workingmen? — A. Yes, sir; I am connected with the Amalgamated Association of Iron and Steel Workers, and I am at present a member of the board of trustees.

---

[1] *puddler*: A worker who stirs molten pig iron in the presence of oxidizing agents to make wrought iron. Hugh Wolfe, in *Life in the Iron-Mills,* is a puddler.

Q. What other position do you hold in that association? — A. No position except as a trustee at the present time.

Q. Are you not the president-elect? — A. Yes, sir; but I do not take possession of the office until some time in October.

Q. But you have been elected president of that association and will take your office in October. Now, what is the condition of the laboring people, skilled and unskilled, in that pursuit, in respect to their surroundings, their manner of living, and the adequacy of their compensation to provide for them comfortably? — A. To some extent their condition is good, and to some extent it is not. As a rule, we have a scale of prices, and we govern ourselves accordingly during the year; different branches of the work receiving different wages per ton, some more and some less. Some branches are more skillful than others, and get a better compensation.

Q. How is it on the average?

A. Well, on the average in certain sections it is very fair, and in other sections it may not be fair. What I mean by fair and unfair is this: Where a mill runs every day men can make a better living than where the mill does not run every day. It depends upon the orders the manufacturers receive, or the demand that is made on the mill, and, of course, the men employed in a locality where the mills run regularly receive a better compensation, that is, they make more money during the year than other men who are employed where the mills are more idle.

Q. As a general rule is it customary to run the mills only a part of the year, or the whole year? — A. Some firms run only a part of the year, others run them more steadily.

Q. You consider the wages very fair, then, for the work really done? — A. Yes, sir; in view of the prices of iron at the present time.

Q. Give us an idea of the prices paid to the men.

The Wages of Iron-Workers

A. Boilers receive $5.50 a ton, or $2.50 card-rate.

Q. At that rate, how much will they make per day? — A. They make five heats[2] in the boiling department for a double turn and six heats a single turn, and the heaters make eight on each turn. The heaters work the iron that the puddlers have made and make it into the finished bar. In some mills they charge heavier than they do in

---

[2] *make . . . heats:* In metallurgy, a heat is a single heating of metal in a furnace.

others, but the average would be between $3.50 and $4 a day for a fair hand in the puddling department. The foremen generally average $25, but they have to pay their helper out of that. The balance remains to the boiler. . . .

Q. In the case of a mill running steadily what will be a man's wages in that department on an average? — A. $3.50 a day.

Q. What will it amount to per month — $3.50 for twenty-six days, I suppose, will give it? — A. They could not work twenty-six days a month; they could only work twenty-two days. . . .

Q. Then the men would only get $3.50 a day for twenty-two days? — A. Yes, sir.

Q. And that, you say, would be the average wages? — A. A pretty fair average.

Q. Is that a reasonable compensation? Does it enable a man to live comfortably? — A. If a man got work all the year round it would, but the business is very laborious and the men that work at it have to live on substantial food, and in connection with that they must make a little more.

Q. Is that the reason why their wages are larger than the wages of others? — A. Not exactly that. The rollers[3] are supposed to have more of the responsibility on them, and their wages will average a little more for that reason.

Q. The rollers, then, are the highest paid? — A. Yes; that is, they make the most.

Q. What do they make? — A. I could not tell you that exactly. Some of the mills are of greater capacity than others, but the rollers average from $5 to $6, and perhaps $7 a day. But there is only one roller at each mill, that is at one train, and he has a number of men under him that he has charge of.

Q. Then he is a kind of superintendent? — A. He works himself, but the same time he has charge of these men under him.

Q. What other classes of workingmen are there in this business besides those you have enumerated? — A. There are the heaters and the roll-hands.

Q. What does a heater get? — A. For a certain brand of iron 70 cents a ton. Some get more for work such as sheet-iron and plate-iron.

Q. What does that rate yield a man? — A. They generally average 7½ tons a day.

---

[3] *rollers:* Workers responsible for rolling metal bars, or sheets.

Q. Is that very severe labor? — A. Yes, sir; very exhausting.

Q. Does it require any great degree of skill? — A. Oh, yes.

Q. Then the man has got to be a trained, skilled laborer? — A. Oh, certainly; a man could not go to any branch of the work in a rolling-mill[4] and do it unless he had got some knowledge or experience before he went there by working at it.

Q. How do you regard that rate of wages, 70 cents a ton? — A. Well, I think that at the present price of iron it is about fair.

Q. You think that that rate of pay will enable a man to live comfortably with his family, do you, particularly out in that region of country where rents are lower than they are farther east? — A. The rents in the city of Pittsburgh are middling high; outside of the city limits they are not.

Q. They are nothing like as high as the rents in the eastern cities, I suppose? — A. But the eastern manufacturers do not pay those prices in all the mills. The eastern men have an advantage. Their food may be as expensive, but their clothing is a good deal cheaper out this way.

Desirable Legislation

Q. Is there anything special which you desire to suggest in the way of legislation or otherwise, for the improvement of the condition of the workingmen in that business? — A. Yes, sir; there can be something done by legislation. During last winter I was a member of the legislature of Pennsylvania, and several laws were passed there that are of benefit to the workingmen, especially the law in regard to convict contract labor and the mining law.

Q. Those laws are satisfactory to the people that you represent, are they? — A. Well, the convict contract labor law is not as satisfactory as it might be. The mining laws are in regard to securing ventilation for the miners, to give the miners an opportunity to have better air in the mines.

Q. Then those are laws designed for the preservation of life and health? — A. Yes, sir.

Q. You don't care, I suppose, to state the specific provisions of those laws? — A. They will only become effective at a certain time, and until that time we are unable to say just what their effect will be. . . .

---

[4] *rolling-mill:* Factory in which metal sheets are rolled out.

Q. What else is there in the way of remedial measures that you can suggest? — A. In regard to the truck system,[5] they had a bill which they were trying to pass, but it failed. The workingmen desired that the truck system should be abolished and a pay system established requiring that the men should be paid every two weeks, and paid in United States money. That bill passed one house but failed to pass the other.

Q. And your people still desire the passage of that bill? — A. Yes, sir; for various reasons. There are men in that part of the country that get paid only once a month, and that have to deal in the employers' stores. If a man goes to work on the first day of one month he will have to work until the third Tuesday (I think it is in some places) in the following month before he receives any pay. That is nearly seven weeks. Before that time arrives the men will have had, of course, to deal in the store, and the wages in those places not being so high as in others, it usually takes every dollar that a man earns to pay his bills in the store by the time pay-day arrives, and consequently he never makes one cent advance in the direction of a better condition.

Q. Then that law is designed to require the payment of the men in money, and at short intervals, every two weeks, you say? — A. Yes, sir.

Q. Are there any other provisions in the law designed to carry that object into effect? — A. Yes.

Q. What other suggestions have you to make in regard to any form of action, legislative or otherwise, for the benefit of the working people that you represent?

A National Bureau of Labor Statistics

A. To establish a national bureau of statistics. There is such a bureau in the State of Pennsylvania now, which has worked well. It collects information from the various branches of labor in the State, and distributes that information in its reports.

Q. The laboring people generally in your trade desire some action on the part of the Government looking to the establishment of a bureau of industrial statistics, I believe? — A. Yes, sir.

Q. Is that desire very general among them? — A. Almost unanimous. I have never heard a dissenting voice yet in regard to it.

---

[5] *truck system:* System of paying wages in goods instead of cash.

Q. What other legislation do you think would be desirable for the benefit of the working classes? — A. Well, I could not suggest anything more just now. There have been so many suggested that if we could carry even a few of them into effect it would do great good.

Q. I am asking now only about those which have assumed a definite form in your association — those measures that have been talked about and agreed upon as something that it would be desirable to have done as a means of affording relief from the evils that the workingmen now suffer. Do you think that those measures that you have suggested are all that your association at present think desirable? — A. As far as they have gone in that line they are satisfactory; but certainly they desire to have improvements made in other directions if they see a chance of having the laws properly carried out. The great trouble is that when there is a law there is no one to enforce it in many cases, and the working classes generally cannot enforce it themselves, and consequently the law is often evaded.

Q. How would you remedy that? — A. By labor organizing and educating the members of the organizations up to that point, so that when a law is evaded they can act in harmony to secure its enforcement.

Q. That is a very wise mode of action — by bringing an intelligent public opinion to bear upon the tribunals charged with the execution of the law; that is the idea, is it not? — A. Yes, sir.

Q. Then there is no form of legislative action which you desire in connection with that? — A. No, sir.

Q. In other words, you mean that you want an organization which will create a public opinion which will enable you to hold a judge responsible for any unreasonable judgment or for failing to execute or carry out the law?

Laws for the Benefit of Workingmen
Not Executed

A. Yes, sir. You see there is a certain class of unskilled workingmen who never have any power to have laws enforced which concern them, and they are the people that are generally most imposed upon. Laws have been passed for the benefit of the working people, but they have not been generally carried out, and, as I have said, very often the workingmen have no means of having them enforced. . . .

Q. Have you any suggestions to make in regard to the importation of labor from abroad under contract — skilled or unskilled labor? — A. We have no objection to labor coming here, but we do object to its being *imported* to take the places of citizens of this country. We do not think it is right to import labor from foreign countries to supersede the American workingman.

Q. What is the difference in effect between importing labor and its coming voluntarily? — A. Oh, there is a great difference.

Q. I know there is a difference in fact in the manner of its coming; but in effect, does not a man who comes here voluntarily as much supersede an American laborer as does a man who is imported? — A. But when they are brought here they are brought for that purpose; while on the other hand, when they come voluntarily, you can do something with them; you can educate them. But when they are brought here in the way that has been described to you by other witnesses you cannot educate them until a considerable time has elapsed, and in the mean while the American workingman has suffered a great deal from their competition.

Q. Those whom you represent, as I understand you, have no objection to the voluntary immigration here of people from any country. — A. No, sir.

Q. I have no other special questions to ask you, unless you can give us some additional facts in regard to the general condition of the people engaged in the different trades, their mode of life, and the sufficiency or insufficiency of their wages to give them a comfortable support. — A. Outside of the branches that I have worked in I could not say very much, because I have not given much attention to any of the other trades.

Q. You live in Pittsburgh? — A. Yes, sir.

Q. Do you consider the general condition of the people engaged in the trades and working in the factories there as favorable and comfortable ones? — A. In some branches it may be so regarded. The unskilled laborers of Pittsburgh often are not employed all the year round, and of course their condition is not so good as that of those who receive steady employment.

Q. Well is their condition positively bad? — A. In the winter months it is.

Q. Generally, or in exceptional cases? — A. It depends on the condition of the market generally.

Q. Putting aside the question of the condition of the market, is there or has there been a good deal of want and destitution among those people at any season of the year during the last seven years? — A. Well, I could not say exactly that there was a great deal of want among them.

Q. You think, then, that as a general rule they are not in absolute want at any season of the year? — A. Not in that section.

Child Labor

Q. In respect to child labor, is there any particular evil that requires examination and the application of a remedy? — A. Oh, yes. I do not think that children should be introduced into any works until they reach a certain age, say from twelve to fourteen.

Q. What is the practice in that respect now? — A. They bring them there into the glass-houses at eight, nine and ten years of age.

Q. And you think there should be legislation to prohibit those children working in factories before the age of twelve years? — A. Some thing like that.

Q. How would you do in cases where they have nothing to eat unless they work? — A. Well, if the parents were placed in such a position that they could have a fair remuneration for their own labor they would be glad to provide for their children.

Q. Yes, but would you let the children starve until the parents got placed in that position? — A. No, sir. I would have the Government clothe them and provide for them where it was necessary.

Q. You think, then, that whenever a man is unable to provide for his children, instead of letting them go into a factory the public should educate them and take care of them? — A. Yes; and if those children were kept out of those factories up to a certain age you see there would be more employment for older people, and they would get better compensation and would generally be able to provide for their families.

Q. Suppose that a man has a large family and says, "I cannot feed and clothe my children unless I put them into the factory," and you say that he shall not put them into the factory, and prevent it — that, you say, will increase your compensation and his compensation so much, but will it increase his compensation in proportion to the number of children he has? — A. Well, no, not in that case; but such instances are very few.

Q. You think that such a law would have a tendency to relieve your people generally of the evils of which they complain? — A. Yes, sir.

The Hours of Labor Should Be Reduced

Q. What have you to say in respect to the hours of labor? — A. Well, we think that the hours of labor should be reduced.

Q. How much? — A. Our members in the rolling-mills could not very well do it, but outside of that branch we believe that it might be so managed that the hours of labor could be curtailed.

Q. You think it impracticable in that branch because of the nature of the business, I suppose? — A. Yes, sir.

Q. Then your own idea is that different employments have different necessities in that respect, which cannot be evaded? — A. Yes, sir.

Q. I don't know of any other questions that I desire to ask, but if anything else occurs to you that you desire to submit you may state it. — A. I don't think of anything else just now.

Imported Labor Again

By the CHAIRMAN:

Q. About this imported labor of which you speak, you make a distinction between that which is imported and that which comes here in the way of voluntary immigration? — A. Yes, sir. Generally this labor that is imported is of a bad quality, and good workingmen, I don't believe, will let themselves be imported. It is the scuff, the bad specimens of the working classes, that are usually selected to be imported.

Q. They are not selected, I suppose, because they are bad, but because they are poor and cheap? — A. Yes, sir; and because they probably can be used for a purpose when they are brought here.

Q. Are those imported laborers, as you have seen them, as a rule, laborers that could have gotten here without assistance? — A. I don't believe they are; there may be some instances of a better class, but very few, I believe.

Q. And therefore, left to the natural laws governing immigration, they would not be here at all? — A. Not unless they came in the way they do.

Q. Those who come naturally, as you call it, must have some means to start with, of course? — A. Certainly. That is what makes me think that these men must be of the lowest grade, when they can be got together in the way they are and brought here in the manner they are. I don't believe that skilled workmen who looked to their own interests could be gathered up and brought over here in that way.

Q. To what extent is that imported labor brought to this country? — A. Well, when a strike occurs, the employers generally go over to Europe or send agents to bring over this labor.

Q. Have these laborers come in large numbers at any time? — A. They have. In 1867 the employers brought quite a number of Belgians over here.

Q. Have any others been brought there that you know of in that interest? — A. Not iron workers. These that I spoke of were iron workers.

Q. What was done with them? — A. There was a strike in the iron mills, and the manufacturers of that district sent agents to Europe and brought over these Belgians.

Q. How extensive was the strike? — A. At that time it was a strike for Pittsburgh only.

Q. How many workmen do you think were on strike at that time? — A. I suppose there were five or six thousand men thrown out of employment by the strike.

Q. How many laborers were imported at that time? — A. The number I could not state, but there was quite a number, perhaps 2,000.

Q. Enough to enable the manufacturers to get along without re-employing the American laborers? — A. For a while they did, but the foreigners did not prove a success.

Q. Why? — A. They were not swift workmen.

Q. Did their importation operate, though, to break down the strike? — A. To a certain extent it did. They were employed until it was found that they were not satisfactory, and then of course the best of the old hands were called upon to work again.

Q. But the average hands that had been in the strike lost their places, I suppose? — A. Yes, sir.

Q. Then they must have been deserted by their leaders, were they not? — A. Well, the organizations at that time were not as complete as they are now.

Q. Do those Belgians still remain in that employment there? — A. I believe there are very few of them there now.

Q. What became of them? Did they go into the iron works or did they go into other pursuits? — A. They went into other work, outdoor work, such as stone quarries and other things out through the country districts.

Q. Then they do not remain permanent competitors with the skilled workmen of Pittsburgh? — A. No; there may be a few of them there yet, but very few.

Q. What sort of men were they? — A. Some were young and some were old.

Q. How were they as to intelligence and as to having some means accumulated? — A. I don't believe they were an educated class of people at all.

Q. They were Belgians, you say? — A. They were Belgians.

Q. Were they a healthy and vigorous people? — A. On the average I think they were.

Q. Physically, were they about the equals of the men who were striking? — A. Oh, yes; physically they were.

Q. Did you ever understand from them or any of them how they got here? — A. I understood that they got here by being imported to take the places of the men who were out on strike.

Q. Who paid the expenses of bringing them here? — A. Of that I have no definite knowledge, but I know it was done.

Q. You only know that the employers got them here? — A. I know they got them here; whether they did it as a body or acting separately as individuals I could not say.

Q. Have you known any other instances in Pittsburgh or that vicinity of such importations of foreign labor when American laborers have been on strike? — A. Not any since that time.

Q. Have there been any importations of foreign laborers who have been introduced into the mills in the ordinary course of the business, when there was no trouble among the workingmen? — A. No, sir.

Q. Have you known any other such cases of importation of laborers in any other pursuits or occupation? — A. I believe that at one time they brought some foreigners over to the mining region in Western Pennsylvania; that was six or seven years ago. I believe the men were Italians. Whether those men were imported direct, or whether the employers came to New York and got them I do not know, but at any rate they were brought there from some other place.

Q. Do you know anything of the condition of the miners? — A. Not very much.

The Small Vices of the Workingmen

Q. To what extent do the evils of drinking, smoking, and other small vices affect the workingmen, to your knowledge? — A. In our association we generally try to prohibit all that. We bring the subject up in the lodge-rooms[6] and warn the men to avoid those things, and

---

[6] *lodge-rooms:* Meeting rooms for an organization or union.

we have been successful in a great many instances in getting people who were in the habit of using stimulants to abandon the habit, or to use them to a much less extent than they had been doing before.

Q. Then, the general attitude of your order is favorable to temperance in such indulgences? — A. Yes, sir.

Q. Is your order made use of for the propagation of new and unusual theories regarding the tenure of property? — A. Well, they bring up all questions that pertain to the branches of labor that are engaged in the iron and steel mills.

Q. That is, you discuss those practical questions rather than questions relating to the ownership of land; changing the form of government, or introducing new and untried theories? — A. We do not take those up much; we have not yet at any rate.

Q. You are rather practical than otherwise in your objects and discussions? — A. Yes, sir.

JESSE CLAXTON, J. G. GOING, AND N. R. FIELDING

Senate Testimony from Workers of Color

Jesse Claxton, J. G. Going, and N. R. Fielding were all southern laborers who had formerly been slaves. In the following excerpts from their 1883 testimony before the Senate Committee, they testify to the fairly good conditions they enjoy, Claxton as a carpenter and contractor, Going as a barber, and Fielding as a bricklayer. All, however, admit that their lives are not without hardships. Each man argues that black children are at a severe disadvantage because of the lack of schools available for them, and each suggests that the government support schools for black children, especially those whose parents cannot afford to pay for their schooling. Fielding also complains of the unequal wages for black and white workers. While these workers describe a time in which black laborers are able to live by their labor, and even to buy real estate and establish savings, they also discuss the difficulties they face in a labor market that favors whites.

The following excerpt is taken from *Report of the Committee of the Senate upon the Relations between Labor and Capital, and Testimony Taken by the Committee,* vol. 3 (Washington, D.C.: Government and Printing Office, 1885).

BIRMINGHAM, ALA., *November* 16, 1883.
JESSE CLAXTON (colored) sworn and examined.
By Mr. PUGH:
Question. Do you live in Birmingham? — Answer. Yes, sir.

Q. What is your business? — A. I am a carpenter.

Q. How long have you been a carpenter? — A. Twenty-nine years.

Q. How did you learn your trade? — A. I was bound out[1] in Richmond, Va., by my owner.

Q. Then you learned your trade when you were a slave? — A. Yes, sir.

Q. And you have been at work at it ever since? — A. Yes, sir.

Q. How long have you been living here? — A. About ten years.

A Colored Contractor

Q. Are you a mechanic working by the day or a contractor? — A. I am a contractor now and have been for a good many years.

Q. Then you employ laborers yourself? — A. Yes, sir.

Q. What wages do you pay the carpenters you employ? — A. From $1.50 to $2.50 per day.

Q. How have you succeeded in your business as a contractor? — A. I have done mighty well. I have had some bad luck, though, but I can blame nobody for it only myself.

Q. Have you been able to save anything? — A. Yes, sir; I have saved a great deal and lost a great deal.

Q. How does your financial condition compare now with what it has been in the past? — A. Well, sir, it is very poor now, but it has been better.

Q. You have been better off than you are now? — A. Oh, yes, sir; I have been worth a good deal of property in this place, but I have not got it now. I have some, though.

Q. How did you lose it? — A. My own misfortunes, bad luck, as other men sometimes have.

Q. What are the opportunities here for men in your trade to make money? — A. Good; very good.

Q. Are they better now than they have been? — A. Well, the opportunity has been better than it is right now, but it is good enough now.

---

[1] *bound out:* Apprenticed.

Q. In what respect has it been better than it is now? — A. Well, when this place first started we got a little better wages for building a house than we can get now.

Q. There is more competition now? — A. Yes, sir; I worked on this very building (the court-house) making those frames. I was getting $3 a day then, working by the day.

Q. If there is anything further that you want to let us know about the condition of your trade or of the working people generally or anything that you think we can do to improve their condition you may go on and state it. — A. I don't suppose that I could state anything to you that you could do for me, because the work is here, and if a man can do it the people will give it to him and pay him for it, and if he tries he can make money. There is some that makes a good deal of money here and some that has a chance to make it and don't make it.

Q. Well, that is the case everywhere, is it not? — A. Oh, yes; this is really about the best part of Alabama for colored people. They can get more work to do, and they can get better pay for it, I believe. The colored people generally have no trouble with the better class of white people in this country; in fact, everywhere that I have been the well raised, wealthy, respectable white people are generally friends to the colored people, but it is the class that is nearly on a level with them that oppresses them, if any at all.

Insufficient School Privileges — Aid Wanted

In some parts of the State the colored people has no chance to get their children to school, somehow. In Saint Clair County, a part of the State that I have been through this year, there is so few colored people living there that the county superintendent says there is not enough colored children to pay the teacher, and consequently they do not get any teaching at all. If they lived in a township where there was a great many colored people then they could get a school.

Q. Do you think of anything else that you would like to state? — A. Nothing else that I know of that is worth stating here.

By the CHAIRMAN:

Q. Are there any trades unions among the colored people, or any institutions of that nature? — A. Not here. I belonged to one or two in Georgia and Virginia.

Q. Were they of any benefit to you? — A. Yes, sir.

Q. I suppose you agree with the other witnesses here in regard to desiring aid from the General Government for your schools? — A.

Yes, sir. If the colored people had the chance to get their children into shops to learn trades, it would be a great help to them. The people here that owns the works, I don't suppose they would have any objection to taking in colored apprentices, but the class that works there won't work with them as a general thing. Now, if there was some way to give the colored people trades it would be a great benefit.

BIRMINGHAM, ALA., *November* 16, 1883.

J. G. GOING (colored) sworn and examined.

By the CHAIRMAN:

Question. Do you live in Birmingham? — Answer. Yes, sir.

Q. What is your business? — A. I am a barber by profession.

Q. You understand the subject of our inquiry; go on and make any statement that you desire on the subject.

The Colored People Doing Well

A. Well, taking everything into consideration, I think the colored people through this section of the country are doing pretty well. They get pretty fair wages for their work and there is a good lot of work here to do; common labor, I think, gets from $1 to $1.25 a day, some more and some less, and an economical man can save something out of that. There is a good number of colored men here that have acquired homes, and some have got very good property. I don't know of any section of country in the State where they are doing as well as they are here.

Q. How badly are they doing anywhere? — A. I don't know that they are doing overly badly anywhere.

Q. How well are they doing outside of Birmingham? — A. I don't know much about what is going on outside of this town, because I don't go much to the country. In the place that I came from the colored men was doing pretty well, some of them living on good farms and having nice property.

Q. Do you think the colored men are buying land more than they used to? — A. Yes, sir; a good deal more.

Q. You think they have generally the idea that they want to own land? — A. Yes, sir.

Q. There is a good deal of talk of their wasting their money, to what extent does that go, according to your observation?

Colored Men Thriftless;
Just Like White People

A. Well, colored people are just like white people in that respect. Plenty of white men work all their lives and don't accumulate anything, and it is the same way with colored people, but it is more general with them, I think, because they are not cultured as much as the white people. It is the more ignorant class of people that are the sufferers in that respect, both white and colored.

Education the Remedy

Q. You think that if they knew more they would save more? — A. Oh, yes, and they would be better citizens in every way. A great amount of the crime that is committed by both whites and blacks is committed by the more or less ignorant people.

Q. You all seem to be thoroughly impressed with the idea that it is well and desirable to be better educated? — A. Yes, sir; that is the thing that our people need mostly. What they need is a common-school system — not colleges, but a common-school system that would meet the wants of the poorer classes, white and black. The colored people, for instance, the poorer classes cannot send their children off to be educated, and it is the same way with the white people; a few colored people and a few white people can, but the poorer classes cannot.

Q. Have you thought anything about the establishment of the postal savings bank system[2] here, and whether it would be a good thing? — A. No sir; I have not thought much of that.

Q. Which do you think is the best way for a colored man who has no home to invest his money, in a bank or in a piece of land? — A. Well, the safest way, I think, is to put it in property.

Q. Then, you think that nobody needs to wait for the establishmen of savings banks in order to save money? — A. Oh, no; they do not need to wait; but there are very few people who are laying up anything.

Q. Is there any difficulty in their getting land here to buy? — A. None at all, if they have got the money to pay for it.

---

[2] *postal savings bank system:* While postal savings banks — savings banks conducted by the government through post offices — had been effectively established in other countries in the nineteenth century, the United States did not create a postal savings bank until 1911.

Q. Can they get trusted like other folks — can they buy a piece of land, paying part down, give a mortgage, and get time to pay the balance? — A. Yes, sir.

Q. Is there any place of which you have knowledge where it is better to buy land than it is here? — A. Well, the tendency around this country is for the value of land to go up.

Q. So that if a man buys a piece of land it may increase in value a great deal faster than his money would increase at interest? — A. Yes, sir.

Q. Is there any other point that you wish to suggest? — A. No, sir; that is all. About the most important thing for our people is to try to have good common schools established.

Federal Aid Wanted

Q. And you want national aid to help that along, do you? — A. Yes, sir. Our school system here is very poor. The State does not appropriate much money for the support of the schools, and the result is that there are very few children in school. The parents are all poor and are not able to send their children to school in many cases. I reckon there are one thousand children in this town of school age that are not in school.

The CHAIRMAN. If you are going to elect Democrats to office in Alabama, you must insist upon it that they shall give you good schools.

The WITNESS. It is always pretty easy to make that bargain, but the sticking up to it is more trouble.

The CHAIRMAN. You do the voting before you get the schools.

The WITNESS. That is the trouble.

The CHAIRMAN. Well, insist upon it that your Representatives in Washington shall vote for a national appropriation to aid your school system.

The WITNESS. Well, I suppose some of them do that.

BIRMINGHAM, ALA., *November* 16, 1883.

N. R. FIELDING (colored) sworn and examined.

By the CHAIRMAN.

Question. You live in Birmingham? — Answer. Yes, sir.

Q. What is your business? — A. I am a bricklayer.

Q. Are you a good one? — A. Well, you know I might say so without other people believing it. I pass for one, anyhow.

Q. Do you get plenty of work? — A. Yes, sir.

Another Colored Contractor

Q. Do you ever take contracts and employ others to help you? —
A. Yes, sir.

Q. How many men have you had in your employ at one time? —
A. I have had six or eight bricklayers apart from laborers. Probably I
have had twenty-five men altogether employed, including laborers.

Q. Then you have yourself superintended the labor of twenty-five
men in your business? — A. Yes, sir.

Q. It is skilled work that you do? — A. Yes.

Q. You understand the general subject of our inquiry. If you have
any ideas that you think would be useful to the committee, just make
your own statement of them. — A. Well, I have not given the subject
much thought. I was just caught up and asked to meet this committee, and I did not know what they wanted with me.

Q. Well, we want to know, in a general way, how you colored
people and other laboring people, are getting along here, and how
you think you are getting along — whether you feel that your condition is improving or is getting worse, and generally how you are situated in this part of the country. — A. A question like that I will answer first in regard to my self, and then, perhaps I can branch out in a
little about other people. My circumstances are very good. Since I
have been in business I have made quite a success as a bricklayer,
while others that have been more advanced and better workmen than
I am, have not made as much as I have. There is a great many men,
you know, that will make a dollar today and spend a dollar, and
there is others that will make only fifty cents, but will save it. Wherever I made any money I saved a part of it.

Q. Have you a family? — A. Yes, sir; I have two children.

Q. You have got a home? — A. Yes, sir.

Q. Do you send your children to school? — A. My oldest girl is
going to school, but not in this county. She is going to school at
Limestone.

Q. How old is she? — A. She is fourteen.

Q. How old is your other child? — A. He is going on two years
of age.

Q. Is your house in this city? — A. Yes, sir.

Q. Do you own it? — A. Yes.

Q. Have you any objection to telling us what your place is
worth? — A. Well, I can get $2,500 cash for it, if I want to sell it.

Q. Is it in a good situation? — A. Yes, sir; I have got a good two-
story house of thirteen rooms.

Q. A brick house? — A. No, sir; it is a frame house.

Q. What did it cost you? — A. It cost me about $900, the way I built it. I paid $250 for the lot, and now the same lot, with nothing on it would be worth $500.

Q. You have made that by saving and managing a little? — A. Yes, sir.

Q. Tell us now about the rest of the colored folks.

Colored Men Who Are Dependent and "Oppressed"

A. Well, the rest suffers themselves to be oppressed in some instances, but in others they do not. What they earn in the week most of them go on Saturday and spend it in rowdiness, and don't have anything left on Monday morning. In old times, you know, we always used to have a living from our master's smoke-house, and if the master did not have anything for us to eat we waited until he got it for us, and a good many of the colored people are of that opinion still — they wait for someone else to provide for them without trying to provide for themselves. But there is others that do better, and there is some others that would probably do better only that they are somewhat oppressed in their labor.

Q. What do you mean by "oppressed?" — A. Well, they are not permitted to get the value of their labor.

Q. In what way does that come about? — A. Suppose I was a journeyman, working for a contractor, he would give me $2.50 a day, and a white man would come along, and if the contractor wanted another man and employed him he might give him $3.50 or $4 a day.

Q. For doing the same work? — A. Yes, sir; and sometimes the white man might not be as good a workman as I was. The highest wages a colored man gets now is $2.50 a day, while the white men get $3 or $4 a day. They always get 50 cents or $1 a day more than colored men, even though the colored man be a better workman.

Q. How does that come to be so? — A. Well, we look at it that it is all on account of color.

Q. They discount your color? — A. Yes, sir; it is not worth a great deal to be black.

Q. There is no compound interest on that? — A. No, sir; not a bit.

Q. The main question, after all, is whether you are not improving under all these difficulties; whether things are not getting better. We have had a big war and lots of trouble all around; but now the question is whether we are improving all over the country? — A. If we are getting along at all, it must be better than it used to be, because it is impossible for us to be in a worse condition than we were in then. If there is any change at all it must be to the better. All the condition wherein we are not better is this being oppressed in our labor, in our work, and deprived of being advanced in skilled labor as we might be. We have no opportunities to learn trades as the whites have.

Q. Do you take any apprentices? — A. Yes, sir; but I do not have work enough to keep them. I have had one.

Q. Do you think that the white man has the preference over the black man as a skilled laborer? — A. Oh, yes; two to one in every respect, in any kind of work from a saw mill up.

Q. In what they call common labor, the lowest paid labor, which will get most wages, the white or the colored? — A. If there is any difference at all in that, the white man will get from 10 cents to 25 cents a day more than the colored man. On the railroads they will pay a colored man 80 cents or 90 cents a day and a white man $1 a day.

Q. Where the work is the same? — A. Yes, sir; the same thing. Take the same tools and the same work, and the men working side by side.

Q. What reason do they give for that discrimination? — A. Some give the reason that it takes more for the white man to live on than the colored man, and that, consequently, they pay him higher wages, so that he may live better. The colored man, they say, gets board for $2.50 a week, while the white man has to pay $3.50, and they have to make up the difference in wages to make the men even.

Q. Do you think that is so? — A. I have some doubt about it. I think the board bill depends upon where the man boards and what he demands for his subsistence.

Q. Have you thought of anything which the General Government ought to do, or that you would like to have it do, for the improvement of your condition here? — A. I really don't know of anything that you could do for us. I have never given much time to matters outside of what comes directly in my business of bricklaying. I profess to know everything connected with that, but I don't know whether the Government could improve that or not. It seems to be a matter left entirely to the contractors.

ROBERT D. LAYTON

Senate Testimony from Grand Secretary of the Knights of Labor

Discerning the conditions under which laborers and skilled workers had to exist was an important goal of the Senate Committee interviews, and Davis attempts to inspire an understanding of these conditions and sympathy for the laborers in *Life in the Iron-Mills*. In his 1883 testimony before the Senate Committee, Robert D. Layton, Grand Secretary of the Knights of Labor, describes in great detail the lives and work of iron-mill laborers and coal miners. He portrays their exhaustion and their inability to save money or to educate themselves or their children, and he calls for a shorter work day and government regulation of monopolies.

Layton's organization, the Knights of Labor, was a workers' labor union organized in 1869 and initially committed to secrecy because of employers' blacklisting and firing of workers in order to suppress unions. The Knights attracted both skilled and unskilled workers and was noteworthy for its inclusion of working-class women, southern blacks, and immigrant factory workers.

The following excerpt is taken from *Report of the Committee of the Senate upon the Relations between Labor and Capital, and Testimony Taken by the Committee*, vol. 1 (Washington, D.C.: Government and Printing Office, 1885).

WASHINGTON, *February* 6, 1883.

Usually the miner in the soft-coal regions, and I think in our hard-coal regions, too, puts his boys to work in the mine very young. I have observed boys of from eight to fourteen years of age working in the hard-coal region, and in the soft-coal mines boys of ten or twelve years of age are able to assist their parents materially in the mine, and unless the miner has a large number of them his boys are usually employed in that way helping their father. If there are only one or two boys in the family the father generally takes them into the mine with him. They go to school some, but their means of education is very limited.

Q. Is that because the father prefers that the boys should assist him in his work or because of a lack of school privileges? — A. The school privileges are generally good enough, but absolute necessity compels the father in many instances to take the child into the mine with him to assist in winning bread for the family.

Q. There is no compulsory school law in Pennsylvania, is there? — A. No, sir.

Q. Do you think of anything further that you are able to state as to the condition of the miner and his family? — A. I think I have covered the ground pretty fully in what I have already stated.

Q. Have they usually any land attached to their houses? — A. No, sir. In the majority of cases they have no fences around the houses. The houses are built in long rows set right out in the sun, without a tree or anything to shelter them. They are usually close to the coal mines.

Q. Do any of those miners ever accumulate any money? — A. There are some instances of that, exceptional cases — as there are in almost every occupation — cases where miners have accumulated a little funds.

Q. What are the personal habits of the miner generally as to economy or a disposition to save his wages? — A. He gets so very little to save from that he rarely saves anything. His desire may be to economize, but his opportunities for it are so poor that he seldom is able to accumulate any savings, let his desire for economy be ever so great.

Q. You call the minor a skilled laborer to some extent. Is there any other class of laborers in or about the mines whose wages are still lower than those of the miner? — A. Yes; but such work is usually done by young boys. Such work as driving the mules in the pit is done generally by the children of the miners. I am speaking of places where they use mules. Some places they do not use them, but dip the coal and permit the miner to push the car along. . . .

WASHINGTON, *February* 7, 1883.

ROBERT D. LAYTON recalled, examination continued: . . .

The CHAIRMAN. . . . You may now, if you please, extend your statement to the condition and domestic situation of the working classes generally so far as you have knowledge on the subject.

The WITNESS. When you leave the miner and go to the iron-worker, the man who works in the iron-mills, you find the social condition and surroundings somewhat improved — more home comforts, more of the little things that go to make the home comfortable and pleasant. The iron-worker has usually more room and better furniture, carpets, and so on, and his children are better clothed, in garments neater and of better quality. The iron-workers have the advantages of the markets in the large centers of industry, the cities, so that they can get a greater variety of food and are not confined, like the miners in isolated situations, to perhaps a visit from the butcher once or twice a week. They eat more fresh beef as a general thing, and as I have said, have usually more living room and that more comfortably furnished. But if you go among the laborers employed in the iron-mills you will find them huddled together in tenement houses and no more comfortable than the miners.

By Mr. GEORGE:

Q. Please state the distinction between the iron-worker and the laborer in the iron-mills. — A. The laborer there performs the heavy work, the unskilled work, and waits upon the skilled worker, the iron-worker. The laborers receive from $1 to $1.25, or perhaps sometimes $1.75, a day. When we speak of a "laborer" in the iron-works, it is understood that we do not mean a man who performs any skilled labor. When you get above the laborer the men are designated by the character of the particular work in which they are engaged; they are called "rollers," "finishers," &c., and are skilled laborers. . . .

Q. I understand you to say that the loss of time resulting from breakages, repairs, &c., falls upon the operative? — A. Yes, sir; he cannot work during such periods, and the time is lost to him.

Q. Are there any holidays allowed in those employments, except Sundays? — A. They allow no holiday whatever. No time that is lost is paid for. The men are paid a per diem rate for services rendered, without any allowance whatever for holidays. If a man takes a day off, or a half day, or any other proportion of the day, so much time is lost to him.

Q. You are an ax-maker? — A. Yes, sir.

Q. And you live in Pittsburgh? — A. In Pittsburgh.

Q. How long have you lived there? — A. Twenty-nine years.

Q. What is your age? — A. Thirty-five years.

Q. How long have you been in the ax business? — A. Off and on since my seventeenth year. I have not been engaged constantly at that work during the whole period, however. I have engaged in other business.

Q. You have spoken of the condition of the laboring classes and their modes of life. I suppose you know something about the condition and mode of life of the employing classes? — A. Only as I can see it externally. I have never mingled with them to any great extent.

Q. State the external appearances which you have observed in connection with their mode of life. — A. Well, speaking generally, they would indicate to me, as a superficial observer, the possession of considerable of the goods of this life.

Q. Describe their dwellings and outside appearances generally, so far as they have come under your observation. You see them every day I suppose? — A. Yes; I see their winter residences, but very rarely their summer residences, for a great many of them aspire to have two residences, one for winter and one for summer.

Q. Well, describe them as they are, so far as you have seen them. — A. I might describe in a general way some of those that are around the city of Pittsburgh. Our iron-masters live, in many instances — there may be a few exceptions where their aspirations do not find vent in that direction, but, as a general thing, they live in very elegant palatial residences, they have carriages and horses, and fine grounds, and servants, and everything that a person would suppose would go to make life enjoyable. I know a man who lives in that condition now who was a warehouse clerk at Pittsburgh at the outbreak of the rebellion. He now owns three iron-mills; I think he owns three wire-works for making barbed wire; and he controls or owns most of the stock in one of our railroads in the city. I know that to be a positive fact.

Q. That is an exceptional case, is it not? — A. Yes, sir; he is the only man now within my recollection who has sprung up to this condition by reason of being an employer; and of course the times were propitious for that sort of advancement. I know another man who in 1862 was working for $3 a day as a saw-maker — a man who is not recognized among his fellow men generally as possessing any superior ability, who is now a part owner in three large establishments, who lives in a very fine residence and has everything about him to make life comfortable and enjoyable. On the other hand, I may state that I have known some of his employés to have earned nice comfortable modest homes of five or six rooms, and to have paid for them and also educated their children well.

By the CHAIRMAN:
Q. Which do you believe is the happier man, the employé or the master — which gets the most out of this life? — A. I cannot give any

positive information on that point, but I can state my belief. If I were to judge by the actions of these men, I would consider that the man that had the most money was the happier, from the way they grab at it and the sordid means they use to get it.

The CHAIRMAN. The question before us is, in what way can a man come to be happiest in this world, not necessarily richest; but happiness in a state of mind which depends, of course, to a considerable extent, upon the bodily condition.

The WITNESS. Well, I might say on that point that the man is happiest who goes to himself for all that he desires, who is independent of outside circumstances. . . .

Q. Have you considered the question enough to be able to say whether it is better for an employé to be employed in a large city or in a village? — A. I consider that upon the whole it is better to have the works outside of a large city, because the men have better air and better chances for gardens to raise vegetables, and usually in this country our school privileges are such that children do not have to go a very long distance to school even in the smaller places. In a place near where large iron works are situated schools usually spring up quite rapidly. . . .

Q. What is your observation as to the effect of iron working on the health of the persons engaged in it? — A. It usually leaves them with a legacy of rheumatism. As to their mental faculties, I do not know that they are affected unfavorably by the business at all.

Q. I am speaking of the physical condition of the men. — A. Well, they run by heats, and then it is necessary to cool off between the heats and the consequence is that they are subject to rheumatism.

Q. What do you mean by running by heats? — A. They fill their furnaces full of iron ore and reduce it to iron by heat, and when that is done they fill it again, and so on; and when the furnace is refilled, then the men have an opportunity to stop for a rest and to cool off.

Q. How is the atmosphere of those works; is there not dust flying all the time? — A. O, yes; there is dust flying constantly; but I never knew any injury to result from that. The buildings are usually open places with large wide doors that you could drive a team through. They are not closed up for the sake of heat, you know. That is not necessary.

Q. How is it as to summer work? — A. The mills are usually shut down through July, in the intensely hot weather. But it is a very common thing to pick up a paper and to read of five or six men having been overcome by the heat in a single day. Many of the men work naked to the waist on account of the heat.

Q. What is the length of life among iron-workers, as a rule? — A. I presume they average as well as in other avocations. I meet a great many old men who have spent the major portions of their lives in iron-working, and, with the exception of rheumatism, and some injury to the eyesight by looking into the heat, they are apt to be as well preserved as other men of their age.

Q. Is there any danger of personal injury from molten iron or anything of that sort? — A. Yes, sir; there is danger. Some portions of the work are more dangerous than others. The man who takes the ball of hot iron on the little car, the "squeezers" as it is called, a machine which rolls the iron into a "bloom" to be fitted for the roller, is liable to injury, and I have known a great many instances where accidents have occurred. The bar that they are pressing it in is liable to be caught and to hurl things around pretty wickedly. A great many accidents occur, too, from the negligence of engineers — incompetent engineers who are employed because they can be hired cheaply. They often blow up the entire works and maim and kill a great many people. There is no law, you know, compelling a stationary engineer to get out a license, and in many instances men are hired for that business without ascertaining their ability to take charge of an engine or machinery. A man in that line is not required to be licensed like a steamboat or a steamship engineer, and many a man who has served in the works awhile will hire as an engineer, and by his negligence or ignorance will blow up things, although such accidents can generally be prevented. We find that skilled engineers seldom or never have any such trouble. . . .

Q. What opportunities have men who [work in these mills] and their families for recreation on Sundays and holidays? What resorts have they? Where do they go to? Do they stay in their houses, or do they go out into the country, or into the parks? — A. If they take the street cars and go to the limits of the city — our lines generally run to the suburbs — they can go out into the country.

Q. I want to know what they usually do? — A. Well, usually they are tired and they stay at home. They may walk around sometimes on Sunday to see a friend, or they may go to church, but if they don't do that they stay at home and rest. The public libraries are closed on Sunday, and our poor men cannot get into them to read or study. And our shop-keepers, who have pretty pictures or paintings in their windows, usually hang something over them in observance of the Sabbath, so that a man engaged at work all through the week in the mill does not get a chance for any entertainment of that kind. If our libraries were open on the Sabbath so that the workingmen could go in and read, it would be better for the morals of the community; there is no doubt about that. Here in Washington I had the pleasure last Sunday of looking at some pretty pictures in windows that were not covered over, but with us the show-windows are usually covered on Sundays and the libraries are locked up.

Q. What are the effects upon the personal habits of the men employed in coal mines as to cleanliness or the contrary? Describe their habits and condition in that respect as well as you can. — A. As far as the peculiar dust in the mines — coal dust — is concerned it is as thick as it can be upon the person and not fall off. The little lamps that the men wear upon their caps to give light always leak more or less and keep them smeared with oil, and the oil and the dust together do certainly combine to make a miner present a fearful picture so far as blackness is concerned. The men are compelled to bathe every day on returning from their work; it is absolutely necessary. In some mines they work where the vein is 7 or 8 or 9 feet thick, and the work there is comparatively comfortable; but where it is only 3½ or 4 feet thick it is very uncomfortable. Then they are constantly in danger; never out of danger; they do not know at what time a piece of "horse flag" may fall and crush them to death; it falls when it is least expected. If it were expected, preparations could be made to avoid the danger in many instances, but that cannot be done. The miner goes to work in the morning just as the sun is coming up above the horizon, and he comes out of the mine in the evening just as it is going down, so that his life is pretty nearly all night. The work is very hard and exhausting. The men have no advantages of society, or very little. Coal mines are not situated in busy centers; they are out in isolated places. The operator does not live in the midst of the mines in ninety-nine cases out of one hundred. The men mingle only with their fellows in their own little villages and communities. In the mines they may work two together. That is pretty nearly the extent of the miner's social habits. In the winter it is night to him all the time. From the shortening of the days to the lengthening of them he seldom sees the sun; it is night all the time, and the only company he has is that the other miners engaged with him in his work. . . .

Q. Have you had occasion to observe the effect of the introduction of improved machinery upon labor? — A. Machinery has lessened the demand for labor in many instances, but it has not lessened the hours of labor at all; while the ability to produce work has been trebled and in many cases much more than trebled.

Q. This matter of machinery is one of the great disturbing elements in the industrial question, and we should be pleased to hear your views in regard to it. Are you, as an order, favorable to further development in that direction? — A. Yes, sir; if we can get the benefit of it.

Q. In order to get the benefit of it what would you have done? — A. We would have the hours of labor shortened.

Q. Without a diminution of wages, of course? — A. Yes, sir.

Q. The ordinary laborer who is accustomed to certain processes of a particular industry would of course be unskilled in the use of new machinery, and unable to work it successfully in the production of the same article which he now produces on the old plan. Upon that point, where the laborer is dispossessed, not only of actual employment, but of his capacity to work, because the work that he can do has been abolished by the introduction of a machine, what is the view of your order? Have you thought out that question, and have you any plan by which you would provide for the difficulty I have suggested? — A. That is one of the most difficult problems. You are aware, no doubt, that the shoemaking trade as a trade has gone. Machinery has superseded handwork, and to-day shoemakers as a class are for the most part cobblers confined to tapping and half-soling and repairing. Some are, of course, employed in that way.

Q. But is it not a fact that the great mass of them are thrown out of employment altogether, and in such a case what are men to do? — A. Those who retain any portion of the trade are engaged in the business of tapping and repairing.

Q. And what are men to do under such circumstances? — A. They are thrown upon the general labor world, and they bring in a new element of competition with other labor.

Q. It is the introduction of a great mass of unskilled labor among the labor engaged in other pursuits? — A. Yes, sir.

Q. Now, when that is done, how is it possible to avoid a reduction of wages in the other pursuits thus inundated with this new and unskilled labor? — A. It is not possible, unless we shorten the hours of labor, and give the surplus a chance. A man working eight hours a day will not do as much as a man working ten hours, and therefore if you shorten the hours of labor you give the surplus labor an opportunity for employment.

Q. Wages now are regulated by demand and supply, and by the price of the articles sold. The more laborers you employ in any given work, of course the less wages will be paid to each individual. One thousand men doing a given work for $1 apiece — when you turn in two thousand men to do the same amount of work, as things at present range in this world, they will get but 50 cents apiece. Now, how can you reach that difficulty? — A. That result which you mention might follow to some extent. But the productiveness of labor has greatly increased. My father made seven dozen axes for a day's work, while I make 145 axes for a day's work.

Q. Well, the demand has increased correspondingly. — A. But the prices have not increased correspondingly. My father received considerably more wages than I do. He lived in a house at a rent of $8 a month, which is now renting at $21 a month; he bought the best beef at 10 cents a pound, while I have to pay 19; he bought eggs at 6 cents a dozen, and they are now worth 32 cents; he bought flour at $4 and $5 a barrel.

Q. How long ago was that? — A. About 1855 or 1856. I do nearly twice as much work as he did in a day. He received $2 a day, and I can make about $3.50.

Q. And the cost of living is about twice as much to you as to him? — A. Yes, sir.

Q. What has made the change? — A. The beating down of wages upon one side and the monopolists raising the cost of living upon the other. . . .

Q. Have you ever taken into consideration the power of the General Government over labor employed in commerce, internal and external, and over transportation routes by land and water? Have you ever considered whether the National Government might not legitimately legislate in that direction? — A. The National Government can assist us materially in that way. We think that it has jurisdiction over the railroads of this country; but the vast monoplies have swallowed up everything and have such general control that they now are virtually the Government, as the case appears to us.

REESE E. LEWIS

"March of the Rolling-Mill Men"

This song, which Reese E. Lewis set to the tune of the Welsh "March of the Men of Harlech," describes the pride of skilled iron and steel craftsmen in the early days of the industry, before mass production machines made individual workers' sense of accomplishment more difficult to achieve. The laborers are described in mythic terms, as noble soldiers who are responsible for the might and wealth of their nation. The song was published in the *National Labor Tribune* on March 30, 1875. The following year, iron and steel workers united in the Amalgamated Association of Iron and Steel Workers, seemingly in response to the song's demand for iron and steel workers to "[a]ll Unite and join the fight."

The text is from *Pennsylvania Songs and Legends*, ed. George Korson (Baltimore: Johns Hopkins UP, 1949).

Moderate

1. Rouse, ye no-ble sons of La-bor, And pro-tect your coun-try's hon-or, Who with bone. and brain. and fi-bre. Make the na-tion's wealth.   Lust-y lads, with souls of fire, Gal-lant sons of no-ble sire,— Lend your voice and raise your ban-ner, Bat-tle for the right.   Heat-er, roll-er, rough-er,   Catch-er, pud-dler, help-er,   All u-nite and join the fight, And might for right en - coun-ter; In the name of truth and jus-tice, Stem the tide of e-vil prac-tice,

Mam-mon's[1] sor-did might and av-'rice, Our land from ru-in save.

2. Ye who aid our locomotion,
   Wield the "cord which binds the nation,"
   Honest types of God's creation,
   Honor to your names.
   Hearts of oak and arms of metal,
   Who by dint of skill and muscle,
   Fashion bridge and iron vessel,
   Ever true and brave.
   Heater, roller, rougher,
   Catcher, puddler, helper,
   All unite and join the fight,
   And might for right encounter;
   Let's be firm, with soul unbending,
   'Mid the flash and sparks ascending,
   Vulcan's[2] sons are now arising,
   Comrades, all unite.

[1] *Mammon:* Syrian god of riches and worldliness, a fallen angel of Milton's *Paradise Lost.*
[2] *Vulcan:* Roman god of fire.

FELIX O'HARE

"The Shoofly"

In 1871, the mine at Valley Furnace in the Schuylkill Valley in Pennsylvania closed. Under normal circumstances, the miners could have been employed at a colliery called Shoofly, but it too was closed, leading unemployed miners to experience the feelings of anxiety and hopelessness expressed in this song, written by Felix O'Hare, a village schoolmaster. The local hardships described in the song were part of the larger depression affecting the entire country in the 1870s, a depression more severe than anything the country had previously suffered, and which was made

worse because of most Americans' reliance on industry for their survival.
The "want and starvation" described in the song, as well as the narraor's
hope for future riches and freedom from debt, were sentiments echoed
throughout the country.

The text is from *Pennsylvania Songs and Legends*, ed. George Korson
(Baltimore: Johns Hopkins UP, 1949).

Moderately fast

1. As I went a-walk-ing one fine sum-mer's morn-ing, It was
   And when I drew nigh her she sat on her hunk-ers,[1] For to

down by the Fur-nace I chanced for to stroll.__ I es-
fill up her scut-tle[2] she just had be-gun __

pied an old la-dy, I'll swear she was eight-y, At the
And to her-self she was sing-ing a dit-ty, And

foot of the dirt banks a-root-ing for coal; __
these are the words the old la-dy did sing: __

Chorus

A__ cry-ing, "Och-one! sure, I'm near-ly dis-tract-ed, __

__ For it's down by the Shoo-fly they cut a bad

---

[1] *hunkers:* Haunches.
[2] *scuttle:* Shallow basket used to carry something, often coal.

vein;[3]_____   And since they con - demned the old

slope at the Fur - nace,_____   Sure all me fine

neigh-bors must leave here a - gain."_____

2. "'Twas only last evenin' that I asked McGinley
   To tell me the reason the Furnace gave o'er.
   He told me the company had spent eighty thousand,
   And finding no prospects they would spend no more.
   He said that the Diamond it was rather bony,
   Besides too much dirt in the seven-foot vein;
   And as for the Mammoth, there's no length of gangway,[4]
   Unless they buy land from old Abel and Swayne.

   CHORUS
   A-crying, "Ochone! sure, I'm nearly distracted,
   For it's down by the Shoofly they cut a bad vein;
   And since they condemned the old slope at the Furnace,
   Sure all me fine neighbors must leave here again."

3. "And as for Michael Rooney, I owe him some money,
   Likewise Patrick Kearns, I owe him some more;
   And as for old John Eagen, I ne'er see his wagon,
   But I think of the debt that I owe in the store.
   I owe butcher and baker, likewise the shoemaker,
   And for plowin' me garden I owe Pat McQuail;
   Likewise his old mother, for one thing and another,
   And to drive away bother, an odd quart of ale.

4. "But if God spares me children until the next summer,
   Instead of a burden, they will be a gain;

---

[3] *cut a bad vein:* The Shoofly, a colliery where the unemployed miners might normally have found work, was shut down because a bad seam, or bed, of coal had been struck.

[4] *gangway:* A passage or way into, through, or out of a place.

And out of their earnin's I'll save an odd dollar,
  And build a snug home at the 'Foot of the Plane.'
Then rolling in riches, in silks, and in satin,
  I ne'er shall forget the days I was poor,
And likewise the neighbors that stood by me children,
  Kept want and starvation away from me door.

5. "And if you should happen to cross the Broad Mountain,
    Step in and sit down on me cane-bottomed chairs;
  Take off your fixin's, lay them on the bureau,
    While I in the kitchen refreshments prepare;
  And while we are seated so snug at the table,
    Enjoying the fruits of a strong cup of tea,
  We'll talk of the quiltin's we had at the Furnace —
    Me heart does rejoice an old neighbor to see."

WALT WHITMAN

"A Song for Occupations"

Walt Whitman (1819–1892) is one of America's great poets. Transitional in numerous ways, Whitman's poetry embodies both romantic sentiments and modernist boldness, early-nineteenth-century caution and early-twentieth-century radical consciousness and experimentation. Fully conscious of his identity as an American poet, Whitman created a masterpiece with his 1855 collection, *Leaves of Grass*. He revised and added to — and relentlessly publicized — *Leaves of Grass* throughout the next four decades. Although Whitman had hoped to touch the working class of America with his poetry, most of his praise came from European intellectuals like Oscar Wilde and Alfred Tennyson. He himself did many working-class jobs, including printing, clerking, news reporting, and nursing Civil War soldiers, although he made enough money from royalties, book sales, and honoraria to live a comfortable life. "A Song for Occupations" demonstrates Whitman's unconventional verse form, his free-form rhyme and meter, and his emphasis on human love and equality. This poem praises the working classes as the fertile ground from which has sprung not only the United States but the world.

The text is from *Leaves of Grass*, ed. Sculley Bradley and Harold W. Blodgett (New York: Norton, 1973; reprint, New York: New York UP, 1965).

1

A song for occupations!
In the labor of engines and trades and the labor of fields I find the
    developments,
And find the eternal meanings.

Workmen and Workwomen!
Were all educations practical and ornamental well display'd out of
    me, what would it amount to?
Were I as the head teacher, charitable proprietor, wise statesman,
    what would it amount to?
Were I to you as the boss employing and paying you, would that
    satisfy you?

The learn'd, virtuous, benevolent, and the usual terms,
A man like me and never the usual terms.

Neither a servant nor a master I,
I take no sooner a large price than a small price, I will have my own
    whoever enjoys me,
I will be even with you and you shall be even with me.

If you stand at work in a shop I stand as nigh as the nighest in the
    same shop,
If you bestow gifts on your brother or dearest friend I demand as
    good as your brother or dearest friend,
If your lover, husband, wife, is welcome by day or night, I must be
    personally as welcome,
If you become degraded, criminal, ill, than I become so for your sake,
If you remember your foolish and outlaw'd deeds, do you think I
    cannot remember my own foolish and outlaw'd deeds?
If you carouse at the table I carouse at the opposite side of the table,
If you meet some stranger in the streets and love him or her, why I
    often meet strangers in the street and love them.

Why what have you thought of yourself?
Is it you then that thought yourself less?
Is it you that thought the President greater than you?
Or the rich better off than you? or the educated wiser than you?

(Because you are greasy or pimpled, or were once drunk, or a thief,
Or that you are diseas'd, or rheumatic, or a prostitute,
Or from frivolity or impotence, or that you are no scholar and never
    saw your name in print,
Do you give in that you are any less immortal?)

2

Souls of men and women! it is not you I call unseen, unheard,
   untouchable and untouching,
It is not you I go argue pro and con about, and to settle whether you
   are alive or no,
I own publicly who you are, if nobody else owns.

Grown, half-grown and babe, of this country and every country, in-
   doors and out-doors, one just as much as the other, I see,
And all else behind or through them.

The wife, and she is not one jot less than the husband,
The daughter, and she is just as good as the son,
The mother, and she is every bit as much as the father.
Offspring of ignorant and poor, boys apprenticed to trades,
Young fellows working on farms and old fellows working on farms,
Sailor-men, merchant-men, coasters, immigrants,
All these I see, but nigher and farther the same I see,
None shall escape me and none shall wish to escape me.

I bring what you much need yet always have,
Not money, amours, dress, eating, erudition, but as good,
I send no agent or medium, offer no representative of value, but offer
   the value itself.

There is something that comes to one now and perpetually,
It is not what is printed, preach'd, discussed, it eludes discussion and
   print,
It is not to be put in a book, it is not in this book,
It is for you whoever you are, it is no farther from you than your
   hearing and sight are from you,
It is hinted by nearest, commonest, readiest, it is ever provoked by
   them.

You may read in many languages, yet read nothing about it,
You may read the President's message and read nothing about it there,
Nothing in the reports from the State department or Treasury
   department, or in the daily papers or weekly papers,
Or in the census or revenue returns, prices current, or any accounts
   of stock.

3

The sun and stars that float in the open air,
The apple-shaped earth and we upon it, surely the drift of them is
   something grand,

I do not know what it is except that it is grand, and that it is
   happiness,
And that the enclosing purport of us here is not a speculation or bon-
   mot or reconnoissance,
And that it is not something which by luck may turn out well for us,
   and without luck must be a failure for us,
And not something which may yet be retracted in a certain
   contingency.

The light and shade, the curious sense of body and identity, the greed
   that with perfect complaisance devours all things,
The endless pride and outstretching of man, unspeakable joys and
   sorrows,
The wonder every one sees in every one else he sees, and the wonders
   that fill each minute of time forever,
What have you reckon'd them for, camerado?
Have you reckon'd them for your trade or farm-work? or for the
   profits of your store?
Or to achieve yourself a position? or to fill a gentleman's leisure, or a
   lady's leisure?

Have you reckon'd that the landscape took substance and form that
   it might be painted in a picture?
Or men and women that they might be written of, and songs sung?
Or the attraction of gravity, and the great laws of harmonious
   combinations and the fluids of the air, as subjects for the savans?[1]
Or the brown land and the blue sea for maps and charts?
Or the stars to be put in constellations and named fancy names?
Or that the growth of seeds is for agricultural tables, or agriculture
   itself?

Old institutions, these arts, libraries, legends, collections, and the
   practice handed along in manufactures, will we rate them so high?
Will we rate our cash and business high? I have no objection,
I rate them as high as the highest — then a child born of a woman
   and man I rate beyond all rate.

We thought our Union grand, and our Constitution grand,
I do not say they are not grand and good, for they are,
I am this day just as much in love with them as you,
Then I am in love with You, and with all my fellows upon the earth.

We consider bibles and religions divine — I do not say they are not
   divine,

---

[1]*savans:* Short for *savants,* learned persons.

I say they have all grown out of you, and may grow out of you still,
It is not they who give the life, it is you who give the life,
Leaves are not more shed from the trees, or trees from the earth, than
  they are shed out of you.

4

The sun of all known reverence I add up in you whoever you are,
The President is there in the White House for you, it is not you who
  are here for him,
The Secretaries act in their bureaus for you, not you here for them,
The Congress convenes every Twelfth-month for you,
Laws, courts, the forming of States, the charters of cities, the going
  and coming of commerce and mails, are all for you.

List close my scholars dear,
Doctrines, politics and civilization exurge from you,
Sculpture and monuments and any thing inscribed anywhere are
  tallied in you,
The gist of histories and statistics as far back as the records reach is
  in you this hour, and myths and tales the same,
If you were not breathing and walking here, where would they all
  be?
The most renown'd poems would be ashes, orations and plays would
  be vacuums.

All architecture is what you do to it when you look upon it,
(Did you think it was in the white or gray stone? or the lines of the
  arches and cornices?)
All music is what awakes from you when you are reminded by the
  instruments,
It is not the violins and the cornets, it is not the oboe nor the beating
  drums, nor the score of the baritone singer singing his sweet
  romanza, nor that of the men's chorus, nor that of the women's
  chorus,
It is nearer and farther than they.

5

Will the whole come back then?
Can each see signs of the best by a look in the looking-glass? is there
  nothing greater or more?
Does all sit there with you, with the mystic unseen soul?

Strange and hard that paradox true I give,
Objects gross and the unseen soul are one.

House-building, measuring, sawing the boards,
Blacksmithing, glass-blowing, nail-making, coopering, tin-roofing,
    shingle-dressing,
Ship-joining, dock-building, fish-curing, flagging of sidewalks by
    flaggers,
The pump, the pile-driver, the great derrick, the coal-kiln and brick-
    kiln,
Coal-mines and all that is down there, the lamps in the darkness,
    echoes, songs, what meditations, what vast native thoughts
    looking through smutch'd faces,
Iron-works, forge-fires in the mountains or by river-banks, men
    around feeling the melt with huge crowbars, lumps of ore, the due
    combining of ore, limestone, coal,
The blast-furnace and the puddling-furnace, the loup-lump[2] at the
    bottom of the melt at last, the rolling-mill, the stumpy bars of pig-
    iron, the strong clean-shaped T-rail for railroads,
Oil-works, silk-works, white-lead-works, the sugar-house, steam-
    saws, the great mills and factories,
Stone-cutting, shapely trimmings for façades or window or door-
    lintels, the mallet, the tooth-chisel, the jib[3] to protect the thumb,
The calking-iron, the kettle of boiling vault-cement, and the fire
    under the kettle,
The cotton-bale, the stevedore's[4] hook, the saw and buck of the
    sawyer, the mould of the moulder, the working-knife of the
    butcher, the ice-saw, and all the work with ice,
The work and tools of the rigger, grappler, sail-maker, block-maker,
Goods of gutta-percha,[5] papier-maché, colors, brushes, brush
    making, glazier's implements,
The veneer and glue-pot, the confectioner's ornaments, the decanter
    and glasses, the shears and flat-iron,
The awl and knee-strap, the pint measure and quart measure, the
    counter and stool, the writing-pen of quill or metal, the making of
    all sorts of edged tools,

---

[2] *loup-lump:* The mass of iron at the bottom of the melt which is the desired result
of the smelting process.
[3] *jib:* Protecting shield.
[4] *stevedore:* One who is responsible for the loading and unloading of a ship in
port.
[5] *gutta-percha:* Rubber-like substance used in the manufacture of insulation and
other products.

The brewery, brewing, the malt, the vats, every thing that is done by
    brewers, wine-makers, vinegar-makers,
Leather-dressing, coach-making, boiler-making, rope-twisting, dis-
    tilling, sign-painting, lime-burning, cotton-picking, electroplating,
    electrotyping, stereotyping,
Stave-machines, planing-machines, reaping-machines, ploughing-
    machines, thrashing-machines, steam-wagons,
The cart of the carman, the omnibus, the ponderous dray,
Pyrotechny letting off color'd fireworks at night, fancy figures and
    jets;
Beef on the butcher's stall, the slaughter-house of the butcher, the
    butcher in his killing-clothes,
The pens of live pork, the killing-hammer, the hog-hook, the
    scalder's tub, gutting, the cutter's cleaver, the packer's maul, and
    the plenteous winterwork of pork-packing,
Flour-works, grinding of wheat, rye, maize, rice, the barrels and the
    half and quarter barrels, the loaded barges, the high piles on
    wharves and levees,
The men and the work of the men on ferries, railroads, coasters, fish-
    boats, canals;
The hourly routine of your own or any man's life, the shop, yard,
    store, or factory,
These shows all near you by day and night — workman! whoever
    you are, your daily life!
In that and them the heft of the heaviest — in that and them far more
    than you estimated, (and far less also,)
In them realities for you and me, in them poems for you and me,
In them, not yourself — you and your soul enclose all things,
    regardless of estimation,
In them the development good — in them all themes, hints,
    possibilities.

I do not affirm that what you see beyond is futile, I do not advise you
    to stop,
I do not say leadings you thought great are not great,
But I say that none lead to greater than these lead to.

6

Will you seek afar off? you surely come back at last,
In things best known to you finding the best, or as good as the best,
In folks nearest to you finding the sweetest, strongest, lovingest,

Happiness, knowledge, not in another place but this place, not for
   another hour but this hour,
Man in the first you see or touch, always in friend, brother, nighest
   neighbor — woman in mother, sister, wife,
The popular tastes and employments taking precedence in poems or
   anywhere,
You workwomen and workmen of these States having your own
   divine and strong life,
And all else giving place to men and women like you.

When the psalm sings instead of the singer,
When the script preaches instead of the preacher,
When the pulpit descends and goes instead of the carver that carved
   the supporting desk,
When I can touch the body of books by night or by day, and when
   they touch by body back again,
When a university course convinces like a slumbering woman and
   child convince,
When the minted gold in the vault smiles like the night-watchman's
   daughter,
When warrantee deeds loafe in chairs opposite and are my friendly
   companions,
I intend to reach them my hand, and make as much of them as I do
   of men and women like you.

1855   1881

OLIVER WENDELL HOLMES

From "A Rhymed Lesson"

   Oliver Wendell Holmes (1809–1894) was a renowned man of letters
known for his conversational wit and his writing. Although by profession he was a medical doctor with a scientific mind, Holmes maintained
an interest in writing poetry and essays throughout his life. He was a
popular public figure, in great demand for giving after-dinner speeches
and composing whimsical and commemorative poems. He titled himself
and other intellectual New Englanders "Brahmins" and remained comfortable in his upper-class position, poking gentle fun at American society without delving into serious social issues or changing his conservative

identity. In "A Rhymed Lesson" from *The Poetical Works of Oliver Wendell Holmes* (Boston: Houghton, 1919), and originally delivered before the Boston Mercantile Library Association on October 14, 1846, Holmes mocks the upper classes and their fashion-consciousness while upholding social conventions of dress and comportment.

> Three pairs of boots one pair of feet demands,
> If polished daily by the owner's hands;
> If the dark menial's visit save from this,
> Have twice the number, for he'll sometimes miss.
> One pair for critics of the nicer sex,
> Close in the instep's clinging circumflex,
> Long, narrow, light; the Gallic boot of love,
> A kind of cross between a boot and glove.
> Compact, but easy, strong, substantial, square,
> Let native art compile the medium pair.
> The third remains, and let your tasteful skill
> Here show some relics of affection still;
> Let no stiff cowhide, reeking from the tan,
> No rough caoutchouc,[1] no deformed brogan,
> Disgrace the tapering outline of your feet,
> Though yellow torrents gurgle through the street.
>
> Wear seemly gloves; not black, nor yet too light,
> And least of all the pair that once was white;
> Let the dead party where you told your loves
> Bury in peace its dead bouquets and gloves;
> Shave like the goat, if so your fancy bids,
> But be a parent, — don't neglect your kids.
>
> Have a good hat; the secret of your looks
> Lives with the beaver in Canadian brooks;
> Virtue may flourish in an old cravat,
> But man and nature scorn the shocking hat.
> Does beauty slight you from her gay abodes?
> Like bright Apollo,[2] you must take to *Rhoades*,[3] —

[1] *caoutchouc:* The chemical compound for rubber.

[2] *Apollo:* The most important of the Greek gods, Apollo was the god of religious law, the future, guilt, crops, and the lyre; he was also associated with the sun.

[3] *Rhoades:* A Greek island whose major city, also called Rhodes, is known for its one-hundred-foot tall bronze statue of the Colossus of Rhodes, a monument to Helios, the sun god.

Mount the new castor, — ice itself will melt;
Boots, gloves, may fail; the hat is always felt!
Be shy of breastpins; plain, well-ironed white,
With small pearl buttons, — two of them in sight, —
Is always genuine, while your gems may pass,
Though real diamonds, for ignoble glass;
But spurn those paltry Cisatlantic lies,
That round his breast the shabby rustic ties;
Breathe not the name, profaned to hallow things
The indignant laundress blushes when she brings!
Our freeborn race, averse to every check,
Has tossed the yoke of Europe from its *neck;*
From the green prairie to the sea-girt town,
The whole wide nation turns its collars down.

The stately neck is manhood's manliest part;
It takes the life-blood freshest from the heart;
With short, curled ringlets close around it spread,
How light and strong it lifts the Grecian head!
Thine, fair Erechtheus[4] of Minerva's[5] wall; —
Or thine, young athlete of the Louvre's hall,
Smooth as the pillar flashing in the sun
That filled the arena where thy wreaths were won, —
Firm as the band that clasps the antlered spoil,
Strained in the winding anaconda's coil!

I spare the contrast; it were only kind
To be a little, nay, intensely blind:
Choose for yourself; I know it cuts your ear;
I know the points will sometimes interfere;
I know that often, like the filial John,
Whom sleep surprised with half his drapery on,
You show your features to the astonished town
With one side standing and the other down; —
But, O my friend! my favorite fellow-man!
If Nature made you on her modern plan,
Sooner than wander with your windpipe bare, —
The fruit of Eden ripening in the air, —

---

[4] *Erechtheus:* Legendary king and divinity of Athens; he was raised by Athena, goddess of wisdom and warfare.
[5] *Minerva:* The Roman goddess associated with the Greek Athena.

With that lean head-stalk, that protruding chin,
Wear standing collars, were they made of tin!
And have a neck-cloth — by the throat of Jove!
Cut from the funnel of a rusty stove!

The long-drawn lesson narrows to its close,
Chill, slender, slow, the dwindled current flows;
Tired of the ripples on its feeble springs,
Once more the Muse unfolds her upward wings.

JAMES RUSSELL LOWELL

" *Without and Within* "

James Russell Lowell (1819–1891), like Longfellow and Holmes, was a Brahmin — an intellectual, upper-class New Englander — who was well-known and respected in the last half of the nineteenth century for his work as a poet, critic, essayist, teacher, and diplomat. Dedicated to American literature, Lowell abandoned his early profession as a lawyer to pursue a literary career, promoting his own writing and that of other American authors. Although interested in political reform, as is suggested in his poem "Without and Within" — first published in *Under the Willows and Other Poems* (1868) and reprinted here from *The Poetical Works of James Russell Lowell* (Boston: Houghton, 1917) — and although opposed to slavery in the years preceding the Civil War, Lowell did not advocate radical political action. Instead, he remained a Brahmin, satisfied with his upper-class status and his literary success.

My coachman, in the moonlight there,
  Looks through the side-light of the door;
I hear him with his brethren swear,
  As I could do, — but only more.

Flattening his nose against the pane,
  He envies me my brilliant lot,
Breathes on his aching fists in vain,
  And dooms me to a place more hot.

He sees me in to supper go,

A silken wonder by my side,
Bare arms, bare shoulders, and a row
    Of flounces, for the door too wide.

He thinks how happy is my arm
    'Neath its white-gloved and jewelled load;
And wishes me some dreadful harm,
    Hearing the merry corks explode.

Meanwhile I inly curse the bore
    Of hunting still the same old coon,
And envy him, outside the door,
    In golden quiets of the moon.

The winter wind is not so cold
    As the bright smile he sees me win,
Nor the host's oldest wine so old
    As our poor gabble sour and thin.

I envy him the ungyved prance
    With which his freezing feet he warms,
And drag my lady's-chains and dance
    The galley-slave of dreary forms.

O, could he have my share of din,
    And I his quiet! — past a doubt
'T would still be one man bored within,
    And just another bored without.

Nay, when, once paid my mortal fee,
    Some idler on my headstone grim
Traces the moss-blurred name, will he
    Think me the happier, or I him?

ANDREW CARNEGIE

From The Gospel of Wealth

One of this nation's wealthiest capitalists and greatest philanthropists, Andrew Carnegie (1835–1919) was born in Scotland and moved to the United States in 1848, where he began working in a cotton factory and educating himself in his spare time. He soon entered the railroad industry and then the iron industry, where he gradually accumulated wealth and authority. In 1873, he invested all his profits in steel, which was then a very young American industry. His investments flourished, and Carnegie became one of the richest and most powerful men in the country. Because Carnegie's father and grandfather had both been active social reformers, and also because throughout his life many of his close friends were writers and philosophers, Carnegie was inclined to think carefully about the responsibilities incumbent upon wealthy people. In his book *The Gospel of Wealth* (1900), Carnegie argues that the rich should view their surplus wealth as held in trust for the public benefit. In 1901 he followed through with this viewpoint, retiring and using his wealth to support libraries, scientific research, public education, and international peace efforts.

The following selection is from *The Gospel of Wealth and Other Timely Essays,* ed. Edward C. Kirkland (Cambridge: Belknap, 1962).

Introduction:
How I Served My Apprenticeship

It is a great pleasure to tell how I served my apprenticeship as a business man. But there seems to be a question preceding this: Why did I become a business man? I am sure that I should never have selected a business career if I had been permitted to choose.

The eldest son of parents who were themselves poor, I had, fortunately, to begin to perform some useful work in the world while still very young in order to earn an honest livelihood, and was thus shown even in early boyhood that my duty was to assist my parents and, like them, become, as soon as possible, a bread-winner in the family. What I could get to do, not what I desired, was the question.

When I was born my father was a well-to-do master weaver in Dunfermline, Scotland. He owned no less than four damask-looms and employed apprentices. This was before the days of steam-factories for the manufacture of linen. A few large merchants took orders, and employed master weavers, such as my father, to weave the cloth, the merchants supplying the materials.

As the factory system developed hand-loom weaving naturally declined, and my father was one of the sufferers by the change. The first serious lesson of my life came to me one day when he had taken in the last of his work to the merchant, and returned to our little home greatly distressed because there was no more work for him to do. I was then just about ten years of age, but the lesson burned into my heart, and I resolved then that the wolf of poverty should be driven from our door some day, if I could do it.

The question of selling the old looms and starting for the United States came up in the family council, and I heard it discussed from day to day. It was finally resolved to take the plunge and join relatives already in Pittsburgh. I well remember that neither father nor mother thought the change would be otherwise than a great sacrifice for them, but that "it would be better for the two boys."

In after life, if you can look back as I do and wonder at the complete surrender of their own desires which parents make for the good of their children, you must reverence their memories with feelings akin to worship.

On arriving in Allegheny City (there were four of us: father, mother, my younger brother, and myself), my father entered a cotton factory. I soon followed, and served as the "bobbin-boy,"[1] and this is how I began my preparation for subsequent apprenticeship as a business man. I received one dollar and twenty cents a week, and was then just about twelve years old.

I cannot tell you how proud I was when I received my first week's own earnings. One dollar and twenty cents made by myself and given to me because I had been of some use in the world! No longer entirely dependent upon my parents, but at last admitted to the family partnership as a contributing member and able to help them! I think this makes a man out of a boy sooner than almost anything else, and a real man, too, if there be any germ of true manhood in him. It is everything to feel that you are useful.

I have had to deal with great sums. Many millions of dollars have since passed through my hands. But the genuine satisfaction I had from that one dollar and twenty cents outweighs any subsequent pleasure in money-getting. It was the direct reward of honest, manual labor; it represented a week of very hard work — so hard that, but for the aim and end which sanctified it, slavery might not be much too strong a term to describe it.

For a lad of twelve to rise and breakfast every morning, except the blessed Sunday morning, and go into the streets and find his way to the factory and begin to work while it was still dark outside, and not be released until after darkness came again in the evening, forty minutes' interval only being allowed at noon, was a terrible task.

---

[1] *"bobbin-boy"*: Child laborer who carried the bobbins, or spools of thread, to the loom workers.

But I was young and had my dreams, and something within always told me that this would not, could not, should not last — I should some day get into a better position. Besides this, I felt myself no longer a mere boy, but quite a little man, and this made me happy.

A change soon came, for a kind old Scotsman, who knew some of our relatives, made bobbins, and took me into his factory before I was thirteen. But here for a time it was even worse than in the cotton factory, because I was set to fire a boiler in the cellar, and actually to run the small steam-engine which drove the machinery. The firing of the boiler was all right, for fortunately we did not use coal, but the refuse wooden chips; and I always liked to work in wood. But the responsibility of keeping the water right and of running the engine, and the danger of my making a mistake and blowing the whole factory to pieces, caused too great a strain, and I often awoke and found myself sitting up in bed through the night, trying the steam-gauges. But I never told them at home that I was having a hard tussle. No, no! everything must be bright to them.

This was a point of honor, for every member of the family was working hard, except, of course, my little brother, who was then a child, and we were telling each other only all the bright things. Besides this, no man would whine and give up — he would die first.

There was no servant in our family, and several dollars per week were earned by the mother by binding shoes after her daily work was done! Father was also hard at work in the factory. And could I complain?

My kind employer, John Hay, — peace to his ashes! — soon relieved me of the undue strain, for he needed someone to make out bills and keep his accounts, and finding that I could write a plain school-boy hand and could "cipher," he made me his only clerk. But still I had to work hard upstairs in the factory, for the clerking took but little time.

You know how people moan about poverty as being a great evil, and it seems to be accepted that if people had only plenty of money and were rich, they would be happy and more useful, and get more out of life.

As a rule, there is more genuine satisfaction, a truer life, and more obtained from life in the humble cottages of the poor than in the palaces of the rich. I always pity the sons and daughters of the rich men, who are attended by servants, and have governesses at a later age, but am glad to remember that they do not know what they have missed.

They have kind fathers and mothers, too, and think that they enjoy the sweetness of these blessings to the fullest: but this they cannot do; for the poor boy who has in his father his constant companion, tutor, and model, and in his mother — holy name! — his nurse, teacher, guardian angel, saint, all in one, has a richer, more precious fortune in life than any rich man's son who is not so favored can possibly know, and compared with which all other fortunes count for little.

It is because I know how sweet and happy and pure the home of honest poverty is, how free from perplexing care, from social envies and emulations, how loving and how united its members may be in the common interest of supporting the family, that I sympathize with the rich man's boy and congratulate the poor man's boy; and it is for these reasons that from the ranks of the poor so many strong, eminent, self-reliant men have always sprung and always must spring.

If you will read the list of the immortals who "were not born to die," you will find that most of them have been born to the precious heritage of poverty.

It seems, nowadays, a matter of universal desire that poverty should be abolished. We should be quite willing to abolish luxury, but to abolish honest, industrious, self-denying poverty would be to destroy the soil upon which mankind produces the virtues which enable our race to reach a still higher civilization than it now possesses. . . .

The Problem of the Administration of Wealth

The problem of our age is the proper administration of wealth, that the ties of brotherhood may still bind together the rich and poor in harmonious relationship. The conditions of human life have not only been changed, but revolutionized, within the past few hundred years. In former days there was little difference between the dwelling, dress, food, and environment of the chief and those of his retainers. The Indians are to-day where civilized man then was. When visiting the Sioux, I was led to the wigwam of the chief. It was like the others in external appearance, and even within the difference was trifling between it and those of the poorest of the braves. The contrast between the palace of the millionaire and the cottage of the laborer with us to-day measures the change which has come with civilization. This change, however, is not to be deplored, but welcomed as highly beneficial. It is well, nay, essential, for the progress of the race that the houses of some should be homes for all that is highest and best in literature and the arts, and for all the refinements of civilization, rather than that none should be so. Much better this great irregularity than universal squalor. Without wealth there can be no Mæcenas.[2] The "good old times" were not good old times. Neither master nor servant was as well situated then as to-day. A relapse to old conditions would be disastrous to both — not the least so to him who serves — and would sweep away civilization with it. But whether the change be for good or ill, it is upon us, beyond our power to alter, and, therefore, to be accepted and made the best of. It is a waste of time to criticize the inevitable.

It is easy to see how the change has come. One illustration will serve for almost every phase of the cause. In the manufacture of products we have the whole story. It applies to all combinations of human industry, as stimulated and enlarged by the inventions of this scientific age. Formerly, articles were manufactured at the domestic hearth, or in small shops which formed part of the household. The master and his apprentices worked side by side, the latter living with the master, and therefore subject to the same conditions. When these apprentices rose to be masters, there was little or no change in their mode of life, and they, in turn, educated succeeding apprentices in the same routine. There was, substantially, social equality, and even political equality, for those engaged in industrial pursuits had then little or no voice in the State.

The inevitable result of such a mode of manufacture was crude articles at high prices. To-day the world obtains commodities of excellent quality at prices which even the preceding generation would have deemed incredible. In the commercial world similar causes have produced similar results, and the race is benefited thereby. The poor enjoy what the rich could not before afford. What were the luxuries have become the necessaries of life. The laborer has now more comforts than the farmer had a few generations ago. The farmer has more luxuries than the landlord had, and is more richly clad and better housed. The landlord has books and pictures rarer and appointments more artistic than the king could then obtain.

The price we pay for this salutary change is, no doubt, great. We assemble thousands of operatives in the factory, and in the mine, of whom the employer can know little or nothing, and to whom he is

---

[2] *Mæcenas:* (d. 8 B.C.) Roman statesman and counsellor to Augustus; his name has come to mean "patron of letters."

little better than a myth. All intercourse between them is at an end. Rigid castes are formed, and, as usual, mutual ignorance breeds mutual distrust. Each caste is without sympathy with the other, and ready to credit anything disparaging in regard to it. Under the law of competition, the employer of thousands is forced into the strictest economies, among which the rates paid to labor figure prominently, and often there is friction between the employer and the employed, between capital and labor, between rich and poor. Human society loses homogeneity.

The price which society pays for the law of competition, like the price it pays for cheap comforts and luxuries, is also great; but the advantages of this law are also greater still than its cost — for it is to this law that we owe our wonderful material development, which brings improved conditions in its train. But, whether the law be benign or not, we must say of it, as we say of the change in the conditions of men to which we have referred: It is here; we cannot evade it; no substitutes for it have been found; and while the law may be sometimes hard for the individual, it is best for the race, because it insures the survival of the fittest in every department. We accept and welcome, therefore, as conditions to which we must accommodate ourselves, great inequality of environment; the concentration of business, industrial and commercial, in the hands of a few; and the law of competition between these, as being not only beneficial, but essential to the future progress of the race. Having accepted these, it follows that there must be great scope for the exercise of special ability in the merchant and in the manufacturer who has to conduct affairs upon a great scale. That this talent for organization and management is rare among men is proved by the fact that it invariably secures enormous rewards for its possessor, no matter where or under what laws or conditions. The experienced in affairs always rate the MAN whose services can be obtained as a partner as not only the first consideration, but such as render the question of his capital scarcely worth considering: for able men soon create capital; in the hands of those without the special talent required, capital soon takes wings. Such men become interested in firms or corporations using millions; and, estimating only simple interest to be made upon the capital invested, it is inevitable that their income must exceed their expenditure and that they must, therefore, accumulate wealth. Nor is there any middle ground which such men can occupy, because the great manufacturing or commercial concern which does not earn at least interest upon its capital soon becomes bankrupt. It must either go forward or fall behind; to stand still is impossible. It is a condition essential to its successful operation that it should be thus far profitable, and even that, in addition to interest on capital, it should make profit. It is a law, as certain as any of the others named, that men possessed of this peculiar talent for affairs, under the free play of economic forces must, of necessity, soon be in receipt of more revenue than can be judiciously expended upon themselves; and this law is as beneficial for the race as the others. . . .

This, then, is held to be the duty of the man of wealth: To set an example of modest, unostentatious living, shunning display or extravagance; to provide moderately for the legitimate wants of those dependent upon him; and, after doing so, to consider all surplus revenues which come to him simply as trust funds, which he is called upon to administer, and strictly bound as a matter of duty to administer in the manner which, in his judgment, is best calculated to produce the most beneficial results for the community — the man of wealth thus becoming the mere trustee and agent for his poorer brethren, bringing to their service his superior wisdom, experience, and ability to administer, doing for them better than they would or could do for themselves.

We are met here with the difficulty of determining what are moderate sums to leave to members of the family; what is modest, unostentatious living; what is the test of extravagance. There must be different standards for different conditions. The answer is that it is as impossible to name exact amounts or actions as it is to define good manners, good taste, or the rules of propriety; but, nevertheless, these are verities, well known, although indefinable. Public sentiment is quick to know and to feel what offends these. So in the case of wealth. The rule in regard to good taste in dress of men or women applies here. Whatever makes one conspicuous offends the canon. If any family be chiefly known for display, for extravagance in home, table, or equipage, for enormous sums ostentatiously spent in any form upon itself — if these be its chief distinctions, we have no difficulty in estimating its nature or culture. So likewise in regard to the use or abuse of its surplus wealth, or to generous, free-handed coöperation in good public uses, or to unabated efforts to accumulate and hoard to the last, or whether they administer or bequeath. The verdict rests with the best and most enlightened public sentiment. The community will surely judge, and its judgments will not often be wrong. . . .

There is room and need for all kinds of wise benefactions for the common weal. The man who builds a university, library, or laboratory performs no more useful work than he who elects to devote himself and his surplus means to the adornment of a park, the gathering together of a collection of pictures for the public, or the building of a memorial arch. These are all true laborers in the vineyard. The only point required by the gospel of wealth is that the surplus which accrues from time to time in the hands of a man should be administered by him in his own lifetime for that purpose which is seen by him, as trustee, to be best for the good of the people. To leave at death what he cannot take away, and place upon others the burden of the work which it was his own duty to perform, is to do nothing worthy. This requires no sacrifice, nor any sense of duty to his fellows.

Time was when the words concerning the rich man entering the kingdom of heaven were regarded as a hard saying. To-day, when all questions are probed to the bottom and the standards of faith receive the most liberal interpretations, the startling verse has been relegated to the rear, to await the next kindly revision as one of those things which cannot be quite understood, but which, meanwhile, it is carefully to be noted, are not to be understood literally. But is it so very improbable that the next stage of thought is to restore the doctrine in all its pristine purity and force, as being in perfect harmony with sound ideas upon the subject of wealth and poverty, the rich and the poor, and the contrasts everywhere seen and deplored? In Christ's day, it is evident, reformers were against the wealthy. It is none the less evident that we are fast recurring to that position to-day; and there will be nothing to surprise the student of sociological development if society should soon approve the text which has caused so much anxiety: "It is easier for the camel to enter the eye of a needle than for a rich man to enter the kingdom of heaven." Even if the needle were the small casement at the gates, the words betoken serious difficulty for the rich. It will be but a step for the theologian from the doctrine that he who dies rich dies disgraced, to that which brings upon the man punishment or deprivation hereafter.

The gospel of wealth but echoes Christ's words. It calls upon the millionaire to sell all that he hath and give it in the highest and best form to the poor by administering his estate himself for the good of his fellows, before he is called upon to lie down and rest upon the bosom of Mother Earth. So doing, he will approach his end no longer the ignoble hoarder of useless millions; poor, very poor indeed, in money, but rich, very rich, twenty times a millionaire still, in the affection, gratitude, and admiration of his fellow-men, and — sweeter far — soothed and sustained by the still, small voice within, which, whispering, tells him that, because he has lived, perhaps one small part of the great world has been bettered just a little. This much is sure: against such riches as these no bar will be found at the gates of Paradise.

FANNY FERN

"Sewing Machines"

"The Working-Girls of New York"

Sara Payson Willis Parton (1811–1872), who identified herself as Fanny Fern in her newspaper columns and books, began writing after the death of her first husband and her divorce from her second. Writing was first and foremost a means of financial support for Parton and her children, and she was quite successful at it. Her collection, *Fern Leaves from Fanny's Port-Folio* (1853), was an immediate bestseller, and she became one of America's first woman columnists with her long-running humorous column in the New York *Ledger*. In the pieces she published in *Ledger* and other magazines, Fern used wit, satire, and sarcasm to champion women's rights and to publicize the difficulties surrounding women's roles in nineteenth-century America. "Sewing Machines" (*True Flag*, January 29, 1853) and "Working-Girls" (*Ledger*, January 26, 1867) were both magazine pieces discussing women's labor, an important and delicate subject to a nineteenth-century public which believed that "labor" and "womanhood" were mutually exclusive categories.

The text is from *Ruth Hall and Other Writings*, ed. Joyce W. Warren (New Brunswick, NJ: Rutgers UP, 1994), 247–48, 346–48.

"Sewing Machines"

There's "nothing new under the sun;" — so I've read, somewhere; either in Ecclesiastes or Uncle Tom's Cabin; but at any rate, I was forcibly reminded of the profound wisdom of the remark, upon seeing a great flourish of trumpets in the papers about a "Sewing Machine," that had been *lately invented.*

Now if *I* know anything of history, that discovery dates back as far as the Garden of Eden. If *Mrs. Adam* wasn't *the first sewing ma-*

chine, I'll give up guessing. Didn't she go right to work making aprons, before she had done receiving her bridal calls from the beasts and beastesses? Certainly she did, and I honor her for it, too.

Well — do you suppose all her pretty little descendants who ply their "busy fingers in the upper lofts of tailors, and hatters, and vest-makers, and 'finding' establishments," are going to be superseded by that dumb old thing? Do you suppose their young and enterprising patrons prefer the creaking of a crazy machine to the music of their young voices? Not by a great deal!

It's something, I can tell you, for them to see their pretty faces light up, when they pay off their wages of a Saturday night (small fee enough! too often, God knows!) Pity that the *shilling heart* so often accompanies the *guinea means.*[1]

Oh, launch out, gentlemen! Don't *always* look at things with a *business* eye. Those fragile forms are young, to toil so unremittingly. God made no distinction of *sex* when he said — "The laborer is worthy of his hire." Man's cupidity puts that interpretation upon it.

Those young operatives in your employ, pass, in their daily walks, forms youthful as their own, "clothed in purple and fine linen," who "*toil not, neither do they spin.*" Oh, teach them not to look after their "satin and sheen," purchased at such a fearful cost, with a discouraged sigh!

For one, I can never pass such a "fallen angel" with a "stand aside" feeling. A neglected youth, an early orphanage, poverty, beauty, coarse fare, the weary day of toil lengthened into night, — a mere pittance its reward. Youth, health, young blood, and the practiced wile of the ready tempter! *Oh, where's the marvel?*

Think of all this, when you poise that hardly earned dollar, on your business finger. What if it were our own delicate sister? Let a LITTLE heart creep into that shrewd bargain. 'Twill be an investment in the Bank of Heaven, that shall return to you four-fold.

"The Working-Girls of New York"

Nowhere more than in New York does the contest between squalor and splendor so sharply present itself. This is the first reflection of the observing stranger who walks its streets. Particularly is this noticeable

---

[1] *shilling heart. . . . guinea means:* That is, that the wealthy are often stingy.

with regard to its women. Jostling on the same pavement with the dainty fashionist is the care-worn working-girl. Looking at both these women, the question arises, which lives the more miserable life — she whom the world styles "fortunate," whose husband belongs to three clubs, and whose only meal with his family is an occasional breakfast, from year's end to year's end; who is as much a stranger to his own children as to the reader; whose young son of seventeen has already a detective on his track employed by his father to ascertain where and how he spends his nights and his father's money; swift retribution for that father who finds food, raiment, shelter, equipages for his household; but love, sympathy, companionship — never? Or she — this other woman — with a heart quite as hungry and unappeased, who also faces day by day the same appalling question: *Is this all life has for me?*

A great book is yet unwritten about women. Michelet[2] has aired his wax-doll theories regarding them. The defender of "woman's rights" has given us her views. Authors and authoresses of little, and big repute, have expressed themselves on this subject, and none of them as yet have begun to grasp it: men — because they lack spirituality, rightly and justly to interpret women; women — because they dare not, or will not tell us that which most interests us to know. Who shall write this bold, frank, truthful book remains to be seen. Meanwhile woman's millennium is yet a great way off; and while it slowly progresses, conservatism and indifference gaze through their spectacles at the seething element of to-day, and wonder "what ails all our women?"

Let me tell you what ails the working-girls. While yet your breakfast is progressing, and your toilet unmade, comes forth through Chatham Street and the Bowery, a long procession of them by twos and threes to their daily labor. Their breakfast, so called, has been hastily swallowed in a tenement house, where two of them share, in a small room, the same miserable bed. Of its quality you may better judge, when you know that each of these girls pay but three dollars a week for board, to the working man and his wife where they lodge.

The room they occupy is close and unventilated, with no accommodations for personal cleanliness, and so near to the little Flinegans that their Celtic night-cries are distinctly heard. They have risen unrefreshed, as a matter of course, and their ill-cooked breakfast does not

---

[2] *Michelet:* Jules Michelet (1798–1874), French historian who described the ideal woman as childlike, docile, and ignorant. By virtue of her inferiority to her husband, she managed the home while he went out to work.

mend the matter. They emerge from the doorway where their passage is obstructed by "nanny goats" and ragged children rooting together in the dirt, and pass out into the street. They shiver as the sharp wind of early morning strikes their temples. There is no look of youth on their faces; hard lines appear there. Their brows are knit; their eyes are sunken; their dress is flimsy, and foolish, and tawdry; always a hat, and feather or soiled artificial flower upon it; the hair dressed with an abortive attempt at style; a soiled petticoat; a greasy dress, a well-worn sacque or shawl, and a gilt breast-pin and earrings.

Now follow them to the large, black-looking building, where several hundred of them are manufacturing hoop-skirts. If you are a woman you have worn plenty; but you little thought what passed in the heads of these girls as their busy fingers glazed the wire, or prepared the spools for covering them, or secured the tapes which held them in their places. *You* could not stay five minutes in that room, where the noise of the machinery used is so deafening, that only by the motion of the lips could you comprehend a person speaking.

Five minutes! Why, these young creatures bear it, from seven in the morning till six in the evening; week after week, month after month, with only half an hour at midday to eat their dinner of a slice of bread and butter or an apple, which they usually eat in the building, some of them having come a long distance. As I said, the roar of machinery in that room is like the roar of Niagara. Observe them as you enter. Not one lifts her head. They might as well be machines, for any interest or curiosity they show, save always to know *what o'clock it is*. Pitiful! pitiful, you almost sob to yourself, as you look at these young girls. *Young?* Alas! it is only in years that they are young.

HARRIET HANSON ROBINSON

From Loom and Spindle

Like many other women in the nineteenth century, Harriet Hanson Robinson (1825–1911) was forced to enter the workforce when the death of her father plunged her family into poverty. At the age of ten she became a laborer in the mill town of Lowell, Massachusetts; eventually she helped bring the Lowell mill girls national and historical prominence. Organized as a factory and a paternalistic support system, the Lowell mill provided its female employees with schools, churches, and libraries through the 1840s. Robinson benefited from publication in the Lowell literary magazine, *The Lowell Offering*. In addition to her active involvement in both the abolitionist and women's suffrage movement, Robinson made a significant historical contribution to our understanding of the nineteenth century with *Loom and Spindle* (New York: Crowell, 1898), a memoir of her time as a Lowell mill girl. In the following selection, Robinson discusses her experiences as a young girl working in the mill and offers insights into the way in which women laborers were viewed by society.

The [textile mill] "Print Works" was a great mystery in its early days. It had its secrets and it was said that no stranger was allowed to enter certain rooms, for fear that the art would be stolen. The first enduring color in print was an indigo blue. This was the groundwork; and a minute white spot sprinkled over it made the goods lively and pretty. It wore like "iron," and its success was the first step toward the high standard in the market once held by the "Merrimack Print."[1]

Before 1840, the foreign element in the factory population was almost an unknown quantity. The first immigrants to come to Lowell were from England. The Irishman soon followed; but not for many years did the Frenchman, Italian, and German come to take possession of the cotton-mills. The English were of the artisan class, but the Irish came as "hewers of wood and drawers of water." The first Irishwomen to work in the Lowell mills were usually scrubbers and waste-pickers. They were always good-natured and when excited used their own language; the little mill-children learned many of the words (which all seemed to be joined together like compound words) and these mites would often answer back, in true Hibernian[2] fashion. These women, as a rule, wore peasant cloaks, red or blue, made with hoods and several capes, in summer (as they told the children), to "kape cool," and in winter to "kape warrum." They were not intemperate, nor "bitterly poor." They earned good wages, and they and their children, especially their children, very soon adapted themselves to their changed conditions of life, and became as "good as anybody."

To show the close connection in family descent of the artisan and the artist, at least in the line of color, it may be said here that a grandson of one of the first blue-dyers in this country is one of the finest

---

[1] "*Merrimack Print*": Lowell, Massachusetts, was located on the banks of the Merrimack River.

[2] *Hibernian*: Relating to or characteristic of the Irish.

American marine painters, and exhibited pictures at the World's Columbian Exposition of 1893.

In 1832 the factory population of Lowell was divided into four classes. The agents of the corporations were the aristocrats, not because of their wealth, but on account of the office they held, which was one of great responsibility, requiring, as it did, not only some knowledge of business, but also a certain tact in managing, or utilizing the great number of operatives so as to secure the best return for their labor. The agent was also something of an autocrat, and there was no appeal from his decision in matters affecting the industrial interests of those who were employed on his corporation.

The agents usually lived in large houses, not too near the boarding-houses, surrounded by beautiful gardens which seemed like Paradise to some of the home-sick girls, who, as they came from their work in the noisy mill, could look with longing eyes into the sometimes open gate in the high fence, and be reminded afresh of their pleasant country homes. And a glimpse of one handsome woman, the wife of an agent, reading by an astral lamp in the early evening, has always been remembered by one young girl, who looked forward to the time when she, too, might have a parlor of her own, lighted by an astral lamp!

The second class were the overseers, a sort of gentry, ambitious mill-hands who had worked up from the lowest grade of factory labor; and they usually lived in the end-tenements of the blocks, the short connected rows of houses in which the operatives were boarded. However, on one corporation, at least, there was a block devoted exclusively to the overseers, and one of the wives, who had been a factory girl, put on so many airs that the wittiest of her former work-mates fastened the name of "Puckersville" to the whole block where the overseers lived. It was related of one of these quondam factory girls, that, with some friends, she once re-visited the room in which she used to work, and, to show her genteel friends her ignorance of her old surroundings, she turned to the overseer, who was with the party, and pointing to some wheels and pulleys over her head, she said, "What's them things up there?"

The third class were the operatives, and were all spoken of as "girls" or "men;" and the "girls," either as a whole, or in part, are the subject of this volume.

The fourth class, lords of the spade and the shovel, by whose constant labor the building of the great factories was made possible, and whose children soon became valuable operatives, lived at first on what was called the "Acre," a locality near the present site of the

North Grammar schoolhouse. Here, clustered around a small stone Catholic Church, were hundreds of little shanties, in which they dwelt with their wives and numerous children. Among them were sometimes found disorder and riot, for they had brought with them from the *ould counthrey* their feuds and quarrels. . . .

I had been to school constantly until I was about ten years of age, when my mother, feeling obliged to have help in her work besides what I could give, and also needing the money which I could earn, allowed me, at my urgent request (for I wanted to earn *money* like the other little girls), to go to work in the mill. I worked first in the spinning-room as a "doffer." The doffers were the very youngest girls, whose work was to doff, or take off, the full bobbins, and replace them with the empty ones.

I can see myself now, racing down the alley, between the spinning-frames, carrying in front of me a bobbin-box bigger than I was. These mites had to be very swift in their movements, so as not to keep the spinning-frames stopped long, and they worked only about fifteen minutes in every hour. The rest of the time was their own, and when the overseer was kind they were allowed to read, knit, or even to go outside the mill-yard to play.

Some of us learned to embroider in crewels, and I still have a lamb worked on cloth, a relic of those early days, when I was first taught to improve my time in the good old New England fashion. When not doffing, we were often allowed to go home, for a time, and thus we were able to help our mothers in their housework. We were paid two dollars a week; and how proud I was when my turn came to stand up on the bobbin-box, and write my name in the paymaster's book, and how indignant I was when he asked me if I could "write." "Of course I can," said I, and he smiled as he looked down on me.

The working-hours of all the girls extended from five o'clock in the morning until seven in the evening, with one-half hour for breakfast and for dinner. Even the doffers were forced to be on duty nearly fourteen hours a day, and this was the greatest hardship in the lives of these children. For it was not until 1842 that the hours of labor for children under twelve years of age were limited to ten per day; but the "ten-hour law" itself was not passed until long after some of these little doffers were old enough to appear before the legislative committee on the subject, and plead, by their presence, for a reduction of the hours of labor.

I do not recall any particular hardship connected with this life, except getting up so early in the morning, and to this habit, I never was, and never shall be, reconciled, for it has taken nearly a lifetime for me to make up the sleep lost at that early age. But in every other respect it was a pleasant life. We were not hurried any more than was for our good, and no more work was required of us than we were able easily to do.

Most of us children lived at home, and we were well fed, drinking both tea and coffee, and eating substantial meals (besides luncheons) three times a day. We had very happy hours with the older girls, many of whom treated us like babies, or talked in a motherly way, and so had a good influence over us. And in the long winter evenings, when we could not run home between the doffings, we gathered in groups and told each other stories, and sung the old-time songs our mothers had sung, such as "Barbara Allen," "Lord Lovell," "Captain Kid," "Hull's Victory," and sometimes a hymn.

Among the ghost stories I remember some that would delight the hearts of the "Society for Psychical Research." The more imaginative ones told of what they had read in fairy books, or related tales of old castles and distressed maidens; and the scene of their adventures was sometimes laid among the foundation stones of the new mill, just building.

And we told each other of our little hopes and desires, and what we meant to do when we grew up. For we had our aspirations; and one of us, who danced the "shawl dance," as she called it, in the spinning-room alley, for the amusement of her admiring companions, discussed seriously with another little girl the scheme of their running away together, and joining the circus. Fortunately, there was a grain of good sense lurking in the mind of this gay little lassie, with the thought of the mother at home, and the scheme was not carried out.

There was another little girl, whose mother was suffering with consumption, and who went out of the mill almost every forenoon, to buy and cook oysters, which she brought in hot, for her mother's luncheon. The mother soon went to her rest, and the little daughter, after tasting the first bitter experience of life, followed her. Dear Lizzie Osborne! little sister of my child-soul, such friendship as ours is not often repeated in after life! Many pathetic stories might be told of these little fatherless mill-children, who worked near their mothers, and who went hand in hand with them to and from the mill.

I cannot tell how it happened that some of us knew about the English factory children, who, it was said, were treated so badly, and were even whipped by their cruel overseers. But we did know of it, and used to sing, to a doleful little tune, some verses called, "The

Factory Girl's Last Day." I do not remember it well enough to quote
it as written, but have refreshed my memory by reading it lately in
Robert Dale Owen's[3] writings: —

The Factory Girl's Last Day

"'Twas on a winter morning,
  The weather wet and wild,
Two hours before the dawning
  The father roused his child,
Her daily morsel bringing,
  The darksome room he paced,
And cried, 'The bell is ringing —
  My hapless darling, haste!'

The overlooker met her
  As to her frame she crept;
And with his thong he beat her,
  And cursed her when she wept.
It seemed as she grew weaker,
  The threads the oftener broke,
The rapid wheels ran quicker,
  And heavier fell the stroke."

The song goes on to tell the sad story of her death while her "pity-
ing comrades" were carrying her home to die, and ends: —

"That night a chariot passed her,
  While on the ground she lay;
The daughters of her master,
  An evening visit pay.
Their tender hearts were sighing,
  As negroes' wrongs were told,
While the white slave was dying
  Who gained her father's gold."

In contrast with this sad picture, we thought of ourselves as well
off, in our cosey corner of the mill, enjoying ourselves in our own
way, with our good mothers and our warm suppers awaiting us when
the going-out bell should ring.

Holidays came when repairs to the great mill-wheel were going on,
or some late spring freshet caused the shutting down of the mill; these
were well improved. With what freedom we enjoyed those happy
times! My summer playhouse was the woodshed, which my mother

---

[3] *Robert Dale Owen:* (1771–1858) British industrialist and socialist.

always had well filled; how orderly and with what precision the logs were sawed and piled with the smooth ends outwards! The catacombs of Paris reminded me of my old playhouse. And here, in my castle of sawed wood, was my vacation retreat, where with my only and beloved wooden doll, I lunched on slices of apple cut in shape so as to represent what I called "German half-moon cakes." I piled up my bits of crockery with sticks of cinnamon to represent candy, and many other semblances of things, drawn from my mother's housekeeping stores.

The yard which led to the shed was always green, and here many half-holiday duties were performed. We children were expected to scour all the knives and forks used by the forty men-boarders, and my brothers often bought themselves off by giving me some trifle, and I was left alone to do the whole. And what a pile of knives and forks it was! But it was no task, for did I not have the open yard to work in, with the sky over me, and the green grass to stand on, as I scrubbed away at my "stent"? I don't know why I did not think such long tasks a burden, nor of my work in the mill as drudgery. Perhaps it was because I *expected* to do my part towards helping my mother to get our living, and had never heard her complain of the hardships of her life.

On other afternoons I went to walk with a playmate, who, like myself, was full of romantic dreams, along the banks of the Merrimack River, where the Indians had still their tents, or on Sundays, to see the "new converts" baptized.[4] These baptizings in the river were very common, as the tanks in the churches were not considered *apostolic* by the early Baptists of Lowell.

Sometimes we rambled by the "race-way" or mill-race, which carried the water into the flume of the mill, along whose inclining sides grew wild roses, and the "rock-loving columbine;" and we used to listen to see if we could hear the blue-bells ring, — this was long before either of us had read a line of poetry.

The North Grammar school building stood at the base of the hilly ridge of rocks, down which we coasted in water, and where in summer, after school-hours, we had a little cave, where we sometimes hid, and played that we were robbers; and together we rehearsed the dramatic scenes in "Alonzo and Melissa," "The Children of the

---

[4] *to see the "new converts" baptized:* Although the Lowell mill girls were not known for their religious fervor, religious values were thought to make better workers, so the mill girls were encouraged to attend religious services.

Abbey," or the "Three Spaniards;"[5] we were turned out of doors with Amanda, we exclaimed "Heavens!" with Melissa, and when night came on we fled from our play-house pursued by the dreadful apparition of old Don Padilla[6] through the dark windings of those old rocks, towards our commonplace home. "Ah!" as some writer has said, "if one could only add the fine imagination of those early days to the knowledge and experience of later years, what books might not be written!"

Our home amusements were very original. We had no toys, except a few homemade articles or devices of our own. I had but a single doll, a wooden-jointed thing, with red cheeks and staring black eyes. Playing-cards were tabooed, but my elder brother (the incipient D.D.), who had somehow learned the game of high-low-jack, set about making a pack. The cards were cut out of thick yellow pasteboard, the spots and figures were made in ink, and, to disguise their real character, the names of the suits were changed. Instead of hearts, diamonds, spades, and clubs, they were called charity, love, benevolence, and faith. The pasteboard was so thick that all together the cards made a pile at least two or three feet high, and they had to be shuffled in sections! He taught my second brother and me the game of high-low-jack; and, with delightful secrecy, as often as we could steal away, we played in the attic, keeping the cards hidden, between whiles, in an old hair trunk. In playing the game we got along very well with the names of the face-cards, — the "queen of charity" the "king of love," and so on; but the "ten-spot of faith," and particularly the "two-spot of benevolence" (we had never heard of the "deuce") was too much for our sense of humor, and almost spoiled the "rigor of the game."

I was a "little doffer" until I became old enough to earn more money; then I tended a spinning-frame for a little while; after that I learned, on the Merrimack corporation, to be a drawing-in girl, which was considered one of the most desirable employments, as about only a dozen girls were needed in each mill. We drew in, one by one, the threads of the warp, through the harness and the reed,

---

[5] *"Alonzo and Melissa"* . . . *"Three Spaniards"*: The Asylum, or Alonzo and Melissa: An American Tale, Founded on Fact (1811) by I. Mitchell; The Children of the Abbey: A Tale (1801) by Regina Maria Roche (ca. 1764–1845); The Three Spaniards: A Romance (1801) by George Walker (1772–1847). All three novels are American.

[6] *Don Padilla:* Juan de Padilla (1490–1521), Spanish rebel and popular hero who headed an insurrection against Charles V.

and so made the beams ready for the weaver's loom. I still have the two hooks I used so long, companions of many a dreaming hour, and preserve them as the "badge of all my tribe" of drawing-in girls.

It may be well to add that, although so many changes have been made in mill-work, during the last fifty years, by the introduction of machinery, this part of it still continues to be done by hand, and the drawing-in girl — I saw her last winter, as in my time — still sits on her high stool, and with her little hook patiently draws in the thousands of threads, one by one. . . .

When I look back into the factory life of fifty or sixty years ago, I do not see what is called "a class" of young men and women going to and from their daily work, like so many ants that cannot be distinguished one from another; I see them as individuals, with personalities of their own. This one has about her the atmosphere of her early home. That one is impelled by a strong and noble purpose. The other, — what she is, has been an influence for good to me and to all womankind.

Yet they were a class of factory operatives, and were spoken of (as the same class is spoken of now) as a set of persons who earned their daily bread, whose condition was fixed, and who must continue to spin and to weave to the end of their natural existence. Nothing but this was expected of them, and they were not supposed to be capable of social and mental improvement. That they could be educated and developed into something more than mere work-people, was an idea that had not yet entered the public mind. So little does one class of persons really know about the thoughts and aspirations of another! It was the good fortune of these early mill-girls to teach the people of that time that this sort of labor is not degrading; that the operative is not only "capable of virtue," but also capable of self-cultivation.

At the time the Lowell cotton-mills were started, the factory girl was the lowest among women. In England, and in France particularly, great injustice had been done to her real character; she was represented as subjected to influences that could not fail to destroy her purity and self-respect. In the eyes of her overseer she was but a brute, a slave, to be beaten, pinched, and pushed about. It was to overcome this prejudice that such high wages had been offered to women that they might be induced to become mill-girls, in spite of the opprobrium that still clung to this "degrading occupation." At first only a few came; for, though tempted by the high wages to be regularly paid in "cash," there were many who still preferred to go on working at some more *genteel* employment at seventy-five cents a week and their board.

But in a short time the prejudice against factory labor wore away, and the Lowell mills became filled with blooming and energetic New England women. They were naturally intelligent, had mother-wit, and fell easily into the ways of their new life. They soon began to associate with those who formed the community in which they had come to live, and were invited to their houses. They went to the same church, and sometimes married into some of the best families. Or if they returned to their secluded homes again, instead of being looked down upon as "factory girls" by the squire's or the lawyer's family, they were more often welcomed as coming from metropolis, bringing new fashions, new books, and new ideas with them. . . .

It must be remembered that at this date woman had no property rights. A widow could be left without her share of her husband's (or the family) property, a legal "incumbrance" to his estate. A father could make his will without reference to his daughter's share of the inheritance. He usually left her a home on the farm as long as she remained single. A woman was not supposed to be capable of spending her own or of using other people's money. In Massachusetts, before 1840, a woman could not legally be treasurer of her own sewing-society unless some man were responsible for her.

The law took no cognizance of woman as a money-spender. She was a ward, an appendage, a relict. Thus it happened, that if a woman did not choose to marry, or, when left a widow, to re-marry, she had no choice but to enter one of the few employments open to her, or to become a burden on the charity of some relative.

In almost every New England home could be found one or more of these women, sometimes welcome, more often unwelcome, and leading joyless, and in more instances unsatisfactory, lives. The cotton-factory was a great opening to these lonely and dependent women. From a condition approaching pauperism they were at once placed above want; they could earn money, and spend it as they pleased; and could gratify their tastes and desires without restraint, and without rendering an account to anybody. At last they had found a place in the universe; they were no longer obliged to finish out their faded lives mere burdens to male relatives. Even the *time* of these women was their own, on Sundays and in the evening after the day's work was done. For the first time in this country woman's labor had a money value. She had become not only an earner and a producer, but also a spender of money, a recognized factor in the political economy of her time. And thus a long upward step in our material civilization was taken; woman had begun to earn and hold her own money, and through its aid had learned to think and to act for herself.

ANONYMOUS

"Factory Life — Romance and Reality"

─────────

"My Experience as a Factory Operative"

"Factory Life — Romance and Reality" (*Voice of Industry*, December 3, 1847) and "My Experience as a Factory Operative" (*Boston Daily Evening Voice*, February 23, 1867), written by anonymous female factory workers, criticize the romance and sentiment attached to the Lowell mill girls. Both selections discuss the physical and mental exhaustion the women suffered after working thirteen-hour days and the discouragement they experienced when this exhaustion prevented them from taking advantage of the moral and educational opportunities that wealthier women enjoyed. Though both women acknowledge the benefits of working, they argue that the Lowell mill system and the system of labor in general has serious flaws that must be addressed.

The text is from *The Factory Girls*, ed. Philip S. Foner (Urbana: U of Illinois P, 1977).

"Factory Life — Romance and Reality"

Aristocratic strangers, in broad cloths and silks, with their imaginations excited by the wonderful stories — romances of Factory Life — which they have heard, have paid hasty visits to Lowell, or Manchester, and have gone away to praise, in prose and verse, the beauty of our "Factory Queens," and the comfort, elegance and almost perfection, of the arrangements by which the very fatherly care of Agents, Superintendents, Overseers, &c., has surrounded them. To these nice visitors everything in and around a Lowell Cotton Mill is bathed in an atmosphere of rose-colored light. They see the bright side of the picture, and that alone. They see the graceful form, the bright and speaking eye, the blushing cheek and the elastic motions of "Industry's Angel daughters," but they fail to see that these belong not to Lowell Cotton Mills, but to New England's country Homes. — There the fair cheek, kissed by the sunlight and the breeze, grew fresh and healthful. There the eye borrowed its brightness from stream and lake and sky, and there too the intellect received the culture which enabled the "Factory Girls" to astonish Europe and America with a LOWELL OFFERING. There a FARLEY, a CURTIS, a HALL and a LAR-COM[1] received the impress which made them what they are in their various departments of effort.

These lovers of the Romance of Labor — they don't like the *reality* very well — see not the pale and emaciated ones. They see not those who wear Consumption's hectic flush. They think little of the weariness and pain of those fair forms, as they stand there, at the loom and spindle, thirteen long hours, each day! They know not *how* long these hours of toil seem to them, as they look out upon the fields, and hills, and woods, which lie beyond the Merrimack, steeped in golden sunlight and radiant with beauty — fields and woods which are to them what the Land of Promise was to Moses on Pisgah,[2] something which *they* may never enjoy. They have no time to ramble and climb the hill-sides. Six days shalt thou labor and do all thy work, and on the seventh thou shalt go to church, is the Commandment as improved by the mammon worshiping Christianity of modern Civilization. The factory girl is required to go to meeting on Sunday, where long, and too often unmeaning, word-prayers are repeated, and dull prosey sermons "delivered," and where God is worshiped, according to law, by pious Agents and Overseers, while the poor Irishman is blasting rocks for them in the Corporation's canal, that the mills may not be stopped on Monday. It would be very wicked, of course, for the "mill girl" to go out upon the hills, where she might worship in the great temple of the universe, without a priest, as proxy, to stand between her and her Maker.

These lovers of the Romance of Labor — here, have much to say of the moral and intellectual advantages by which the operatives are surrounded. These may be over-rated or they may not be, it matters not. It is true there are Churches and ministers "in any quantity," with many good influences, and with some that are at least questionable.

There are lectures of various kinds, some of them *free*, and others requiring only a trifling fee to secure admission, to all who wish it. Then there are also libraries of well selected books, to which all can have access.

---

[1] *FARLEY . . . LARCOM:* Harriet Farley, Harriot F. Curtis, Lydia S. Hall, and Lucy Larcom were associated with *The Lowell Offering;* Hall also edited *Operative's Magazine.*

[2] *Land . . . Pisgah:* Moses did not go into the promised land himself; he was permitted to go only to Pisgah, the mountain range east of the northern end of the Dead Sea.

Those who recollect the fable of *Tantalus*[3] in the old Mythology, will be able to appreciate the position of a large portion of the population with respect to these exalted privileges. They are all around them, on every side, but they cannot grasp them — they continually invite to the soul-feast, those who, tho' they hunger and thirst, cannot partake. Do you ask why they cannot partake? Simply from physical and mental exhaustion. The unremitted toil of thirteen long hours, drains off the vital energy and unfits for study or reflection. They need amusement, relaxation, *rest*, and not mental exertion of any kind. A really sound and instructive lecture cannot, under such circumstances, be appreciated, and the lecturer fails, to a great extent, in making an impression. — "Jim Crow" performances[4] are much better patronized than scientific lectures, and the trashy, milk-and-water sentimentalities of the *Lady's Book*[5] and *Olive Branch*,[6] are more read than the works of Gibbon,[7] or Goldsmith,[8] or Bancroft.[9]

If each factory girl could suspend her labors in the Mill for a few months each year, for the purpose of availing herself of the advantages for intellectual culture by which she is surrounded, much good might be derived. A few can and do thus avail themselves of these advantages; but the great mass are there to toil and toil only. Among these are some of the earth's noblest spirits. Theirs is Love's *willing* toil. The old homestead must be redeemed, — a poor sick mother or an aged and infirm father needs their little savings to keep them from that dreadful place, Civilization's only guarantee, the "Poor House," — or a loved brother at Dartmouth or Harvard, is to be assisted in his manful efforts to secure an education; so they must not think of schools and books for themselves. They must toil on, and they do toil on. But day by day they feel their over-tasked systems give way. — A dizziness in the head or a

---

[3] *Tantalus:* A king in Greek mythology who was condemned in Hades to stand in a pool of water that receded when he tried to drink and under a fruit tree whose branches receded when he reached for them.

[4] *"Jim Crow" performances:* Jim Crow is thought to have been a black stable hand in Louisville whom Thomas D. Rice imitated in his "Jim Crow" act, which was the first minstrel show. The term came to designate blacks in general and became associated with segregation laws and policies.

[5] *Lady's Book: Godey's Lady's Book*, edited by Sarah J. Hale, was published in Philadelphia.

[6] *Olive Branch:* Published in Boston from 1830 to 1860.

[7] *Gibbon:* Edward Gibbon (1737–1794), English historian and author of *Decline and Fall of the Roman Empire.*

[8] *Goldsmith:* Oliver Goldsmith (1728–1774), British poet, dramatist, and novelist.

[9] *Bancroft:* George Bancroft (1800–1891), American historian and author of *History of the United States* and *History of the Formation of the Constitution of the United States.*

pain in the side, or the shoulders or the back, admonishes them to return to their country homes before it is too late. But too often these
friendly monitions are unheeded. They resolve to toil a *little longer.* —
But nature cannot be cheated, and the poor victim of a false system of
Industrial Oppression is carried home — *to die!* Or, if her home is far
away and disease comes on too rapidly, she goes to the Hospital, and
soon, in the Strangers' Burial Ground may be seen another unmarked
grave! This is no fancy of mine — no studied fiction — (would to God
it were) but sober truth. There are now in our very midst hundreds of
these loving, self-sacrificing martyr-spirits. They will die unhonored
and unsung, but not unwept; for the poor factory girl has a *home* and
loved ones, and dark will be that home, and sad those loved ones when
the light of her smile shines on them no more.

"My Experience as a Factory Operative"

To the Editor of the Daily Evening Voice:
    Thirty years ago I was a factory girl in the city of Lowell. I was
ambitious to do something for myself in the way of earning money to
pay my expenses at an Academy; and being too young to teach school
in the country, not strong enough to do housework or learn a trade, I
went into the card-room on the Fremont Corporation. My work was
easy; I could sit down part of the time, and received ($1.75) one dol-
lar and seventy-five cents per week beside my board. Being fond of
reverie, and in the habit of constructing scenes and building castles in
the air, I enjoyed factory life very well.
    After a few months my parents removed from a country town to
Lowell, and I went to board with them on the street, and then I began
seriously to reflect on the realities of life.
    For a delicate girl of fourteen years of age to be called out of bed and
be obliged to eat her breakfast without any light, and then frequently
wallow through the snow to the factory, stay there until half-past
twelve, then run home and swallow her dinner without mastication,
run back and stay there until half-past seven, is, to say the least, very
unpleasant and unnatural, and exceedingly hurtful to the constitution.
    I attended school three months during the following summer; then
worked about eighteen months longer in the factory; afterwards
worked in the weave-room, in all three years, but only about six
months at a time, as my health would not allow me to work longer.

The labor of attending three or four looms thirteen hours per day, with no time for recreation or mental improvement is very severe.

The habit of standing on the feet frequently produces varicose veins; and though the girls seldom complain, for they know it is useless, yet it is a fact that factory girls are great sufferers in this respect.

In those days the morals of the girls were well guarded, and they were generally treated respectfully by the overseers, and I think lived well on the corporations.

They were generally daughters of our New England farmers and mechanics, some of them were well educated. Many of them had learned trades. Some of them were of a literary turn and get up improvement circles. And I will say in truth that if the hours of labor had been only eight instead of thirteen, I should prefer working in the mill to house work, enjoyed the society of the girls, and the noise of the machinery was not displeasing to me; but after one has worked from daylight until dark, the prospect of working two or three hours more by lamp light is very discouraging.

In 1849 I was thrown into the society of several young women who were daughters of mill owners; and the contrast between their condition and that of the operatives was so great that it led me to serious reflection on the injustice of society. These girls had an abundance of leisure, could attend school when and where they pleased, were fashionably dressed, were not obliged to work any except when they pleased; indeed, they suffered for want of exercise; and while they were so tenderly cared for, lest the "winds of heaven should visit their faces too roughly," the operatives toiled on through summer's heat and winter's cold; many passing into an early grave in consequence of protracted labor, and many others making themselves invalids for life.

For one, I could never see the justice of one set of girls working all the time in order that another set should live in ease and idleness. Cowper says, "I would not have a slave to till my ground, to fan me while I sleep, and tremble when I wake, for all the wealth that sinews bought and sold have ever earned." But many of our people in Massachusetts are quite willing to make fat dividends on the labor of anybody they can hire, widows and orphans, boys and girls of tender age; and when they cannot obtain American girls, they send across the ocean for operatives, and then allow them just enough to keep them from starvation.

I am satisfied from my own experience, as well as from observation of the working classes for many years, that nothing can be done for their education or elevation, until the hours of labor are reduced. After one has worked from ten to fourteen hours at manual labor, it is impossible to study History, Philosophy, or Science.

I well remember the chagrin I often felt when attending lectures, to find myself unable to keep awake; or perhaps so far from the speaker on account of being late, that the ringing in my ears caused by the noise of the looms during the day, prevented my hearing scarcely a sentence he uttered. I am sure few possessed a more ardent desire for knowledge than I did, but such was the effect of the long hour system, that my chief delight was, after the evening meal, to place my aching feet in any easy position, and read a novel. I was never too tired, however, to listen to the lectures given by the friends of Labor Reform, such as John Allen, John C. Cluer or Mike Walsh. I assisted in getting signers to a Ten Hour petitions to the Legislature, and since I have resided in Boston and vicinity have seen and enjoyed the good results of that improvement in the condition of the working classes.

A Working Woman

ELIZABETH E. TURNER

"Factory Girl's Reverie"

The Lowell Offering was a well-known literary publication of the Lowell factory, which employed young women and offered them education, religion, and access to libraries in addition to the independence of wage-earning employment. Elizabeth E. Turner's "Factory Girl's Reverie" was published in *The Lowell Offering* in 1845. Although the very existence of the text proves that the Lowell mill girls had opportunities to voice their opinions that may not have been available to other nineteenth-century women, Turner expresses harsh thoughts on life as a factory girl.

The text is from *The Lowell Offering: Writings by New England Mill Women (1840–1845)*, ed. Benita Eisler (Philadelphia: Lippincott, 1977).

'Tis evening. The glorious sun has sunk behind the western horizon. The golden rays, of sunset hues, are fast fading from the western sky. Gray twilight comes stealing over the landscape. One star after another sparkles in the firmament. The bird, that warbled its plaintive song through the long day, has pillowed its head beneath its wing. The prattle of playful children is hushed. The smith's hammer is no more heard upon the anvil. The rattle of noisy wheels has ceased. All nature is at rest.

Evening is the time for thought and reflection. All is lovely without, and am I not happy? I *cannot* be, for a feeling of sadness comes stealing over me. I am far, far from that loved spot, where I spent the evenings of childhood's years. I am here, among strangers — a factory girl — yes, a *factory girl;* that name which is thought so degrading by many, though, in truth, I neither see nor feel its degradation.

But here I am. I toil day after day in the noisy mill. When the bell calls I must go: and must I always stay here, and spend my days within these pent-up walls, with this ceaseless din my only music?

O that I were a *child* again, and could wander in my little flower garden, and cull its choicest blossoms, and while away the hours in that bower, with cousin Rachel. But alas! that dear cousin has long since ceased to pluck the flowers, and they now bloom over her grave. That garden is now cultivated by stranger's hands. I fear they take but little care of those vines I loved to trail so well; and my bower has gone to decay. But what is that to me? I shall never spend the sweet hours there again.

I am sometimes asked, "When are you going home?" "*Home,* that name ever dear to me." But they would not often ask me, if they only knew what sadness it creates to say, "*I have no home*" — if they knew that Death hath taken for his own those dear presiding spirits, and that strangers now move in their places. Ah! I have

> "No kind-hearted mother to wipe the sad tear,
> No brother or sister my bosom to cheer."

I *will* once more visit the home of my childhood. I will cast one long lingering look at the grave of my parents and brothers, and bid farewell to the spot. I have many friends who would not see me in want. I have uncles, aunts and cousins, who have kindly urged me to share their homes. But I have a little pride yet. I will not be dependent upon friends while I have health and ability to earn bread for myself. I will no more allow this sadness. I will wear a cheerful countenance, and make myself happy by contentment. I will earn all I can, and "lay by something against a *stormy* day." I will do all the good I can, and make those around me happy as far as lies in my power. I see many whose brows are marked with sorrow and gloom; with them I will sympathize, and dispel their gloom if I can. I will while away my leisure hours in reading good books, and trying to acquire what useful knowledge I can. I will ever strive to be contented with my lot, though humble, and not make myself unhappy by repining. I will try to live in reference to that great day of accounts, and ever hope to meet my parents in a land of bliss.

One boon of kind Heaven I ask, though far from that loved spot, that I may be laid beside my mother, "'neath the dew-drooping willow."

T********

HERMAN MELVILLE

"The Tartarus[1] *of Maids"*

Herman Melville (1819–1891), best known in his lifetime as a popular travel writer, is now considered one of America's greatest authors. As a young man, Melville worked at a variety of jobs in search of a career that would enable him to support his family and eventually turned to work on whaling ships. Although his South Sea adventure novels *Typee* (1846) and *Omoo* (1847) sold well, Melville's later, more serious novels such as *Moby-Dick* (1851) were not well received by the public or by critics. The influential critic Everett Duyckinck, for example, saw *Moby-Dick* as immoral. Because of the disappointing sales of the book, Melville had difficulty supporting his family.

"The Tartarus of Maids" is the second part of a double sketch called "The Paradise of Bachelors and the Tartarus of Maids" (*Harper's*, 1855). In these stories, Melville contrasts the easy, almost decadent lives of bachelors living in London's Temple with the lives of women working in a paper factory in New England. Images of frigidity, thwarted and dangerous sexuality, and female suffering propel "The Tartarus of Maids," a story that implicates anyone who makes use of paper products — including the story's reader — as being part of the factory system.

The text is from *The Piazza Tales and Other Prose Pieces, 1839–1860* (Evanston: Northwestern UP, 1987).

---

[1]*Tartarus:* The underworld, a sunless abyss below hell.

It lies not far from Woedolor Mountain in New England. Turning to the east, right out from among bright farms and sunny meadows, nodding in early June with odorous grasses, you enter ascendingly among bleak hills. These gradually close in upon a dusky pass, which, from the violent Gulf Stream of air unceasingly driving between its cloven walls of haggard rock, as well as from the tradition of a crazy spinster's hut having long ago stood somewhere hereabouts, is called the Mad Maid's Bellows'-pipe.

Winding along at the bottom of the gorge is a dangerously narrow wheel-road, occupying the bed of a former torrent. Following this road to its highest point, you stand as within a Dantean gateway. From the steepness of the walls here, their strangely ebon hue, and the sudden contraction of the gorge, this particular point is called the Black Notch. The ravine now expandingly descends into a great, purple, hopper-shaped hollow, far sunk among many Plutonian, shaggy-wooded mountains. By the country people this hollow is called the Devil's Dungeon. Sounds of torrents fall on all sides upon the ear. These rapid waters unite at last in one turbid brick-colored stream, boiling through a flume among enormous boulders. They call this strange-colored torrent Blood River. Gaining a dark precipice it wheels suddenly to the west, and makes one maniac spring of sixty feet into the arms of a stunted wood of gray-haired pines, between which it thence eddies on its further way down to the invisible lowlands.

Conspicuously crowning a rocky bluff high to one side, at the cataract's verge, is the ruin of an old saw-mill, built in those primitive times when vast pines and hemlocks superabounded throughout the neighboring region. The black-mossed bulk of those immense, rough-hewn, and spike-knotted logs, here and there tumbled all together, in long abandonment and decay, or left in solitary, perilous projection over the cataract's gloomy brink, impart to this rude wooden ruin not only much of the aspect of one of rough-quarried stone, but also a sort of feudal, Rhineland,[2] and Thurmberg look, derived from the pinnacled wildness of the neighboring scenery.

Not far from the bottom of the Dungeon stands a large white-washed building, relieved, like some great whited sepulchre, against the sullen background of mountain-side firs, and other hardy evergreens, inaccessibly rising in grim terraces for some two thousand feet.

---

[2] *Rhineland:* The Rhineland consists of the land along both banks of the middle Rhine River; Melville uses the association to suggest the medieval character of the landscape.

The building is a paper-mill.

Having embarked on a large scale in the seedsman's business (so extensively and broadcast, indeed, that at length my seeds were distributed through all the Eastern and Northern States, and even fell into the far soil of Missouri and the Carolinas), the demand for paper at my place became so great, that the expenditure soon amounted to a most important item in the general account. It need hardly be hinted how paper comes into use with seedsmen, as envelopes. These are mostly made of yellowish paper, folded square; and when filled, are all but flat, and being stamped, and superscribed with the nature of the seeds contained, assume not a little the appearance of business-letters ready for the mail. Of these small envelopes I used an incredible quantity — several hundreds of thousands in a year. For a time I had purchased my paper from the wholesale dealers in a neighboring town. For economy's sake, and partly for the adventure of the trip, I now resolved to cross the mountains, some sixty miles, and order my future paper at the Devil's Dungeon paper-mill.

The sleighing being uncommonly fine toward the end of January, and promising to hold so for no small period, in spite of the bitter cold I started one gray Friday noon in my pung,[3] well fitted with buffalo and wolf robes; and, spending one night on the road, next noon came in sight of Woedolor Mountain.

The far summit fairly smoked with frost; white vapors curled up from its white-wooded top, as from a chimney. The intense congelation made the whole country look like one petrifaction. The steel shoes of my pung craunched and gritted over the vitreous, chippy snow, as if it had been broken glass. The forests here and there skirting the route, feeling the same all-stiffening influence, their inmost fibres penetrated with the cold, strangely groaned — not in the swaying branches merely, but likewise in the vertical trunk — as the fitful gusts remorselessly swept through them. Brittle with excessive frost, many colossal tough-grained maples, snapped in twain like pipe-stems, cumbered the unfeeling earth.

Flaked all over with frozen sweat, white as a milky ram, his nostrils at each breath sending forth two horn-shaped shoots of heated respiration, Black, my good horse, but six years old, started at a sudden turn, where, right across the track — not ten minutes fallen — an old distorted hemlock lay, darkly undulatory as an anaconda.

Gaining the Bellows'-pipe, the violent blast, dead from behind, all but shoved my high-backed pung up-hill. The gust shrieked through

---

[3] *pung:* Boxlike sleigh drawn by one horse.

the shivered pass, as if laden with lost spirits bound to the unhappy world. Ere gaining the summit, Black, my horse, as if exasperated by the cutting wind, slung out with his strong hind legs, tore the light pung straight up-hill, and sweeping grazingly through the narrow notch, sped downward madly past the ruined saw-mill. Into the Devil's Dungeon horse and cataract rushed together.

With might and main, quitting my seat and robes, and standing backward, with one foot braced against the dash-board, I rasped and churned the bit, and stopped him just in time to avoid collision, at a turn, with the bleak nozzle of a rock, couchant like a lion in the way — a road-side rock.

At first I could not discover the paper-mill.

The whole hollow gleamed with the white, except, here and there, where a pinnacle of granite showed one wind-swept angle bare. The mountains stood pinned in shrouds — a pass of Alpine corpses. Where stands the mill? Suddenly a whirling, humming sound broke upon my ear. I looked, and there, like an arrested avalanche, lay the large white-washed factory. It was subordinately surrounded by a cluster of other and smaller buildings, some of which, from their cheap, blank air, great length, gregarious windows, and comfortless expression, no doubt were boarding-houses of the operatives. A snow-white hamlet amidst the snows. Various rude, irregular squares and courts resulted from the somewhat picturesque clusterings of these buildings, owing to the broken, rocky nature of the ground, which forbade all method in their relative arrangement. Several narrow lanes and alleys, too, partly blocked with snow fallen from the roof, cut up the hamlet in all directions.

When, turning from the traveled highway, jingling with bells of numerous farmers — who, availing themselves of the fine sleighing, were dragging their wood to market — and frequently diversified with swift cutters dashing from inn to inn of the scattered villages — when, I say, turning from that bustling main-road, I by degrees wound into the Mad Maid's Bellows'-pipe, and saw the grim Black Notch beyond, then something latent, as well as something obvious in the time and scene, strangely brought back to my mind my first sight of dark and grimy Temple-Bar.[4] And when Black, my horse, went darting through the Notch, perilously grazing its rocky wall, I remembered being in a runaway London omnibus, which in much the same sort of style, though by no means at an equal rate, dashed

---

[4] *Temple-Bar:* In the first half of this double sketch, Melville discusses the lives of bachelors living in the externally grim but internally comfortable Temple-Bar in London.

through the ancient arch of Wren. Though the two objects did by no means completely correspond, yet this partial inadequacy but served to tinge the similitude not less with the vividness than the disorder of a dream. So that, when upon reining up at the protruding rock I at last caught sight of the quaint groupings of the factory-buildings, and with the traveled highway and the Notch behind, found myself all alone, silently and privily stealing through deep-cloven passages into this sequestered spot, and saw the long, high-gabled main factory edifice, with a rude tower — for hoisting heavy boxes — at one end, standing among its crowded outbuildings and boarding-houses, as the Temple Church amidst the surrounding offices and dormitories, and when the marvelous retirement of this mysterious mountain nook fastened its whole spell upon me, then, what memory lacked, all tributary imagination furnished, and I said to myself, "This is the very counterpart of the Paradise of Bachelors, but snowed upon, and frost-painted to a sepulchre."

Dismounting, and warily picking my way down the dangerous declivity — horse and man both sliding now and then upon the icy ledges — at length I drove, or the blast drove me, into the largest square, before one side of the main edifice. Piercingly and shrilly the shotted blast blew by the corner; and redly and demoniacally boiled Blood River at one side. A long wood-pile, of many scores of cords, all glittering in mail of crusted ice, stood crosswise in the square. A row of horse-posts, their north sides plastered with adhesive snow, flanked the factory wall. The bleak frost packed and paved the square as with some ringing metal.

The inverted similitude recurred — "The sweet, tranquil Temple garden, with the Thames bordering its green beds," strangely meditated I.

But where are the gay bachelors?

Then, as I and my horse stood shivering in the wind-spray, a girl ran from a neighboring dormitory door, and throwing her thin apron over her bare head, made for the opposite building.

"One moment, my girl; is there no shed hereabouts which I may drive into?"

Pausing, she turned upon me a face pale with work, and blue with cold; an eye supernatural with unrelated misery.

"Nay," faltered I, "I mistook you. Go on; I want nothing."

Leading my horse close to the door from which she had come, I knocked. Another pale, blue girl appeared, shivering in the doorway as, to prevent the blast, she jealously held the door ajar.

"Nay, I mistake again. In God's name shut the door. But hold, is there no man about?"

That moment a dark-complexioned well-wrapped personage passed, making for the factory door, and spying him coming, the girl rapidly closed the other one.

"Is there no horse-shed here, Sir?"

"Yonder, to the wood-shed," he replied, and disappeared inside the factory.

With much ado I managed to wedge in horse and pung between the scattered piles of wood all sawn and split. Then, blanketing my horse, and piling my buffalo on the blanket's top, and tucking in its edges well around the breast-band and breeching, so that the wind might not strip him bare, I tied him fast, and ran lamely for the factory door, stiff with frost, and cumbered with my driver's dread-naught.[5]

Immediately I found myself standing in a spacious place, intolerably lighted by long rows of windows, focusing inward the snowy scene without.

At rows of blank-looking counters sat rows of blank-looking girls, with blank, white folders in their blank hands, all blankly folding blank paper.

In one corner stood some huge frame of ponderous iron, with a vertical thing like a piston periodically rising and falling upon a heavy wooden block. Before it — its tame minister — stood a tall girl, feeding the iron animal with half-quires[6] of rose-hued note paper, which, at every downward dab of the piston-like machine, received in the corner the impress of a wreath of roses. I looked from the rosy paper to the pallid cheek, but said nothing.

Seated before a long apparatus, strung with long, slender strings like any harp, another girl was feeding it with foolscap sheets,[7] which, so soon as they curiously traveled from her on the cords, were withdrawn at the opposite end of the machine by a second girl. They came to the first girl blank; they went to the second girl ruled.

I looked upon the first girl's brow, and saw it was young and fair; I looked upon the second girl's brow, and saw it was ruled and wrinkled. Then, as I still looked, the two — for some small variety to the monotony — changed places; and where had stood the young, fair brow, now stood the ruled and wrinkled one.

Perched high upon a narrow platform, and still higher upon a high stool crowning it, sat another figure serving some other iron animal;

[5] *dread-naught:* Coat made of a thick woolen cloth.
[6] *half-quires:* A quire is four sheets of paper folded into eight leaves.
[7] *foolscap sheets:* Large pieces of writing paper.

while below the platform sat her mate in some sort of reciprocal attendance.

Not a syllable was breathed. Nothing was heard but the low, steady, overruling hum of the iron animals. The human voice was banished from the spot. Machinery — that vaunted slave of humanity — here stood menially served by human beings, who serve mutely and cringingly as the slave serves the Sultan. The girls did not so much seem accessory wheels to the general machinery as mere cogs to the wheels.

All this scene around me was instantaneously taken in at one sweeping glance — even before I had proceeded to unwind the heavy fur tippet from around my neck. But as soon as this fell from me the dark-complexioned man, standing close by, raised a sudden cry, and seizing my arm, dragged me out into the open air, and without pausing for a word instantly caught up some congealed snow and began rubbing both my cheeks.

"Two white spots like the whites of your eyes," he said; "man, your cheeks are frozen."

"That may well be," muttered I; "'tis some wonder the frost of the Devil's Dungeon strikes in no deeper. Rub away."

Soon a horrible, tearing pain caught at my reviving cheeks. Two gaunt blood-hounds, one on each side, seemed mumbling them. I seemed Actæon.[8]

Presently, when all was over, I re-entered the factory, made known my business, concluded it satisfactorily, and then begged to be conducted throughout the place to view it.

"Cupid is the boy for that," said the dark-complexioned man. "Cupid!" and by this odd fancy-name calling a dimpled, red-cheeked, spirited-looking, forward little fellow, who was rather impudently, I thought, gliding about among the passive-looking girls — like a gold fish through hueless waves — yet doing nothing in particular that I could see, the man bade him lead the stranger through the edifice.

"Come first and see the water-wheel," said this lively lad, with the air of boyishly-brisk importance.

Quitting the folding-room, we crossed some damp, cold boards, and stood beneath a great wet shed, incessantly showering with foam, like the green barnacled bow of some East Indiaman in a gale. Round and round here went the enormous revolutions of the dark colossal water-wheel, grim with its one immutable purpose.

[8] *Actæon:* A hunter in Greek mythology whom the goddess Artemis turned into a stag because he saw her bathing; his own hounds then killed him.

"This sets our whole machinery a-going, Sir; in every part of all these buildings; where the girls work and all."

I looked, and saw that the turbid waters of Blood River had not changed their hue by coming under the use of man.

"You make only blank paper; no printing of any sort, I suppose? All blank paper, don't you?"

"Certainly; what else should a paper-factory make?"

The lad here looked at me as if suspicious of my common-sense.

"Oh, to be sure!" said I, confused and stammering; "it only struck me as so strange that red waters should turn out pale chee — paper, I mean."

He took me up a wet and rickety stair to a great light room, furnished with no visible thing but rude, manger-like receptacles running all round its sides; and up to these mangers, like so many mares haltered to the rack, stood rows of girls. Before each was vertically thrust up a long, glittering scythe, immovably fixed at bottom to the manger-edge. The curve of the scythe, and its having no snath to it, made it look exactly like a sword. To and fro, across the sharp edge, the girls forever dragged long strips of rags, washed white, picked from baskets at one side; thus ripping asunder every seam, and converting the tatters almost into lint. The air swam with the fine, poisonous particles, which from all sides darted, subtilely, as motes in sun-beams, into the lungs.

"This is the rag-room," coughed the boy.

"You find it rather stifling here," coughed I, in answer; "but the girls don't cough."

"Oh, they are used to it."

"Where do you get such hosts of rags?" picking up a handful from a basket.

"Some from the country round about; some from far over sea — Leghorn and London."

"'Tis not unlikely, then," murmured I, "that among these heaps of rags there may be some old shirts, gathered from the dormitories of the Paradise of Bachelors. But the buttons are all dropped off. Pray, my lad, do you ever find any bachelor's buttons hereabouts?"

"None grow in this part of the country. The Devil's Dungeon is no place for flowers."

"Oh! you mean the *flowers* so called — the Bachelor's Buttons?"

"And was not that what you asked about? Or did you mean the gold bosom-buttons of our boss, Old Bach, as our whispering girls all call him?"

"The man, then, I saw below is a bachelor, is he?"

"Oh, yes, he's a Bach."

"The edges of those swords, they are turned outward from the girls, if I see right; but their rags and fingers fly so, I can not distinctly see."

"Turned outward."

Yes, murmured I to myself; I see it now; turned outward; and each erected sword is so borne, edge-outward, before each girl. If my reading fails me not, just so, of old, condemned state-prisoners went from the hall of judgment to their doom: an officer before, bearing a sword, its edge turned outward, in significance of their fatal sentence. So, through consumptive pallors of this blank, raggy life, go these white girls to death.

"Those scythes look very sharp," again turning toward the boy.

"Yes; they have to keep them so. Look!"

That moment two of the girls, dropping their rags, plied each a whet-stone up and down the sword-blade. My unaccustomed blood curdled at the sharp shriek of the tormented steel.

Their own executioners; themselves whetting the very swords that slay them; meditated I.

"What makes those girls so sheet-white, my lad?"

"Why" — with a roguish twinkle, pure ignorant drollery, not knowing heartlessness — "I suppose the handling of such white bits of sheets all the time makes them so sheety."

"Let us leave the rag-room now, my lad."

More tragical and more inscrutably mysterious than any mystic sight, human or machine, throughout the factory, was the strange innocence of cruel-heartedness in this usage-hardened boy.

"And now," said he, cheerily, "I suppose you want to see our great machine, which cost us twelve thousand dollars only last autumn. That's the machine that makes the paper, too. This way, Sir."

Following him, I crossed a large, bespattered place, with two great round vats in it, full of a white, wet, woolly-looking stuff, not unlike the albuminous part of an egg, soft-boiled.

"There," said Cupid, tapping the vats carelessly, "these are the first beginnings of the paper; this white pulp you see. Look how it swims bubbling round and round, moved by the paddle here. From hence it pours from both vats into that one common channel yonder; and so goes, mixed up and leisurely, to the great machine. And now for that."

He led me into a room, stifling with a strange, blood-like, abdominal heat, as if here, true enough, were being finally developed the germinous particles lately seen.

Before me, rolled out like some long Eastern manuscript, lay stretched one continuous length of iron frame-work — multitudinous and mystical, with all sorts of rollers, wheels, and cylinders, in slowly-measured and unceasing motion.

"Here first comes the pulp now," said Cupid, pointing to the nighest end of the machine. "See; first it pours out and spreads itself upon this wide, sloping board; and then — look — slides, thin and quivering, beneath the first roller there. Follow on now, and see it as it slides from under that to the next cylinder. There; see how it has become just a very little less pulpy now. One step more, and it grows still more to some slight consistence. Still another cylinder, and it is so knitted — though as yet mere dragon-fly wing — that it forms an air-bridge here, like a suspended cobweb, between two more separated rollers; and flowing over the last one, and under again, and doubling about there out of sight for a minute among all those mixed cylinders you indistinctly see, it reappears here, looking now at last a little less like pulp and more like paper, but still quite delicate and defective yet awhile. But — a little further onward, Sir, if you please — here now, at this further point, it puts on something of a real look, as if it might turn out to be something you might possibly handle in the end. But it's not yet done, Sir. Good way to travel yet, and plenty more of cylinders must roll it."

"Bless my soul!" said I, amazed at the elongation, interminable convolutions, and deliberate slowness of the machine; "it must take a long time for the pulp to pass from end to end, and come out paper."

"Oh! not so long," smiled the precocious lad, with a superior and patronizing air; "only nine minutes. But look; you may try it for yourself. Have you a bit of paper? Ah! here's a bit on the floor. Now mark that with any word you please, and let me dab it on here, and we'll see how long before it comes out at the other end."

"Well, let me see," said I, taking out my pencil; "come, I'll mark it with your name."

Bidding me take out my watch, Cupid adroitly dropped the inscribed slip on an exposed part of the incipient mass.

Instantly my eye marked the second-hand on my dial-plate.

Slowly I followed the slip, inch by inch; sometimes pausing for full half a minute as it disappeared beneath inscrutable groups of the lower cylinders, but only gradually to emerge again; and so, on, and on, and on — inch by inch; now in open sight, sliding along like a freckle on the quivering sheet; and then again wholly vanished; and so, on, and on, and on — inch by inch; all the time the main sheet growing more and more to final firmness — when, suddenly, I saw a sort of paper-fall, not wholly unlike a water-fall; a scissory sound smote my ear, as of some cord being snapped; and down dropped an unfolded sheet of perfect foolscap, with my "Cupid" half faded out of it, and still moist and warm.

My travels were at an end, for here was the end of the machine.

"Well, how long was it?" said Cupid.

"Nine minutes to the second," replied I, watch in hand.

"I told you so."

For a moment a curious emotion filled me, not wholly unlike that which one might experience at the fulfillment of some mysterious prophecy. But how absurd, thought I again; the thing is a mere machine, the essence of which is unvarying punctuality and precision.

Previously absorbed by the wheels and cylinders, my attention was now directed to a sad-looking woman standing by.

"That is rather an elderly person so silently tending the machine-end here. She would not seem wholly used to it either."

"Oh," knowingly whispered Cupid, through the din, "she only came last week. She was a nurse formerly. But the business is poor in these parts, and she's left it. But look at the paper she is piling there."

"Ay, foolscap," handling the piles of moist, warm sheets, which continually were being delivered into the woman's waiting hands. "Don't you turn out any thing but foolscap at this machine?"

"Oh, sometimes, but not often, we turn out finer work — cream-laid and royal sheets, we call them. But foolscap being in chief demand, we turn out foolscap most."

It was very curious. Looking at that blank paper continually dropping, dropping, dropping, my mind ran on in wonderings of those strange uses to which those thousand sheets eventually would be put. All sorts of writings would be writ on those now vacant things — sermons, lawyers' briefs, physicians' prescriptions, love-letters, marriage certificates, bills of divorce, registers of births, death-warrants, and so on, without end. Then, recurring back to them as they here lay all blank, I could not but bethink me of that celebrated comparison of John Locke,[9] who, in demonstration of his theory that man had no innate ideas, compared the human mind at birth to a sheet of blank paper; something destined to be scribbled on, but what sort of characters no soul might tell.

---

[9] *John Locke:* (1632–1704) English philosopher.

Pacing slowly to and fro along the involved machine, still humming with its play, I was struck as well by the inevitability as the evolvement-power in all its motions.

"Does that thin cobweb there," said I, pointing to the sheet in its more imperfect stage, "does that never tear or break? It is marvelous fragile, and yet this machine it passes through is so mighty."

"It never is known to tear a hair's point."

"Does it never stop — get clogged?"

"No. It *must* go. The machinery makes it go just *so*; just that very way, and at that very pace you there plainly *see* it go. The pulp can't help going."

Something of awe now stole over me, as I gazed upon this inflexible iron animal. Always, more or less, machinery of this ponderous, elaborate sort strikes, in some moods, strange dread into the human heart, as some living, panting Behemoth might. But what made the thing I saw so specially terrible to me was the metallic necessity, the unbudging fatality which governed it. Though, here and there, I could not follow the thin, gauzy vail of pulp in the course of its more mysterious or entirely invisible advance, yet it was indubitable that, at those points where it eluded me, it still marched on in unvarying docility to the autocratic cunning of the machine. A fascination fastened on me. I stood spell-bound and wandering in my soul. Before my eyes — there, passing in slow procession along the wheeling cylinders, I seemed to see, glued to the pallid incipience of the pulp, the yet more pallid faces of all the pallid girls I had eyed that heavy day. Slowly, mournfully, beseechingly, yet unresistingly, they gleamed along, their agony dimly outlined on the imperfect paper, like the print of the tormented face on the handkerchief of Saint Veronica.[10]

"Halloa! the heat of the room is too much for you," cried Cupid, staring at me.

"No — I am rather chill, if any thing."

"Come out, Sir — out — out," and, with the protecting air of a careful father, the precocious lad hurried me outside.

In a few moments, feeling revived a little, I went into the folding-room — the first room I had entered, and where the desk for transacting business stood, surrounded by the blank counters and blank girls engaged at them.

"Cupid here has led me a strange tour," said I to the dark-complexioned man before mentioned, whom I had ere this discovered

---

[10] *Saint Veronica:* A woman who is supposed to have met Christ and allowed him to wipe his face on her handkerchief, which then retained the features of his face.

not only to be an old bachelor, but also the principal proprietor. "Yours is a most wonderful factory. Your great machine is a miracle of inscrutable intricacy."

"Yes, all our visitors think it so. But we don't have many. We are in a very out-of-the-way corner here. Few inhabitants, too. Most of our girls come from far-off villages."

"The girls," echoed I, glancing round at their silent forms. "Why is it, Sir, that in most factories, female operatives, of whatever age, are indiscriminately called girls, never women?"

"Oh! as to that — why, I suppose, the fact of their being generally unmarried — that's the reason, I should think. But it never struck me before. For our factory here, we will not have married women; they are apt to be off-and-on too much. We want none but steady workers: twelve hours to the day, day after day, through the three hundred and sixty-five days, excepting Sundays, Thanksgiving, and Fast-days. That's our rule. And so, having no married women, what females we have are rightly enough called girls."

"Then these are all maids," said I, while some pained homage to their pale virginity made me involuntarily bow.

"All maids."

Again the strange emotion filled me.

"Your cheeks look whitish yet, Sir," said the man, gazing at me narrowly. "You must be careful going home. Do they pain you at all now? It's a bad sign, if they do."

"No doubt, Sir," answered I, "when once I have got out of the Devil's Dungeon, I shall feel them mending."

"Ah, yes; the winter air in valleys, or gorges, or any sunken place, is far colder and more bitter than elsewhere. You would hardly believe it now, but it is colder here than at the top of Woedolor Mountain."

"I dare say it is, Sir. But time presses me; I must depart."

With that, remuffling myself in dread-naught and tippet,[11] thrusting my hands into my huge seal-skin mittens, I sallied out into the nipping air, and found poor Black, my horse, all cringing and doubled up with the cold.

Soon, wrapped in furs and meditations, I ascended from the Devil's Dungeon.

At the Black Notch I paused, and once more bethought me of Temple-Bar. Then, shooting through the pass, all alone with inscrutable nature, I exclaimed — Oh! Paradise of Bachelors! and oh! Tartarus of Maids!

---

[11] *tippet:* Wool or fur scarf.

THE MANUFACTURE OF IRON—FILLING THE FURNACE.

Figure 2. *The Manufacture of Iron*, from *Harper's Weekly*, November 1, 1873. Illustration by Tavernier and Frenzeny. These two images are part of a series of three showing the steps in the process of iron manufacture. Handcarts of coal or coke are dumped into the hot smelting furnace (top), and the waste ash, scorle — or korl, as it is termed in *Life in the Iron-Mills* — is removed hours later when sufficiently cooled (bottom). Finally, workmen open, or tap, the sealed furnace to extract the iron product (see Figure 1, p. 76).

Figure 3. *Forging the Shaft,* by John Ferguson Weir, 1877. Replica of a destroyed 1867 painting. The Metropolitan Museum of Art, Purchase, Lyman G. Bloomingdale Gift, 1901. (01.7.1)

Figure 4. *The Workers and Their Dwellings at Pittsburgh Coke Ovens,* from *Harper's Weekly,* July 7, 1888. Illustration by W. A. Rogers. Note the "dwellings" above, almost concealed by smoke as the workers hasten to fuel the coke ovens.

Figure 5. *The Iron-Workers' Noon-Time,* from *Harper's Weekly,* August 30, 1884. Engraved by F. Juengling from the painting by Thomas Anshutz.

COMPOSITE IRON WORKS.

IRA HUTCHINSON, *Pres't and Treas.*
IRAH CHASE, *Vice-Pres't and Sec'y.*

Figure 6. Advertisement from *Harper's Weekly*, April 12, 1873. Located on Mercer Street in New York City, the Composite Iron Works produced ornamental products for personal, commercial, and public use.

Figure 7. Advertisement from *Harper's Weekly*, March 1, 1873.

Figure 8 (above). *Emigrant Wagon — On the Way to the Railroad Station*, from *Harper's Weekly*, October 25, 1873. Illustration by Frenzeny and Tavernier.

Figure 9 (below). *Immigrants Waiting to Be Distributed to the Coal [and Iron] Regions of Pennsylvania*, from *Harper's Weekly*, July 28, 1888. Illustration by W. A. Rogers.

Figure 10. *A Question of Labor*, from *Harper's Weekly*, July, 1888. This image shows Chinese immigrant workers in a Massachusetts shoe factory.

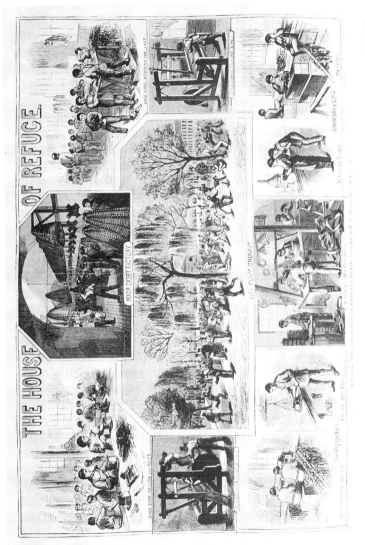

Figure 11. *New York House of Refuge on Randall's Island*, from *Harper's Weekly*, May 23, 1868. Illustration by W. H. Davenport. Children convicted of a crime were sent to houses of refuge like this one, where they worked at such jobs as making shoes and hoop skirts. The facility on Randall's Island held one thousand children in 1868.

Figure 12. *Small Motor Running Sewing Machine,* from *Harper's Weekly,*
February 25, 1888. The writer Fanny Fern satirized the notion of labor-
saving devices when she termed women garment workers "sewing machines."
This image shows the sewing machine in use in a scene of middle-class
domesticity.

Figure 13. *Cutting and Sorting in a Paper Mill*, from *The Growth of Industrial Art*, 1892. Published by the U.S. government to celebrate the development of the nation's technology, *The Growth of Industrial Art* depicted scenes of work in numerous industries, including papermaking.

Figure 14. *Jack Frost among the Rich and the Poor*, from *Harper's Weekly*, January 27, 1866.

Figure 15. *The Mill and the Still*, from *Harper's Weekly*, August 18, 1883. Illustration by Jessie Shepherd. The production of bread and alcoholic beverages from the same sheaf of grain provides the basis for this allegory of family life.

Figure 16. *Rich and Poor*, from *Harper's Weekly*, January 11, 1873. Illustration by Sol Gytinge.

2

Social Reform and the Promise of the Dawn

In 1830, the future U.S. President Andrew Jackson praised the United States as a nation of "happy people . . . filled with all the blessings of liberty, civilization, and religion." But within a decade, an English traveler to the United States, Thomas Brothers, registered the opposite impression, describing daily events in the new nation in scathing terms: "lynching, firing, stabbing, shooting, and rioting are daily taking place" (qtd. in Mintz 15). The world of *Life in the Iron-Mills* lies between these two extremes of utopia and anarchy. The novella depicts a nation riddled with social problems but concludes with a vision of an imminent, hopeful sunrise wherein "God has set the promise of the dawn."

To bring about dawn's godly promise was seen as a duty and obligation by nineteenth-century Americans who identified themselves as the socially responsible middle class. Although Rebecca Harding Davis was not linked with any particular reform movement, her portrayal of the wretched conditions under which the Wolfe family subsists in *Life in the Iron-Mills* — "laired by day in dens of drunkenness and infamy . . . incessant labor, sleeping in kennel-like rooms, eating rank pork and molasses" — can be said to constitute an argument for social improvement through education, social reform, and Christian Protestant faith and works. Though Davis's novella does not proselytize on behalf of a particular cause, such as temperance or prison reform, it fully belongs in a nineteenth-century social context in which reform was considered a national mandate for secular progress and spiritual salvation.

Several factors contributed to the growing sense of urgency surrounding nineteenth-century American reform movements. First, in terms of national identity, Americans earlier in the century had experienced a kind of crisis of sociopolitical authority. A self-proclaimed nation that was just one generation removed from its rejection of a "mother" country against which it had fought two wars, the United States seemed to many to have a precarious hold on social order. Not only did mob uprisings, lynchings, and gang violence appear to be endemic in the growing cities but frontier life seemed equally rough and chaotic. One spokesperson felt that children had become "difficult to govern" because they heard "so much about liberty and equality." A Virginia newspaper reported that "shooting and cutting of throats appear to be the order of the day." In 1835, the New England minister William Ellery Channing remarked on "jarring interests and passions, invasions of rights, resistance of authority, violence, force" (qtd. in Mintz 3).

Amid scenes of violence were those of shocking destitution as urban children begged and scavenged for food in rat-infested heaps of refuse, as adults gleaned coal or wood for fires, and as young girls and boys struggled to survive as prostitutes. In 1816, one Boston slum, dubbed "Mount Whoredom," exhibited "scenes of iniquity and debauchery too dreadful to be named," according to a female reform society. By 1820, New York City had some two hundred brothels, and by 1850, the number of female prostitutes in the city approached six thousand. It was not uncommon to see destitute children swallow the dregs of whiskey from bottles they found in garbage-choked gutters. Understandably, many observers believed that the social order was imperiled, if not in a state of outright disintegration. In 1872, the reformer Charles Loring Brace wrote of urban "street-girls," some of whom "have come from the country, from kind and respectable homes, to seek work in the city," but who "gradually consume their scanty means, and are driven from one refuge to another, till they stand on the street, with the gayly-lighted house of vice and the gloomy police-station to choose between" (see p. 235). Many social analysts blamed a self-seeking materialism as the root cause of these and other problems the nation faced.

Reform movements arose in response to these conditions, though American social guardianship was a tradition predating the nineteenth century and originally centered in patriarchal, familial relationships.

William Penn's colonial Philadelphia was supposedly the City of Brotherly Love, and throughout colonial New England, certain respected men held the office of tithingmen, whose duties involved the oversight of several families' domestic and economic affairs. In 1710, the New England minister Cotton Mather published a civics guidebook, *Bonifacius, an Essay Upon the Good*, which enjoins readers to be loving and responsible parents and neighbors in their communities. "Whatever *snare* you see anyone in, be so kind, as to tell him of his danger to be *ensnared*, and save him from it" (60), wrote Mather in this text, which was reprinted well into the nineteenth century. Mather, however, lived in a New England of towns and villages centered around churches and could not have foreseen a United States transformed by the immigration, urbanization, and industrialization that were well under way in Davis's era.

It has been argued that much of the social turbulence that characterized the nineteenth century was rooted in racial and class antagonisms, as one social group acted out its resentment of the privileges it felt were accorded to another. For instance, the 1863 Civil War draft riots in New York City were an expression of hostility toward both blacks and the rich on the part of white workers. Many of these workers were Irish immigrants whose own wages and working conditions were deplorable and who resented the monied class and the war apparently being fought for blacks, with whom the immigrants competed for scarce jobs.

Yet the reformers, who readily acknowledged the existence of "the laboring classes" (or "the rowdies," as Charles Loring Brace terms them), did not concentrate their efforts solely on the working-class. They struggled simultaneously to change the attitudes and behavior of the affluent, whom they held responsible for fomenting discontent through their elitist greed and callousness. *Life in the Iron-Mills* shows the cool, even cynical disregard for the workers on the part of the wealthy mill visitors. Social reformers such as Orestes Brownson attempted to explore the motives and behavior of the elite in order to bring about change. In "The Laboring Classes" (1840), Brownson admonishes the well-to-do employer who has the power of life and death over his employee-laborer: "He is at your mercy . . . if he have not employment, he must die" (see p. 213).

Brownson chides employers who justify low wages on the basis of a "market price" that is fixed to enrich employers at the expense of their workers. He poses this challenge to employers: "You would regard, as the greatest of calamities which could befall you, that of losing your property, and being reduced to . . . supporting yourselves and families on the wages you could receive as common laborers" (see p. 213). Edward Bellamy, in his best-selling socially reformist novel, *Looking Backward, 2000–1887*, attempts to persuade American elites that social reform is in their best interest by depicting the nineteenth-century American upper classes as riding comfortably atop a capitalist coach that is subject to periodic jolts and accidents. Pitched to the ground in the event of economic crashes and depressions, those once prosperous are "instantly compelled to take hold of the rope and help to drag the coach on which they had before ridden so pleasantly" (see p. 275). *Looking Backward* attempts to convince the well-to-do that an equal distribution of the nation's wealth will in fact be beneficial to themselves.

Like Bellamy, most nineteenth-century American reformers defined personal and social life in the context of the developing middle class. They portrayed reform as both providing a pathway toward social stability and involving the inculcation of enlightened self-control. After all, the creation of a nation based on principles of self-government meant that civic order could not be maintained by authoritarian means. In the Old World, populations could be held in check by "the bayonet of the Czar and the scimitar of the Sultan," said the president of Amherst College in 1840. In the United States, however, the populace was thought to need education that would result in a citizenry collectively exercising civic and personal self-control. These qualities, in turn, would bring about social stability. Thus, Henry Ward Beecher writes that "if a man has nothing to do but to turn a grindstone [or] . . . stick pins on a paper [or] . . . sweep the streets, he had better be educated." Beecher continues, "'A man may be a workingman and follow a menial calling, and yet carry within him a noble soul and have a cultivated and refined nature'" (see pp. 222, 226).

The reformers therefore emphasized self-discipline as a means of controlling passions and appetites ranging from greed to lust. At stake was the very character of the nation. The poet John Greenleaf Whittier presents his ideal, "The Quaker of the Olden Time," as an exemplum for the contemporary movement, describing the inwardly pure Quaker as "calm and firm and true" / Unspotted by . . . wrong and crime" (see p. 271). Similarly, Ralph Waldo Emerson writes of a "moral order through the medium of individual nature" (see p. 221). Beecher, as a Protestant minister, conveys a sense of moral urgency when he writes in 1873, "We must show that knowledge is not the monopoly of the professions, not the privilege of wealth, not the prerogative of leisure, but that knowledge and refinement belong to hard-working men as much as to any other class of men" (see p. 223).

A major concern of reform movements throughout the nineteenth century was the maintenance of a moral, socially stable order in a more equal society. The various reform groups — which focused on a range of issues from etiquette to abolition, labor unions, education, temperance, prison reform, dietary improvement, and women's rights — all held the common goal of carrying forward the principles of the American Revolution in a social context of assiduous character development. Undergirding the reform movement, moreover, was a strong Christian ethos. "According to Christianity, all men are equal before God," writes Orestes Brownson, proceeding to the corollary statement that "democracy [is] the creature of this truth." Not surprisingly, the life of Christ was often held up by the reformers as one of moral perfection. In 1831, Channing published an essay, "The Perfect Life," in which he states as the purpose of Christianity "the perfection of human nature, the elevation of men into nobler beings" (qtd. in Mintz 22).

It must be noted that some commentators revealed a racist dimension in their Christian reformism. Josiah Strong writes that "most of the spiritual Christianity in the world is found among Anglo-Saxons and their converts" (see p. 250–51); and some reform organizations, such as the Woman's Christian Temperance Union, propounded similar views, reflecting the identity of their membership and leaders. When such groups resisted the inclusion of African Americans, the latter organized their own societies. As early as 1832, the Hartford Colored People's Temperance Society was formed when black temperance advocates were denied admission to the white organization.

Reform provided a particular focus for women's energies. Excluded from direct involvement in political and business life, women exerted political influence largely through religious means. "Women are happily formed for religion," wrote an early nineteenth-century Protestant minister, Daniel Chapman, who referred to women's "natural endowments" as presumed traits of compassion, service to others, and self-sacrifice (qtd. in Mintz 27). The nineteenth-century evangelical movement taught that Christian morality encompassed such qualities as personal self-discipline, thrift, sobriety, and industry, and the reform movement readily became an extension of Protestant thought (though it was a Catholic, Dorothea Dix, who worked

tirelessly for the cause of the mentally ill). The names of male ministers abound in the numerous reform efforts, but a striking number of
women's names appear as colleagues, including Frances Willard,
president of the Woman's Christian Temperance Union, and Harriet
Beecher Stowe, who found her abolitionist platform in fiction.
Women's work in religious reform paved the way for other notable
women reformers, including Elizabeth Cady Stanton and Lucretia
Mott, who worked for women's suffrage; Catharine Beecher, author
of *Physiology and Calesthenics* (1856) and a leader in the cause of
improved health for women; and Caroline H. Wood, whose *Woman
in Prison* (1869) took up the cause of penal justice. Anna Gordon,
founder of the Kitchen Garden movement, defines her reform work in
her Senate testimony of 1883: "The young ladies of our Society go to
the workhouse, and have a class among the girls who are confined
there for petty offences; and they say that these children brighten
their homes greatly by carrying to them the ideas of cleanliness and
tidiness they glean in these Kitchen Garden classes" (see p. 256). Gordon then describes the workhouse girls demonstrating their new
skills, making beds, setting tables, serving food, washing dishes, and
thus showing preparation to become respectable wage-earners in domestic service.

The name of Rebecca Harding Davis is not ordinarily found in the
roll call of reformers. Davis tended to subscribe to the school of
thought linked to the transcendentalists, who felt that individual spiritual renewal would result in beneficial social changes as a matter of
course. "If we would indeed restore mankind," wrote the transcendentalist Henry David Thoreau in *Walden* (1854), "let us first be as
simple and well as Nature ourselves, dispel the clouds which hang
over our own brows, and take up a little life into our pores"
(*Portable* 350). This sentiment is echoed at the conclusion of *Life in
the Iron-Mills* when the Quaker woman points to the "hills . . . over
the river" where "the light lies warm" and "the winds of God blow
all day." On those hills, the refugee from the foul mill and slum can
finally "begin . . . life again" with "long years of sunshine, and fresh
air, and slow, patient Christ-love needed to make healthy and hopeful [an] impure body and soul." Ultimately, however, the readers of
Life in the Iron-Mills may find the scenes of mill-town squalor and
degradation to be the most memorable in the novella, and on this
basis the text situates itself firmly in the tradition of nineteenth-
century reform.

ORESTES BROWNSON

From "The Laboring Classes"

Orestes Brownson (1803–1876), editor and author, espoused many different viewpoints in his lifetime. Initially a strict Puritan, he moved through Universalism, Unitarianism, and finally settled with Catholicism until he was branded as a heretic by the Catholic Church. In terms of his social philosophy, he was a socialist who helped organize a Workingmen's Party, moved to the Democratic Party, and eventually adopted a more conservative worldview. He edited *The Boston Quarterly Review* (1838–1844), later called *Brownson's Quarterly Review* (1844–1865, 1872–1875), which gave him an outlet for his opinions. In the following essay, published in *The Boston Quarterly Review* (July 1840 and October 1840), Brownson critiques those who blame the problems of the laboring classes on the laziness or inherent inadequacy of the individual members of that class. He compares the working-class population with slaves, lacking social, financial, or legal power. Arguing for radical measures to alleviate the problems of the poor, Brownson implicates every American in the class system, which oppresses workers and their families; moreover, he asserts that every American suffers from the class system as it stands.

We are not ignorant that there is a class of our fellow citizens, who stare at us as if we were out of our wits, or possessed of no ordinary malignancy, when we represent the workingman as still a slave, and demand his enfranchisement. In their estimation he is already enfranchised, already a free man, in the full significance of the term; and no more dependent on the capitalist, than the capitalist is on him. These people, who think so, are, we must admit, very decent people in their way, and we desire to have for them all becoming respect. On several subjects they unquestionably have considerable intelligence and sound views. Did we wish to ascertain the rates of exchange on England or France, the prices of stocks, broadcloths, cottons, or tape, and such like matters, there are no people in the world we would more willingly consult, or with greater deference. But in questions like those which now concern us, — questions which relate to the bearing of social or economical systems, the actual progress of civi-

lization, or the means of advancing it, we must be held excusable, if
we cannot in all respects take them for our masters. . . .

For ourselves, we were born and reared in the class of proletaries;
and we have merely given utterance to their views and feelings. . . .

The class of persons, who have been loudest in their condemnation
of us, are the *Nouveaux riches, parvenus,* upstarts, men who have
themselves come up from the class of proletaries, and who have made
it a virtue to forget "the rock whence they were hewn." Standing now
on the shoulders of their brethren, they are too elevated to see what is
going on at the base of the social organization. Would you know
what is going on down there, you must interrogate those who dwell
there, and feel the pressure that is on them. One would not interrogate the rider in order to ascertain the sensations the horse has in
being ridden.

Then, again, these persons never had any sympathy with the class
of proletaries. They early adopted that convenient morality, pithily
expressed in the maxim, "Look out for Number One;" and consequently have never studied their condition, except so far as they
could avail themselves of it as a means of their own elevation. They
have found the condition of the workingmen a very convenient help
to those, who are skilful enough to avail themselves of it as a means
of rising to the top of the social ladder; and therefore they have inferred that it is good enough for those who are always to remain in it.
Would these upstarts be willing to exchange places with the workingmen? If so, let us see them do it; if not, let them be silent.

Moreover, these people have risen in the social scale to be, what
one of their number calls, "the better sort," and they very naturally
are anxious to have us understand that it has been by the blessing of
God and their own virtue. They wish us to believe that they are what
they are, because they are wiser, more talented, more skilful, and
more virtuous than those they have left behind them. They wish to be
able to say, "God, I thank thee, that I am better than these poor
wretches, who toil on from one year's end to another, and yet accumulate nothing." This is no doubt a very pleasant manner of addressing the Deity; it puts one in admirable humor with oneself, and saves
one from any compunctious twinges of conscience, one might have
on hearing the cry of the poor and needy. Now, if you say the proletaries are in a hopeless condition, if you say they cannot of themselves rise from their condition, you take away a considerable portion
of these people's merit, and lower their fancied superiority several degrees. It therefore behooves them to maintain that the condition of

the proletaries is good enough. If the proletaries are poor and wretched, the fault is all their own. It is owing to their incapacity, their indolence, or their vice. Were we not once poor, and are we not now rich and respectable? . . .

"But *we* have risen and so may others." Yes, doubtless; *some* others; but *all* others? How have you risen? By the productive industry of your own hands? By hard work. Aye, but by what kind of hard work? Has it not been by hard work in studying how you could turn the labors of others to your own profit; that is, transfer the proceeds of labor from the pockets of the laborer to your own? If you had had no laboring class, dependent entirely on its labor for the means of living, whose industry you could lay under contribution, would you ever have risen to your present wealth? Of course not. Of course, then, only a certain number of individuals of the laboring classes could, even with your talents, skill, and matchless virtues, rise as you have done. One rises from the class of proletaries only by making those he leaves behind the lever of his elevation. This, therefore, necessarily implies that there must always be a laboring class, and of course that the means, which this or that laborer uses for his individual elevation, cannot in the nature of things be used by all of his class.

But our conservative friends shift their ground, when driven to this point, and take refuge in Providence; or rather seek to make Providence the scapegoat for their social sins. They allege that Providence has ordained all these distinctions, has made some to be rich and others to be poor. It is all God's doing. That vain pretender to piety, who grows rich out of the labors of those half-starved sempstresses, and who tells the poor girl when she asks for more wages, "My dear, I give you all I can afford; I have to pay so much now for what I have done, that I can hardly live by my business, and I would throw it up, were it not a Christian duty to give employment to those who otherwise might starve or do worse," — this base hypocrite, who, as the Abbé de La Mennais[1] says, "has no name out of hell," grows rich by Divine Appointment, does he? And you accuse us of infidelity, for uttering the natural indignation of a virtuous soul at such foul blasphemy? We have looked now and then into the upper classes of society, if not often, at least often enough to see their hollow-heartedness and loathsome depravity; and we assure them, that not to us will it

---

[1] *Abbé de La Mennais:* Hughes Félicité de Lamennais (1782–1854), Catholic priest who became a socialist and staunchly defended the rights of the oppressed.

answer to preach, that they are the distinguished favorites of Heaven. The miserable vagrant, who has no lodging but the bare earth, and whom your police punishes for sleeping on the only bed he can procure, often surpasses, in a true, manly virtue, many a loud-boasting and loud-boasted pharisee, whose praises may be read in the public journals, and heard from the pulpit. No; "Go to, now, ye rich men, weep and howl for your miseries that shall come upon you. Your riches are corrupted, and your garments are moth-eaten. Your gold and silver are cankered, and the rust of them shall be a witness against you, and shall eat your flesh as it were fire. Ye have heaped up treasure for the last days, (or the last time.) Behold the hire of the laborers, who have reaped down your fields, which of you is kept back by fraud, crieth; and the cries of them that have reaped have entered into the ears of the Lord of Sabbaoth. Ye have lived in pleasure on the earth, and been wanton; ye have nourished your hearts as in a day of slaughter. Ye have condemned and killed the just; and he doth not resist you."[2]

So does an inspired Apostle address you, ye rich men; and Jesus himself tells you, that it is "easier for a camel to go through the eye of a needle, than for a rich man to enter the kingdom of heaven" and that "if ye would be perfect, ye must sell what ye have and give it to the poor, and follow him." Have ye the effrontery then to tell a man who has the New Testament before him, and who can read it, that ye are rich by the express appointment of God, as a reward for your superior capacities and virtues? Say rather through God's forbearance and long suffering, waiting to be gracious to the sinner that repents and turns from his evil ways. A terrible book for you, ye scribes and pharisees, ye rich and great of this world, is this same New Testament! "Woe unto you," it says, "for ye are like unto whited sepulchres, which indeed appear beautiful outward, but within are full of dead men's bones, and all uncleanness; because ye build the tombs of the prophets, and garnish the sepulchres of the righteous, and say, If we had been in the days of our fathers, we would not have been partakers with them in the blood of the prophets. Wherefore ye be witnesses that ye are the children of them that killed the prophets. Fill ye up then the measure of your fathers. Ye serpents, ye generation of vipers, how can ye escape the damnation of hell!" A terrible book, this New Testament! And did ye but believe it, there would be to you nothing but a fearful looking for of wrath and fiery indignation to

---

[2] James, v. 1–8, — a good lesson for the rich. [Brownson's note.]

devour you as the adversaries of God and his children. Be sure now, and call him who reads this terrible book in your hearing an infidel, as the thief, when the hue and cry is up, is loudest in calling out "stop thief," that he may turn the pursuit from himself.

"But what would you that we should do? Do we not pay the market price for labor?" Ay, the market price; but who fixes the market price; you, or the laborer? Why do you employ him? Is it not that you may grow rich? Why does he seek employment? Is it not that he may not die of hunger, he, his wife, and little ones? Which is the more urgent necessity, that of growing rich, or that of guarding against hunger? You can live, though you do not employ the laborer; but, if he find not employment, he must die. He is then at your mercy. You have over him the power of life and death. It is then of his necessity that you avail yourselves, and by taking advantage of that you reduce the price of labor to the minimum of human subsistence,[3] and then grow rich by purchasing it. Would you be willing to labor through life as he does, and live on the income he receives? Not at all. You would regard, as the greatest of calamities which could befall you, that of losing your property, and being reduced to the necessity of supporting yourselves and families on the wages you could receive as common laborers. Do you not then see that you condemn in the most positive terms the condition of the proletary, that you declare plainer than any words we can use, that you look upon that condition as a serious calamity? What right have you then to maintain that a condition, which you regard with horror so far as concerns yourselves, is good enough for your brethren? And why complain of us for calling upon you to do all in your power, so to arrange matters, that no one shall be doomed to that condition? Why do you not, as the Christian law, of doing unto others as you would be done by, commands you, set yourselves at work in earnest to remodel the institution of property, so that all shall be proprietors, and you be relieved from paying wages, and the proletary from the necessity of receiving them? This is what we would have you do; what we hold you bound to do, and which you must do, or the wrongs and sufferings of the laborer will lie at your door, and his cries will ascend to the ears of an avenging God against you, — a God who espouses the cause of the poor and needy, and has sworn to avenge them on their oppressors. This you know, if you believe at all in that Gospel, which you so wrongfully accuse us of denying.

---

[3] The only drawback on this statement is the competition among capitalists themselves. [Brownson's note.]

It is said that we have preferred the slave system to that of free labor, and in so doing have slandered the laboring classes. We understand this objection. It is a device of the Devil. No doubt, they who thrive on the labors of their brethren, would fain make the laboring classes feel that we have wronged them, and have shown contempt for them. But this device will not succeed. It is not contempt for the workingman we have shown, but sympathy with his wrongs; and if we have pointed out the evils of his condition, it has not been to exult over him, but to rebuke the upper classes for their injustice. It has been to show the hollowness of that friendship which these classes profess for him.

We have never pretended that the proletary is no advance on the slave; he is in advance of the slave; for his rights as a man are legally recognised, though not in fact enjoyed; for he is nearer the day of his complete enfranchisement, and has a greater moral force and more instruments with which to effect it. It is only on the supposition that one or the other is to be a permanent system, that we have given the preference to the slave system over that of labor at wages. We however oppose with all our might both systems. We would have neither the slave nor the proletary. We would combine labor and capital in the same individual. What we object to, is the division of society into two classes, of which one class owns the capital, and the other performs the labor. If, however, this division must always take place, we prefer the slave system which prevails at the South, to the free labor system which prevails here at the North. And we are not alone in this opinion. We have conversed with many intelligent mechanics of this city, who have resided at the South, and they all with one voice sustain the view we have here given. They all tell us that, if the present condition of the laborer here must remain forever, they should regard it as worse than that of the Southern slave.

Why is it, we would ask, that so few of the real workingmen here are abolitionists? Why do they interest themselves so little in the freedom of the negro slave? It is because they feel that they themselves are virtually slaves, while mocked with the name of freemen, and that the movements in behalf of freedom should be first directed towards their emancipation. With them we find friends and supporters in the course we take, and we become endeared to them, just in proportion as the upper classes condemn us; for they feel the truth of what we say.

We know that the law declares these workingmen equal to any other members of society and the body-politic; but what avails the declaration of the law, when those, in whose favor it is, cannot take advantage of it? What avails the theoretic recognition of their rights, when they want the power to make them recognised in fact? Nor, in truth, is the law so impartial as it would seem. The laws of this Commonwealth, as interpreted by the courts, allow, we believe, the employer to inflict corporal punishment on the employed. In the State of New York, laborers have been fined and imprisoned for refusing to work at the wages offered them; or rather, for agreeing together, not to sell their labor unless at higher price than they had hitherto been paid. Yet manufacturers, flour dealers, physicians, and lawyers, may band together on the same principle, for a similar end, form their Trades Unions, and no law is violated. A rich man may get drunk in a gentlemanly way in his own house, and be carried by his servants to his bed, and the law is silent, while the poor man, who has taken a glass too much, and is seen intoxicated, shall be fined, or imprisoned, or both. A man who belongs to the upper classes, may be an habitual drunkard, and the law shall not interfere; but if a poor man is convicted of habitual drunkenness, he shall be sent to the House of Correction. A poor man accused of a crime is convicted in advance, — for he is poor, — and is pretty sure to be punished. A rich man accused, and convicted even, is pretty sure to get clear of the punishment.

Our penal code bears with peculiar severity on the poor. In numerous cases, the punishment is fine or imprisonment. Now, in all these cases, the poor alone are really punished. The rich man, if guilty, can easily pay the fine, without feeling it. The poor can rarely pay the fine; and if they do, it is generally by surrendering all they have, and by drawing some months in advance on their labor; in which case, the punishment of a fine of twenty dollars falls as heavy on the poor man as a fine of as many hundreds would on a rich man. But generally the poor man cannot pay his fine, and consequently must be imprisoned three or six months for an offence, from which a rich man may get clear by paying five, ten, or twenty dollars out of his superfluity. This too in a land of equal laws!

Then, again, the administration of justice is so expensive, that the poor man is rarely able to resort to it. It costs too much. Is he injured in his person? He must give security for the expenses of the court, before he can have even the process for his redress commence. Are his wages withheld? It will cost him more to compel their payment, even if successful, which he can rarely count on being, than they amount to. He must pocket the insults offered him, and abandon his righteous claims, when not freely allowed. . . .

We see society as it is. We see whence it has become what it is. It is the growth of ages. No one man, and no class of men now living are wholly responsible for its vices. All classes are victims of systems and organizations, which have come down to us from the past. We know not in reality, who suffer the most by the present order of things. If we deplore the condition of the laborer, we by no means envy that of the capitalist. We know not, indeed, which most to pity. All are sufferers. The cry of distress comes to us from all classes of society. All are in a false position; all are out of their true condition, as free, high-minded, virtuous men. And instead of weeping, or criminating, we would call upon all, whether high or low, rich or poor, to look at things as they are, and set themselves at work in earnest, and in good faith, to ascertain the remedy needed, and to apply it.

The great evil of all modern society, in relation to the material order, is the separation of the capitalist from the laborer, — the division of the community into two classes, one of which owns the funds, and the other of which performs the labor, of production.

This division obtains throughout the civilized world, but is less clearly marked with us, than anywhere else. To a considerable extent, our agricultural population combines the proprietor and laborer in the same individual; and where this is not the case, the condition of the proletaries, or hired men, as we call them, presents its most favorable aspect, — at least so far as the non-slaveholding states are concerned. The hired men in the agricultural districts are hardly distinguished from their employers. They are as well dressed, as well educated, work no harder, and mingle with them very nearly on terms of equality in the general intercourse of society.

But this is not universally true, and is becoming less and less so every year. It is said that our agricultural population is rising in wealth, intelligence, and refinement, and this is unquestionably true of landed proprietors. The proportion of what we term gentlemen farmers is, no doubt, rapidly increasing. But this, while it speaks well for the proprietor, tells a mournful tale for the proletary. Where the man who owns the plough holds it, there can be no great disparity between the employer and employed; but this disparity necessarily increases just in proportion as the owner of the plough employs another to hold it. The distance between the owner of the farm, and the men who cultivate it, is, therefore, becoming every day greater and greater.

But it is in our cities, large towns, and manufacturing villages, that the condition of the laboring population is the most unfavorable. The distinction between the capitalist and the proletary, in these, is as strongly marked as it is in the old world. The distance between the wife and daughters of an Abbot Lawrence, and the poor factory girl employed in his mills, is as great as that between the wife and daughters of an English nobleman, and the daughter of one of his tenants, and the intercourse less frequent. Intermarriage between the families of the wealthy factory owners, and those of the operatives, is as much an outrage on the public sense of propriety, as it was in ancient Rome between the patricians and plebeians, — almost as much as it would be at the south between the family of a planter and that of one of his slaves.

Still, taking our country throughout, the condition of the proletary population has been, and is altogether superior here to what it is in any other part of the civilized world. We do not, however, attribute this fact to our democratic institutions, nor to the adoption of more enlightened systems of social, political, or domestic economy, than are adopted elsewhere. It is owing to causes purely accidental, and which are rapidly disappearing. The first of these accidental causes may be traced to the original equality of the first settlers of this country. But this equality no longer exists. Fortunes are said to be more unequal with us than they are in France. The second cause, and the main one, has consisted in the low price of land. The ease with which individuals have been able to procure them farms, and pass from the class of proletaries to that of proprietors, has had a constant tendency to diminish the number of proletaries, and to raise the price of labor. But this cause becomes less and less powerful. Few, comparatively speaking, of the proletaries, in any of the old states, can ever become land-owners. Land there, is already too high for that. The new lands are rapidly receding to the west, and can even now be reached only by those who have some little capital in advance. Moreover, these new lands are not inexhaustible. Fifty years to come, if emigration go on at the rate it has for fifty years past, will leave very little for the new emigrant.

The causes removed, which have hitherto favored the working-man, and lessened the distance between him and the proprietor, what is to prevent the reproduction here, in our land of boasted equality, of the order of things which now exists in the old world? As yet, that order does not exist here in all its revolting details; but who can fail to see that there is a strong tendency to it? Our economical systems are virtually those of England; our passions, our views, and feelings are similar; and what is to prevent the reproduction of the same state of things in relation to our laboring population with that which gangrenes English society? We confess, we cannot see any causes at work among us likely to prevent it.

The remedies relied on by the political reformers are free trade, and universal suffrage; by the moral reformers, universal education, and religious culture. We agree with both, and sustain them as far as they go; but they are insufficient. These measures are all good and necessary; but inadequate, unless something more radical still be adopted along with them. Alone they are mere palliatives. They may serve to conceal the sore, perhaps assuage its pain; but they cannot cure it.

Universal suffrage is little better than a mockery, where the voters are not socially equal. No matter what party you support, no matter what men you elect, property is always the basis of your governmental action. No policy has ever yet been pursued by our government, state or federal, under one party or another, notwithstanding our system of universal suffrage, which has had for its aim the elevation of man, independent of his relation as a possessor of property. . . .

The system of free trade, so far as it has as yet been advocated in this country, we approve, as a means of social amelioration; but we cannot rely on it, as alone sufficient. Because, to amount to much, the competitors must start even, and with nearly equal chances of success, which cannot be, with our present constitution of property, nor, indeed, with our present constitution of human nature. Moreover, if the system of free trade be pushed to its last results, it becomes the introduction of a system of universal competition, a system of universal strife, where each man is for himself, and no man for another. It would be a return to the pure individuality of the savage state, the abolition of all government, and the adoption, as the practical rule of conduct, of the maxim, "save who can." . . .

In universal education and religious culture, we have faith indeed; but not as final measures. Their office is to generate the moral force needed; but the generation of that force is not the reform. Mind is undoubtedly superior to matter, and all reforms must come from within; but the mental and moral reform, effected in the interior of man, will prove insufficient, unless it come out of the interior, and remodel the exterior. What we contend is not, that free trade, universal suffrage, universal education, and religious culture, are not essential, indispensable means to the social regeneration we are in pursuit of; but that, if we stop with them, and leave the material order of society untouched, they will prove inadequate. We make no war on the political reformer, nor on the moral reformer. Our plan includes all they propose, and more too. Ours includes that, without which theirs would accomplish little.

With this view of the case, it becomes necessary to seek something more ultimate, more radical than our most approved reformers have as yet ventured upon. This something we have professed to find in the abolition of hereditary property, a measure foreshadowed in the first number of this Journal, and implied, at least in our own mind, by almost every article we have ever written on the subject of social reform. We have long been thoroughly convinced that, without resorting to some such measure, it would be useless to talk of social progress, or to speak in behalf of the laborer.

The doctrine we have long labored to maintain is, that the work of this country is to emancipate labor, by raising up the laborer from a mere workman, without capital, to be a proprietor, and a workman on his own farm, or in his own shop. Those who have read our writings, or listened to our public lectures and addresses, must have perceived this. In maintaining this doctrine, we have been seconded by not a few. We have been censured for it by no party, and by no individuals, save a few who have never accepted the doctrine, that all men are born with equal rights. . . .

Equal chances imply equal starting points. Nobody, it would seem, could pretend that where the points of departure were unequal the chances could be equal. Do the young man inheriting ten thousand pounds, and the one whose inheritance is merely the gutter, start even? Have they equal chances? It may be said both are free to rise as high as they can, — one starting with ten thousand pounds in advance, and the other starting with the gutter. But it might as well be said the chances of the eldest son of the Duke of Newcastle, and those of the eldest son of one of the lowest of the Duke's tenants, are equal, since both unquestionably are free to rise as high as they can, — one starting with a dukedom in advance, and the other with nothing. But to pretend this is mere jesting.

But why stop with hereditary property? why not have hereditary magistrates, hereditary professors, hereditary priests, hereditary legislators, hereditary governors, and an hereditary president? Hereditary distinction, that is to say, distinction founded on birth, once admitted as just in principle, we see not how can you consistently stop without pushing it to its last consequences. Be this, however, as it may; if society, so far as it depends on her, — as Americans, to say the least, very generally believe, — is bound to furnish equal chances to all her members, hereditary property must unquestionably be abolished; unless, what will amount to the same thing, a plan be devised and carried into operation, by which the portion inherited by each shall be absolutely equal. . . .

But property we are told is a sacred institution. Touch it and you throw everything into confusion, cut society loose from all its old fastenings, and send us all back to the savage state, to live by plundering and devouring one another. So said the defenders of hereditary monarchy, of hereditary nobility, of an hereditary priesthood, of primogeniture and entail. Yet society survives, and, for aught we can see, looks as likely for a long life as ever it did. Now, for ourselves, we are not quite so squeamish on this subject as some others are. We believe property should be held subordinate to man, and not man to property; and therefore that it is always lawful to make such modifications of its constitution as the good of Humanity requires.

RALPH WALDO EMERSON

From "American Civilization"

Ralph Waldo Emerson (1803–1882) was one of the most important intellectual and literary influences on nineteenth-century American culture. A foundational figure in the transcendentalist movement, Emerson's lectures and essays were both controversial and popular during his lifetime. His most famous works include his book *Nature* (1836), which argues that individuals should build their own worlds based on their perceptions of reality; his lecture "The American Scholar" (1837), which calls for truly American literature and thought; and his essay "Self-Reliance" (1841), which rejects any ideal of social conformity or consistency in favor of the autonomous self. Although Emerson was sometimes criticized by his contemporaries for being too abstract and insufficiently political, he was politically engaged, especially later in life. In this essay, which is part of a lecture he delivered in the presence of President Abraham Lincoln in 1862 and published in *Society and Solitude* (1870), Emerson praises labor and criticizes those who, by "stealing" the labor of others, refrain from working and declare labor disgraceful. He also compares slavery and the treatment of the working class, arguing that if the injustices of both are not eliminated, class war may result.

The text is from *Miscellanies* (Boston: Houghton, 1884).

Use, labor of each for all, is the health and virtue of all beings. *Ich dien*, I serve, is a truly royal motto. And it is the mark of nobleness to volunteer the lowest service, the greatest spirit only attaining to humility. Nay, God is God because he is the servant of all. Well, now here comes this conspiracy of slavery, — they call it an institution, I call it a destitution, — this stealing of men and setting them to work, stealing their labor, and the thief sitting idle himself; and for two or three ages it has lasted, and has yielded a certain quantity of rice, cotton and sugar. And, standing on this doleful experience, these people have endeavored to reverse the natural sentiments of mankind, and to pronouce labor disgraceful, and the well-being of a man to consist in eating the fruit of other men's labor. Labor: a man coins himself into his labor; turns his day, his strength, his thought, his affection into some product which remains as the visible sign of his power; and to protect that, to secure that to him, to secure his past self to his future self, is the object of all government. There is no interest in any country so imperative as that of labor; it covers all, and constitutions and governments exist for that, — to protect and insure it to the laborer. All honest men are daily striving to earn their bread by their industry. And who is this who tosses his empty head at this blessing in disguise, the constitution of human nature, and calls labor vile, and insults the faithful workman at his daily toil? I see for such madness no hellebore,[1] — for such calamity no solution but servile war and the Africanization of the country that permits it.

[1] *hellebore:* Medicinal herb.

HENRY WARD BEECHER

"Practical Hints"

Henry Ward Beecher (1813–1887) was a popular and controversial clergyman, author, and lecturer. Brother of Harriet Beecher Stowe (author of *Uncle Tom's Cabin*), he was strongly opposed to slavery and favored women's suffrage. His renowned sermons at Plymouth Church in

Boston reflected the philosophical influence of Ralph Waldo Emerson.
Lectures to Young Men (New York: Ford, 1873), first published as *Seven
Lectures to Young Men* (1844), was his most popular work. These essays
were addressed to clerks, mechanics, and other members of the lower —
but not lowest — classes. In "Practical Hints," excerpted here from the
1873 edition of the *Lectures*, Beecher speaks in favor of education for all
people, especially the working classes, for whom education has often
been considered unimportant. Note that Beecher describes a "hunger"
for knowledge and beauty that accords with the hunger apparent in
Hugh Wolfe's korl woman sculpture.

I pass, next, to speak of the care and culture of your minds; and
this part of my discourse relates especially to the young who are
under employers, and are learning occupations that are not themselves directly intellectual. It is not a small thing for a man to be able
to make his hands light by supplementing them with his head. The
advantage which intelligence gives a man is very great. It oftentimes
increases one's mere physical ability full one half. Active thought, or
quickness in the use of the mind, is very important in teaching us how
to use our hands rightly in every possible relation and situation in
life. The use of the head abridges the labor of the hands. There is no
drudgery, there is no mechanical routine, there is no minuteness of
function, that is not advantaged by education. If a man has nothing
to do but to turn a grindstone, he had better be educated; if a man
has nothing to do but to stick pins on a paper, he had better be educated; if he has to sweep the streets, he had better be educated. It
makes no difference what you do, you will do it better if you are educated. An intelligent man knows how to bring knowledge to bear
upon whatever he has to do. It is a mistake to suppose that a stupid
man makes a better laborer than one who is intelligent. If I wanted a
man to drain my farm, or merely to throw the dirt out from a ditch, I
would not get a stupid drudge if I could help it. In times when armies
have to pass through great hardships, it is the stupid soldiers that
break down quickest; while the men of intelligence, who have mental
resources, hold out longest. It is a common saying that blood will always tell in horses: I know that intelligence will tell in men.

Whatever your occupation may be, it is worth your while to be a
man of thought and intellectual resources. It is worth your while to
be educated thoroughly for any business. If you are a mechanic or

tradesman, education is good enough for you, and you are good enough for it. Sometimes wonder is expressed that a man who has been through college, and who is therefore supposed to be educated, should bury himself in business. But why should he not? Has not a merchant a right to be an educated man? Do you suppose a man has no right to an education unless he is going to be a doctor, a minister, a lawyer, or some kind of a public man? I affirm the right of every man in the community to an education. A man should educate himself for his own sake, even if his education should benefit no one else in the world. Every man's education does, however, benefit others besides himself. There is no calling, except that of slave-catching, for Christian governments, that is not made better by brains. No matter what a man's work is, he is a better man for having had a thorough mind-drilling. If you are to be a farmer, go to college or to the academy, first. If you are to be a mechanic, and you have an opportunity of getting an education, get that first. If you mean to follow the lowest calling, — one of those callings termed "menial," — do not be ignorant; have knowledge. A man can do without luxuries and wealth and public honors, but not without knowledge. Poverty is not disreputable, but ignorance is.

One of the things which our age and which this land has to develop, is the compatibility of manual labor with real refinement and education. This is to be one of the problems of the age. We must show that knowledge is not the monopoly of professions, not the privilege of wealth, not the prerogative of leisure, but that knowledge and refinement belong to hard-working men as much as to any other class of men. And I hope to see the day when there will be educated day-laborers, educated mechanics, refined and educated farmers and ship-masters; for we must carry out into practice our theory of men's equality, and of common worth in matters of education. We must endeavor to inspire every calling in life with an honest ambition for intelligence. There is no calling that will not be lifted up by it. Whatever may be your business, then, make it a point to get from it, or in spite of it, a good education.

Never whine over what you may suppose to be the loss of early opportunities. A great many men have good early opportunities who never improve them; and many have lost their early opportunities without losing much. Every man may educate himself that wishes to. It is the will that makes the way. Many a slave that wanted knowledge has listened while his master's children were saying their letters and putting them together to form easy words, and thus caught the first elements of spelling; and then, lying flat on his belly before the raked-up coals and embers, with a stolen book, has learned to read and write. If a man has such a thirst for knowledge as that, I do not care where you put him, he will become an educated man.

Hugh Miller,[1] the quarry man, became one of the most learned men in natural science in the Old World. Roger Sherman[2] came up from a shoemaker's bench. A blacksmith may become a universal linguist. You can educate yourself. Where there is a will there is a way; and in almost every business of life there is much which demands reading, study, and thinking. Every mechanic should make himself a respectable mathematician. He ought to understand the principles of his business; and if, when he has been engaged in it five or ten years, he has never had the interest to search out such of those principles as are within his reach, it is a sign that he is without laudable ambition. Every man who has to do with construction should have a knowledge of the philosophy of mechanics. . . .

Life itself, moreover, is an academy. There is something to be learned from everybody, in every place, about everything. A man that has eyes and ears, and uses them, can go nowhere without finding himself a pupil and everybody a teacher. Conceit it is, a contemptible satisfaction with your present state, a complacent pride, that stagnates all your faculties, and leads you up and down the street, among all sorts of men, collecting nothing. Every ride in a car, every walk in the street, every sail in a boat, every visit to the store, the shop, or the dwelling, should make you a richer man in knowledge. . . .

A history of the institutions of the country, its laws and its polity; a history of the principal nations of the world, their manners and their customs; a history of the physical globe, its geology, its geography, and its natural productions; and some knowledge of the arts and of the fine arts, — may be had by every laboring man, every clerk, and every woman. There is no excuse for you if you do not understand these things. You do not need to go to school, to a college, or to an academy to learn them. They are published in books, and the books are accessible. Somebody has got them. You need not advertise in the newspapers, asking for a man who will lend you an encyclopædia. You can learn something everywhere. Everybody can tell you something. Ask for knowledge, if you desire it. If you were hungry, I

---

[1] *Hugh Miller:* (1802–1856) Scottish geologist and man of letters.
[2] *Roger Sherman:* (1721–1793) American statesman and patriot who took a prominent part in the debates on the Constitution.

do not believe you would starve. I think you would ask for food before you would die. I think you would work for bread before you would perish. And you ought to be ten times as hungry for knowledge as for food for the body. . . .

Why should you, an apprentice or a clerk or a day-workman, not wish to see galleries of pictures as much as I or any other man? I see that there is a great deal of enthusiasm about Church's picture,[3] and I do not wonder at it. I am proud of the picture and of the man who painted it. But I go among some classes of people, and hear not one word about it. Now, why should not a blacksmith, as well as any other man, say, "I have heard that there is a splendid picture on exhibition up town, and I am going to see it"? Why should not a man who wields the broad-axe say, "I am going to see it"? Then there is the Academy of Design. I look, and those I see there are principally richly dressed people. I am not sorry to see persons in silk and satin and broadcloth there; but I am sorry not to see there more clerks and workingmen. I am astonished that I do not see more there from among the fifty thousand clerks and the two hundred and fifty thousand laboring men in New York, when I remember that fifty cents will give a person permission to go there as much as he pleases during a whole season. The trouble is, they are hungry in the stomach and not in the head. People should be hungry with the eye and the ear as well as with the mouth. If all a man's necessaries of life go in at the port-hole of the stomach, it is a bad sign. A man's intelligence should be regarded by him as of more importance than the gratification of his physical desires. I long to see my countrymen universally intelligent. I long to see those in the lower walks of life building themselves up in all true appetites and relishes and tastes. I love to see them aspiring after knowledge and refinement, and employing the means required to obtain them. In this way, should you never become rich, you can afford to be poor. A woman who does not know anything cannot afford to live in an attic, and sew for five cents a shirt, half so well as one who is intelligent. A woman who has a soul that can appreciate God's blessings, that can read his secrets in nature, that can see his love for his creatures displayed in all his works, — she, if anybody, can bear that hardship. I pity the drudge that has no intelligence or refinement. If I see poor people that have cultivated minds, I

---

[3] *Church's picture:* American artist Frederick Edwin Church (1826–1900) painted large landscapes of New England, South America, and the Middle East; his works were exhibited in U.S. cities in the 1840s.

say, "Thank God, they have so much, at least." There are none that stand hardship so well as those who are cultivated. If, having secured intelligence and refinement, you ever do become rich, you will not be dependent upon your wealth for happiness, and therefore you will not be in danger of the vulgar ostentation of crude riches.

There are two things that delight my very soul. First, I delight to see a hard-working and honest laboring man, especially if he has some dirty calling like that, for instance, of a butcher, a tallow-chandler, or a dealer in fish or oil, — I delight to see such a man get rich, by fair and open methods, and then go and build him a house in the best neighborhood in the place, and build it so that everybody says, "He has got a fine house, and it is in good taste too." It does me good, it makes me fat to the very marrow, to see him do that. And, next, when he prospers, I delight to see him, after he has built his house so as to adapt it to all the purposes of a household, employ his wealth with such judicious taste, and manifest such an appreciation of things fine and beautiful, that it shall say to the world, with silent words louder than any vocalization, "A man may be a workingman and follow a menial calling, and yet carry within him a noble soul and have a cultivated and refined nature." I like to see men that have been chrysalids break their covering and come out with all the beautiful colors of the butterfly. . . .

In the last place, I must not fail to urge upon every one the importance of personal religion in his toil and strife of life. I urge it upon every man as a duty which he owes to God. I urge it upon every man as a joy and comfort which he owes to himself. The sweetest life that a man can live is that which is keyed to love toward God and love toward man. . . .

CHARLES LORING BRACE

From The Dangerous Classes of New York

In the following excerpts from *The Dangerous Classes of New York, and Twenty Years' Work Among Them* (New York: Wynkoop, 1872), Charles Loring Brace (1826–1890) discusses the successes and failures of reform movements in which he has participated. As the principal founder in 1853 of the Children's Aid Society of New York, Brace was immersed in the reform culture. The experiences he relates are typical of many nineteenth-century reformers. He and the other members of his charity organization emphasized Christianity, self-control, and the removal of people from negative influences. Brace maintains an optimistic tone, for even in the face of the failures he describes, he believes that the work of the reformers is necessary for secular and spiritual salvation.

Reform among the Rowdies — Free Reading-rooms

At first sight, it would seem very obvious that a place of mental improvement and social resort, with agreeable surroundings, offered gratuitously to the laboring-people, would be eagerly frequented. On its face, the "FREE READING-ROOM" appears a most natural, feasible method of applying the great lever of sociality (without temptations) to lifting up the poorer classes. The working-man and the street-boy get here what they so much desire, a pleasant place, warmed and lighted, for meeting their companions, for talking, playing innocent games, or reading the papers; they get it, too, for nothing. When we remember how these people live, in what crowded and slatternly rooms, or damp cellars, or close attics, some even having no home at all, and that their only social resort is the grog-shop, we might suppose that they would jump at the chance of a pleasant and Free Saloon and Reading-room. But this is by no means the case. This instrument of improvement requires peculiar management to be successful. Our own experience is instructive.

The writer of this had had the Reading-room "on the brain" for many years, when, at length, on talking over the subject with a gentleman in the eastern part of the city — one whose name has since been a tower of strength to this whole movement — he consented to father the enterprise, and be the treasurer — an office in young charities, be it remembered, no sinecure

We opened, accordingly, near the Novelty Iron-Works, under the best auspices,

The Eleventh Ward Free Reading-room.

The rooms were spacious and pleasant, furnished with a plenty of papers and pamphlets, and, to add to the attractions and help pay expenses, the superintendent was to sell coffee and simple refreshments. Our theory was, that coffee would compete with liquor as a stimulus, and that the profits of the sale would pay most of the running cost. We were right among a crowded working population, and everything promised success.

At first there were considerable numbers of laboring-men present every day and evening; but, to our dismay, they began to fall off. We tried another superintendent; still the working-man preferred his "dreary rooms," or the ruinous liquor-shops, to our pleasant Reading-room. The coffee did not suit him; the refreshments were not to his taste; he would not read, because he thought he ought to call for something to eat or drink if he did; and so at length he dropped off. Finally, the attendance became so thin and the expenses were accumulating to such a degree, that we closed the room, and our magnanimous treasurer footed the bills. This failure discouraged us for some years, but the idea seemed to me sound, and I was resolved to try it once more under better circumstances.

In looking about for some specially-adapted instrument for influencing "the dangerous classes," I chanced, just after the remarkable religious "Revival" of 1858,[1] on a singular character,

A Reformed Pugilist.

This was a reformed or converted prize-fighter, named Orville (and nicknamed "Awful") Gardner. He was a broad-shouldered, burly individual, with a tremendous neck, and an arm as thick as a moderate-sized man's leg. His career had been notorious and infamous in the extreme, he having been one of the roughs employed by politicians, and engaged in rows and fights without number, figuring several times in the prize-ring, and once having bitten off a man's nose!

Yet the man must have been less brutal than his life would show. He was a person evidently of volcanic emotions and great capacity of affection. I was curious about his case, and watched it closely for some years, as showing what is so often disputed in modern times — the reforming power of Christianity on the most abandoned characters.

The point through which his brutalized nature had been touched, had been evidently his affection for an only child — a little boy. He described to me once, in very simple, touching language, his affection and love for this child; how he dressed him in the best, and did all he could for him, but always keeping him away from all knowledge of

---

[1] *"Revival" of 1858:* A religious revival that began in New York City and Philadelphia and swept across America; it was characterized by daily prayer meetings and huge numbers of conversions.

his own dissipation. One day he was off on some devilish errand among the immigrants on Staten Island, when he saw a boat approaching quickly with one of his "pals." The man rowed up near him, and stopped and looked at him "very queer," and didn't say anything.

"What the devil are you looking at me in that way for?" said Gardner.

"Your boy is drownded!" replied the other.

Gardner says he fell back in the boat, as if you'd hit him right straight from the shoulder behind the ear, and did not know anything for a long time. When he recovered, he kept himself drunk for three weeks, and smashed a number of policemen, and was "put up," just so as to forget the bright little fellow who had been the pride of his heart.

This great loss, however, must have opened his nature to other influences. When the deep religious sympathy pervaded the community, there came over him suddenly one of those Revelations which, in some form or other, visit most human beings at least once in their lives. They are almost too deep and intricate to be described in these pages. The human soul sees itself, for the first time, as reflected in the mirror of divine purity. It has for the moment a conception of what CHRIST is, and what Love means. Singularly enough, the thought and sentiment which took possession of this ruffian and debauchee and prize-fighter, and made him as one just cured of leprosy, was the Platonic conception of Love, and that embodied in the ideal form of Christianity. Under it he became as a little child; he abandoned his vices, gave up his associates, and resolved to consecrate his life to humanity and the service of Him to whom he owed so much. The spirit, when I first met him, with which he used to encounter his old companions must have been something like that of the early Christian converts.

Thus, an old boon companion meets him in the street: "Why, Orful, what the h — ll's this about your bein' converted?"

And the other turns to him with such pent-up feeling bursting forth, telling him of the new things that have come to him, that the "rough" is quite melted, and begins a better course of life.

Again, he is going down a narrow street, when he suddenly sees coming up a bitter enemy. His old fire flames up, but he quenches it, walks to the other, and, with the tears streaming down his cheeks, he takes him by the hand and tells him "the old story" which is always new, and the two ruffians forget their feuds and are friends.

Could the old Greek philosopher[2] have seen this imbruted athlete, so mysteriously and suddenly fired with the ideal of Love till his past crimes seemed melted in the heat of this great sentiment, and his rough nature appeared transformed, he would have rejoiced in beholding at length the living embodiment of an ideal theory for so many ages held but as the dream of a poetic philosopher.

Gardner was only a modern and striking instance of the natural and eternal power of Christianity.

We resolved to put him where he could reach the class s from which he had come. With considerable exertion the necessary sums were raised to open a "Coffee and Reading Room" in the worst district of the city — the Fourth Ward. Great numbers of papers and publications were furnished gratuitously by that body who have always been so generous to this enterprise — the conductors of the press of the city. A bar for coffee and cheap refreshments was established, and Gardner was put at the head of the whole as superintendent.

The Drunkards' Club

The opening is thus described in our Journal: —

"We must confess, as one of the managers of that institution, we felt particularly nervous about that opening meeting.

"Messrs Beecher and Cochrane[3] and other eminent speakers had been invited to speak, and the Mayor was to preside. It was certainly an act of some self-denial to leave their country-seats or cool rooms, and spend a hot summer evening in talking to Fourth-ward rowdies. To requite this with any sort of 'accident' should have been very awkward. Where would we of the committee have hid our heads if our friends the 'roughs' had thought best to have a little bit of a shindy, and had knocked Brother Beecher's hat in, and had tossed the Hon. John Cochrane out of the window, or rolled the Mayor down-stairs? We confess all such possible eventualities did present themselves, and we imagined the sturdy form of our eminent clerical friend breasting the opposing waves of rowdies, and showing himself as skillful in demolishing corporeal enemies as he is in overthrowing spiritual. We were comforted in spirit, however, by remembering that the saint at the head of our establishment — the renowned Gardner — would

[2] *the old Greek philosopher:* Plato (427?–347? B.C.).
[3] *Messrs Beecher and Cochrane:* Henry Ward Beecher (1813–1887), clergyman and lecturer; John Cochrane (1813–1898), American general from New York.

now easily take a place in the church militant, and perhaps not object to a new exercise of muscle in a good cause.

      *   *   *   *   *   *   *   *

"After other addresses, Gardner — 'Awful Gardner' — was called for. He came forward — and a great trial it must have been to have faced that crowd, where there were hundreds who had once been with him in all kinds of debaucheries and deviltries — men who had drunk and fought and gambled and acted the rowdy with him — men very quick to detect any trace of vanity or cant in him. He spoke very simply and humbly; said that he had more solid peace and comfort in one month now than he had in years once; spoke of his 'black life,' his sins and disgrace, and then of his most cordial desire to welcome all his old companions there. In the midst of these remarks there seemed to come up before him suddenly a memory of Him who had saved him, his eyes filled with tears, and, with a manly and deep feeling that swept right through the wild audience, he made his acknowledgment to 'Him who sticketh closer than a brother — even the Lord Jesus Christ.'

"No sermon could have been half so effective as these stammering ungrammatical, but manly remarks."

Our Reading-room under this guidance became soon a very popular resort; in fact, it deserved the nickname one gentleman gave it, "The Drunkards' Club." The marked, simple, and genuine reform in a man of such habits as this pugilist, attracted numbers of that large class of young men who are always trying to break from the tyranny of evil habits and vices. The rooms used to be thronged with reformed or reforming young men. The great difficulty with a man under vices is to make him believe that change for him is possible. The sight of Gardner always demonstrated this possibility. Those men who are sunk in such courses cannot get rid of them gradually, and nothing can arouse them and break the iron rule of habits but the most tremendous truths.

"Awful Gardner" had but one theory of reform — absolute and immediate change, in view of the love of Christ, and of a deserved and certain damnation.

The men to whom he spoke needed no soft words; they knew they were "in hell" now; some of them could sometimes for a moment realize what such a character as Christ was, and bow before it in unspeakable humility. No one whom I have ever seen could so influence the "roughs" of this city. He ought to have been kept as a missionary to the rowdies.

I extract from our Journal: —

"The moral success of the room has been all that we could have desired. Hundreds of young men have come there continually to read or chat with their friends — many of them even who had habitually frequented the liquor-saloons, and many persons with literally no homes. The place, too, has become a kind of central point for all those who have become more or less addicted to excessive drinking, and who are desirous of escaping from the habit.

"There are days when the spectacle presented there is a most affecting one; the room filled with young men, each of whom has a history of sorrow or degradation — broken-down gentlemen, ruined merchants, penniless clerks, homeless laboring-men and printers (for somehow this most intelligent profession seems to contain a large number of cases who have been ruined by drunkenness), and outcast men of no assignable occupation. These have been attracted in part by the cheerfulness of the room and the chances for reading, and in part by Gardner's influence, who has labored indefatigably in behalf of these poor wretches. Under the influences of the Room, incredible as it may seem, over *seven hundred* of these men have been started in sober courses and provided with honest employments, and many of them have become hopefully religious. It is believed that the whole quarter has been improved by the opening of this agreeable and temperate place of resort."

But, alas! even with a man so truly repentant and reformed, Nature does not let him off so easily. He had to bear in his body the fruits of his vices. His nervous system began to give way under the fearful strain both of his sins and his reform. He found it necessary to leave this post of work and retire to a quiet place in New Jersey, where he has since passed a calm and virtuous life, working, I suppose, at his trade, and, so far as I know, he has never been false to the great truths which once inspired him. With his departure, however, we thought it best to close the Reading-room, especially as we could not realize our hope of making it self-supporting. So ended the second of our experiments at "virtuous amusements."

I now resolved to try the experiment, without any expectation of sustaining the room with sales of refreshments. The working classes seem to be utterly indifferent to such attractions. They probably cannot compete a moment with those of the liquor-shops. With the aid of friends, who are always ready in this city to liberally support rational experiments of philanthropy, we have since then opened various Free Reading-rooms in different quarters of the city.

One of the most successful was carried on by Mr. Macy at Cottage Place for his "lambs."

Here sufficient books and papers were supplied by friends, little temperance and other societies were formed, the room was pleasant and cozy, and, above all, Mr. Macy presided or infused into it his spirit. The "lambs" were occasionally obstreperous and given to smashing windows, but to this Mr. M. was sufficiently accustomed, and in time the wild young barbarians began to feel the influences thrown around the place, until now one may see of a winter evening eighty or a hundred lads and young men quietly reading, or playing backgammon or checkers.

The room answers exactly its object as a place of innocent amusement and improvement, competing with the liquor-saloons. The citizens of the neighborhood have testified to its excellent moral influences on the young men.

A similar room was opened in the First Ward by the kind aid of the late Mr. J. Couper Lord, and the good influences of the place have been much increased by the exertions of Mr. D. E. Hawley and a committee of gentlemen.

There are other Reading-rooms connected with the Boys' Lodging-houses. Most of them are doing an invaluable work; the First ward room especially being a centre for cricket-clubs and various social re-unions of the laboring classes, and undoubtedly saving great numbers of young men from the most dangerous temptations. Mr. Hawley has inaugurated here also a very useful course of popular lectures to the laboring people.

This Reading-room is crowded with young men every night, of the class who should be reached, and who would otherwise spend their leisure hours at the liquor-saloons. Many of them have spoken with much gratitude of the benefit the place has been to them.

The Reading-rooms connected with Boys' Lodging-houses, though sometimes doing well, are not uniformly successful, perhaps from the fact that working-men do not like to be associated with homeless boys.

Besides those connected with the Children's Aid Society, the City Mission and various churches have founded others, so that now the Free Reading-room is recognized as one of the means for improving the "dangerous classes," as much as the Sunday School, Chapel, or Mission.

The true theory of the formation of the Reading-room is undoubtedly the inducing the laboring class to engage in the matter themselves, and then to assist them in meeting the expenses. But the lowest poor and the young men who frequent the grog-shops are so indifferent to mental improvement, and so seldom associate themselves for any virtuous object, that it is extremely difficult to induce them to combine for this.

Moreover, as they rise in the social scale, they find organizations ready to hand, like the "Cooper Union,"[4] where Reading-rooms and Libraries are provided gratuitously. For the present, the Reading-room may be looked upon, like the Public School, as a means of improvement offered by society, in its own interest, to all.

Homeless Girls

It was a fortunate event for our charity which led, in 1861, a certain New York merchant to accept the position of President of our Society.

Mr. William A. Booth had the rare combination of qualities which form a thorough presiding officer, and at the same time he was inspired by a spirit of consecration to what he believed his Master's service, rarely seen among men. His faculty of "rolling off" business, of keeping his assembly or board on the points before them — for even business men have sometimes the female tendency of rather wide-reaching discussions and conversations — his wonderful clearness of comprehension, and a judicial faculty which nearly always enabled him to balance with remarkable fairness both sides of a question, made him beyond comparison the best presiding officer for a business-board I have ever seen. With him, we always had short and very full sessions, and reached our points rapidly and efficiently. He had, too, the capacity, rare among men of organizing brains, of accepting a rejection or rebuff to any proposition he may have made (though this happened seldom) with perfect good humor. Perhaps more than with his public services in our Board, I was struck with his private career. Hour after hour in his little office, I have seen different committees and officials of numerous societies, charities, and financial associations come to him with their knotty points, and watched with admiration as he disentangled each question, seeming always to strike upon the course at once wise and just. A very small portion of his busy time was then given to his own interests, though he had been singularly successful in his private affairs. He seemed to me to carry out wonderfully the Christian ideal in practical life in a busy city; liv-

---

[4] *"Cooper Union"*: Tuition-free undergraduate college in New York City endowed in 1859 by Peter Cooper, a wealthy merchant and philanthropist.

ing day after day " for others," and to do the will of Him whom he followed.

In our first labors together, I feared that, owing to his stricter school of Presbyterian theology, we might not agree in some of our aims and plans; but the practical test of true benefit to these unfortunate children soon brought our theoretic views to a harmony in religious practice; and as we both held that the first and best of all truths to an outcast boy is the belief and love of Christ as a friend and Saviour, we agreed on the substantial matter. I came, year by year, greatly to value his judgment and his clear insight as to the *via media.*

Both with him and our Treasurer, Mr. Williams, the services of love rendered so many years to this cause of humanity, could not, as mere labor, have been purchased with very lucrative salaries.

Mr. Booth's wise policy with the Society was to encourage whatever would give it a more permanent foot-hold in the city, and, in this view, to stimulate especially the founding of our Lodging-houses by means of "funds," or by purchasing buildings.

How this plan succeeded, I shall detail hereafter.

At this present stage in our history, his attention was especially fixed on the miserable condition of the young street-girls, and he suggested to me what I had long been hoping for, the formation of a Lodging-house for them, corresponding to that which had been so successful with the newsboys.

As a preparatory step, I consulted carefully the police. They were sufficiently definite as to the evil, but not very hopeful as to the cure.

The Street-girls

I can truly say that no class we have ever labored for seemed to combine so many elements of human misfortune and to present so many discouraging features as this. They form, indeed, a class by themselves.

Their histories are as various as are the different lots of the inhabitants of a populous town. Some have come from the country, from kind and respectable homes, to seek work in the city; here they gradually consume their scanty means, and are driven from one refuge to another, till they stand on the street, with the gayly-lighted house of vice and the gloomy police-station to choose between. Others have sought amusement in the town, and have been finally induced to enter some house of bad character as a boarding-house, and have been thus entrapped; and finally, in despair, and cursed with disease, they break loose, and take shelter even in the prison-cell, if necessary. Others still have abandoned an ill-tempered step-mother or father, and rushed out on the streets to find a refuge, or get employment anywhere.

Drunkenness has darkened the childhood of some, and made home a hideous place, till they have been glad to sleep in the crowded cellar or the bare attic of some thronged "tenement," and then go forth to pick up a living as they could in the great metropolis. Some are orphans, some have parents whom they detest, some are children of misfortune, and others of vice; some are foreigners, some native. They come from the north and the south, the east and the west; all races and countries are represented among them. They are not habitually vicious, or they would not be on the streets. They are unlucky, unfortunate, getting a situation only to lose it, and finding a home, to be soon driven from it. Their habits are irregular, they do not like steady labor, they have learned nothing well, they have no discipline, their clothes are neglected, they have no appreciation of what neatness is, yet if they earn a few shillings extra, they are sure to spend them on some foolish gewgaw. Many of them are pretty and bright, with apparently fine capacities, but inheriting an unusual quantity of the human tendencies to evil. They are incessantly deceived and betrayed, and they as constantly deceive others. Their cunning in concealing their indulgences or vices surpasses all conception. Untruth seems often more familiar to them than truth. Their worst quality is their superficiality. There is no depth either to their virtues or vices. They sin, and immediately repent with alacrity; they live virtuously for years, and a straw seems suddenly to turn them. They weep at the presentation of the divine character in Christ, and pray with fervency; and, the very next day, may ruin their virtue or steal their neighbor's garment, or take to drinking, or set a whole block in ferment with some biting scandal. They seem to be children, but with woman's passion, and woman's jealousy and scathing tongue. They trust a superior as a child; they neglect themselves, and injure body and mind as a child might; they have a child's generosity, and occasional freshness of impulse and desire of purity; but their passions sweep over them with the force of maturity, and their temper, and power of setting persons by the ears, and backbiting, and occasional intensity of hate, belong to a later period of life. Not unfrequently, when real danger or severe sickness arouses them, they show the wonderful qualities of womanhood in a power of sacrifice which utterly forgets self, and a love which shines brightly, even through the shadow of death.

But their combination of childishness and undisciplined maturity is an extremely difficult one to manage practically, and exposes them to endless sufferings and dangers. Their condition fifteen years ago seemed a thoroughly hopeless one.

There was then, if we mistake not, but a single refuge in the whole city, where these unfortunate creatures could take shelter, and that was Mr. Pease's Five Points[5] Mission, which contained so many women who had been long in vicious course, as to make it unsuitable for those who were just on the dividing line.

Our plan for their relief took the shape of

The Girls' Lodging-house.

It is no exaggeration to say that this instrument of charity and reform has cost us more trouble than all our enterprises together.

The simple purpose and plan of it was, like that of our other efforts, to reform habits and character through material and moral appliances, and subsequently through an entire change of circumstances, and at the same time to relieve suffering and misfortune.

We opened first a shelter, where any drifting, friendless girl could go for a night's lodging. If she had means, she was to pay a trifling sum — five or six cents; if not, she aided in the labor of the house, and thus in part defrayed the expense of her board. Agents were sent out on the docks and among the slums of the city to pick up the wayfarers; notices were posted in the station-houses, and near the ferries and railroads depots, and even advertisements put into the cheap papers. We made a business of scattering the news of this charity wherever there were forlorn girls seeking for home or protection, or street-wandering young women who had no place to lay their heads.

We hoped to reach down the hand of welcome to the darkest dens of the city, and call back to virtue some poor, unbefriended creature, who was trembling on the very line between purity and vice. Our charity seemed to stand by the ferries, the docks, the police-stations, and prisons, and open a door of kindness and virtue to these hard-driven, tired wanderers on the ways of life. Our design was that no young girl, suddenly cast out on the streets of a great city, should be without a shelter and a place where good influences could surround her. We opened a House for the houseless; an abode of Christian sympathy for the utterly unbefriended and misguided; a place of work for the idle and unthrifty.

---

[5] *Five Points:* Notorious slum in New York City.

The plan seemed at once to reach its object: the doors opened on a forlorn procession of unfortunates. Girls broke out of houses of vice, where they had been entrapped, leaving every article of dress, except what they wore, behind them; the police brought wretched young wanderers, who had slept on the station-floors; the daughters of decent country-people, who had come to the town for amusement or employment, and, losing or wasting their means, had walked the streets all the night long, applied for shelter; orphans selling flowers, or peddling about the theatres; the children of drunkards; the unhappy daughters of families where quarreling and abuse were the rule; girls who had run away; girls who had been driven away; girls who sought a respite in intervals of vice, — all this most unfortunate throng began to beset the doors of the "Girls' Lodging-house."

We had indeed reached the class intended, but now our difficulties only began.

It would not do to turn our Lodging-house into a Reformatory for Magdalens, nor to make it into a convenient resting-place for those who lived on the wages of lust. To keep a house for reforming young women of bad character would only pervert those of good, and shut out the decent and honest poor. We must draw a line; but where? We attempted to receive only those of apparent honesty and virtue, and to exclude those who were too mature; keeping, if possible, below the age of eighteen years. We sought to shut out the professional "street-walkers." This at once involved us in endless difficulties. Sweet young maidens, whom we guilelessly admitted, and who gave most touching stories of early bereavement and present loneliness, and whose voices arose in moving hymns of penitence, and whose bright eyes filled with tears under the Sunday exhortation, turned out perhaps the most skillful and thorough-going deceivers, plying their bad trade in the day, and filling the minds of their comrades with all sorts of wickedness in the evening. We came to the conviction that these girls would deceive the very elect. Then some "erring child of poverty," as the reporters called her, would apply at a late hour at the door, after an unsuccessful evening, her breath showing her habit, and be refused, and go to the station-house, and in the morning a fearful narrative would appear in some paper, of the shameful hypocrisy and cruel machinery of charitable institutions.

Or, perhaps, she would be admitted, and cover the house with disgrace by her conduct in the night. One wayfarer, thus received, scattered a contagious disease, which emptied the whole house, and carried off the housekeeper and several lodgers. Another, in the night dropped her newly-born dead babe into the vault.

The rule, too, of excluding all over eighteen years of age caused great discontent with the poor, and with certain portions of the public. And yet, as rigidly as humanity would allow, we must follow our plan of benefiting children and youth.

It soon turned out, however, that the young street-children who were engaged in street-trades, had some relative to whom their labor was of profit, so that they gradually drifted back to their cellars and attics, and only occasionally took a night's lodging when out late near the theatre. Those who were the greatest frequenters of the House proved to be the young girls between fourteen and eighteen.

And a more difficult class than these to manage, no philanthropic mortal ever came in contact with. The most had a constitutional objection to work; they had learned to do nothing well, and therefore got but little wages anywhere; they were shockingly careless, both of their persons and their clothing; and, worse than all, they showed a cunning and skill of deceit and a capacity of scandal, and of setting the family by the ears in petty quarrels and jealousies, which might have discouraged the most sanguine reformer.

The matron, Mrs. Trott, who had especially to struggle with these evils, had received a fitting preparatory training: she had taught in the "Five Points." She was a thorough disciplinarian; believed in work, and was animated by the highest Christian earnestness.

As years passed by, the only defect that appeared in her was, perhaps, what was perfectly natural in such circumstances. The sins of the world, and the calamities of the poor, began to weigh on her mind, until its spring was fairly bent. Society seemed to her diseased with the sin against purity. The outcast daughters of the poor had no chance in this hard world. All the circumstances of life were against the friendless girl. Often, after most self-denying, and, to other minds, successful efforts to benefit these poor creatures, some enthusiastic spectator would say, "How much good you are doing!" "Well," she would say, with a sigh, "I sometimes hope so!"

Once, I asked her if she could not write a cheerful report for our trustees, giving some of the many encouraging facts she knew.

To my dismay, when the document appeared, the first two pages were devoted to a melancholy recollection of the horrible typhus which had once desolated the household! I think, finally, her mind took almost a sad pleasure in dwelling on the woes and miseries of humanity. Still, even with this constitutional weight on her, she did her work for those unfortunate girls faithfully and devotedly.

The great danger and temptation of such establishments, as I have always found, are in the desire of keeping the inmates, and showing to the public your "reforms." My instruction always was, that the "Girls' Lodging-house" was not to be a "Home." We did not want to make an asylum of it. We hoped to begin the work of improvement with these young girls, and then leave them to the natural agencies of society. To teach them to work, to be clean, and to understand the virtues of order and punctuality; to lay the foundations of a housekeeper or servant; to bring the influences of discipline, of kindness, and religion to bear on these wild and ungoverned creatures — these were to be the great objects of the "Lodging-house;" then some good home or respectable family were to do the rest. We were to keep lodgers a little while only, and then to pass them along to situations or places of work.

The struggles of Mr. and Mrs. Trott, the superintendent and matron, against these discouraging evils in the condition and character of this class, would make a history in itself. They set themselves to work upon details, with an abounding patience, and with a humanity which was not to be wearied.

The first effort was to teach the girls something like a habit of personal cleanliness; then, to enforce order and punctuality, of which they knew nothing; next, to require early rising, and going to bed at a reasonable hour. The lessons of housekeeping were begun at the foundation, being tasks in scrubbing and cleaning; then, bed-making, and finally plain cooking, sewing, and machine-work. Some of the inmates went out for their daily labor in shops or factories; but the most had to be employed in house-work, and thus paid for their support. They soon carried on the work of a large establishment, and at the same time made thousands of articles of clothing for the poor children elsewhere under the charge of the Society.

A great deal of stress, of course, was laid on religious and moral instruction. The girls always "listened gladly," and were easily moved by earnest and sympathetic teaching and oratory.

Fortunately for the success of this Charity, one of our trustees, a man filled with "the milk of human kindness," Mr. B. J. Howland, took part in it, as if it were his main occupation in life. Twice in the week, he was present with these poor girls for many years, teaching them the principles of morality and religion, training them in singing, contriving amusements and festivals for them, sympathizing in their sorrows and troubles, until he became like a father and counselor to these wild, heedless young creatures.

When, at length, the good old man departs — *et serus in cœlum redeat!* — the tears of the friendless and forgotten will fall on his grave,

"And the blessings of the poor
Shall waft him to the other shore."

Of the effects of the patient labors of years, we will quote a few instances from Mrs. Trott's journal. She is writing, in the first extract, of a journey at the West: —

"Several stations were pointed out, where our Lodging-house girls are located; and we envied them their quiet, rural homes, wishing that others might follow their example. Maggie M., a bright American girl, who left us last spring, was fresh in our memory, as we almost passed her door. The friendless child bids fair to make an educated, respectable woman. She writes of her advantages and privileges, and says she intends to improve them, and make the very best use of her time.

"Our old friend, Mary F., is still contented and happy; she shows no inclination to return, and remains in the place procured for her two years ago. She often expresses a great anxiety for several of the girls whom she left here, and have turned out very bad. We were rather doubtful of Mary's intentions when she left us, but have reason for thankfulness that thus far she tries to do right, and leads a Christian life. She was a girl well informed, of good common-sense, rather attractive, and, we doubt not, is 'a brand plucked from the burning.'

"Emma H., a very interesting, amiable young girl, who spent several months at the Lodge, while waiting for a good opening, has just been to visit us. She is living with Mrs. H., Judge B —— 's daughter, on the Hudson. They are mutually, pleased with each other; and Mrs. B. says that 'Emma takes an adopted daughter's place, and nothing would tempt me to par[t] with her.' Emma was well dressed, and as comfortably situated as one could wish. There is no reason why she should not educate herself, and fill a higher position in the future.

"S. A. was a cigar-girl when she came to the Lodging-house six years ago. An orphan, friendless and homeless — we all knew her desire to obtain an education, her willingness to make any sacrifice, and put up with the humblest fare, that she might accomplish this end; and then her earnest desire to do good, and her consistent Christian character, since she united with the Church, and the real missionary she proved among the girls, when death was in the house, leaving her school, and assisting night and day among the sick. She is now completing her education, and will soon graduate with honors. Her teacher speaks of her in the highest terms.

"There was another, J. L., a very pretty little girl, who was with us at the same time, who was guilty of the most aggravating petty thefts. She was so modest and pleasing in her demeanor, so sincere in her attachments, that it was difficult to believe, until she acknowledged her guilt, that she had picked the pockets of the very persons to whom she had made showy presents. Vanity was her ruling motive — a desire to appear smart and generous, and to show that she had rich friends, who supplied her with money. She was expostulated with long and tenderly, promised to reform, and has lately united with a church where she is an active and zealous member. We have never heard a word respecting her dishonesty since she left us, and she now occupies a responsible position as forewoman in a Broadway store.

"P. E. was also a Lodging-house girl, a year or more, at the same time. She came to us in a very friendless, destitute condition. She was one of the unfortunates with the usual story of shame and desertion — she had just buried her child, and needed an asylum. We have every reason to believe her repentance sincere, and that she made no false pretensions to piety when her name was added to the list of professing Christians. The church took an unusual interest in her, and have paid her school expenses several years. She is now teaching.

"Our next is Mary M. Here is a bit of romance. When she first entered our home, she was reduced to the very lowest extremity of poverty and wretchedness. She remained with us some time, and then went to a situation in Connecticut, where she married a young Southern gentleman, who fell desperately in love with her (because she cared for him when ill), returned to New York, and, when she called upon us, was boarding at the Fifth-avenue Hotel. This was noticed at the time in several Eastern and New York papers. She showed her gratitude to us by calling and making presents to members of the House — looking up an associate, whom she found in a miserable garret, clothing her, and returning her to her friends. She greatly surprised us in the exhibition of the true womanly traits which she always manifested. This is a true instance of the saying that a resident of the Five Points to-day may be found in her home in Fifth Avenue to-morrow.

"Without going into details, we could also mention S. H., who has often been in our reports as unmanageable; the two D —— girls, who came from Miss Tracy's school; the two M —— sisters, who had a fierce drunken mother, that pawned their shoes for rum one cold winter's morn, before they had arisen from their wretched bed; two R —— sisters, turned into the streets by drunken parents, brought to our house by a kind-hearted expressman, dripping with rain; and little May, received, cold and hungry, one winter's day — all comfortably settled in country homes; most of them married, and living out West — not forgetting Maggie, the Irish girl who wrote us, soon after she went West, that her husband had his little farm, pigs, cow, etc.; requesting us to send them a little girl for adoption. Her prospect here never would have been above a garret or cellar.

"We have L. M. in New York, married to a mechanic. Every few months she brings a bundle of clothing for those who were once her companions. She is very energetic and industrious, and highly respected.

"M. E., another excellent Christian girl. She has been greatly tried in trying to save a reckless sister from destruction; once she took her West; then she returned with her when she found her sister's condition made it necessary. Such sisterly affection is seldom manifested as this girl has shown. She bought her clothing out of her own earnings, when she had scarcely a change for herself; and, after the erring sister's death, paid her child's board, working night and day to do so.

"These cases are true in every particular, and none of recent date. There are many more hopeful ones among our young girls, who have not been away from us long, and of whom we hear excellent reports."

One of the best features of this most practical "institution" for poor girls is a Sewing-machine School, where lessons are given gratuitously. In three weeks, a girl who had previously depended wholly on her needle, and could hardly earn her three dollars a week, will learn the use of the machine, and earn from one dollar to two dollars per day.

During one year this Sewing-machine School sent forth some one thousand two hundred poor girls, who earned a good living through their instruction there. The expense was trifling, as the machines were all given or loaned by the manufacturers, and for the room, we employed the parlor of the Lodging-house.

During the winter of 1870–71, the trustees determined to try to secure a permanent and convenient house for these girls.

Two well-known gentlemen of our city headed the subscription with $1,000 each; the trustees came forward liberally, and the two or three who have done so much for this charity took on themselves the disagreeable task of soliciting funds, so that in two months we had some $27,000 subscribed, with which we both secured an excellent building in St. Mark's Place, and adapted it for our purposes. Our effort is in this to make the house more attractive and tasteful than such places usually are; and various ladies have co-operated with us, to exert a more profound and renovating influence on these girls.

Training-school for Servants

We have already engrafted on this Lodging-house a School to train ordinary house-servants; to teach plain cooking, waiting, the care of bedrooms, and good laundry-work. Nothing is more needed among this class, or by the public generally, than such a "Training-school."

Of the statistics of the Lodging-house, Mrs. Trott writes as follows: —

"Ten thousand two hundred and twenty-five lodgers. What an army would the registered names make, since a forlorn, wretched child of thirteen years, from the old Trinity station-house, headed the lists in 1861!

"Among this number there are many cozily sitting by their own hearth-stones; others are filling positions of usefulness and trust in families and stores; some have been adopted in distant towns, where they fill a daughter's place; and some have gone to return no more. A large number we cannot trace.

"During this period, three thousand one hundred and one have found employment, and gone to situations, or returned to friends.

"Fifteen thousand four hundred and twenty-nine garments have been cut and made, and distributed among the poor, or used as outfits in sending companies West."

ANONYMOUS

"In Soho on Saturday Night"

Soho was one of the roughest neighborhoods in Pittsburgh in the 1890s. Its population consisted mostly of steelworkers who had little respect for the law. Fighting, prostitution, and, as the song explains, drinking were common recreations. Because of the strains and hazards of police assignments in Soho, the inhabitants experienced little police interference with their activities. The song describes the failure of "the new license plan," part of a reform movement meant to clean up Soho. The drinking and carousing continued in spite of attempts at reform.

The text is from *Pennsylvania Songs and Legends*, ed. George Korson (Baltimore: Johns Hopkins UP, 1949).

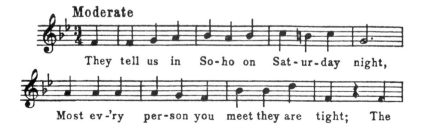

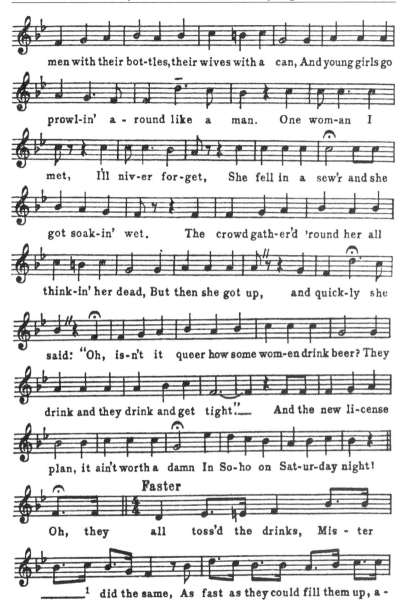

men with their bot-tles, their wives with a can, And young girls go prowl-in' a - round like a man. One wom-an I met, I'll niv-er for-get, She fell in a sew'r and she got soak-in' wet. The crowd gath-er'd 'round her all think-in' her dead, But then she got up, and quick-ly she said: "Oh, is-n't it queer how some wom-en drink beer? They drink and they drink and get tight."__ And the new li-cense plan, it ain't worth a damn In So-ho on Sat-ur-day night!

Faster

Oh, they all toss'd the drinks, Mis - ter _____¹ did the same, As fast as they could fill them up, a -

---

¹*Mister* —— : Singers would insert the names of prominent contemporary Pittsburgh citizens in these blanks.

round the drinks they came; Mis - ter
_____ got blind drunk, Mis-ter _____ could-n't see;
I was bad, but Mis-ter _____ was a
damned sight worse than me. Oh, the new li-cense plan, it
ain't worth a damn in So-ho on Sat-ur-day night!

JOSIAH STRONG

"Perils — Immigration"

"The Anglo-Saxon and the World's Future"

Josiah Strong (1847–1916) was a clergyman and social reformer. Anguished by the lack of moral values he saw resulting from the transition of a nation based on agriculture to one based on industry, Strong advocated a return to humanitarian ideals. In "Perils — Immigration," he blames many of America's urban problems on immigrants who, he argues, degrade popular morals, intellect, and religious observance, as well as corrupt the political system. Similarly, in "The Anglo-Saxon and the World's Future," Strong puts forth the argument that the Anglo-Saxon race has brought the ideals of civil liberty and pure Christianity to the world, virtues which give Anglo-Saxons — and, by extension, the United States — the right to control the rest of the world. Strong's essays, which are reprinted from the 1890 revised edition of *Our Country: Its Possible Future and Its Present Crisis*, originally published in 1885, demonstrate the racism that often infiltrated nineteenth-century reform movements.

"Perils — Immigration"

Consider briefly the moral and political influence of immigration. 1. Influence on morals. Let me hasten to recognize the high worth of many of our citizens of foreign birth, not a few of whom are eminent in the pulpit and in all the learned professions. Many come to us in full sympathy with our free institutions, and desiring to aid us in promoting a Christian civilization. But no one knows better than these same intelligent and Christian foreigners that they do not represent the mass of immigrants. The typical immigrant is a European peasant, whose horizon has been narrow, whose moral and religious training has been meager or false, and whose ideas of life are low. Not a few belong to the pauper and criminal classes. "From a late report of the Howard Society of London, it appears that 'seventy-four per cent of the Irish discharged convicts have found their way to the United States.'" "Every detective in New York knows that there is scarcely a ship landing immigrants that does not bring English, French, German, or Italian 'crooks.'" Moreover, immigration is demoralizing. No man is held upright simply by the strength of his own roots; his branches interlock with those of other men, and thus society is formed, with all its laws and customs and force of public opinion. Few men appreciate the extent to which they are indebted to their surroundings for the strength with which they resist, or do, or suffer. All this strength the emigrant leaves behind him. He is isolated in a strange land, perhaps doubly so by reason of a strange speech. He is transplanted from a forest to an open prairie, where, before he is rooted, he is smitten with the blasts of temptation. . . .

Moreover, immigration not only furnishes the greater portion of our criminals, it is also seriously affecting the morals of the native population. It is disease and not health which is contagious. Most foreigners bring with them continental ideas of the Sabbath, and the result is sadly manifest in all our cities, where it is being transformed from a holy day into a holiday. But by far the most effective instrumentality for debauching popular morals is the liquor traffic, and this is chiefly carried on by foreigners. In 1880, of the "Traders and dealers in liquors and wines," (I suppose this means wholesale dealers) sixty-three per cent were foreign-born, and of the brewers and maltsters seventy-five per cent, while a large proportion of the remainder were of foreign parentage. Of saloon-keepers about sixty per cent were foreign-born, while many of the remaining forty per cent of these corrupters of youth, these western Arabs, whose hand is against every man, were of foreign extraction.

2. We can only glance at the political aspects of immigration. As we have already seen, it is immigration which has fed fat the liquor power; and there is a liquor vote. Immigration furnishes most of the victims of Mormonism; and there is a Mormon vote. Immigration is the strength of the Catholic church; and there is a Catholic vote. Immigration is the mother and nurse of American socialism; and there is to be a socialist vote. Immigration tends strongly to the cities, and gives to them their political complexion. And there is no more serious menace to our civilization than our rabble-ruled cities. These several perils, all of which are enhanced by immigration, will be considered in succeeding chapters.

Many American citizens are not Americanized. It is as unfortunate as it is natural, that foreigners in this country should cherish their own language and peculiar customs, and carry their nationality, as a distinct factor, into our politics. Immigration has created the "German vote" and the "Irish vote," for which politicians bid, and which have already been decisive of state elections, and might easily determine national. A mass of men but little acquainted with our institutions, who will act in concert and who are controlled largely by their appetites and prejudices, constitute a very paradise for demagogues.

We have seen that immigration is detrimental to popular morals. It has a like influence upon popular intelligence, for the percentage of illiteracy among the foreign-born population is thirty-eight per cent, greater than among the native-born whites. Thus immigration complicates our moral and political problems by swelling our dangerous classes. And as immigration will probably increase more rapidly than the population, we may infer that the dangerous classes will probably increase more rapidly than hitherto. It goes without saying, that there is a dead-line of ignorance and vice in every republic, and when it is touched by the average citizen, free institutions perish; for intelligence and virtue are as essential to the life of a republic as are brain and heart to the life of a man.

A severe strain upon a bridge may be borne with safety if evenly distributed, which, if concentrated, would ruin the whole structure. There is among our population of alien birth an unhappy tendency toward aggregation, which concentrates the strain upon portions of our social and political fabric. Certain quarters of many of the cities are, in language, customs and costumes, essentially foreign. Many colonies have bought up lands and so set themselves apart from Americanizing influences. In 1845, New Glarus, in southern Wisconsin, was settled by a colony of 108 persons from one of the cantons of Switzerland. In 1880 they numbered 1,000 souls; and in 1885 it was said, "No Yankee lives within a ring of six miles round the first built dug-out." This Helvetian settlement, founded three years before Wisconsin became a state, has preserved its race, its language, its worship, and its customs in their integrity. Similar colonies are now being planted in the West. In some cases 100,000 or 200,000 acres in one block, have been purchased by foreigners of one nationality and religion; thus building up states within a state, having different languages, different antecedents, different religions, different ideas and habits, preparing mutual jealousies, and perpetuating race antipathies. In New England, conventions are held to which only French Canadian Catholics are admitted. At such a convention in Nashua in 1888, attended by eighty priests, the following mottoes were displayed: "Our tongue, our nationality, and our religion." "Before everything else let us remain French." If our noble domain were tenfold larger than it is, it would still be too small to embrace with safety to our national future, little Germanies here, little Scandinavias there, and little Irelands yonder. A strong centralized government, like that of Rome under the Caesars, can control heterogeneous populations, but local self-government implies close relations between man and man, a measure of sympathy, and, to a certain extent, community of ideas. Our safety demands the assimilation of these strange populations, and the process of assimilation will become slower and more difficult as the proportion of foreigners increases.

When we consider the influence of immigration, it is by no means reassuring to reflect that so large a share of it is pouring into the formative West. Already is the proportion of foreigners in the territories from two to three times greater than in the states east of the Mississippi. In the East, institutions have been long established and are, therefore, less easily modified by foreign influence, but in the West, where institutions are formative, that influence is far more powerful. We may well ask — and with special reference to the West — whether this in-sweeping immigration is to foreignize us, or we are to Americanize it. Mr. [Henry Ward] Beecher once said, "When the lion eats an ox, the ox becomes lion, not the lion, ox." The illustration would be very neat if it only illustrated. The lion happily has an instinct controlled by an unfailing law which determines what, and when, and how much he shall eat. If that instinct should fail, and he should some day eat a badly diseased ox, or should very much over-eat, we might have on our hands a very sick lion. I can even conceive that under such conditions the ignoble ox might slay the king of beasts.

Foreigners are not coming to the United States in answer to any appetite of ours, controlled by an unfailing moral or political instinct. They naturally consult their own interests in coming, not ours. The lion, without being consulted as to time, quantity or quality, is having the food thrust down his throat, and his only alternative is, digest or die.

"The Anglo-Saxon and the World's Future"

Every race which has deeply impressed itself on the human family has been the representative of some great idea — one or more — which has given direction to the nation's life and form to its civilization. Among the Egyptians this seminal idea was life, among the Persians it was light, among the Hebrews it was purity, among the Greeks it was beauty, among the Romans it was law. The Anglo-Saxon is the representative of two great ideas, which are closely related. One of them is that of civil liberty. Nearly all of the civil liberty of the world is enjoyed by Anglo-Saxons: the English, the British colonists, and the people of the United States. . . . In modern times, the peoples whose love of liberty has won it, and whose genius for self-government has preserved it, have been Anglo-Saxons. The noblest races have always been lovers of liberty. The love ran strong in early German blood, and has profoundly influenced the institutions of all the branches of the great German family; but it was left for the Anglo-Saxon branch fully to recognize the right of the individual to himself, and formally to declare it the foundation stone of government.

The other great idea of which the Anglo-Saxon is the exponent is that of a pure *spiritual* Christianity. It was no accident that the great reformation of the sixteenth century originated among a Teutonic, rather than a Latin people. It was the fire of liberty burning in the Saxon heart that flamed up against the absolutism of the Pope. Speaking roughly, the peoples of Europe which are Celtic are Roman Catholic, and those which are Teutonic are Protestant; and where the Teutonic race was purest, there Protestantism spread with the greatest rapidity. But, with beautiful exceptions, Protestantism on the continent has degenerated into mere formalism. By confirmation at a certain age, the state churches are filled with members who generally know nothing of a personal spiritual experience. . . . Most of the spiritual Christianity in the world is found among Anglo-Saxons and their converts; for this is the great missionary race. . . .

It is not necessary to argue to those for whom I write that the two great needs of mankind, that all men may be lifted up into the light of the highest Christian civilization, are, first, a pure, spiritual Christianity, and second, civil liberty. Without controversy, these are the forces which, in the past, have contributed most to the elevation of the human race, and they must continue to be, in the future, the most efficient ministers to its progress. It follows, then, that the Anglo-Saxon, as the great representative of these two ideas, the depositary of these two greatest blessings, sustains peculiar relations to the world's future, is divinely commissioned to be, in a peculiar sense, his brother's keeper. . . .

When we consider how much more favorable are the conditions for the increase of population in Anglo-Saxon countries than in continental Europe, and remember that we have reckoned the growth of European population at its rate of increase from 1870 to 1880, while we have reckoned Anglo-Saxon growth at much less than its rate of increase during the same ten years, we may be reasonably confident that a hundred years hence this one race will outnumber all the peoples of continental Europe. And it is possible that, by the close of the next century, the Anglo-Saxons will outnumber all the other civilized races of the world. Does it not look as if God were not only preparing in our Anglo-Saxon civilization the die with which to stamp the peoples of the earth, but as if he were also massing behind that die the mighty power with which to press it? My confidence that this race is eventually to give its civilization to mankind is not based on mere numbers — China forbid! I look forward to what the world has never yet seen united in the same race; viz., the greatest numbers, *and* the highest civilization.

There can be no reasonable doubt that North America is to be the great home of the Anglo-Saxon, the principal seat of his power, the center of his life and influence. Not only does it constitute seven-elevenths of his possessions, but here his empire is unsevered, while the remaining four-elevenths are fragmentary and scattered over the earth. . . .

America is to have the great preponderance of numbers and of wealth, and by the logic of events will follow the scepter of controlling influence. This will be but the consummation of a movement as old as civilization — a result to which men have looked forward for centuries. John Adams records that nothing was "more ancient in his memory than the observation that arts, sciences and empire had traveled westward; and in conversation it was always added that their next leap would be over the Atlantic into America." He recalled a couplet that had been "inscribed" or rather drilled, into a rock on the shore of Monument Bay in our old colony of Plymouth:

> 'The Eastern nations sink, their glory ends,
> And empire rises where the sun descends.'[1]

. . . It surely needs no prophet's eye to see that the civilization of the *United States* is to be the civilization of America, and that the future of the continent is ours. In 1880, the United States had already become the home of more than one-half of the Anglo-Saxon race; and, if the computations already given, are correct, a much larger proportion will be here a hundred years hence. It has been shown that we have room for at least a thousand millions. . . .

Our national genius is Anglo-Saxon, but not English, its distinctive type is the result of a finer nervous organization, which is certainly being developed in this country. "The history of the world's progress from savagery to barbarism, from barbarism to civilization, and, in civilization, from the lower degrees toward the higher, is the history of increase in average longevity, corresponding to, and accompanied by, increase of nervousness. Mankind has grown to be at once more delicate and more enduring, more sensitive to weariness and yet more patient of toil, impressible, but capable of bearing powerful irritation; we are woven of finer fiber, which, though apparently frail, yet outlasts the coarser, as rich and costly garments oftentimes wear better than those of rougher workmanship." The roots of civilization are the nerves; and other things being equal, the finest nervous organization will produce the highest civilization. Heretofore, war has been almost the chief occupation of strong races. The mission of the Anglo-Saxon has been largely that of the soldier; but the world is making progress, we are leaving behind the barbarism of war; as civilization advances, it will learn less of war, and concern itself more with the arts of peace, and for these the massive battle-ax must be wrought into tools of finer temper. The physical changes accompanied by mental, which are taking place in the people of the United States are apparently to adapt men to the demands of a higher civilization. . . .

---

[1]'*The Eastern . . . descends*': See *The Works of John Adams*, vol. 9 (Boston: Little, 1854), 597–99.

Mr. Darwin is not only disposed to see, in the superior vigor of our people, an illustration of his favorite theory of natural selection, but even intimates that the world's history thus far has been simply preparatory for our future, and tributary to it. He says: "There is apparently much truth in the belief that the wonderful progress of the United States, as well as the character of the people, are the results of natural selection; for the more energetic, restless, and courageous men from all parts of Europe have emigrated during the last ten or twelve generations to that great country, and have there succeeded best."[2] . . .

There is abundant reason to believe that the Anglo-Saxon race is to be, is, indeed, already becoming, more effective here than in the mother country. The marked superiority of this race is due, in large measure, to its highly mixed origin. Says Rawlinson:[3] "It is a general rule, now almost universally admitted by ethnologists, that the mixed races of mankind are superior to the pure ones"; and adds: "Even the Jews, who are so often cited as an example of a race at once pure and strong, may, with more reason, be adduced on the opposite side of the argument." The ancient Egyptians, the Greeks, and the Romans, were all mixed races. Among modern races, the most conspicuous example is afforded by the Anglo-Saxons. Mr. Green's studies show that Mr. Tennyson's poetic line,

"Saxon and Norman and Dane are we,"

must be supplemented with Celt and Gaul, Welshman and Irishman, Frisian and Flamand, French Huguenot and German Palatine. What took place a thousand years ago and more in England again transpires to-day in the United States. "History repeats itself"; but, as the wheels of history are the chariot wheels of the Almighty, there is, with every revolution, an onward movement toward the goal of His eternal purposes. There is here a new commingling of races; and, while the largest injections of foreign blood are substantially the same elements that constituted the original Anglo-Saxon admixture, so that we may infer the general type will be preserved, there are strains of other bloods being added, which, if Mr. Emerson's remark is true,

---

[2]"*There is . . . best*": See Charles Darwin's *Descent of Man and Selection in Relation to Sex* (London: Murray, 1871), 142. *Descent of Man* propounds Darwin's theory of natural selection and evolution and profoundly influenced the scientific world at the time.

[3]*Rawlinson*: Sir Henry Creswicke Rawlinson (1810–1895), English diplomat and scholar of Assyria. See "Duties of Higher Towards Lower Races," *Princeton Review*, Nov. 1878: 804–47.

that "the best nations are those most widely related," may be expected to improve the stock, and aid it to a higher destiny. If the dangers of immigration, which have been pointed out, can be successfully met for the next few years, until it has passed its climax, it may be expected to add value to the amalgam which will constitute the new Anglo-Saxon race of the New World. . . .

Is there room for reasonable doubt that this race, unless devitalized by alcohol and tobacco, is destined to dispossess many weaker races, assimilate others, and mold the remainder, until, in a very true and important sense, it has Anglo-Saxonized mankind? Already "the English language, saturated with Christian ideas, gathering up into itself the best thought of all the ages, is the great agent of Christian civilization throughout the world; at this moment affecting the destinies and molding the character of half the human race." . . .

In my own mind, there is no doubt that the Anglo-Saxon is to exercise the commanding influence in the world's future; but the exact nature of that influence is, as yet, undetermined. How far his civilization will be materialistic and atheistic, and how long it will take thoroughly to Christianize and sweeten it, how rapidly he will hasten the coming of the kingdom wherein dwelleth righteousness, or how many ages he may retard it, is still uncertain; but *is now being swiftly determined*. Let us weld together in a chain the various links of our logic which we have endeavored to forge. Is it manifest that the Anglo-Saxon holds in his hands the destinies of mankind for ages to come? Is it evident that the United States is to be the home of this race, the principal seat of his power, the great center of his influence? . . . We stretch our hand into the future with power to mold the destinies of unborn millions. . . .

Notwithstanding the great perils which threaten it, I cannot think our civilization will perish; but I believe it is fully in the hands of the Christians of the United States, during the next ten or fifteen years, to hasten or retard the coming of Christ's kingdom in the world by hundreds, and perhaps thousands, of years. We of this generation and nation occupy the Gibraltar of the ages which commands the world's future.

ANNA GORDON

Senate Testimony on the Kitchen Garden Movement

Anna Adams Gordon (1853–1931) is best known for her work in temperance reform, which dominated her adult life. She was an officer and a crucial force within the Woman's Christian Temperance Union (WCTU) from 1879 to 1925, becoming the president of the World's WCTU in 1921. Her special focus within her temperance work was always on children, and this area of interest is clear in the following excerpt from her testimony before the Senate Committee on Education and Labor, 1883. The "Miss Willard" who appears in the testimony is Frances Willard (1839–1898), for whom Gordon worked as secretary and then as a companion reformer and with whom Gordon had a very close friendship.

The following excerpt is taken from *Report of the Committee of the Senate upon the Relations between Labor and Capital, and Testimony Taken by the Committee,* vol. 2 (Washington, D.C.: Government and Printing Office, 1885).

NEW YORK, *October* 2, 1883.

Miss ANNA GORDON examined.

The Kitchen Garden:
What It Is and What It Does

By the CHAIRMAN:

Question. Please tell us something about the Kitchen Garden work? — Answer. The Kitchen Garden work is a comparatively new philanthropy. I think it came first to the thought of Miss Huntington, of this city. It was her idea to reach the children of the poorer classes, who are in very wretched homes, and homes often of drunkenness.

She gathered a number of these children together and taught them, much on the Kindergarten plan, by which lessons are given in all the household arts. At the close of their teaching, when graduated from these classes, they have been able to enter into house service, and have commanded high wages. The women of our Temperance Union have obtained permission to teach this method only to members of the Woman's Christian Temperance Union. They have established schools in Yonkers and Oswego, in this State, at Baltimore, Md., Louisville, Ky., and also in Cleveland, Ohio. In Cleveland the young ladies of our Society go to the workhouse, and have a class among the girls who are confined there for petty offenses; and they say that these children brighten their homes greatly by carrying to them the ideas of cleanliness and tidiness they glean in these Kitchen Garden classes, and, if they go into service, they are prepared to obtain good wages, and to give good service in the families to which they are sent. In the presence of those ladies of so much more experience, I hope the committee will be good enough to excuse me now.

Miss WILLARD. I thought Miss Gordon might give an idea of an exhibition that the Kitchen Garden ladies gave us in Cleveland.

The WITNESS. Yes. They gave us an exhibition of a class in Cleveland at the time that the reception was given to Miss Willard. Little girls, twelve or fifteen in number, marched into a hall to the music of a spirited march, carrying toy beds, and, placing them on tables that were in a row, made the beds properly. Then they set a table, four of the girls taking seats and four others coming in and serving properly the dishes on the table. Then followed a variety of household avocations, such as sweeping, waiting on the door, washing dishes, &c. The work was done while keeping time to music, is very bright and pleasant in its influences, and full of instruction for the girls.

Q. How extensively are you applying this; is it a part of your work everywhere? — A. No, sir. A superintendent of our National Society has only been appointed this last year — Miss Mary McClees, of Yonkers, N. Y. She has established a society in Louisville under the charge of young ladies, also in her own home in New York, and is now in Minnesota on the same errand.

Q. Is it contemplated to introduce this feature everywhere? — A. Just as far as possible in large cities.

By Mr. CALL:

Q. Why is it named the "Kitchen Garden"? — A. Because they are taught so much of the kitchen art, cooking, washing, &c., so that they can become reliable servants.

Miss WILLARD. As I understand it, they are taught just as they would be taught in a regular industrial school where they set out to make good servants, only our ladies begin with them when they are children, and teach this work in the form of play, and add music to it in order to teach them habits of order. As the children get older the ladies take them to the markets, and teach them how to select meats, and then of course they are taught to cook them; and everything is taught which will enable them to keep their homes in nice order, or, if they are at service, to enable them to render good and acceptable service, so that they may be able to command better wages.

Mr. CALL. That is a little outside of the regular work of your organization?

Miss WILLARD. Oh, yes; but we believe that temperance, like the atmosphere, goes into everything. We think that if the people were taught to prepare food in a simple, hygienic, manner, it would greatly redound to their benefit in establishing simple, unartificial habits. Besides, very many fashionable and elegant young ladies, who would not come in with us on our more solid lines of work, the lines which we veterans are devoted to, would think it entirely enjoyable work, and perhaps, from their stand-point, more elegant, to do work of this character.

Mr. CALL. You are catching them with a little guile, then?

Miss WILLARD. Yes, a little, only we think it is the most guileless guile that can be imagined. We want to be all things to all women, if by that means we can do the most good. We have these elegant and interesting young ladies to do this kitchen garden work; it is a noble work. Of course, we talk a great deal to these little girls about the duty of not using liquors, and perhaps these young ladies who come with us may do us much good by fostering temperance sentiment in the refined society in which they move. It is really an outside department for reaching young ladies who have not hitherto been specially with us. Our latest department is the Flower Mission. That was organized for the purpose of getting those same lovely girls to take to the hospitals the prettiest posies they can find, bound up with a nice white ribbon and a pretty motto. I was at the recent Kentucky Exhibition, and spoke to the young ladies there. We found a young lady in Louisville, Miss Jennie Cassidy, a lifelong invalid, who had telephones all over the city communicating with her flower girls. We have found a re-enforcement there in the flower mission, and it has been an *entrez* to us really, which, perhaps, with our more sturdy methods, we could not find.

The CHAIRMAN [to Miss Gordon]. Won't you please give us an account of this trip which you made recently?

Miss GORDON. Yes, sir. We left Boston early in March, and organized the Woman's Christian Temperance Union where it had not been organized, in New Mexico and Arizona, at Santa Fé, Albuquerque, and Tucson. Then we went to California and visited, I think, thirty towns; then to Oregon, visiting there six towns, and holding a convention of the Oregon women in Portland, organizing the State Woman's Christian Temperance Union. Then we went on to Washington Territory and British Columbia, and then back through Montana and Idaho; then to Utah, and home through Colorado, Wyoming, Nebraska, and Dakota. In nearly all these localities we held conventions, so that the principal towns and cities of those Territories were then reached for the first time by our Union.

The CHAIRMAN. How much time was occupied?

Miss GORDON. We reached home by the last of August.

The CHAIRMAN. Were you "loafing" most of the time?

Miss GORDON. No, indeed, sir. We averaged a meeting a day, but very often the meetings were two or three a day. We always met the women by themselves first, to talk over the plans of work, and then would hold a public meeting. We averaged, really, two meetings a day while absent on that trip.

Miss WILLARD. Miss Gordon's special work was to organize the Bands of Hope. She met the children in almost every place, and also the young ladies, wherever practicable, introducing these lighter methods with the young ladies, and forming Bands of Hope on the plan that I spoke of in Iowa, a systematic method by which the boys were taught the military drill. We found a captain or colonel in some one of the forts, who would come to some adjacent point where we were, and teach the boys the military drill; then we would have banners painted with little mottoes, such as "Tremble, King Alcohol; we shall grow up;" and these banners they were very proud of. We taught them that they were to be the great strength of the future, for the temperance cause. By the introduction of this military drill we were actually able to bring in the sons of saloon keepers themselves, and young boys who would not come into any other sort of temperance organization. I have heard of a saloon keeper who said to a friend, "You should have seen my boy marching in a procession of rabid prohibitionists — and my boy walked the straightest of the lot." So by little means of this kind we get even the saloon keepers interested in letting their boys become temperance soldiers. I think that of all the methods adopted for the furtherance of the cause of temperance, this method is perhaps the most hopeful.

The women of the West take great interest in it. In San Francisco, Mrs. P. D. Brown is organizing what she calls "The Royal Legion," and she has pledged herself that it shall be organized in every town in California; it is an open society for boys.

May I say, before Mrs. Hunt makes her statement, that we have had no more fortunate feature of our work than that the inevitable duty always finds a worker ready. Wherever a new branch of work, or a new evolution, comes to us, there is some lady especially well equipped for it and ready to take it up. I wish to say that Mrs. Hunt has been second to none in the success of her efforts for our great cause. She is a graduate of Mrs. Lincoln Phelps' Institute, near Baltimore — a sister of Emma Willard, of Troy — and particularly gifted in the sciences. I remember one of my first books of study was Elmira Phelps' Botany. Mrs. Hunt's especial delight, also, has been in the natural sciences: she stood very high in all branches, but especially in the natural sciences. When the idea came to us that scientific instruction in the public schools, as a part of the regular curriculum, would be the mightiest leverage possible, and that it would perhaps unite the people most, Mrs. Hunt seemed to have an inspiration for the work, and has dedicated her life to it with so much devotion, and so much success, as I have never known similar worker to meet with in the same degree. Through Mrs. Hunt's influence we have been able to secure the influence of the educational journals of this country on our side. She has spoken at the National Educational Convention, and a book upon the topics in which she is interested is now being prepared under her suggestion for use in the public schools. I merely mention these things because it may be interesting to you gentlemen of the committee, as it is to us to know that when we have had a department ready we have always found a specialist willing to devote her time to it. Mrs. Hunt's work is to address legislature, conventions, &c., on the subject of the scientific relations of temperance, and to influence the temperance sentiment as far as possible through scientific teaching in the public schools, and also, of course, in private schools.

T. S. ARTHUR

From Ten Nights in a Bar-Room

A watchmaker who became an author and reformer, Timothy Shay Arthur (1809–1885) wrote stories about the domestic virtues for magazines like *Godey's Lady's Book* and, later, for his own magazines, such as *Arthur's Home Magazine*. He also wrote novels that addressed gambling, drinking, and other vices. His *Ten Nights in a Bar-Room: And What I Saw There* (Philadelphia: Altemus, 1854), the melodramatic story of a drunkard who ruins his family, was very popular, so much so that it has become a minor classic of American literature. When it was made into a play, only *Uncle Tom's Cabin* exceeded its popularity. The story and the play led to the passage of many temperance laws. The selection included here shows the final dissolution of the family of the onetime miller whose career as a tavern-keeper leads to drunkenness and bankruptcy.

Night the Ninth

A Fearful Consummation

Neither Slade nor his son was present at the breakfast table on the next morning. As for myself, I did not eat with much appetite. Whether this defect arose from the state of my mind or the state of the food set before me I did not stop to inquire, but left the stifling, offensive atmosphere of the dining-room in a very few moments after entering that usually attractive place for a hungry man.

A few early drinkers were already in the bar-room — men with shattered nerves and cadaverous faces, who could not begin the day's work without the stimulus of brandy or whisky. They came in with gliding footsteps, asked for what they wanted in low voices, drank in silence, and departed. It was a melancholy sight to look upon.

About nine o'clock the landlord made his appearance. He, too, came gliding into the bar-room, and his first act was to seize upon a brandy decanter, pour out nearly half a pint of the fiery liquid and drink it off. How badly his hand shook — so badly that he spilled the brandy both in pouring it out and in lifting the glass to his lips! What a shattered wreck he was! He looked really worse now than he did on the day before, when drink gave an artificial vitality to his system, a tension to his muscles, and light to his countenance. The miller of ten years ago, and the tavern-keeper of to-day! Who could have identified them as one?

Slade was turning from the bar when a man came in. I noticed an instant change in the landlord's countenance. He looked startled, almost frightened. The man drew a small package from his pocket, and after selecting a paper therefrom, presented it to Slade, who received it with a nervous reluctance, opened and let his eye fall upon the writing within. I was observing him closely at the time, and saw his countenance flush deeply. In a moment or two it became pale again — paler even than before.

"Very well — all right. I'll attend to it," said the landlord, trying to recover himself, yet swallowing with every sentence.

The man, who was no other than the sheriff's deputy, and who gave him a sober, professional look, then went out with a firm step and an air of importance. As he passed through the outer door Slade retired from the bar-room.

"Trouble coming," I heard the bar-keeper remark, speaking partly to himself and partly with the view, as was evident from his manner, of leading me to question him. But this I did not feel that it was right to do.

"Got the sheriff on him at last," added the bar-keeper.

"What's the matter, Bill?" inquired a man who now came in with a bustling, important air, and leaned familiarly over the bar. "Who was Jenkins after?"

"The old man," replied the bar-keeper, in a voice that showed pleasure rather than regret.

"No!"

"It's a fact." Bill, the bar-keeper, actually smiled.

"What's to pay?" said the man.

"Don't know, and don't care much."

"Did he serve a summons or an execution?"[1]

"Can't tell."

"Judge Lyman's suit went against him."

"Did it?"

"Yes; and I heard Judge Lyman swear that if he got him on the hip he'd sell him out, bag and basket. And he's the man to keep his word."

"I never could just make out," said the bar-keeper, "how he ever came to owe Judge Lyman so much. I've never known of any business transactions between them."

"It's been dog eat dog, I rather guess," said the man.

"What do you mean by that?" inquired the bar-keeper.

"You've heard of dogs hunting in pairs?"

"Oh, yes."

"Well, since Harvey Green got his deserts, the business of fleecing our silly young fellows who happened to have more money than wit

---

[1] *a summons or an execution:* A *summons* is a citation to appear in court; an *execution* is a judicial writ empowering an officer to make a judgment.

or discretion has been in the hands of Judge Lyman and Slade. They hunted together, Slade holding the game while the Judge acted as blood-sucker. But that business was interrupted about a year ago, and game got so scarce that, as I suggested, dog began to eat dog. And here comes the end of the matter, if I'm not mistaken. So mix us a stiff toddy. I want one more good drink at the 'Sickle and Sheaf' before the colors are struck."

And the man chuckled at his witty effort.

During the day I learned that affairs stood pretty much as this man had conjectured. Lyman's suits had been on sundry notes, payable on demand; but nobody knew of any property transactions between him and Slade. On the part of Slade no defense had been made, the suit going by default. The visit of the sheriff's officer was for the purpose of serving an execution.

As I walked through Cedarville on that day the whole aspect of the place seemed changed. I questioned with myself often whether this were really so or only the effect of imagination. The change was from cheerfulness and thrift to gloom and neglect. There was to me a brooding silence in the air, a pause in the life-movement, a folding of the hands, so to speak, because hope had failed from the heart. The residence of Mr. Harrison, who some two years before had suddenly awakened to a lively sense of the evil of rum-selling, because his own sons were discovered to be in danger, had been one of the most tasteful in Cedarville. I had often stopped to admire the beautiful shrubbery and flowers with which it was surrounded; the walks so clear — the borders so fresh and even — the arbors so cool and inviting. There was not a spot upon which the eye could rest that did not show the hand of taste. When I now came opposite to this house I was no longer in doubt as to the actuality of a change. There was no marked evidences of neglect, but the high cultivation and nice regard for the small details were lacking. The walks were cleanly swept; but the box-borders were not so carefully trimmed. The vines and bushes, that in former times were cut and tied so evenly, could hardly have felt the keen touch of the pruning-knife for months.

As I paused to note the change, a lady, somewhat beyond the middle age, came from the house. I was struck by the deep gloom that overshadowed her countenance. Ah! said I to myself, as I passed on, how many dear hopes that once lived in that heart must have been scattered to the winds. As I conjectured, this was Mrs. Harrison, and I was not unprepared to hear, as I did a few hours afterward, that her two sons had fallen into drinking habits; and not only this, had been enticed to the gaming-table. Unhappy mother! What a lifetime of wretchedness was compressed for thee into a few short years!

I walked on, noting here and there changes even more marked than appeared about the residence of Mr. Harrison. Judge Lyman's beautiful place showed utter neglect; and so did one or two others that on my first visit to Cedarville charmed me with their order, neatness, and cultivation. In every instance I learned, on inquiring, that the owners of these, or some members of their families, were, or had been, visitors at the "Sickle and Sheaf," and that the ruin, in progress or completed, began after the establishment of that point of attraction in the village.

Something of a morbid curiosity, excited by what I saw, led me on to take a closer view of the residence of Judge Hammond than I had obtained on the day before. The first thing that I noticed on approaching the old, decaying mansion were handbills posted on the gate, the front door, and on one of the windows. A nearer inspection revealed their import. The property had been seized, and was now offered at sheriff's sale!

Ten years before Judge Hammond was known as the richest man in Cedarville; and now the homestead he had once so loved to beautify — where all that was dearest to him in life once gathered — worn, disfigured and in ruins, was about being wrested from him. I paused at the gate, and leaning over it looked with saddened feelings upon the dreary waste within. No sign of life was visible. The door was shut — the windows closed — not the faintest wreath of smoke was seen above the blackened chimney-tops. How vividly did imagination restore the life, and beauty, and happiness that made their home there only a few years before — the mother and her noble boy, one looking with trembling hope, the other with joyous confidence, into the future — the father proud of his household treasures, but not their wise and jealous guardian.

Ah! that his hands should have unbarred the door and thrown it wide for the wolf to enter that precious fold! I saw them all in their sunny life before me, yet even as I looked upon them their sky began to darken. I heard the distant mutterings of the storm, and soon the desolating tempest swept down fearfully upon them. I shuddered, as it passed away, to look upon the wrecks left scattered around. What a change!

"And all this," said I, "that one man, tired of being useful and eager to get gain, might gather in accursed gold!"

Pushing open the gate I entered the yard and walked around the dwelling, my footsteps echoing in the hushed solitude of the deserted place. Hark! was that a human voice?

I paused to listen.

The sound came once more distinctly to my ears. I looked around, above, everywhere, but perceived no living sign. For nearly a minute I stood still, listening. Yes, there it was again — a low, moaning voice, as of one in pain or grief. I stepped onward a few paces, and now saw one of the doors standing ajar. As I pushed this door wide open the moan was repeated. Following the direction from which the sound came, I entered one of the large drawing-rooms. The atmosphere was stifling, and all as dark as if it were midnight. Groping my way to a window, I drew back the bolt and threw open a shutter. Broadly the light fell across the dusty, uncarpeted floor, and on the dingy furniture of the room. As it did so the moaning voice which had drawn me thither swelled on the air again, and now I saw lying upon an old sofa the form of a man. It needed no second glance to tell me that this was Judge Hammond. I put my hand upon him and uttered his name, but he answered not. I spoke more firmly, and slightly shook him, but only a piteous moan was returned.

"Judge Hammond!" I now called aloud, and somewhat imperatively.

But it availed nothing. The poor old man aroused not from the stupor in which mind and body were enshrouded.

"He is dying!" thought I, and instantly left the house in search of some friends to take charge of him in his last sad extremity. The first person to whom I made known the fact shrugged his shoulders, and said it was no affair of his, and that I must find somebody whose business it was to attend to him. My next application was met in the same spirit, and no better success attended my reference of the matter to a third party. No one to whom I spoke seemed to have any sympathy for the broken-down old man. Shocked by this indifference, I went to one of the county officers, who, on learning the condition of Judge Hammond, took immediate steps to have him removed to the Almshouse, some miles distant.

"But why to the Almshouse?" I inquired, on learning his purpose. "He has property."

"Everything has been seized for debt," was the reply.

"Will there be nothing left after his creditors are satisfied?"

"Very few, if any, will be satisfied," he answered. "There will not be enough to pay half the judgments against him."

"And is there no friend to take him in, — no one, of all who moved by his side in the days of prosperity, to give a few hours' shelter and soothe the last moments of his unhappy life?"

"Why did you make application here?" was the officer's significant question.

I was silent.

"Your earnest appeals for the poor old man met with no words of sympathy?"

"None."

"He has, indeed, fallen low. In the days of his prosperity he had many friends, so-called. Adversity has shaken them all like dead leaves from sapless branches."

"But why? This is not always so."

"Judge Hammond was a selfish, worldly man. People never liked him much. His favoring so strongly the tavern of Slade, and his distillery operations, turned from him some of his best friends. The corruption and terrible fate of his son — and the insanity and death of his wife — all were charged upon him in people's minds, and everyone seemed to turn from him instinctively after the fearful tragedy was completed. He never held up his head afterward. Neighbors shunned him as they would a criminal. And here has come the end at last. He will be taken to the Poorhouse, to die there — a pauper!"

"And all," said I, partly speaking to myself, "because a man too lazy to work at an honest calling must needs go to rum-selling."

"The truth, the whole truth, and nothing but the truth," remarked the officer with emphasis, as he turned from me to see that his directions touching the removal of Mr. Hammond to the Poorhouse were promptly executed.

In my wanderings about Cedarville during that day I noticed a small but very neat cottage a little way from the centre of the village. There was not around it a great profusion of flowers and shrubbery, but the few vines, flowers and bushes that grew green and flourishing about the door and along the clean walks added to the air of taste and comfort that so peculiarly marked the dwelling.

"Who lives in that pleasant little spot?" I asked of a man whom I had frequently seen in Slade's bar-room. He happened to be passing the house at the same time that I was.

"Joe Morgan," was answered.

"Indeed!" I spoke in some surprise. "And what of Morgan? How is he doing?"

"Very well."

"Doesn't he drink?"

"No. Since the death of his child he has never taken a drop. That event sobered him, and he has remained sober ever since."

"What is he doing?"

"Working at his old trade."

"That of a miller?"

"Yes. After Judge Hammond broke down, the distillery apparatus and cotton-spinning machinery were all sold and removed from Cedarville. The purchaser of what remained, having something of the fear of God, as well as regard for man in his heart, set himself to the restoration of the old order of things, and in due time the revolving millwheel was at its old and better work of grinding corn and wheat for bread. The only two men in Cedarville competent to take charge of the mill were Simon Slade and Joe Morgan. The first could not be had, and the second came in as a matter of course."

"And he remains sober and industrious?"

"As any man in the village," was the answer.

I saw but little of Slade or his son during the day. But both were in the bar-room at night, and both in a condition sorrowful to look upon. Their presence, together, in the bar-room, half-intoxicated as they were, seemed to revive the unhappy temper of the previous evening as freshly as if the sun had not risen and set upon their anger.

During the early part of the evening considerable company was present, though not of a very select class. A large proportion were young men. To most of them the fact that Slade had fallen into the sheriff's hands was known; and I gathered from some aside conversation which reached my ears that Frank's idle, spendthrift habits had hastened the present crisis in his father's affairs. He too was in debt to Judge Lyman — on what account it was not hard to infer.

It was after nine o'clock, and there was not half a dozen persons in the room, when I noticed Frank Slade go behind the bar for the third or fourth time. He was just lifting a decanter of brandy when his father, who was considerably under the influence of drink, started forward and laid his hand upon that of his son. Instantly a fierce light gleamed from the eyes of the young man.

"Let go of my hand!" he exclaimed.

"No, I won't. Put up that brandy bottle — you're drunk now."

"Don't meddle with me, old man!" angrily retorted Frank. "I'm not in the mood to bear anything more from *you*."

"You're drunk as a fool now," returned Slade, who had seized the decanter. "Let go the bottle!"

For only an instant did the young man hesitate. Then he drove his half-clenched hand against the breast of his father, who went staggering away several paces from the counter. Recovering himself, and now almost furious, the landlord rushed forward upon his son, his hand raised to strike him.

"Keep off!" cried Frank. "Keep off! If you touch me, I'll strike you down!" at the same time raising the half-filled bottle threateningly.

But his father was in too maddened a state to fear any consequences, and so pressed forward upon his son, striking him in the face the moment he came near enough to do so.

Instantly the young man, infuriated by drink and evil passions, threw the bottle at his father's head. The dangerous missile fell, crashing upon one of his temples, shivering it into a hundred pieces. A heavy, jarring fall too surely marked the fearful consequences of the blow. When we gathered around the fallen man, and made an effort to lift him from the floor, a thrill of horror went through every heart. A mortal paleness was already on his marred face and the death-gurgle in his throat! In three minutes from the time the blow was struck his spirit had gone upward to give an account of the deeds done in the body.

"Frank Slade, you have murdered your father!"

Sternly were these terrible words uttered. It was some time before the young man seemed to comprehend their meaning. But the moment he realized the awful truth he uttered an exclamation of horror. Almost at the same instant a pistol-shot came sharply on the ear. But the meditated self-destruction was not accomplished. The aim was not surely taken, and the ball struck harmlessly against the ceiling.

Half an hour afterward and Frank Slade was a lonely prisoner in the county jail!

Does the reader need a word of comment on this fearful consummation? No: and we will offer none.

Night the Tenth
The Closing Scene at the "Sickle and Sheaf"

On the day that succeeded the evening of this fearful tragedy, placards were to be seen all over the village announcing a mass meeting at the "Sickle and Sheaf" that night.

By early twilight the people commenced assembling. The bar, which had been closed all day, was now thrown open and lighted, and in this room where so much of evil had been originated, encouraged and consummated, a crowd of earnest-looking men were soon gathered. Among them I saw the fine person of Mr. Hargrove. Joe Morgan — or rather Mr. Morgan — was also of the number. The latter I would scarcely have recognized had not some one near me called him by name. He was well dressed, stood erect, and, though there were many deep lines on his thoughtful countenance, all traces of his former habits were gone. While I was observing him he arose, and addressing a few words to the assemblage, nominated Mr. Hargrove as chairman of the meeting. To this a unanimous assent was given.

On taking the chair, Mr. Hargrove made a brief address, something to this effect:

"Ten years ago," said he, his voice evincing a slight unsteadiness as he began, but growing firmer as he proceeded, "there was not a happier spot in Bolton county than Cedarville. Now the marks of ruin are everywhere. Ten years ago there was a kind-hearted, industrious miller in Cedarville, liked by everyone, and as harmless as a little child. Now his bloated, disfigured body lies in that room. His death was violent, and by the hand of his own son!"

Mr. Hargrove's words fell slowly, distinctly, and marked by the most forcible emphasis. There was scarcely one present who did not feel a low shudder run along his nerves as the last words were spoken in a husky whisper.

"Ten years ago," he proceeded, "the miller had a happy wife and two innocent, glad-hearted children. Now his wife, bereft of reason, is in a mad-house, and his son the occupant of a felon's cell, charged with the awful crime of parricide!"

Briefly he paused, while his audience stood gazing upon him with half-suspended respiration.

"Ten years ago," he went on, "Judge Hammond was accounted the richest man in Cedarville. Yesterday he was carried, a friendless pauper, to the Almshouse, and today he is the unmourned occupant of a pauper's grave! Ten years ago his wife was the proud, hopeful, living mother of a most promising son. I need not describe what Willy Hammond was. All here knew him well. Ah! what shattered the fine intellect of that noble-minded woman? Why did her heart break? Where is she? Where is Willy Hammond?"

A low, half-repressed groan answered the speaker.

"Ten years ago you, sir," pointing to a sad-looking old man and calling him by name, "had two sons — generous, promising, manly-hearted boys. What are they now? You need not answer the question.

Too well is their history and your sorrow known. Ten years ago I had a son, — amiable, kind, loving, but weak. Heaven knows how I sought to guard and protect him! But he fell also. The arrows of destruction darkened the very air of our once secure and happy village. And who was safe? Not mine, nor yours!

"Shall I go on? Shall I call up and pass in review before you, one after another, all the wretched victims who have fallen in Cedarville during the last ten years? Time does not permit. It would take hours for the enumeration! No, I will not throw additional darkness into the picture. Heaven knows it is black enough already! But what is the root of this great evil? Where lies the fearful secret? Who understands the disease? A direful pestilence is in the air — it walketh in darkness and wasteth at noonday. It is slaying the first-born in our houses, and the cry of anguish is swelling on every gale. Is there no remedy?"

"Yes! yes! There is a remedy!" was the spontaneous answer from many voices.

"Be it our task, then, to find and apply it this night," answered the chairman, as he took his seat.

"And there is but one remedy," said Morgan, as Mr. Hargrove sat down. "The accursed traffic must cease among us. You must cut off the fountain if you would dry up the stream. If you would save the young, the weak and the innocent — on you God has laid the solemn duty of their protection — you must cover them from the tempter. Evil is strong, wily, fierce and active in the pursuit of its ends. The young, the weak and the innocent can no more resist its assaults than the lamb can resist the wolf. They are helpless, if you abandon them to the powers of evil. Men and brethren! as one who has himself been wellnigh lost — as one who daily feels and trembles at the dangers that beset his path — I do conjure you to stay the fiery stream that is bearing everything good and beautiful among you to destruction. Fathers! for the sake of your young children, be up now and doing. Think of Willy Hammond, Frank Slade, and a dozen more whose names I could repeat, and hesitate no longer! Let us resolve this night that from henceforth the traffic shall cease in Cedarville. Is there not a large majority of citizens in favor of such a measure? And whose rights or interests can be affected by such a restriction? Who, in fact, has any right to sow disease and death in our community? The liberty, under sufferance to do so, wrongs the individual who uses it as well as those who become its victims. Do you want proof of this? Look at Simon Slade, the happy, kind-hearted miller, and at Simon

Slade, the tavern-keeper. Was he benefited by the liberty to work harm to his neighbor? No! no! In heaven's name, then, let the traffic cease! To this end I offer these resolutions: —

"Be it resolved by the inhabitants of Cedarville, That from this day henceforth no more intoxicating drink shall be sold within the limits of the corporation.

"Resolved, further, That all the liquors in the 'Sickle and Sheaf' be forthwith destroyed, and that a fund be raised to pay the creditors of Simon Slade therefor, should they demand compensation.

"Resolved, That in closing up all other places where liquor is sold regard shall be had to the right of property which the law secures to every man.

"Resolved, That with the consent of the legal authorities all the liquor for sale in Cedarville be destroyed, provided the owners thereof be paid its full value out of a fund specially raised for that purpose."

But for the calm yet resolute opposition of one or two men these resolutions would have passed by acclamation. A little sober argument showed the excited company that no good end is ever secured by the adoption of wrong means.

There were in Cedarville regularly constituted authorities, which alone had the power to determine public measures, or to say what business might or might not be pursued by individuals. And through these authorities they must act in an orderly way.

There was some little chafing at this view of the case. But good sense and reason prevailed. Somewhat modified, the resolutions passed, and the more ultra-inclined contented themselves with carrying out the second resolution — to destroy forthwith all the liquor to be found on the premises — which was immediately done. After which the people dispersed to their homes, each with a lighter heart and better hopes for the future of their village.

On the next day, as I entered the stage that was to bear me from Cedarville, I saw a man strike his sharp axe into the worn, faded and leaning post that had for so many years borne aloft the "Sickle and Sheaf;" and just as the driver gave word to his horses, the false emblem which had invited so many to enter the way of destruction fell crashing to the earth.

JOHN GREENLEAF WHITTIER

"The Quaker of the Olden Time"

John Greenleaf Whittier (1807–1892) was a poet and an abolitionist as well as a Quaker. In the decades before the Civil War, he published abolitionist poems and essays, becoming one of the most eloquent voices in the abolitionist movement and forming friendships with such prominent literary figures as Robert Lowell and Oliver Wendell Holmes. By the mid-1860s, Whittier was recognized by the literary community as a major poet. He experienced increased popularity as his life progressed and became a schoolroom classic and a well-loved public figure. In "The Quaker of the Olden Time," originally published in the collection *Songs of Labor and Reform* (Boston: Ticknor, 1850), Whittier displays his respect for values like simplicity and moral strength.

The text reprinted here is that of the Cambridge Edition of *The Complete Poetical Works of John Greenleaf Whittier* (Boston: Houghton, 1894).

The Quaker of the olden time!
   How calm and firm and true,
Unspotted by its wrong and crime,
   He walked the dark earth through.
The lust of power, the love of gain,
   The thousand lures of sin
Around him, had no power to stain
   The purity within.

With that deep insight which detects
   All great things in the small,
And knows how each man's life affects
   The spiritual life of all,
He walked by faith and not by sight,
   By love and not by law;
The presence of the wrong or right
   He rather felt than saw.

He felt that wrong with wrong partakes,
   That nothing stands alone,
That whoso gives the motive, makes

His brother's sin his own.
And, pausing not for doubtful choice
  Of evils great or small,
He listened to that inward voice
  Which called away from all.

O Spirit of that early day,
  So pure and strong and true,
Be with us in the narrow way
  Our faithful fathers knew.
Give strength the evil to forsake,
  The cross of Truth to bear,
And love and reverent fear to make
  Our daily lives a prayer!

HARRIET BEECHER STOWE

"The Quaker Settlement"
(*From* Uncle Tom's Cabin)

Uncle Tom's Cabin was one of the most popular, controversial, and important books in the mid-nineteenth century. Published in serial form in the anti-slavery magazine *National Era* from June 1851 to April 1852, the novel immediately sold out when it was published in book form. In 1852 alone, the novel sold three hundred thousand copies, and by 1860 it had sold one million copies in the United States. The strength of the novel's anti-slavery message was such that when Harriet Beecher Stowe (1811–1896) met President Lincoln in 1862, he is said to have joked, "So this is the little lady who made this big war." Stowe deplored slavery's violation of Christian values, especially its disregard for the family structure. In the following excerpt from a chapter of *Uncle Tom's Cabin,* she describes the family utopia that is possible when slavery is eliminated. This utopia is governed by the ideal nineteenth-century maternal figure, Rachel Halliday.

The text is that of the original 1852 edition of the novel.

A quiet scene now rises before us. A large, roomy, neatly painted kitchen, its yellow floor glossy and smooth, and without a particle of dust; a neat, well-blacked cooking-stove; rows of shining tin, suggestive of unmentionable good things to the appetite; glossy, green, wood chairs, old and firm; a small flag-bottomed rocking-chair, with a patchwork cushion in it, neatly contrived out of small pieces of different colored woolen goods, and a larger-sized one, motherly and old, whose wide arms breathed hospitable invitation, seconded by the solicitation of its feather cushions, — a real comfortable, persuasive old chair, and worth, in the way of honest, homely enjoyment, a dozen of your plush or brocatelle[1] drawing-room gentry; and in the chair, gently swaying back and forward, her eyes bent on some fine sewing, sat our old friend Eliza.[2] Yes, there she is, paler and thinner than in her Kentucky home, with a world of quiet sorrow lying under the shadow of her long eyelashes, and marking the outline of her gentle mouth! It was plain to see how old and firm the girlish heart was grown under the discipline of heavy sorrow; and when, anon, her large dark eye was raised to follow the gambols of her little Harry, who was sporting, like some tropical butterfly, hither and thither over the floor, she showed a depth of firmness and steady resolve that was never there in her earlier and happier days.

By her side sat a woman with a bright tin pan in her lap, into which she was carefully sorting some dried peaches. She might be fifty-five or sixty; but hers was one of those faces that time seems to touch only to brighten and adorn. The snowy lisse crape cap, made after the strait Quaker pattern, — the plain white muslin handkerchief, lying in placid folds across her bosom, — the drab shawl and dress, — showed at once the community to which she belonged. Her face was round and rosy, with a healthful downy softness, suggestive of a ripe peach. Her hair, partially silvered by age, was parted smoothly back from a high placid forehead, on which time had written no inscription, except peace on earth, good will to men, and beneath shone a large pair of clear, honest, loving brown eyes; you only needed to look straight into them, to feel that you saw to the bottom of a heart as good and true as ever throbbed in woman's bosom. So much has been said and sung of beautiful young girls, why don't somebody wake up to the beauty of old women? If any want to get

---

[1] *brocatelle:* Embroidered or brocaded.
[2] *Eliza:* Eliza Harris and her son Harry have escaped from slavery and are reunited with Eliza's husband, George, in this Quaker settlement in Ohio.

up an inspiration under this head, we refer them to our good friend Rachel Halliday, just as she sits there in her little rocking-chair. It had a turn for quacking and squeaking — that chair had, — either from having taken cold in early life, or from some asthmatic affection, or perhaps from nervous derangement; but, as she gently swung backward and forward, the chair kept up a kind of subdued "creechy-crawchy," that would have been intolerable in any other chair. But old Simeon Halliday often declared it was as good as any music to him, and the children all avowed that they wouldn't miss of hearing mother's chair for anything in the world. For why? For twenty years or more, nothing but loving words, and gentle moralities, and motherly loving kindness, had come from that chair; — headaches and heartaches innumerable had been cured there, — difficulties spiritual and temporal solved there, — all by one good, loving woman, God bless her!

EDWARD BELLAMY

From Looking Backward: 2000–1887

Edward Bellamy (1850–1898) was a reformer and the author of several successful short stories and novels. *Looking Backward* (Boston: Ticknor, 1888) was his greatest success — both extremely popular, selling nearly one million copies in ten years, and influential. This utopian novel advocates state capitalism as a nonviolent step toward the eventual goal of state socialism. Its sequel, *Equality* (1897), which was more theoretical and therefore less popular, advocated even more strongly the eradication of the profit system and the establishment of economic equality.

Both *Equality* and *Looking Backward* are narrated by Julian West, Bellamy's fictional upper-class Bostonian. In the selection from *Looking Backward* reprinted here, West, who has awoken from a century-long sleep to find himself in the year 2000, describes the perils of late-nineteenth-century socioeconomic insecurity. He then listens to Dr. Leete's explanation of how, over the course of a century, U.S. society has reorganized itself into a utopia.

The text is from the second edition (Boston: Houghton, 1888), in which Bellamy altered spelling, punctuation, and paragraphing and revised some sentences and paragraphs.

By way of attempting to give the reader some general impression of the way people lived together in those days, and especially of the relations of the rich and poor to one another, perhaps I cannot do better than to compare society as it then was to a prodigious coach which the masses of humanity were harnessed to and dragged toilsomely along a very hilly and sandy road. The driver was hunger, and permitted no lagging, though the pace was necessarily very slow. Despite the difficulty of drawing the coach at all along so hard a road, the top was covered with passengers who never got down, even at the steepest ascents. These seats on top were very breezy and comfortable. Well up out of the dust, their occupants could enjoy the scenery at their leisure, or critically discuss the merits of the straining team. Naturally such places were in great demand and the competition for them was keen, every one seeking as the first end in life to secure a seat on the coach for himself and to leave it to his child after him. By the rule of the coach a man could leave his seat to whom he wished, but on the other hand there were so many accidents by which it might at any time be wholly lost. For all that they were so easy, the seats were very insecure, and at every sudden jolt of the coach persons were slipping out of them and falling to the ground, where they were instantly compelled to take hold of the rope and help to drag the coach on which they had before ridden so pleasantly. It was naturally regarded as a terrible misfortune to lose one's seat, and the apprehension that this might happen to them or their friends was a constant cloud upon the happiness of those who rode.

But did they think only of themselves? you ask. Was not their very luxury rendered intolerable to them by comparison with the lot of their brothers and sisters in the harness, and the knowledge that their own weight added to their toil? Had they no compassion for fellow beings from whom fortune only distinguished them? Oh, yes, commiseration was frequently expressed by those who rode for those who had to pull the coach, especially when the vehicle came to a bad place in the road, as it was constantly doing, or to a particularly steep hill. At such times, the desperate straining of the team, their agonized leaping and plunging under the pitiless lashing of hunger, the many who fainted at the rope and were trampled in the mire, made a very distressing spectacle, which often called forth highly creditable displays of feeling on the top of the coach. At such times the passengers would call down encouragingly to the toilers of the rope, exhorting them to patience, and holding out hopes of possible compensation in another world for the hardness of their lot, while others contributed to buy salves and liniments for the crippled and injured. It was agreed that it was a great pity that the coach should be so hard to pull, and there was a sense of general relief when the specially bad piece of road was gotten over. This relief was not, indeed, wholly on account of the team, for there was always some danger at these bad places of a general overturn in which all would lose their seats.

It must in truth be admitted that the main effect of the spectacle of the misery of the toilers at the rope was to enhance the passengers' sense of the value of their seats upon the coach, and to cause them to hold on to them more desperately than before. If the passengers could only have felt assured that neither they nor their friends would ever fall from the top, it is probable that, beyond contributing to the funds for liniments and bandages, they would have troubled themselves extremely little about those who dragged the coach.

I am well aware that this will appear to the men and women of the twentieth century an incredible inhumanity, but there are two facts, both very curious, which partly explain it. In the first place, it was firmly and sincerely believed that there was no other way in which Society could get along, except when the many pulled at the rope and the few rode, and not only this, but that no very radical improvement even was possible, either in the harness, the coach, the roadway, or the distribution of the toil. It had always been as it was, and it always would be so. It was a pity, but it could not be helped, and philosophy forbade wasting compassion on what was beyond remedy.

The other fact is yet more curious, consisting in a singular hallucination which those on the top of the coach generally shared, that they were not exactly like their brothers and sisters who pulled at the rope, but of finer clay, in some way belonging to a higher order of beings who might justly expect to be drawn. This seems unaccountable, but, as I once rode on this very coach and shared that very hallucination, I ought to be believed. The strangest thing about the hallucination was that those who had but just climbed up from the ground, before they had outgrown the marks of the rope upon their hands, began to fall under its influence. As for those whose parents and grandparents before them had been so fortunate as to keep their seats on the top, the conviction they cherished of the essential difference between their sort of humanity and the common article was absolute. The effect of such a delusion in moderating fellow feeling for the sufferings of the mass of men into a distant and philosophical compassion is obvious. To it I refer as the only extenuation I can offer for the indifference which, at the period I write of, marked my own attitude toward the misery of my brothers. . . .

[In this next scene, the narrator spends an evening with Dr. Leete, who explains the new social changes that have eliminated strife and peril.]

When, in the course of the evening the ladies retired, leaving Doctor Leete and myself alone, he sounded me as to my disposition for sleep,[1] saying that if I felt like it my bed was ready for me; but if I was inclined to wakefulness nothing would please him better than to bear me company. "I am a late bird, myself," he said, "and, without suspicion of flattery, I may say that a companion more interesting than yourself could scarcely be imagined. It is decidedly not often that one has a chance to converse with a man of the nineteenth century."

Now I had been looking forward all the evening with some dread to the time when I should be alone, on retiring for the night. Surrounded by these most friendly strangers, stimulated and supported by their sympathetic interest, I had been able to keep my mental balance. Even then, however, in pauses of the conversation I had had glimpses, vivid as lightning flashes, of the horror of strangeness that was waiting to be faced when I could no longer command diversion. I knew I could not sleep that night, and as for lying awake and thinking, it argues no cowardice, I am sure, to confess that I was afraid of it. When, in reply to my host's question, I frankly told him this, he replied that it would be strange if I did not feel just so, but that I need have no anxiety about sleeping; whenever I wanted to go to bed, he would give me a dose which would insure me a sound night's sleep without fail. Next morning, no doubt, I would awake with the feeling of an old citizen.

"Before I acquire that," I replied, "I must know a little more about the sort of Boston I have come back to. You told me when we were upon the housetop that though a century only had elapsed since I fell asleep, it had been marked by greater changes in the conditions of

---

[1] *my disposition for sleep:* The narrator, Julian West, suffers from insomnia and had formerly relied on the services of a "Professor of Animal Magnetism" to send him into a sleeping trance. When West's house burned to the ground on the night of May 30, 1887, the servant whose job it was to bring him out of the trance died. West, whose sleeping chamber was in an underground vault, survived the fire and was discovered, still in his trance, on September 10, 2000, by Dr. Leete and his family.

humanity than many a previous millennium. With the city before me I could well believe that, but I am very curious to know what some of the changes have been. To make a beginning somewhere, for the subject is doubtless a large one, what solution, if any, have you found for the labor question? It was the Sphinx's riddle of the nineteenth century, and when I dropped out the Sphinx was threatening to devour society, because the answer was not forthcoming. It is well worth sleeping a hundred years to learn what the right answer was, if, indeed, you have found it yet."

"As no such thing as the labor question is known nowadays," replied Doctor Leete, "and there is no way in which it could arise, I suppose we may claim to have solved it. Society would indeed have fully deserved being devoured if it had failed to answer a riddle so entirely simple. In fact, to speak by the book, it was not necessary for society to solve the riddle at all. It may be said to have solved itself. The solution came as the result of a process of industrial evolution which could not have terminated otherwise. All that society had to do was to recognize and cooperate with that evolution, when its tendency had become unmistakable."

"I can only say," I answered, "that at the time I fell asleep no such evolution had been recognized."

"It was in 1887 that you fell into this sleep, I think you said."

"Yes, May 30, 1887."

My companion regarded me musingly for some moments. Then he observed, "And you tell me that even then there was no general recognition of the nature of the crisis which society was nearing? Of course, I fully credit your statement. The singular blindness of your contemporaries to the signs of the times is a phenomenon commented on by many of our historians, but few facts of history are more difficult for us to realize, so obvious and unmistakable as we look back seem the indications, which must also have come under your eyes, of the transformation about to come to pass. I should be interested, Mr. West, if you would give me a little more definite idea of the view which you and men of your grade of intellect took of the state and prospects of society in 1887. You must, at least, have realized that the widespread industrial and social troubles, and the underlying dissatisfaction of all classes with the inequalities of society, and the general misery of mankind, were portents of great changes of some sort."

"We did, indeed, fully realize that," I replied. "We felt that society was dragging anchor and in danger of going adrift. Whither it would drift nobody could say, but all feared the rocks."

"Nevertheless," said Doctor Leete, "the set of the current was perfectly perceptible if you had but taken pains to observe it, and it was not toward the rocks, but toward a deeper channel."

"We had a popular proverb," I replied, "that 'hindsight is better than foresight,' the force of which I shall now, no doubt, appreciate more fully than ever. All I can say is, that the prospect was such when I went into that long sleep that I should not have been surprised had I looked down from your housetop today on a heap of charred and moss-grown ruins instead of this glorious city."

Doctor Leete had listened to me with close attention and nodded thoughtfully as I finished speaking. "What you have said," he observed, "will be regarded as a most valuable vindication of Storiot, whose account of your era has been generally thought exaggerated in its picture of the gloom and confusion of men's minds. That a period of transition like that should be full of excitement and agitation was indeed to be looked for; but seeing how plain was the tendency of the forces in operation, it was natural to believe that hope rather than fear would have been the prevailing temper of the popular mind."

"You have not yet told me what was the answer to the riddle which you found," I said. "I am impatient to know by what contradiction of natural sequence the peace and prosperity which you now seem to enjoy could have been the outcome of an era like my own."

"Excuse me," replied by host, "but do you smoke?" It was not till our cigars were lighted and drawing well that he resumed. "Since you are in the humor to talk rather than to sleep, as I certainly am, perhaps I cannot do better than to try to give you enough idea of our modern industrial system to dissipate at least the impression that there is any mystery about the process of its evolution. The Bostonians of your day had the reputation of being great askers of questions, and I am going to show my descent by asking you one to begin with. What should you name as the most prominent feature of the labor troubles of your day?"

"Why, the strikes, of course," I replied.

"Exactly. But what made the strikes so formidable?"

"The great labor organizations."

"And what was the motive of these great organizations?"

"The workmen claimed they had to organize to get their rights from the big corporations," I replied.

"That is just it," said Doctor Leete. "The organization of labor and the strikes were an effect, merely, of the concentration of capital in greater masses than had ever been known before. Before this concentration began, while as yet commerce and industry were conducted by innumerable petty concerns with small capital, instead of a small number of great concerns with vast capital, the individual workman was relatively important and independent in his relations to the employer. Moreover, when a little capital or a new idea was enough to start a man in business for himself, workingmen were constantly becoming employers and there was no hard and fast line between the two classes. Labor unions were needless then, and general strikes out of the question. But when the era of small concerns with small capital was succeeded by that of the great aggregations of capital, all this was changed. The individual laborer, who had been relatively important to the small employer, was reduced to insignificance and powerlessness over against the great corporation, while at the same time the way upward to the grade of employer was closed to him. Self-defense drove him to union with his fellows.

"The records of the period show that the outcry against the concentration of capital was furious. Men believed that it threatened society with a form of tyranny more abhorrent than it had ever endured. They believed that the great corporations were preparing for them the yoke of a baser servitude than had ever been imposed on the race, servitude not to men but to soulless machines incapable of any motive but insatiable greed. Looking back, we cannot wonder at their desperation, for certainly humanity was never confronted with a fate more sordid and hideous than would have been the era of corporate tyranny which they anticipated.

"Meanwhile, without being in the smallest degree checked by the clamor against it, the absorption of business by ever-larger monopolies continued. In the United States there was not, after the beginning of the last quarter of the century, any opportunity whatever for individual enterprise in any important field of industry, unless backed by a great capital. During the last decade of the century, such small businesses as still remained were fast-failing survivals of a past epoch, or mere parasites on the great corporations, or else existed in fields too small to attract the great capitalists. Small businesses, as far as they still remained, were reduced to the condition of rats and mice, living in holes and corners, and counting on evading notice for the enjoyment of existence. The railroads had gone on combining till a few great syndicates controlled every rail in the land. In manufactories, every important staple was controlled by a syndicate. These syndicates, pools, trusts, or whatever their name, fixed prices and crushed all competition except when combinations as vast as themselves arose. Then a struggle, resulting in a still greater consolidation, ensued. The great city bazaar crushed its country rivals with branch stores, and in the city itself absorbed its smaller rivals till the business of a whole quarter was concentrated under one roof, with a hundred former proprietors of shops serving as clerks. Having no business of his own to put his money in, the small capitalist, at the same time that he took service under the corporation, found no other investment for his money but its stocks and bonds, thus becoming doubly dependent upon it.

"The fact that the desperate popular opposition to the consolidation of business in a few powerful hands had no effect to check it proves that there must have been a strong economical reason for it. The small capitalists, with their innumerable petty concerns, had in fact yielded the field to the great aggregations of capital, because they belonged to a day of small things and were totally incompetent to the demands of an age of steam and telegraphs and the gigantic scale of its enterprises. To restore the former order of things, even if possible, would have involved returning to the day of stagecoaches. Oppressive and intolerable as was the regime of the great consolidations of capital, even its victims, while they cursed it, were forced to admit the prodigious increase of efficiency which had been imparted to the national industries, the vast economies effected by concentration of management and unity of organization, and to confess that since the new system had taken the place of the old the wealth of the world had increased at a rate before undreamed of. To be sure this vast increase had gone chiefly to make the rich richer, increasing the gap between them and the poor; but the fact remained that, as a means merely of producing wealth, capital had been proved efficient in proportion to its consolidation. The restoration of the old system with the subdivision of capital, if it were possible, might indeed bring back a greater equality of conditions, with more individual dignity and freedom, but it would be at the price of general poverty and the arrest of material progress.

"Was there, then, no way of commanding the services of the mighty wealth-producing principle of consolidated capital without bowing down to a plutocracy like that of Carthage? As soon as men began to ask themselves these questions, they found the answer ready for them. The movement toward the conduct of business by larger and larger aggregations of capital, the tendency toward monopolies, which had been so desperately and vainly resisted, was recognized at last, in its true significance, as a process which only needed to complete its logical evolution to open a golden future to humanity.

"Early in the last century the evolution was completed by the final consolidation of the entire capital of the nation. The industry and commerce of the country, ceasing to be conducted by a set of irresponsible corporations and syndicates of private persons at their caprice and for their profit, were entrusted to a single syndicate representing the people, to be conducted in the common interest for the common profit. The nation, that is to say, organized as the one great business corporation in which all other corporations were absorbed; it became the one capitalist in the place of all other capitalists, the sole employer, the final monopoly in which all previous and lesser monopolies were swallowed up, a monopoly in the profits and economies of which all citizens shared. The epoch of trusts had ended in The Great Trust. In a word, the people of the United States concluded to assume the conduct of their own business, just as one hundred-odd years before they had assumed the conduct of their own government, organizing now for industrial purposes on precisely the same grounds that they had then organized for political purposes. At last, strangely late in the world's history, the obvious fact was perceived that no business is so essentially the public business as the industry and commerce on which the people's livelihood depends, and that to entrust it to private persons to be managed for private profit is a folly similar in kind, though vastly greater in magnitude, to that of surrendering the functions of political government to kings and nobles to be conducted for their personal glorification."

"Such a stupendous change as you describe," said I, "did not, of course, take place without great bloodshed and terrible convulsions."

"On the contrary," replied Doctor Leete, "there was absolutely no violence. The change had been long foreseen. Public opinion had become fully ripe for it, and the whole mass of the people was behind it. There was no more possibility of opposing it by force than by argument. On the other hand the popular sentiment toward the great corporations and those identified with them had ceased to be one of bitterness, as they came to realize their necessity as a link, a transition phase, in the evolution of the true industrial system. The most violent foes of the great private monopolies were now forced to recognize how invaluable and indispensable had been their office in educating the people up to the point of assuming control of their own business. Fifty years before, the consolidation of the industries of the country under national control would have seemed a very daring experiment to the most sanguine. But by a series of object lessons, seen and studied by all men, the great corporations had taught the people an entirely new set of ideas on this subject. They had seen for many years syndicates handling revenues greater than those of states, and directing the labors of hundreds of thousands of men with an efficiency and economy unattainable in smaller operations. It had come to be recognized as an axiom that the larger the business the simpler the principles that can be applied to it; that, as the machine is truer than the hand, so the system, which in a great concern does the work of the master's eye in a small business, turns out more accurate results. Thus it came about that, thanks to the corporations themselves, when it was proposed that the nation should assume their functions, the suggestion implied nothing which seemed impracticable even to the timid. To be sure, it was a step beyond any yet taken, a broader generalization, but the very fact that the nation would be the sole corporation in the field would, it was seen, relieve the undertaking of many difficulties with which the partial monopolies had contended."

Doctor Leete ceased speaking, and I remained silent, endeavoring to form some general conception of the changes in the arrangements of society implied in the tremendous revolution which he had described.

Finally I said, "The idea of such an extension of the functions of government is, to say the least, rather overwhelming."

"Extension!" he repeated. "Where is the extension?"

"In my day," I replied, "it was considered that the proper functions of government, strictly speaking, were limited to keeping the peace and defending the people against the public enemy, that is, to the military and police powers."

"And, in heaven's name, who are the public enemies?" exclaimed Doctor Leete. "Are they France, England, Germany, or hunger, cold, and nakedness? In your day governments were accustomed, on the slightest international misunderstanding, to seize upon the bodies of citizens and deliver them over by hundreds of thousands to death and mutilation, wasting their treasures the while like water; and all this oftenest for no imaginable profit to the victims. We have no wars now, and our governments no war powers, but in order to protect every citizen against hunger, cold, and nakedness, and provide for all his physical and mental needs, the function is assumed of directing his industry for a term of years. No, Mr. West, I am sure on reflection you will perceive that it was in your age, not in ours, that the extension of the functions of governments was extraordinary. Not even for the best ends would men now allow their governments such powers as were then used for the most maleficent."

"Leaving comparisons aside," I said, "the demagoguery and corruption of our public men would have been considered, in my day, insuperable objections to any assumption by government of the charge of the national industries. We should have thought that no arrangement could be worse than to entrust the politicians with control of the wealth-producing machinery of the country. Its material interests were quite too much the football of parties as it was."

"No doubt you were right," rejoined Doctor Leete, "but all that is changed now. We have no parties or politicians, and as for demagoguery and corruption, they are words having only an historical significance."

"Human nature itself must have changed very much," I said.

"Not at all," was Doctor Leete's reply, "but the conditions of human life have changed, and with them the motives of human action. The organization of society with you was such that officials were under a constant temptation to misuse their power for the private profit of themselves or others. Under such circumstances it seems almost strange that you dared entrust them with any of your affairs. Nowadays, on the contrary, society is so constituted that there is absolutely no way in which an official, however ill-disposed, could possibly make any profit for himself or any one else by a misuse of his power. Let him be as bad an official as you please, he cannot be a corrupt one. There is no motive to be. The social system no longer offers a premium on dishonesty. But these are matters which you can only understand as you come, with time, to know us better."

"But you have not yet told me how you have settled the labor problem. It is the problem of capital which we have been discussing," I said. "After the nation had assumed conduct of the mills, machinery, railroads, farms, mines, and capital in general of the country, the labor question still remained. In assuming the responsibilities of capital the nation had assumed the difficulties of the capitalist's position."

"The moment the nation assumed the responsibilities of capital those difficulties vanished," replied Doctor Leete. "The national organization of labor under one direction was the complete solution of what was, in your day and under your system, justly regarded as the insoluble labor problem. When the nation became the sole employer, all the citizens, by virtue of their citizenship, became employees, to be distributed according to the needs of industry."

"That is," I suggested, "you have simply applied the principle of universal military service, as it was understood in our day, to the labor question."

"Yes," said Doctor Leete, "that was something which followed as a matter of course as soon as the nation had become the sole capitalist. The people were already accustomed to the idea that the obligation of every citizen, not physically disabled, to contribute his military services to the defense of the nation was equal and absolute. That it was equally the duty of every citizen to contribute his quota of industrial or intellectual services to the maintenance of the nation was equally evident, though it was not until the nation became the employer of labor that citizens were able to render this sort of service with any pretense either of universality or equity. No organization of labor was possible when the employing power was divided among hundreds or thousands of individuals and corporations, between which concert of any kind was neither desired, nor indeed feasible. It constantly happened then that vast numbers who desired to labor could find no opportunity, and on the other hand, those who desired to evade a part or all of their debt could easily do so."

"Service, now, I suppose, is compulsory upon all," I suggested.

"It is rather a matter of course than of compulsion," replied Doctor Leete. "It is regarded as so absolutely natural and reasonable that the idea of its being compulsory has ceased to be thought of. He would be thought to be an incredibly contemptible person who should need compulsion in such a case. Nevertheless, to speak of service being compulsory would be a weak way to state its absolute inevitableness. Our entire social order is so wholly based upon and deduced from it that if it were conceivable that a man could escape it, he would be left with no possible way to provide for his existence. He would have excluded himself from the world, cut himself off from his kind, in a word, committed suicide."

"Is the term of service in this industrial army for life?"

"Oh, no; it both begins later and ends earlier than the average working period in your day. Your workshops were filled with children and old men, but we hold the period of youth sacred to education, and the period of maturity, when the physical forces begin to flag, equally sacred to ease and agreeable relaxation. The period of industrial service is twenty-four years, beginning at the close of the course of education at twenty-one and terminating at forty-five. After

forty-five, while discharged from labor, the citizen still remains liable
to special calls, in case of emergencies causing a sudden great increase
in the demand for labor, till he reaches the age of fifty-five, but such
calls are rarely, in fact almost never, made. The fifteenth day of October of every year is what we call Muster Day, because those who
have reached the age of twenty-one are then mustered into the industrial service, and at the same time those who, after twenty-four years'
service, have reached the age of forty-five are honorably mustered
out. It is the great day of the year with us, whence we reckon all
other events, our Olympiad, save that it is annual."

"It is after you have mustered your industrial army into service," I
said, "that I should expect the difficulty to arise, for there its analogy
with a military army must cease. Soldiers have all the same thing, and
a very simple thing, to do, namely, to practice the manual of arms, to
march and stand guard. But the industrial army must learn and follow two or three hundred diverse trades and avocations. What ad-
ministrative talent can be equal to determine wisely what trade or
business every individual in a great nation shall pursue?"

"The administration has nothing to do with determining that
point."

"Who does determine it, then?" I asked.

"Every man for himself in accordance with his natural aptitude,
the utmost pains being taken to enable him to find out what his natural aptitude really is. The principle on which our industrial army is
organized is that a man's natural endowments, mental and physical,
determine what he can work at most profitably to the nation and
most satisfactorily to himself. While the obligation of service in some
form is not to be evaded, voluntary election, subject only to necessary
regulation, is depended on to determine the particular sort of service
every man is to render. As an individual's satisfaction during his term
of service depends on his having an occupation to his taste, parents
and teachers watch from early years for indications of special aptitudes in children. A thorough study of the national industrial system,
with the history and rudiments of all the great trades, is an essential
part of our educational system. While manual training is not allowed
to encroach on the general intellectual culture to which our schools
are devoted, it is carried far enough to give our youth, in addition to
their theoretical knowledge of the national industries, mechanical and
agricultural, a certain familiarity with their tools and methods. Our
schools are constantly visiting our workshops, and often are taken on

long excursions to inspect particular industrial enterprises. In your day a man was not ashamed to be grossly ignorant of all trades except his own, but such ignorance would not be consistent with our idea of placing every one in a position to select intelligently the occupation for which he has most taste. Usually long before he is mustered into service a young man has found out the pursuit he wants to follow, has acquired a great deal of knowledge about it, and is waiting impatiently the time when he can enlist in its ranks."

"Surely," I said, "it can hardly be that the number of volunteers for any trade is exactly the number needed in that trade. It must be generally either under or over the demand."

"The supply of volunteers is always expected to fully equal the demand," replied Doctor Leete. "It is the business of the administration to see that this is the case. The rate of volunteering for each trade is closely watched. If there be a noticeably greater excess of volunteers over men needed in any trade, it is inferred that the trade offers greater attractions than others. On the other hand, if the number of volunteers for a trade tends to drop below the demand, it is inferred that it is thought more arduous. It is the business of the administration to seek constantly to equalize the attractions of the trades, so far as the conditions of labor in them are concerned, so that all trades shall be equally attractive to persons having natural tastes for them. This is done by making the hours of labor in different trades to differ according to their arduousness. The lighter trades, prosecuted under the most agreeable circumstances, have in this way the longest hours, while an arduous trade, such as mining, has very short hours. There is no theory, no a priori rule, by which the respective attractiveness of industries is determined. The administration, in taking burdens off one class of workers and adding them to other classes, simply follows the fluctuations of opinion among the workers themselves as indicated by the rate of volunteering. The principle is that no man's work ought to be, on the whole, harder for him than any other man's for him, the workers themselves to be the judges. There are no limits to the application of this rule. If any particular occupation is in itself so arduous or so oppressive that, in order to induce volunteers, the day's work in it had to be reduced to ten minutes, it would be done. If, even then, no man was willing to do it, it would remain undone. But of course, in point of fact, a moderate reduction in the hours of labor, or addition of other privileges, suffices to secure all needed volunteers for any occupation necessary to men. If, indeed, the unavoidable difficulties and dangers of such a necessary pursuit were so great that no

inducement of compensating advantages would overcome men's re-
pugnance to it, the administration would only need to take it out of
the common order of occupations by declaring it 'extra hazardous,'
and those who pursued it especially worthy of the national gratitude,
to be overrun with volunteers. Our young men are very greedy of
honor, and do not let slip such opportunities. Of course you will see
that dependence on the purely voluntary choice of avocations in-
volves the abolition in all of anything like unhygienic conditions or
special peril to life and limb. Health and safety are conditions common to all industries. The nation does not maim and slaughter its
workmen by thousands, as did the private capitalists and corporations of your day."

"When there are more who want to enter a particular trade than
there is room for, how do you decide between the applicants?" I
inquired.

"Preference is given to those who have acquired the most knowledge of the trade they wish to follow. No man, however, who
through successive years remains persistent in his desire to show what
he can do at any particular trade, is in the end denied an opportunity.
Meanwhile, if a man cannot at first win entrance into the business he
prefers, he has usually one or more alternative preferences, pursuits
for which he has some degree of aptitude, although not the highest.
Everyone, indeed, is expected to study his aptitudes so as to have not
only a first choice as to occupation, but a second or third, so that if,
either at the outset of his career or subsequently, owing to the
progress of invention or changes in demand, he is unable to follow
his first vocation, he can still find reasonably congenial employment.
This principle of secondary choices as to occupation is quite important in our system. I should add, in reference to the counter-
possibility of some sudden failure of volunteers in a particular trade,
or some sudden necessity of an increased force, that the administration, while depending on the voluntary system for filling up the trades
as a rule, holds always in reserve the power to call for special volunteers, or draft any force needed from any quarter. Generally, however, all needs of this sort can be met by details from the class of unskilled or common laborers."

"How is this class of common laborers recruited?" I asked.
"Surely nobody voluntarily enters that."

"It is the grade to which all new recruits belong for the first three
years of their service. It is not till after this period, during which he is
assignable to do any work at the discretion of his superiors, that the

young man is allowed to elect a special avocation. These three years of stringent discipline none are exempt from, and very glad our young men are to pass from this severe school into the comparative liberty of the trades. If a man were so stupid as to have no choice as to occupation, he would simply remain a common laborer; but such cases, as you may suppose, are not common."

"Having once elected and entered on a trade or occupation," I remarked, "I suppose he has to stick to it the rest of his life."

"Not necessarily," replied Doctor Leete. "While frequent and merely capricious changes of occupation are not encouraged or even permitted, every worker is allowed, of course, under certain regulations and in accordance with the exigencies of the service, to volunteer for another industry which he thinks would suit him better than his first choice. In this case his application is received just as if he were volunteering for the first time, and on the same terms. Not only this, but a worker may likewise, under suitable regulations and not too frequently, obtain a transfer to an establishment of the same industry in another part of the country which for any reason he may prefer. Under your system a discontented man could indeed leave his work at will, but he left his means of support at the same time, and took his chances as to future livelihood. We find that the number of men who wish to abandon an accustomed occupation for a new one, and old friends and associations for strange ones, is small. It is only the poorer sort of workmen who desire to change even as frequently as our regulations permit. Of course transfers or discharges, when health demands them, are always given."

"As an industrial system, I should think this might be extremely efficient," I said, "but I don't see that it makes any provision for the professional classes, the men who serve the nation with brains instead of hands. Of course you can't get along without the brain workers. How, then, are they selected from those who are to serve as farmers and mechanics? That must require a very delicate sort of sifting process, I should say."

"So it does," replied Doctor Leete. "The most delicate possible test is needed here, and so we leave the question whether a man shall be a brain or hand worker entirely to him to settle. At the end of the term of three years as a common laborer, which every man must serve, it is for him to choose, in accordance to his natural tastes, whether he will fit himself for an art or profession, or be a farmer or mechanic. If he feels that he can do better work with his brains than his muscles, he finds every facility for testing the reality of his supposed bent, of cultivating it, and, if fit, of pursuing it as his avocation. The schools of technology, of medicine, of art, of music, of histrionics, and of higher liberal learning are always open to aspirants without condition."

"Are not the schools flooded with young men whose only motive is to avoid work?"

Doctor Leete smiled a little grimly.

"No one is at all likely to enter the professional schools for the purpose of avoiding work, I assure you," he said. "They are intended for those with special aptitude for the branches they teach, and anyone without it would find it easier to do double hours at his trade than try to keep up with the classes. Of course many honestly mistake their vocation, and, finding themselves unequal to the requirements of the schools, drop out and return to the industrial service; no discredit attaches to such persons, for the public policy is to encourage all to develop suspected talents which only actual tests can prove the reality of. The professional and scientific schools of your day depended on the patronage of their pupils for support, and the practice appears to have been common of giving diplomas to unfit persons, who afterward found their way into the professions. Our schools are national institutions, and to have passed their tests is a proof of special abilities not to be questioned.

"This opportunity for a professional training," the doctor continued, "remains opens to every man till the age of thirty is reached, after which students are not received, as there would remain too brief a period before the age of discharge in which to serve the nation in their professions. In your day young men had to choose their professions very young, and therefore, in a large proportion of instances, wholly mistook their vocations. It is recognized nowadays that the natural aptitudes of some are later than those of others in developing, and therefore, while the choice of profession may be made as early as twenty-four, it remains open for six years longer."

A question which had a dozen times before been on my lips now found utterance, a question which touched upon what, in my time, had been regarded the most vital difficulty in the way of any final settlement of the industrial problem. "It is an extraordinary thing," I said, "that you should not yet have said a word about the method of adjusting wages. Since the nation is the sole employer, the government must fix the rate of wages and determine just how much everybody shall earn, from the doctors to the diggers. All I can say is, that this plan would never have worked with us, and I don't see how it can now unless human nature has changed. In my day, nobody was satisfied with his wages or salary. Even if he felt he received enough, he was sure his neighbor had too much, which was as bad. If the universal discontent on this subject, instead of being dissipated in curses and strikes directed against innumerable employers, could have been concentrated upon one, and that the government, the strongest ever devised would not have seen two pay days."

Doctor Leete laughed heartily.

"Very true, very true," he said, "a general strike would most probably have followed the first pay day, and a strike directed against a government is a revolution."

"How, then, do you avoid a revolution every pay day?" I demanded. "Has some prodigious philosopher devised a new system of calculus satisfactory to all for determining the exact and comparative value of all sorts of service, whether by brawn or brain, by hand or voice, by ear or eye? Or has human nature itself changed, so that no man looks upon his own things but 'every man on the things of his neighbor'? One or the other of these events must be the explanation."

"Neither one nor the other, however, is," was my host's laughing response. "And now, Mr. West," he continued, "you must remember that you are my patient as well as my guest, and permit me to prescribe sleep for you before we have any more conversation. It is after three o'clock."

"The prescription is, no doubt, a wise one," I said. "I only hope it can be filled."

"I will see to that," the doctor replied, and he did, for he gave me a wineglass of something or other which sent me to sleep as soon as my head touched the pillow.

Figure 17. *The Greek Slave,* by Hiram Powers, ca. 1843. Marble, 65.5 inches high. Yale University Art Gallery. Purchase — Olive Louise Dann Fund.

3

Art and Artists

Life in the Iron-Mills seeks to portray nineteenth-century American industrial conditions, but its plot hinges on the presence of a crude yet powerful sculpture, so lifelike that one character mistakes it for a living person — "a woman, white, of giant proportions, crouching on the ground, her arms flung out in some wild gesture of waving." By giving a central place to a sculptural form, Davis calls on her readers to juxtapose two realms ordinarily kept separate in nineteenth-century culture: fine arts and heavy industry. Her use of Hugh Wolfe's korl woman as a central symbol in the novella elicits associations from a world of art objects, which were understood in educated and genteel American circles as signposts of civilization. By characterizing Hugh Wolfe as a sculptor, Davis invites readers to link the iron worker with such successful contemporary sculptors as Horatio Greenough and Hiram Powers, as well as to associate him with the world of art production, art criticism, education, exhibition, patronage, and connoisseurship. Davis also urges readers to consider the opportunities — or lack of them — available in a self-proclaimed democratic society for the schooling of a raw, native talent desperate for knowledgeable mentors and guidance.

Fine-arts sculpting in America began with the seventeenth- and eighteenth-century low-relief carvings of gravestones, furniture, ship figureheads, moldings, mantles, and stairwells produced by stonemasons, carpenters, and cabinetmakers, some of whom, like Salem's

Samuel McIntire, distinguished themselves in the history of American decorative arts. Certain women modeled wax flowers and portraits, which were considered desirable as ornaments for the home and memorials for deceased loved ones.

By the 1740s, elaborate marble memorials, many with portrait busts, were imported to the colonies to be inset into church wall-niches. After the Revolution, European sculptors and sculpture were brought to the new nation in order to satisfy demands for funeral monuments and desires for classical edification. Casts of Venus and Apollo, for instance, were shipped to Boston and Philadelphia. In 1784, the state of Virginia commissioned "a statue of George Washington, to be of the finest marble and best workmanship" by the renowned French sculptor Jean Antoine Houdon; and Thomas Jefferson planned a sculpture gallery for his Virginia estate, Monticello.

By 1805, the architect Benjamin Latrobe arranged for the first sculptural carvings on the U.S. Capitol by the Italian sculptors Giovanni Andrei and Giuseppe Franzoni, who carved large, allegorical figures of Agriculture, Art, Science, and Commerce. Following the War of 1812 and the burning of the U.S. Capitol, Congress commissioned artworks of various kinds, executed by skilled Italian sculptors and representing iconic events in the history of the new nation (for example, Enrico Causici's 1825 *Landing of the Pilgrims,* in which the Indian Squanto proffers an ear of maize to a family of disembarking Pilgrims).

Early in the nineteenth century, Americans became more conscious of sculpture as a result of the exhibition of several collections. An exhibition at the newly established American Academy of Fine Arts in New York City included plaster casts of such famous statues as the *Apollo Belvedere, The Dying Gladiator,* and *Laocoön* grouping, and similar collections were exhibited at the Boston Athenaeum, the Pennsylvania Academy of Fine Arts, and the South Carolina Academy of Fine Arts in Charleston. These institutions were emerging because of national pride. The new nation likened itself to the ancient Roman Republic and based its democratic ideals on those of ancient Greece. If the United States were to become a major civilization, then surely in time it, like these ancient civilizations, would need to demonstrate its status through great achievement in art. Many believed that the Christian enlightenment of the United States would ultimately express itself in art that would supersede the pagan productions of classical civilization.

Just as the nation's capital and private estates and academies displayed sculpture, so by the 1820s did prominent citizens begin to consider it appropriate to have art objects in the home. In James Fenimore Cooper's novel, *The Pioneers* (1823), the home furnishings of the gentry in the upstate New York Adirondack Mountains include pedestal-mounted plaster-of-paris busts of Homer and Shakespeare, Franklin and Washington. The sculpture-filled halls, galleries, and great parlors of such late-nineteenth-century residences as that of the New York department store magnate A. T. Stewart were built on a decades-long tradition of such artistic and deliberately edifying home furnishing (see Figure 27, p. 352).

Yet Cooper also called attention to the problems of insufficient public education in the arts in a new nation whose citizens had little exposure to the paintings, frescoes, sculpture, and architecture that had been on view for centuries in European churches, cathedrals, public squares, and state buildings. In 1829, Cooper, who traveled extensively in Europe, happened upon an Italian warehouse filled with copies of classical sculpture bound for English and American markets. He was horrified. "Grosser caricatures," he said, "were never fabricated," and he itemized the aesthetic offenses: "attenuated nymphs and Venuses, clumsy Herculeses, hobbledehoy Apollos, and grinning Fauns."

Cooper feared that the American consumers of these ridiculous travesties of classical sculpture would mistake them for accurate copies of the originals. Lacking any basis for critical comparison, they would learn to respect and appreciate caricature instead of authentic art. Cooper's dismay is echoed by one of the first well-informed nineteenth-century American critics of art, James Jackson Jarves, who reflects in *The Art-Idea* that the "art-feeling" in America remains "dormant" because the nation is but "half rescued from the wild embrace of the wilderness." Jarves compares Americans experiencing art for the first time with children let into a toy shop. Though he is heartened that the American public are eager students gradually developing "an intelligent perception of art-motives and . . . principles," he regrets that academies of design in the United States are few and that private collections are not open to the general public.

In 1879, in an article on the private collection of A. T. Stewart, *Harper's Weekly* magazine stated that "time must elapse . . . before we shall have public galleries filled with the rarest products of artistic genius, such as abound in the Old World" (see p. 317), and the problem of democratizing art remained through the nineteenth century. Henry Ward Beecher asked, "Why should you, an apprentice or a clerk or a day-workman, not wish to see galleries of pictures as much as I or any other man? . . . [W]hy should not a blacksmith, as well as any other man, say, 'I have heard that there is a splendid picture on exhibition up town, and I am going to see it'? Why should not a man who wields the broad-axe say, 'I am going to see it'?" Beecher, instead, noticed that the art exhibition attracted "richly dressed people . . . in silk and satin and broadcloth." By his own count, New York in 1873 employed fifty thousand clerks and two hundred and fifty thousand laboring men; however, these individuals were not present at art exhibitions or concerts, preferring instead such amusements as circuses, the theater, blackface minstrel shows, and boxing matches. Beecher concludes, "People should be hungry with the eye and the ear as well as with the mouth. . . . A man's intelligence should be regarded by him as of more importance than the gratification of his physical desires" (see p. 225). The history of popular entertainment in nineteenth-century America, however, suggests that in terms of the laboring classes whom Beecher and his cohorts yearned to reform and educate to the appreciation of the fine arts, such exhortations fell on deaf ears.

Though class division persisted in artistic taste and judgment, the increasing presence of sculpture in the United States nonetheless intensified the demand for that art form; it also stimulated the patronage of wealthy individuals willing to commission sculpture from American artists and to support the schooling of young artists who previously could have sculpted only as a hobby. Thus, toward the mid-nineteenth century, a new American school of sculpture came into existence that included such artists as Horatio Greenough, Hiram Powers, Thomas Crawford, Randolph Rogers, Harriet Hosmer, and Louisa Lander.

The backgrounds of the members of this group provide some insight into Davis's decision to make her iron worker a protosculptor. Though Greenough belonged to a wealthy mercantile family that had copies of antique art in its garden, and though both Hosmer and Lander were from genteel backgrounds, the other sculptors came from the trades or artisanry. Rogers earned his living by working in a drygoods store. Powers worked as a mechanic in a clock and organ factory and also repaired figures in a wax museum, while Crawford worked as a stonecutter and made marble mantelpieces. In his novel *The Marble Faun* Nathaniel Hawthorne links fine arts with artisanry by describing the studio of a sculptor as a "dreary-looking place, with a good deal the aspect, indeed, of a stone-mason's workshop" (see p. 322). The onetime tradesmen or artisans who aspired to become sculptors frequently gained the financial support and encouragement of patrons willing to underwrite the costs of their schooling and educational travel, including long sojourns abroad. The wealthy businessman Nicholas Longworth, for example, backed Powers's East Coast travel, after which another patron sponsored his art studies in Italy. The story lines of *The Marble Faun* and Henry James's *Roderick Hudson* are based on such patterns of patronage.

In Davis's novella, Hugh Wolfe represents raw, native talent from that portion of the population toiling without the benefit of formal art education or patronage. Through her portrayal of Wolfe's encounter with the group of wealthy visitors to the mill, Davis surely wished to stimulate considerations of the plight of a self-taught artist unable to advance without assistance.

It is significant that Hugh Wolfe makes his korl figures with a hands-on directness. It was customary for a sculptor to fashion a clay model of a statue which was turned over to skilled studio craftspeople who made the plaster mold and model used to produce the object in marble. For large works, the plaster models were often shipped to Carrara, the Italian quarry renowned from classical antiquity for its pure white marble. There, Italian craftspeople would cut the block marble and undertake finishing work by a system called "pointing," which involved precise, machine-assisted measurement and drilling, with excess stone finally removed by a mason. For small sculptures, though, the steps from clay to plaster to marble, including the "pointing," were often completed at the artist's studio. The most creative part of the sculptural process was thought to be the fashioning of the original clay model. Thus Hugh Wolfe's carving of korl figures is analogous to the creative clay modeling of the sculptors whose work had gained respect and acclaim in the United States for some twenty years prior to the publication of *Life in the Iron-Mills*.

The example of successful American sculptors suggests the difference that an education would have made to a laborer like Hugh Wolfe. As beneficiaries of educational patronage, artists like Hiram Powers earned their livings from orders, or commissions, for portrait busts and other works. In Italy, sculptors such as Powers maintained studios that opened their doors to affluent travelers eager to visit the sites of artistic creation and to hear the artists explain their work. Frequently, these visitors would commission the portrait bust of a family member or a figure with classical or literary resonance. In addition, some artists undertook entrepreneurial exhibitions. With the help of a manager, Powers was able to exploit the public's willingness to buy tickets to view his sculpture when it was exhibited from city to city in the United States.

This process was particularly lucrative when a statue caused as much stir as his celebrated *Greek Slave* (1843).

Powers's *The Greek Slave* (see Figure 17, p. 292) is a prime example of what was termed ideal sculpture in nineteenth-century America. It is a figure of a woman standing with her hands chained together and gazing sideways with a modest and downcast look. Both her body and the chains are rendered in white marble, which was characteristic of figures of the ideal school. Although *The Greek Slave* — like many other ideal sculptural figures — was entirely nude, viewers were cautioned to suppress any erotic or sensual responses and were instructed instead to see the sculpture as representative of a higher plane of religious-aesthetic thought. Powers himself deflected inappropriate responses by insisting that *The Greek Slave* represented a young Greek woman who had been kidnapped by Turks; the Turks had likely destroyed her entire family, leaving her wholly dependent on the providence of God. Indeed, the artist could expect the audience for his *Greek Slave* to recall the 1831 struggle of the Greeks to liberate themselves from the Turks.

Other authorities, including ministers, also admonished viewers on appropriate interpretive responses. James Jackson Jarves typifies the instructional mentality of the critic when he denounces erotic reactions as "ignoble" and proposes a formula for "female loveliness": "If to the physical ideal be added the greater loveliness of mind, which radiates from the features as light from the sun, elevating and purifying all things on which its glances rest, we have all that Art might aspire to and yet not reach, unless its lamp were replenished at the divine fountain from which beauty itself was created." The magazine *Literary World* speaks similarly of the "elevating effect" of *The Greek Slave*: "Every sensitive and ingenuous lover of art recognizes a high and pure ideal, which gives significance and vitality to the graceful form" (see p. 319).

Rebecca Harding Davis does not portray Hugh Wolfe's korl woman as a work of ideal sculpture, though its whiteness allies it with the uniformly white marble figures of the ideal school. The strong impact of the korl woman on the educated, affluent mill visitors, however, suggests that Hugh Wolfe's statue is as powerful in its own way as *The Greek Slave* had been in the 1840s. Just as *The Greek Slave* and other ideal sculptures were meant to evoke high-minded feelings, so, Davis suggests, Hugh's korl woman ought to incite feelings about high ideals of social justice in a democracy. If the United States traced its ideological lineage to democratic Greece and to the Roman Republic, then its art ought also to respond to its own republican, democratic values. Through Hugh Wolfe's korl woman, Davis suggests that an art that prompts thought about social conditions in the United States is an art that is worthy of high-minded fervor.

JAMES JACKSON JARVES

"An Inquiry into the Art-Conditions and Prospects of America"

From Art Thoughts

Journalist, travel writer, diplomat, and well-informed art critic James Jackson Jarves (1818–1888) founded the first newspaper in Hawaii in 1840. His first visit to Italy, however, inspired him to resign from his post in Hawaii and settle in Italy. He later became the United States vice consul at Florence. In "An Inquiry," from *The Art-Idea* (1864), Jarves calls for a recognition of America's artistic disadvantages and for a realistic — even harsh — criticism that honestly evaluates American artistic efforts so that America can become a respectable nation with art that displays American greatness. *Art Thoughts: The Experiences and Observations of an American Amateur in Europe* (Cambridge: Riverside, 1869) discusses the importance of art and its contribution to the world.

The text of "An Inquiry" is reprinted from James Jackson Jarves, *The Art Idea,* ed. Benjamin Rowland Jr. (Cambridge: Belknap, 1960), 148–54.

"An Inquiry into the Art-Conditions and Prospects of America"

American soil, but half rescued from the wild embrace of the wilderness, is a virgin field of art. By America we mean that agglomerate of European civilizations welded by Anglo-Saxon institutions into the Federal Union. The other portions of the continent are simply offshoots of their parent countries, without national life in art or literature. Consequently, our inquiries belong to that people which, in virtue of their power and progress, have taken to themselves the designation of Americans, sanctioned by the tacit consent of the world, prophetically foreshadowing a period in their destiny, when, by the noble conquest of ideas, the entire continent shall of right be theirs.

An inquiry of this nature, under the circumstances of newness and inexperience which everywhere present themselves, is, in many respects, embarrassing. At the same time, it is interesting, involving as it does not only the previous points of our investigations, whether by inheritance, transmission, or imitation, but new forms, rooted in novel conditions of national being; in short, the future of the art of the intermingling races of a new world, fused into a democracy which is now passing through its gravest struggle for existence, to reissue, as we believe, the most powerful because the most enlightened, the most peaceful because the most free, and the most influential people of the globe, because having sacrificed the most for justice and liberty. . . .

For the present, America, like England, prefers the knowledge which makes her rich and strong, to the art that implies cultivation as well as feeling rightly to enjoy it. In either country, climate, race, and religion are adverse, as compared with Southern lands, to its spontaneous and general growth. Americans calculate, interrogate, accumulate, debate. They yet find their chief success in getting, rather than enjoying; in having, rather than being: hence, material wealth is the great prize of life. Their character tends to thrift, comfort, and means, rather than final aims. It clings earthward, from faith in the substantial advantages of things of sense. We are laying up a capital for great achievements by and by. Our world is still of the flesh, with bounteous loyalty to the devil. Religion, on the side either of heaven or hell, has but little of the fervid, poetical, affectionate sentiment of the Roman creed and ritual. In divorcing it from the supersensuous and superstitious, Protestantism has gone to the other extreme, making it too much a dogma. Franklin[1] most rules the common mind. He was eminently great and wise. But his greatness and wisdom was unspiritual, exhibiting the advantages that spring from intellectual foresight and homely virtue; in short, the practical craft of the scientist, politician, and merchant. His maxims have fallen upon understandings but too well disposed by will and temperament to go beyond his meaning, so that we need the counteracting element which is to be found in the art-sentiment.

---

[1] *Franklin:* Benjamin Franklin (1706–1790), American philosopher and statesman.

What progress has it made in America?

To get at this there are three points of view: the individual, national, and universal. American art must be submitted to each, to get a correct idea of it as a whole. Yet it can scarcely be said to have fairly begun its existence, because, in addition to the disadvantages art is subjected to in America in common with England, it has others more distinctively its own.

The popular faith is more rigidly puritanical in tone. This not only deprives art of the lofty stimulus of religious feeling, but subjects it to suspicion, as of doubtful morality.

Art also is choked by the stern cares and homely necessities of an incipient civilization. Men must work to live, before they can live to enjoy the beautiful.

It has no antecedent art: no abbeys in picturesque ruins; no stately cathedrals, the legacies of another faith and generation; no mediaeval architecture, rich in crimson and gold, eloquent with sculpture and color, and venerable with age; no aristocratic mansions, in which art enshrines itself in a selfish and unappreciating era, to come forth to the people in more auspicious times; no state collections to guide a growing taste; no caste of persons of whom fashion demands encouragement to art-growth; no ancestral homes, replete with a storied portraiture of the past; no legendary lore more dignified than forest or savage life; no history more poetical or fabulous than the deeds of men almost of our own generation, too like ourselves in virtues and vices to seem heroic — men noble, good, and wise, but not yet arrived to be gods; and, the greatest loss of all, no lofty and sublime poetry.

Involuntarily, the European public is trained to love and know art. The most stolid brain cannot wholly evade or be insensible to the subtle influences of so many means constantly about it calculated to attract the senses into sympathy with the Beautiful. The eye of the laborer is trained and his understanding enlightened as he goes to and fro the streets to his daily labor; so, too, the perceptions and sentiments of the idle and fashionable throng in their pursuit of pleasure. A vast school of art equally surrounds the student and non-student. None can remain entirely unconscious of its presence, any more than of the invigorating sensations of fine weather. Hence the individual aptness of Italians, Germans, and Frenchmen to appreciate and pronounce upon art, independent of the press and academic axioms, thus creating for their artists an outside school, which perhaps is of more real benefit to them than the one within doors in which they acquired their elementary knowledge and skill. Of these incentives to art-progress America is still destitute.

To this loss of what may be termed a floating aesthetic capital must be added the almost equal destitution of institutions for instruction in the science of art, except in a crude and elementary way. Academies and schools of design are few, and but imperfectly established. Public galleries exist only in idea. Private collections are limited in range, destitute of masterpieces, inaccessible to the multitude. Studios would effect much for the development of taste and knowledge, were they freely visited, by bringing our public into more cordial relations with artists, who do not yet exercise their legitimate influence. In a nation of lyceums and lecturers, every topic except art is heard. Indeed, outside of occasional didactic teaching and a few works not much read, we are without other resources of aesthetic education on a public scale than meagre exhibitions of pictures on private speculation in some of the chief cities.

This leads us to enlarge on the special disadvantages to American art arising from false criticism. The ordinary productions of men who handle brush or chisel are spoken of in public prints as "works of consummate taste and ability," "perfect gems," proofs of "astonishing genius," and with similar puffery. These vague, swelling words would be received at their real value, did not so many of our people, just awakening to aesthetic sensations, have such a mistaken estimate of art. They view it as an undefined something above and apart from themselves and their daily lives, an Eleusinian mystery of a sacred priesthood, to be seen only through the veil of the imagination, not amenable to the laws of science or the results of experience, nor to be spoken of except in high-sounding phrases and wanton praise. Feeding artists on this diet is like cramming children with colored candies. Every true artist shrinks from it, and yearns for a remedy. This will appear as soon as the public comprehend that it is as feasible to teach the young to draw, paint, and model, presupposing average intellectual faculties, as much else they are required to learn; and that the result would equal much that now passes for fine art. We can educate clever external artists as readily as clever artisans; a certain knack of hand, and development of taste and of the perceptive faculties being sufficient. When the public see this, they will cast aside their nonsense and mummery about art, and judge its mechanical qualities with the same intelligent freedom and decision that they do the manual arts with which they are acquainted. In fact, design and the science of color should be made an elementary branch of instruction in our system of common education, precisely as we are now training the ear to music, and the muscles to strength and suppleness. Genius is not essential to mere painting and modeling, certainly not to a knowledge of principles, and a respectable degree of skill or dexterity in their manifestation. These qualities can be acquired by study and application. Genius is the exception, talent the rule, of art and literature. It is as fatal an error to postpone the acquisition of knowledge, or the development of a faculty, from the want of genius, as to fancy that genius exists because we have a facility of doing certain things. Unless we conform our language to truth, we shall lose sight of the right distinction of words. An artisan who makes a good coat is more useful and respectable than a painter who makes bad pictures. Even a child would laugh at the absurdity of calling "dime-novels" or "Rollo story-books" works of astonishing genius, or of applying to them any of the hyperbolical expressions of admiration which are so lavishly showered by excited friendship or an indiscriminating press upon almost every effort of an American artist. Yet the larger portion of productions are no more matchless or divine than the common run of books, nor imply any more intellect to produce them. If we should begin with exhausting the capacity for praise of our tongue on penny-a-line writers, what would be left for Irving, Emerson, Hawthorne, Bryant, or Poe?[2] And could we invent words suitable to their merits, which would be doubtful on the scale applied to art, imagination would utterly fail us in coining terms to measure the genius of the absolutely great lights of literature, the Dantes, Homers, Goethes, and Shakespeares.[3] Common sense must stop this debasing flattery by exposing its fallacy. It will be a fortunate day, when our public and our artists meet understandingly face to face, having put out of sight the present pernicious system of befogging and befooling. The reform lies more with the artists than the public, for they are its teachers. Eschewing clap-trap, let them recognize only that sort of criticism which justifies its faith by reason and honest likings.

From Art Thoughts

What is the origin and scope of the art-idea? What has it done for men, and what may it still do? What are its relations to nature, sci-

---

[2] *Irving . . . Poe:* Washington Irving (1783–1859), Ralph Waldo Emerson (1803–1882), Nathaniel Hawthorne (1804–1864), William Cullen Bryant (1794–1878), and Edgar Allan Poe (1809–1849).
[3] *Dantes . . . Shakespeares:* Dante (1265–1321), Homer (ca. 1000 B.C.), Johann Wolfgang Goethe (1749–1832), and William Shakespeare (1564–1616).

ence, and religion? How are communities made better or worse by it? To what extent is it indispensable to our individual happiness? These questions cover all the ground we need examine.

Our first difficulty arises from the fact that words are vague in the ratio of their generalization. Comprehensive nouns like Art, Science, Religion, Philosophy, or God, convey to different minds varied conceptions. Each degree of knowledge, and even of temperament, has its formula of expression. Thus language is largely conventional. As minds grow, the significance of words changes to them. I cannot, therefore, hope to be understood by all exactly as I could desire; but I may make my use of essential terms intelligible to thinkers.

Art has its origin deep in a human want. I would not exclude animals from a certain consciousness of its presence, for even they enjoy something above and beyond physical functions, indicative of a receptive sense of pleasure, as if they too welcomed their ideal. If man were solely a being of abstract reason, the exercise of thought would be sufficient to his happiness. But he has also heart and imagination which demand gratification. Both clamor for more than they ever obtain. This unfulfilled wish constitutes their ideal, or that subtle aspiration of the soul which is the essence of noble art. This it is which gives a halo to the beauty it evokes; which fires the sentiments and exalts the intellect, imparting an undefinable joy as the object responds to our amorous appeal: a language felt rather than heard. Our happiness is the more complete inasmuch that it is dissociated with notions of labor or utility. Fine art suggests neither. As with the fragrance of a flower or the radiance of a sunset, we inhale its sweetness in unconscious gratitude, forming the while close friendships with its images. No one need expect to comprehend art in its ultimate sense, unless he is capable of receiving its impressions as spontaneously and supersensuously as he would those of love; for art is first passion, then conviction. Whence its power is not to be ciphered. Ends, not means, it affirms. Unless we apprehend the spiritual element, our satisfaction must limit itself to its technical and material functions.

Both science and art aspire to sublime things; the former to discover and use, the latter to represent and suggest. Science tells us of what salts a tear is made, but can give no insight into its cause, as can art. Analyzing the excretions of the kidneys, it decides with mathematical accuracy on the relative activity of mind and muscle, informing us how much passion, thought, or repose a man has had in a given time, and even claims that thought itself is only one form of matter. In this way it treats movement and character, which art also embodies in solid material in a different fashion. We can thus understand the kinship of art and science, and their diverging technical offices.

Some of these are confounded in popular apprehension by an endeavor to enhance the credit of certain occupations. Photography is not art, but a process of science to which art may add grace and beauty. As commonly practiced, it is chemical handicraft, and not to be spoken of as art, though, under its guidance, capable of making one forget its scientific origin in aesthetic satisfaction. Further, it is a useful servant of the artist, in many familiar ways, besides disseminating copies of the works of art in a cheap and portable form. Chromolithography is another manual process of less importance and truth of characterization. We should not confuse the shadow with the substance of art any more than we do the abstract idea with the printed word.

Cookery, hair-dressing, and tailoring, owing to the transcendental importance given them in France, have trespassed on the domain of art. In that country, tailors, cooks, and barbers are often called artists. This misnomer may be exhilarating to individual vanity; but it does not elevate these occupations though it does tend to degrade art, by vulgarizing its associations and lowering its mental standard. Moreover, it is a sad commentary on the aspirations of a people to permit any handicraft to rank as art; for it virtually says that muscle is entitled to the highest honors of mind, and puts the servant in the place of his master. To cook a meal, stitch clothes, or dress hair no more makes an artist than to blow glass or shoe horses. There is no need of jumbling art and manual labor. One is the product of thought, imagination, feeling; the other is work done according to rule, receipt, or pattern, in which dexterity of hand is of more account than mental action. Art can benefit a handicraft by making its product ornamental and pleasurable instead of plain or ugly; but ugliness and coarseness, as we perceive in things in general, do not diminish their absolute utility.

An artist is called to higher functions than the craftsman. By the same election no cook, barber, or photographer can be an artist, or else he would not be what he is. Whenever handicraft aspires to the ornamental, the artist must be called in. Calling charcoal a diamond does not make it one; nevertheless the smutty wood can be transformed into the brilliant gem. No man of taste is taken in by names, for ugliness does not become beauty by the addition of a lie. I emphasize these points now, that I may not be misunderstood later in my application of the art-idea.

As there are many artificers who boast themselves artists, so there are many men who pass current as artists in virtue of prodigious self-assertion, maybe deception, and turning out work as a printer prints books. They create nothing; recast nothing; fulfill no law of art; but execute terribly, in acres of canvas and tons of stone, which, being called pictures and statues, impose on the credulous by sheer nomenclature. These forgeries abound in all countries and times; for art, being pleasanter in garb and more readily perverted into shams, has more parasites than science. Nevertheless there is a rule whereby to detect the real artist. His tools are in his brain rather than his hands. His creed is in his work, not his cash-book. Having a detective taste for beauty in any guise, he accumulates artistic things even less as practical hints than as objects to be enjoyed. No matter how famous an artist is in type or lucky in "orders," unless he shows style in his work and taste in his home, he is no true man, but only a shrewd guller of the public. I would gladly omit all reference to fictitious work, for the same reason that I would not waste eyesight on it; but some examples will be needed to correct common misconceptions.

By style I mean more particularly that character given to the artist's work which comes of thought, whether new in conception and treatment, or the recasting of older ideas and forms into fresh life. The style of a school is an aggregation of the forces of its masters. In art, therefore, it is a positive, indispensable element, as character is, to manhood. Taste enters into style in the same way that polite manners help form the gentleman. There may be style with but little taste; still it is essential to complete work. By putting into harmony diverse forms and qualities, it acts as a barometer of art-feeling and intelligence. A man without taste is a mental cripple. His aesthetic faculty being unformed, he is virtually deaf and blind to the most refined pleasures of life.

No one will deny that the most intense and diffused of human joys spring from the passion of love. Without pretending to define art in precise terms, I venture to call it the love of the soul, in the sense that science is its law. As a civilizing process, each is the complement of the other. Practically, art is the ornamental side of life, as science is its utilitarian; the one having to do with the appearance of things, the other with their substance. Whatever is produced by man of which beauty is the main feature, and enjoyment the chief aim, that has its origin in the art-idea; while things of simple use are the fruit of the opposite faculty. This is, however, only a superficial view. A more profound apprehension of their attributes makes science the representative of Divine Wisdom, and art the image of Divine Love; both bringing down to the level of our senses, by a sort of incarnation, the unseen and infinite.

Two fundamental distinctions underlie art. I call them Realism and Idealism, from want of clearer words to express my meaning. The former applies to the portraiture of the external world, and partakes more or less of copying and imitation. It affects local and particular truths; is circumscribed in action and motive; inclines to inventories of things in its poorer estate; is apt to be cold, pedantic, minutely fine, or broadly rough; and seldom rises above consummate dexterity and intellectual appreciation.

Idealism bases itself on universal truths. It deals more with emotions and ideas than facts and action, opposing imagination to perception, on which realism chiefly rests. Inventing, suggesting, creating, the former is the poetry of fine art; the latter, its prose. How to combine perfect execution with profound thought, and while rendering temporal and special truths to endow them with the spirit of the ideal and eternal, is the great problem of art. Great artists ever struggle to solve it. But owing to the bias which the mind early takes for one or the other of these phases, and the limitations of their materials, few succeed in combining their best points.

The motives which determine the generic directions of art are of three kinds. . . . First, DECORATION; having for its object ornament, and addressing itself chiefly to the sensuous faculties. This is the most common, and enters largely into food, clothing, furniture, building, manufacture, and polite manners; in fine, into everything which besides its utility has scope for beauty.

Secondly, ILLUSTRATION; teaching, representation, preservation, and reminiscence under aesthetic forms being its chief aims. This includes more especially landscape, historical, and dramatic art, and portraiture, whether realistic or idealistic.

Thirdly, REVELATION, in the sense of invention, suggestion, creation, and discovery, inspired by the imagination. All supersensuous and supernal imagery that has no exact likeness to things in the world about us comes under this distinction. Its real mission is spiritual truth, but not unseldom it is prostituted to sensualism and diabolism, for it goes to either extreme just as it is controlled by a pure or a debauched mind.

Frequently the above distinctions commingle, but in general one of them marks the ruling thought. Art of itself is neither good nor evil, but passively obeys the human will, so that it affords a sure test of culture and morals, individually and nationally. I include in it polite literature, poetry, music, and the drama, because in each, as in painting and sculpture, either forms, colors, sounds, action, or thought are given under pleasurable combinations, and we are harmoniously let into the mysteries of nature, as Orpheus[4] led the beasts, trees, and stones to follow him by the sweetness of his lyre. Whatever, therefore, has the power so to affect mankind, which is neither the direct product of pure reason or science, nor is the manifest form of nature itself, but suggests it or reveals the unseen in aesthetic guise, that is ART!

[4] *Orpheus:* In Greek mythology, a poet, musician, and inventor; he enchanted animals with the music from his lyre.

ANONYMOUS

"Hints to American Artists"

This essay was published in *The Crayon, A Journal Devoted to the Graphic Arts, and the Literature Related to Them* (vol. 6, part 1) in January 1859. The introductory issue of *The Crayon* (1855) explained, "In the midst of a great commercial crisis, while fortunes of years' growth have been falling around us, and the panic-stricken world of business has been gathering in its resources, to save what it may from wreck, an effort has been organized, having for its object the education of our countrymen to the perception and enjoyment of Beauty." "Hints to American Artists" further describes art as a tool for reform, asking, in imagery surprisingly similar to that in *Life in the Iron-Mills,* "Could we but throw more flowers in the way of earth's unfortunates, who could tell what might be done by the ever-growing, never satiated thirst for Beauty?"

"Hints to American Artists" calls for an American art that responds to the unique identity of America; rather than relying on the conventions of European art, American artists must look to America, commemorating Protestant values, the American frontier, and American virtues.

Recent developments in our American world of Art are among the most hopeful and beautiful signs of the times. Art-exhibitions and artists' receptions are increasing in number, popularity, and magnitude. Artists from all parts of the land rush to New York to avail themselves of the executive facilities which no other city on this continent possesses in a similar degree, while Boston — the great nursery of thought of the new world — contemplates the establishment of an American school of Art. The new field which modern civilization opens for Art is well calculated to arrest the attention of the American artist. In the religious and moral world changes have taken place within the last few hundred years which have not yet been duly appreciated by the artists of the old world, but the elasticity of thought that distinguishes the new world seems to point to greater quickness of perception. Madonnas and saints have hitherto been the Alpha and Omega of sacred art, but has the time not arrived when the practical results achieved by Christianity might be illustrated in a different way by the sculptor and the painter? The various religious denominations which have sprung into existence since the Reformation are as yet entirely unrepresented in the fine arts. The stately Episcopalian, the sturdy Presbyterian, the plain Methodist, the thoughtful Unitarian, the rapturous Spiritualist, offer not only striking relative contrasts, but contrasts equally striking side by side with the gorgeous pageantry of the church of Rome. Art might heal, to some extent, the wounds of sectarian strife, and by doing pictorial justice to all denominations show that each, according to its kind, endeavors to serve the good cause. Pictures illustrative of the religious exploits of the different denominations would soon be welcomed as a relief to the excessive baldness of Protestant worship. If the followers of Rome cover their churches with their saints, why should not we begin to adorn our sanctuaries with pictures of the great Protestant reformers, heroes, poets, sages, and philanthropists, whom we honor in our hearts, if we do not put their figures into material form. Take John Howard and Florence Nightingale, the English philanthropists! If their fate had been cast among Roman Catholics, they would probably be canonized in due time, as St. John and St. Philomela. Why should we Protestants, then, not imitate all that is elevating and beautifying in the Roman church, embellish our churches in commemoration of our holy women and men, and thus hold out at the same time a new incentive to the genius of the artist and the progress of aesthetic and religious culture. The immense missionary enterprises of the day also offer themes of remarkable capabilities. Think of the heroic Judson,[1] or some other gallant soldier of Christ, surrounded

---

[1] *Judson:* (1788–1850) American Baptist missionary to Burma.

by a parcel of savage Hindoos and Chinese, and in the background the glowing scenery of Asia, with diverse pictorial elements, almost unparalleled in grandeur. Again, the charitable institutions, the free schools, the myriad agencies for philanthropic and educational purposes, which have been called into life within the last hundred years should receive some consideration at the hands of artists. We have visited so-called school-loghouses in the far West, where noble women of refinement and learning gather around them the Indian, Yankee, Irish, and miscellaneous urchins of the neighborhood, repeating to them in the wilderness the master-thoughts of the great sages and poets of the old world. The desolated spot, the rugged schoolhouse, the ragged but appreciative look of the children; the gentle but vigorous-minded teacher, and withal the moral beauty of the occasion; the natural beauty of the scenery, all present a combination of the picturesque and the pathetic, the artistic and the humane, well calculated to rouse the ambition and to test the genius of the artist.

But this is only one instance out of a thousand. In every direction we find institutions and aspects of life which did not exist one hundred years ago, which have hitherto escaped the attention of the artist. It should be borne in mind that we possess in this country a greater amount of executive power than in older countries, where a lesser degree of mental and moral independence militates against boldness and directness of action. From this condition proceeds more intelligence and thoughtfulness among us; many persons who are supposed to be only mere "business men" (as the vulgar phrase goes), will be the first to commission an artist to illustrate on canvas or marble, one or the other of those striking modern manifestations of civilization and humanity to which we have referred. It is evident that our artists cannot all depend on portraits and landscapes. Some may possess faculties which disqualify them for these, but which qualify them for other spheres of Art. We do not wish to hold forth grandiloquently about the possibilities of American art; but on the other hand, it must be freely admitted that the discovery of new worlds, the advent of a new civilization, the rise of new institutions, the supremacy of new social powers, argue of better and vaster things for Art, than portraits for the mere gratification of Mr. Smith or Mr. Brown. There is no reason why the taste of these worthy gentlemen should not be amply gratified, and why the industrious artist should be deterred from reaping a rich harvest therefrom. Yet, other spheres and schools of Art may at the same time find disciples and admirers, and we believe the first successful American picture of the kind alluded to will at once dispel all doubts about the public appreciation for ideas of a higher order.

We behold in this country a strife of races and an amalgamation of nationalities, which the cunning hand of the artist may strip of all their bitterness, and at the same time show forth in all their psychological and picturesque significance. Extremes meet here as they meet nowhere else. We have the feudal barons of the Middle Ages ruling in the South, and the thrifty business man of the 19th century asserting his power in the North. The one full of sentiment and chivalric notions, the other tremulous with activity, and palpitating with speculative enterprise. The knowledge which can now only be gleaned by a long study of history might thus be brought home to the mind by a felicitous perception; a few bold strokes of distinct individualities, as representative men of their class, would accomplish it. The streets and highways of this continent teem with such ambulating pieces of history and civilization. The future historian, in taking his information from the press and statistics, will be unable to give a graphic description of the rise and progress of this republic, unless the artist assists him in his task by affording some glimpses of the inner life, of the personal idiosyncrasies of those races, nationalities, men and women, who are very conveniently, but rather vaguely, designated as the American people.

But not only our own national life, but also the events of other parts of the world should receive fuller consideration in an artistic point of view. Take, for instance, the kidnapping of the Jewish boy, Mortara, by the papal authorities. This is an appropriate subject for the artist. It derives elements of popularity from the world-wide sensation it has excited, while at the same time the romance, pathos, and filth of the Ghetto of Bologna present fine contrasts with the gloom and awful beauty of the church of Rome. Or take Poerio's[2] companion, the young Sicilian mate, forcing the captain to steer towards the coast of Britain. Here, again, are good elements of popularity and picturesqueness. The poetry and sadness and glory of the exiles, the terrors and the grandeur of the sea, the resolute spirit of the patriotic sailor, and the gracefulness of marine objects, all combine to form a groundwork of a noble, truthful, and successful picture. This is what we call eliminating the ideal from the gross reality. To grapple with

---

[2] *Poerio:* Carlo Poerio (1803–1867), liberal Italian politician persecuted by the Neapolitan government.

the life which daily passes before us, and to illustrate with the touch of genius all events which bear a striking relation — this is the greatest privilege of the artist and the poet.

WILLIAM WETMORE STORY

From Conversations in a Studio

William Wetmore Story (1819–1895) had a diversified career, working at various times as a lawyer, sculptor, novelist, and poet, as well as an author of travel books. He disliked New England, his birthplace, and lived in Italy for most of his life. Henry James examined the lives of nineteenth-century expatriates like Story in his little-known book *William Wetmore Story and His Friends* (1903). Story was best known for his sculpture, and in this excerpt from *Conversations in a Studio* (Boston: Houghton, 1890), he provides a glowing report of the life of an artist and describes the way in which a sculpture came into being in the nineteenth century. Story also speaks to the need for American artists and audiences to be educated in order to foster the creation and appreciation of art.

Belton. How pleasant it is to get into a studio! There is always something attractive to me in its atmosphere. It seems to be a little ideal world in itself, outside the turmoil and confusion of common life, and having different interests and influences. An artist ought to be very happy in his life. His occupation leads him into harmony with nature and man, lifts him into ideal regions and sympathies, and gives to the outward world a peculiar charm and beauty.

Mallett. It is a happy life; all other occupations after art seem flat and tasteless. The world has for the artist a different aspect from what it wears to the common eye. Beauty starts forth to greet him from the vulgarest corners, and Nature shows him new delights of color, light, and form at every turn. He is her lover, and "love lends a precious seeing to the eye." If art be pursued in a high spirit and pure love, I know nothing more delightful. It gives a new meaning and value to everything. Life is only too short for the wooing.

M. Still, one enjoys the present through the ministrations of art more than by any other means. Every day has its happiness and its work; and it is the union of the mechanical and the poetic — the real and the ideal — which gives it a special charm. The body and mind are working together. Artists are generally long-lived — and particularly sculptors — for the simple reason that the mind and body are both kept constantly in harmonious action.

B. I suppose irritation and worry kill far more than hard work, and this is the reason why business and commerce use men up so rapidly.

M. Besides, in art one is always learning, and that begets a kind of cheerfulness, under the influence of which the mind works more easily, and with less wear and tear. The labor we delight in physics pain, and as long as we enjoy our work there is no danger of overworking. It is only when we get irritated and worried that work begins to tell on us and wear us out.

B. I suppose artists have their black days too? I hope you have. You have no right to have all your lives pleasant.

M. Black enough days we have, undoubtedly, when nothing will come to our hand; when we get confused and tormented, and know we are going wrong, and cannot see the right way. Then our work haunts us and harries us, and pursues us in our dreams, and will not give us peace. But these days pass, and we get over the trouble; the sun shines again, and all goes well. . . .

[The dialogue moves to the step-by-step production of sculpture.]

M. The matter is very simple. It is the invariable habit of a sculptor first to make his sketch, or small model, of the figure or group. This he does solely with his own hand and from his own mind, and in making this no assistance is permissible. In this the action, the composition, the character, the general masses, the lines, the draperies, in a word the whole creative part, is achieved. The details only are left unfinished. Some sculptors carry their small models much farther on in details and execution than others; and in case a sculptor intends to intrust to others the putting up of the large model from this, he determines every particular. The small model is then placed in the hands of a workman, who enlarges it by proportional compasses, mechanically, makes a framework of iron and wire, and packs upon this the clay, following by measurement all the forms and masses, and copying it in large in all its parts. He gives the general form, and makes what may be called a large, rude sketch of the small model. How much further he may go in his work depends upon the extent to which the small model is finished. If it be carefully thought out in all its details, his business is to imitate these as well as he can. The sculptor himself generally works with him in all these beginnings, though that is by no means necessary. The work being thus set up and put into general form and mass, after the small model, the sculptor makes what changes and deviations he deems necessary, sometimes entirely altering one action, distributing differently the masses, varying the composition of lines, and working out the details. From the time the general masses are arranged, the assistant is of little or no use, save to copy, under direction of the sculptor, bits of drapery arranged by him on a lay-figure, or from casts in plaster of fragments from nature, or to render him, in a word, any mere mechanical service. All the rest is done by the sculptor's own hands. The assistant's work is purely preparation. Nothing of the arrangement, or of the finish, or of the feeling is his, and as the work approximates to completion he becomes useless, and the sculptor works alone. Practically speaking, the assistant's work, being mere rough preparation, is invariably again worked over and varied in every part, often entirely pulled down and remodeled, so that nothing remains of it; and it not unfrequently occurs that, after the first packing on of the clay, he is rather an embarrassment than a help, however clever he may be. If you pause to think for a moment, you will see that, however well he may do merely mechanical work, it is impossible, from the nature of things, that he can divine the wishes or convey the spirit and feeling of the artist himself. As to all the essential parts, they must and can be done only by the artist's own hands. He alone knows, or feels rather, what he seeks and wants, and no one can help him. How can any one aid him, for instance, in the character and expression of the face, in the arrangement of the draperies, in the pose of the figure, in the *finesse* of feeling and touch, that constitutes all the difference between a good and a bad work? These things cannot be left to any assistant; they require the artist's own mind and hand.

B. In a word, all that any assistant does is purely mechanical, under the direction of the sculptor. He invents nothing, he designs nothing, and he only copies at best, or prepares the parts for the hand of the sculptor to finish. He is no more the creator of the statue than the copyist of a rough manuscript is the author; or the mason who executes the material work of a building after the plans of an architect is the architect. . . .

[The dialogue turns to the subject of the sculptor's education.]

B. It is a common notion that no general education or high culture is necessary to the artist, but that art is a special faculty, a handicraft, a gift requiring no education save in its practice. No mistake could, as it seems to me, be greater. It is only from the pressure of full and lofty streams that the fountain owes the exultant spring of its column. The imagination needs to be fed from high sources, and strengthened and enriched to fullness, before it can freely develop its native force. The mere drilling of hand and eye, the mere technical skill, nay, even the natural bias and faculty of the mind, are not sufficient. They are indeed necessary, but they are not all. It is from the soul and mind that the germs of thought and feeling must spring; and in proportion as these are nourished and expanded by culture do they flower forth in richer hues and forms. It is by these means that the taint of the vulgar and common is eradicated, that ideas are purified and exalted, that feeling and thought are stimulated, and taste refined. Out of the fullness of the whole being each word is spoken, and each act takes the force of the whole man. It is not alone the athlete's arm that strikes — it is his whole body. The blacksmith's arm in itself may be stronger, but his blow is far less effective.

M. Undoubtedly; but on the other hand, the public, on whose approbation the artist to a certain extent depends, requires equally to be educated, for without this the higher fruit of art cannot be tasted or appreciated. While the general education of the public in art is so deficient, criticism must necessarily be low and ignorant. All that we can ask is that it be not also arrogant.

ANONYMOUS

"The Stewart Art Gallery"

New York department store magnate A.T. Stewart amassed one of the largest collections of idealized American sculpture during the 1860s (see Figure 27, p. 352). This article from the May 3, 1879, issue of *Harper's Weekly* discusses with particular enthusiasm the inclusion in Stewart's collection of *The Greek Slave* (see Figure 17, p. 292), a renowned sculpture by the American sculptor Hiram Powers, and contains Powers's description of the story told by the statue.

The mansion of the late Mr. STEWART contains, as is well known, one of the most magnificent private art galleries in the world. However the treasures within its walls may compare with the collections of many connoisseurs, the apartment itself exceeds in luxury and splendor any shrine of its size ever dedicated to art. Situated at the rear of the mansion, it is approached by the main hall, and as the visitor enters he finds himself in a sort of fairy-land, surrounded on all sides by products of human genius. Here may be found the works of such artists as ROSA BONHEUR, CHURCH, MEISSONIER, FORTUNY, POWERS,[1] and others of high distinction.

Among the many exquisite pieces of statuary in the gallery are three by our own great American sculptor, [Hiram] POWERS. Here will be found the original "Greek Slave," which at the time of its first exhibition in this country produced so much consternation, our people at that time having little knowledge or appreciation of nude beauty in art. The story is told of a gang of juvenile burglars discovering a case containing a copy of this remarkable work, and concluding from the weight that it contained silver plate, broke it open. When the white form of the marble sleeper, seen by the light of a dim lantern, caught their eyes, they dropped their tools and incontinently fled, without a particle of spoil. This work was the one which gave POWERS renown, and was the realization of an ideal of which he had long dreamed. He describes the spirit which he had designed to imprison in the marble as follows: "The slave has been taken from one of the Greek islands by the Turks in the time of the Greek revolution, which is familiar to all. Her father and mother, and perhaps all her kindred, have been destroyed by her foes, and she alone preserved as a treasure too valuable to be thrown away. She is now among barbarian strangers, under the pressure of a full recollection of the calamitous events which have brought her to her present state, and she stands exposed to the gaze of the people she abhors, and awaits her fate with intense anxiety, tempered, indeed, by the support of her reliance upon the goodness of God." The two other statues by POWERS both represent EVE. The one shows the mother of our race before the Fall. The second is called "Paradise Lost," and she stands with the apple held to her breast, gazing down at the serpent whose wiles have caused her ruin.

[1] ROSA BONHEUR . . . POWERS: Rosa Bonheur (1822–1899), French painter of animals; Frederick Church (1826–1900), American landscape painter; Jean Louis Ernest Meissonier (1815–1891), French painter; Marian Fortuny (1838–1874), Spanish painter; Hiram Powers (1805–1873), American sculptor.

It is impossible in the space allowed us to even mention all the positively world-renowned works of art that have found their way into this gallery. . . . It has been suggested that it was Mr. STEWART's intention that some day his collection of art treasures should be placed within reach of the public. Since his death nothing has been heard of the matter, neither were the details of any scheme ever promulgated. Did these treasures exist abroad, they would probably be the property of the government, and thus open to the view of the people. Time must elapse, however, before we shall have public galleries filled with the rarest products of artistic genius, such as abound in the Old World.

ANONYMOUS

"The Process of Sculpture"

In this article from the September 18, 1847, issue of *The Literary World*, the discussion of Hiram Powers's sculpture *The Greek Slave* continues. The article describes Powers's creation of the clay sculpture on which the final marble sculpture was modeled. Because nineteenth-century sculptors made only the clay models and left the marble-work to the artisans' "uninspired hands," the working of the clay was considered the true act of artistry. This article describes Powers as a kind of god, bringing *The Greek Slave* to life under his hands.

The Greek Slave is the second ideal work of the American sculptor, Hiram Powers; the Eve being his first. The clay model was begun and finished in the summer and autumn of 1842. American sculptors having been hitherto obliged to work abroad, but few of our citizens have had opportunities of witnessing the labors of the studio; acceptable, therefore, will be some explanation of the several processes through which a work in sculpture must pass, ere the artist can present his conception smoothly embodied in marble. The visitors to the "Slave" will thus be made acquainted with the bodily birth and growth of the wonderful creation that stands before them in dazzling beauty.

The conception being matured in the artist's mind, the first step in the process of giving form to it is to erect, on a firm pedestal, a skeleton of iron, whose height, breadth, and limbs are determined by the size and shape of the proposed statue. In this case it would be about five feet high, with branches, first at the shoulders, running down forwards for the arms, then at the hips, to support the large mass of clay in the trunk, and thence divided in two for the legs. About this strong, simple frame is now roughly built, with wet clay, the predetermined image. Rapidly is this moulded into an approximation to the human form, and when the trunk, head, and limbs have been definitely shaped, then begins the close labor of the mind. The living models are summoned, and by their aid the surface is wrought to its last stage of finish. I say models, for to achieve adequately a high ideal, several are needed. Nature rarely centres in one individual all her gifts of corporeal beauty. For the Eve, Powers had more than a score of models. The modern Christian artist cannot be favored as was the painter Zeuxis[1] of old, to whom a Grecian city, that had ordered from him a picture of Helen, sent a number of its choicest maidens, that out of their various graces and beauties he might, as it were, extract one matchless form. For the "Slave," the character Powers had established in Florence, for purity and uprightness, obtained for him one model (who was not a professional sitter) of such perfection of form as to furnish nearly all that he could derive from a model. With this breathing figure before him, and through his precise knowledge of the form and expression of every part of the human body, obtained from the study of nature, and his own deep artistic intuitions, the clay under his hand gradually grew into life, and assumed the elastic, vital look, which no mere anatomical knowledge or craft of hand can give, but which is imparted by the genial sympathy with nature's living forms in alliance with a warm sensibility to the beautiful, — qualities which crown and render effectual the other less elevated endowments for art. Thus, by the most minute manual labor, directed by those high and refined mental gifts, the clay model of the "Slave" was wrought out; and there the artist's work ended: the creation was complete. The processes whereby it was now to be transferred to marble, though of a delicate, difficult kind, and requiring labor and time, are purely mechanical, and are performed, under the artist's directions, by uninspired hands.

---

[1] *Zeuxis:* Zeuxis, of Heraclea in southern Italy (fifth century B.C.), was one of the most famous painters of ancient Greece, renowned for representing female beauty.

ANONYMOUS

"The Greek Slave"

In 1848, Hiram Powers sent his statue *The Greek Slave* on a profitable tour of the United States, exhibiting it in several cities for a fee, and thus capitalizing on the growing desire for a national appreciation of and ability to create art in the United States. This excerpt from the booklet *Powers' Statue of the Greek Slave, Exhibiting at the Pennsylvania Academy of the Fine Arts* (Philadelphia: Collins, 1848), describes the powerful emotions and ideas the writers felt the statue should elicit from its audience.

The exhibition of a statue by a native artist, which has successfully passed the ordeal of European criticism, and achieved an established renown before reaching our shores, is an event comparatively so rare, and in itself so worthy of consideration, that a natural curiosity is excited to learn the circumstances attending its production, the history of the sculptor, and the true design of the work. In order to meet the numerous inquiries to which the exhibition daily gives birth, it has been thought advisable to collect such notices of the Greek Slave as best serve to illustrate the subject. The reader will find in the following pages a brief but authentic memoir of POWERS, an account of the process by which works of statuary are designed and completed, and several criticisms on the statue, as well as an analysis of the sculptor's genius. All the tributes to the merits of the Greek Slave have been spontaneous. As regards the perfection of its mechanical details, and the exquisite beauty of its finish, there has been expressed but one opinion. Of the peculiar moral impression it conveys, and the sentiments its contemplation awakens, a very natural and interesting variety of feeling is manifest. As may be expected in regard to all works of true genius, each spectator is affected according to his particular point of view, or the individual cast of his mind. All, however, agree in the elevating effect of the work; all feel, in gazing upon it, that "a thing of beauty is a joy for ever;" and every sensitive and ingenuous lover of art recognizes a high and pure ideal, which gives significance and vitality to the graceful form. The ostensible subject is merely a Grecian maiden, made captive by the Turks and exposed at Constantinople, for sale. The cross and locket, visible amid the drapery, indicate that she is a Christian and beloved. But this simple phase by no means completes the meaning of the statue. It represents a being superior to suffering, and raised above degradation, by inward purity and force of character. Thus the Greek Slave is an emblem of all trial to which humanity is subject, and may be regarded as a type of resignation, uncompromising virtue, or sublime patience. Accordingly, we find that all who approach or comment upon the work are not satisfied with designating its material perfection, but eloquently claim for it high moral and intellectual beauty. From the many articles which have appeared since the exhibition was commenced, and those previously written by European travelers, it is difficult to make a selection; but it is believed that the following point out what is most essential to enable the spectator to appreciate the character of the work and the genius of the artist.

The GREEK SLAVE was finished, in plaster, in 1842, and the first copy in marble was sold to Captain Grant of the British Navy, and exhibited in London about two years since; the second, which is the one now exhibiting, was executed immediately after, from the original plaster cast, for Lord Ward, a liberal patron of the arts, who, upon hearing that Mr. POWERS was desirous of sending a statue to his native country, generously offered to relinquish his claims upon this for the purpose, and receive, in its stead, a third statue, at the convenience of the sculptor. Mr. POWERS gratefully availed himself of this kind proposal, and committed the Greek Slave to the charge of a friend in Florence, who brought it to America.

The figure is about five feet five inches in height, and is cut from a single piece of Serravezza marble, quarries of which adjoin those of Carrara in the Duchy of Lucca, and first opened about ten years ago, and the marble brought into notice by the busts of Mr. POWERS. Its texture is finer and harder than that of Carrara, and more free from blemishes, the block used in the present instance being a very fine specimen.

NATHANIEL HAWTHORNE

"A Sculptor's Studio"
(From The Marble Faun)

The Marble Faun is considered to be Nathaniel Hawthorne's (1804–1864) last great book. Written in 1860, it follows the life of the Italian count Donatello, the sculptor Kenyon, and the art students Miriam and Hilda. Kenyon is a young sculptor with the advantages not available to Davis's Hugh Wolfe, including a patron who provides the money for his education and materials. In the chapter excerpted here, Hawthorne's discussion of the sculptor's minimal work in the process of making a sculpture creates an interesting context for reading Davis's description of Wolfe's work in *Life in the Iron-Mills*. While Hawthorne's narrator disparages sculptors for removing themselves from the physical labor of sculpting, leaving the work to "some nameless machine," Davis has Wolfe create his sculpture from start to finish, thus functioning as both artist and craftsman.

The text is from *The Marble Faun* (New York: Burt, 1902).

About this period, Miriam seems to have been goaded by a weary restlessness that drove her abroad on any errand or none. She went one morning to visit Kenyon in his studio, whither he had invited her to see a new statue, on which he had staked many hopes, and which was now almost completed in the clay. Next to Hilda, the person for whom Miriam felt most affection and confidence was Kenyon; and in all the difficulties that beset her life, it was her impulse to draw near Hilda for feminine sympathy, and the sculptor for brotherly counsel.

Yet it was to little purpose that she approached the edge of the voiceless gulf between herself and them. Standing on the utmost verge of that dark chasm, she might stretch out her hand, and never clasp a hand of theirs; she might strive to call out, "Help, friends! help!" but, as with dreamers when they shout, her voice would perish inaudibly in the remoteness that seemed such a little way. This perception of an infinite, shivering solitude, amid which we cannot come close enough to human beings to be warmed by them, and where they turn to cold, chilly shapes of mist, is one of the most forlorn results of any accident, misfortune, crime, or peculiarity of character, that puts an individual ajar with the world. Very often, as in Miriam's case, there is an insatiable instinct that demands friendship, love, and intimate communion, but is forced to pine in empty forms; a hunger of the heart, which finds only shadows to feed upon.

Kenyon's studio was in a cross-street, or, rather, an ugly and dirty little lane, between the Corso and the Via della Ripetta; and though chill, narrow, gloomy, and bordered with tall and shabby structures, the lane was not a whit more disagreeable than nine tenths of the Roman streets. Over the door of one of the houses was a marble tablet, bearing an inscription, to the purpose that the sculpture-rooms within had formerly been occupied by the illustrious artist Canova. In these precincts (which Canova's genius was not quite of a character to render sacred, though it certainly made them interesting) the young American sculptor had now established himself.

The studio of a sculptor is generally but a rough and dreary-looking place, with a good deal the aspect, indeed, of a stone-mason's workshop. Bare floors of brick or plank, and plastered walls; an old chair or two, or perhaps only a block of marble (containing, however, the possibility of ideal grace within it) to sit down upon; some hastily scrawled sketches of nude figures on the whitewash of the wall. These last are probably the sculptor's earliest glimpses of ideas that may hereafter be solidified into imperishable stone, or perhaps may remain as impalpable as a dream. Next there are a few very roughly modelled little figures in clay or plaster, exhibiting the second stage of the idea as it advances towards a marble immortality; and then is seen the exquisitely designed shape of clay, more interesting than even the final marble, as being the intimate production of the sculptor himself, moulded throughout with his loving hands, and nearest to his imagination and heart. In the plaster-cast, from this clay model, the beauty of the statue strangely disappears, to shine forth again with pure, white radiance, in the precious marble of Carrara. Works in all these stages of advancement, and some with the final touch upon them, might be found in Kenyon's studio.

Here might be witnessed the process of actually chiselling the marble, with which (as it is not quite satisfactory to think) a sculptor, in these days, has very little to do. In Italy, there is a class of men whose merely mechanical skill is perhaps more exquisite than was possessed by the ancient artificers, who wrought out the designs of Praxiteles;[1] or, very possibly, by Praxiteles himself. Whatever of illusive representation can be effected in marble, they are capable of achieving, if the object be before their eyes. The sculptor has but to present these men with a plaster-cast of his design, and a sufficient block of marble, and tell them that the figure is imbedded in the stone, and must be freed from its encumbering superfluities; and, in due time, without the necessity of his touching the work with his own finger, he will see before him the statue that is to make him renowned. His creative power has wrought it with a word.

In no other art, surely, does genius find such effective instruments, and so happily relieve itself of the drudgery of actual performance;

---

[1] *Praxiteles:* (ca. 360 B.C.) Great Greek sculptor.

doing wonderfully nice things by the hands of other people, when it may be suspected they could not always be done by the sculptor's own. And how much of the admiration which our artists get for their buttons and buttonholes, their shoeties, their neckcloths, — and these, at our present epoch of taste, make a large share of the renown, — would be abated, if we were generally aware that the sculptor can claim no credit for such pretty performances, as immortalized in marble! They are not his work, but that of some nameless machine in human shape.

Miriam stopped an instant in an antechamber, to look at a half-finished bust, the features of which seemed to be struggling out of the stone; and, as it were, scattering and dissolving its hard substance by the glow of feeling and intelligence. As the skilful workman gave stroke after stroke of the chisel with apparent carelessness, but sure effect, it was impossible not to think that the outer marble was merely an extraneous environment; the human countenance within its embrace must have existed there since the limestone ledges of Carrara were first made. Another bust was nearly completed, though still one of Kenyon's most trustworthy assistants was at work, giving delicate touches, shaving off an impalpable something, and leaving little heaps of marble-dust to attest it.

"As these busts in the block of marble," thought Miriam, "so does our individual fate exist in the limestone of time. We fancy that we carve it out; but its ultimate shape is prior to all our action."

Kenyon was in the inner room, but, hearing a step in the antechamber, he threw a veil over what he was at work upon, and came out to receive his visitor. He was dressed in a gray blouse, with a little cap on the top of his head; a costume which became him better than the formal garments which he wore, whenever he passed out of his own domains. The sculptor had a face which, when time had done a little more for it, would offer a worthy subject for as good an artist as himself; features finely cut, as if already marble; an ideal forehead, deeply set eyes, and mouth much hidden in a light-brown beard, but apparently sensitive and delicate.

"I will not offer you my hand," said he; "it is grimy with Cleopatra's clay."

"No; I will not touch clay; it is earthy and human," answered Miriam. "I have come to try whether there is any calm and coolness among your marbles. My own art is too nervous, too passionate, too full of agitation, for me to work at it whole days together, without intervals of repose. So, what have you to show me?"

"Pray look at everything here," said Kenyon. "I love to have painters see my work. Their judgment is unprejudiced, and more valuable than that of the world generally, from the light which their own art throws on mine. More valuable, too, than that of my brother sculptors, who never judge me fairly — nor I them, perhaps."

To gratify him, Miriam looked round at the specimens in marble or plaster, of which there were several in the room, comprising originals or casts of most of the designs that Kenyon had thus far produced. He was still too young to have accumulated a large gallery of such things. What he had to show were chiefly the attempts and experiments, in various directions, of a beginner in art, acting as a stern tutor to himself, and profiting more by his failures than by any successes of which he was yet capable. Some of them, however, had great merit; and, in the pure, fine glow of the new marble, it may be, they dazzled the judgment into awarding them higher praise than they deserved. Miriam admired the statue of a beautiful youth, a pearl-fisher, who had got entangled in the weeds at the bottom of the sea, and lay dead among the pearl-oysters, the rich shells, and the seaweeds, all of like value to him now.

"The poor young man has perished among the prizes that he sought," remarked she. "But what a strange efficacy there is in death! If we cannot all win pearls, it causes an empty shell to satisfy us just as well. I like this statue, though it is too cold and stern in its moral lesson; and, physically, the form has not settled itself into sufficient repose."

In another style, there was a grand, calm head of Milton, not copied from any one bust or picture, yet more authentic than any of them, because all known representations of the poet had been profoundly studied, and solved in the artist's mind. The bust over the tomb in Grey Friars Church, the original miniatures and pictures, wherever to be found, had mingled each its special truth in this one work; wherein, likewise, by long perusal and deep love of the *Paradise Lost*, the *Comus*, the *Lycidas*, and *L'Allegro*,[2] the sculptor had succeeded even better than he knew, in spiritualizing his marble with the poet's mighty genius. And this was a great thing to have achieved, such a length of time after the dry bones and dust of Milton were like those of any other dead man.

---

[2] *Paradise Lost . . . L'Allegro: Paradise Lost* (1665), *Comus, Lycidas,* and *L'Allegro* (1637) are literary works by the English writer John Milton (1608–1674).

There were also several portrait-busts, comprising those of two or three of the illustrious men of our own country, whom Kenyon, before he left America, had asked permission to model. He had done so, because he sincerely believed that, whether he wrought the busts in marble or bronze, the one would corrode and the other crumble, in the long lapse of time, beneath these great men's immortality. Possibly, however, the young artist may have under-estimated the durability of his material. Other faces there were, too, of men who (if the brevity of their remembrance, after death, can be argued from their little value in life) should have been represented in snow rather than marble. Posterity will be puzzled what to do with busts like these, the concretions and petrifactions of a vain self-estimate; but will find, no doubt, that they serve to build into stone walls, or burn into quick-lime, as well as if the marble had never been blocked into the guise of human heads.

But it is an awful thing, indeed, this endless endurance, this almost indestructibility, of a marble bust! Whether in our own case, or that of other men, it bids us sadly measure the little, little time, during which our lineaments are likely to be of interest to any human being. It is especially singular that Americans should care about perpetuating themselves in this mode. The brief duration of our families, as a hereditary household, renders it next to a certainty that the great-grandchildren will not know their father's grandfather, and that half a century hence, at farthest, the hammer of the auctioneer will thump its knock-down blow against his blockhead, sold at so much for the pound of stone! And it ought to make us shiver, the idea of leaving our features to be a dusty-white ghost among strangers of another generation, who will take our nose between their thumb and fingers (as we have seen men do by Cæsar's), and infallibly break it off, if they can do so without detection!

"Yes," said Miriam, who had been revolving some such thoughts as the above, "it is a good state of mind for mortal man, when he is content to leave no more definite memorial than the grass, which will sprout kindly and speedily over his grave, if we do not make the spot barren with marble. Methinks, too, it will be a fresher and better world, when it flings off this great burden of stony memories, which the ages have deemed it a piety to heap upon its back."

"What you say," remarked Kenyon, "goes against my whole art. Sculpture, and the delight which men naturally take in it, appear to me a proof that it is good to work with all time before our view."

"Well, well," answered Miriam, "I must not quarrel with you for flinging your heavy stones at poor Posterity; and, to say the truth, I think you are as likely to hit the mark as anybody. These busts, now, much as I seem to scorn them, make me feel as if you were a magician. You turn feverish men into cool, quiet marble. What a blessed change for them!"

HENRY JAMES

From Roderick Hudson

Roderick Hudson (first serialized in *The Atlantic Monthly*, 1875) was the first major work by the American author Henry James (1843–1916), although it is typical of James's later work in that it centers on a group of American expatriates in Italy. The title character, Hudson, is a precocious young sculptor whose untutored work wins him the patronage of the wealthy Rowland Mallet. The first section excerpted here describes Mallet's introduction to Hudson and Hudson's sculpture, depicting the kind of praise and support that Davis's Hugh Wolfe desperately needs but does not receive. The second excerpt discusses the fine, often nonexistent, line between beauty and ugliness, putting forth a realist's view of beauty similar to that which Wolfe and Davis seem to espouse.

She threw open a window and pointed to a statuette which occupied the place of honor among the ornaments of the room. Rowland looked at it a moment and then turned to her with an exclamation of surprise. She gave him a rapid glance, perceived that her statuette was of altogether exceptional merit, and then smiled, knowingly, as if this had long been an agreeable certainty.

"Who did it? where did you get it?" Rowland demanded.

"Oh," said Cecilia, adjusting the light, "it's a little thing of Mr. Hudson's."

"And who the deuce is Mr. Hudson?" asked Rowland. But he was absorbed; he lost her immediate reply. The statuette, in bronze, something less than two feet high, represented a naked youth drinking from a gourd. The attitude was perfectly simple. The lad was squarely planted on his feet, with his legs a little apart; his back was slightly hollowed, his head thrown back, and both hands raised to support the rustic cup. There was a loosened fillet of wild flowers about his head, and his eyes, under their dropped lids, looked straight into the cup. On the base was scratched the Greek word Δίψα, Thirst. The figure might have been some beautiful youth of ancient fable, — Hylas or Narcissus, Paris or Endymion.[1] Its beauty was the beauty of natural movement; nothing had been sought to be represented but the perfection of an attitude. This had been most attentively studied, and it was exquisitely rendered. Rowland demanded more light, dropped his head on this side and that, uttered vague exclamations. He said to himself, as he had said more than once in the Louvre and the Vatican, "We ugly mortals, what beautiful creatures we are!" Nothing, in a long time, had given him so much pleasure. "Hudson — Hudson," he asked again; "who is Hudson?"

"A young man of this place," said Cecilia.

"A young man? How old?"

"I suppose he is three or four and twenty."

"Of this place, you say — of Northampton, Massachusetts?"

"He lives here, but he comes from Virginia."

"Is he a sculptor by profession?"

"He's a law-student."

Rowland burst out laughing. "He has found something in Blackstone that I never did. He makes statues then simply for his pleasure?"

Cecilia, with a smile, gave a little toss of her head. "For mine!"

"I congratulate you," said Rowland. "I wonder whether he could be induced to do anything for me?"

"This was a matter of friendship. I saw the figure when he had modeled it in clay, and of course greatly admired it. He said nothing at the time, but a week ago, on my birthday, he arrived in a buggy, with this. He had had it cast at the foundry at Chicopee; I believe it's a beautiful piece of bronze. He begged me to accept."

"Upon my word," said Mallet, "he does things handsomely!" And he fell to admiring the statue again.

"So then," said Cecilia, "it's very remarkable?"

"Why, my dear cousin," Rowland answered, "Mr. Hudson, of Virginia, is an extraordinary" — Then suddenly stopping: "Is he a great friend of yours?" he asked.

---

[1] *Hylas . . . Endymion:* Characters from Greek mythology.

"A great friend?" and Cecilia hesitated. "I regard him as a child!"

"Well," said Rowland, "he's a very clever child. Tell me something about him: I should like to see him."

Cecilia was obliged to go to her daughter's music-lesson, but she assured Rowland that she would arrange for him a meeting with the young sculptor. He was a frequent visitor, and as he had not called for some days, it was likely he would come that evening. Rowland, left alone, examined the statuette at his leisure, and returned more than once during the day to take another look at it. He discovered its weak points, but it wore well. It had the stamp of genius. Rowland envied the happy youth who, in a New England village, without aid or encouragement, without models or resources, had found it so easy to produce a lovely work. . . .

[Rowland Mallet meets the young sculptor, then discusses him with Cecilia once again.]

"Well, what do you make of him?" asked Cecilia, returning a short time afterwards from a visit of investigation as to the sufficiency of Bessie's bedclothes.

"I confess I like him," said Rowland. "He's very immature, — but there's stuff in him."

"He's a strange being," said Cecilia, musingly.

"Who are his people? what has been his education?" Rowland asked.

"He has had no education, beyond what he has picked up, with little trouble, for himself. His mother is a widow, of a Massachusetts country family, a little timid, tremulous woman, who is always on pins and needles about her son. . . .

"Roderick . . . has given her plenty to think about, and she has induced him, by some mysterious art, to abide, nominally at least, in a profession that he abhors, and for which he is about as fit, I should say, as I am to drive a locomotive. He grew up *à la grâce de Dieu*, and was horribly spoiled. Three or four years ago he graduated at a small college in this neighborhood, where I am afraid he had given a good deal more attention to novels and billiards than to mathematics and Greek. Since then he has been reading law, at the rate of a page a day. If he is ever admitted to practice I'm afraid my friendship won't avail to make me give him my business. Good, bad, or indifferent, the boy is essentially an artist — an artist to his fingers' ends."

"Why, then," asked Rowland, "doesn't he deliberately take up the chisel?"

"For several reasons. In the first place, I don't think he more than half suspects his talent. The flame is smoldering, but it is never fanned by the breath of criticism. He sees nothing, hears nothing, to help him to self-knowledge. He's hopelessly discontented, but he doesn't know where to look for help. Then his mother, as she one day confessed to me, has a holy horror of a profession which consists exclusively, as she supposes, in making figures of people without their clothes on. Sculpture, to her mind, is an insidious form of immorality, and for a young man of a passionate disposition she considers the law a much safer investment. Her father was a judge, she has two brothers at the bar, and her elder son had made a very promising beginning in the same line. She wishes the tradition to be perpetuated. I'm pretty sure the law won't make Roderick's fortune, and I'm afraid it will, in the long run, spoil his temper." . . .

"Has he then no society? Who is Miss Garland, whom you asked about?"

"A young girl staying with his mother, a sort of far-away cousin; a good plain girl, but not a person to delight a sculptor's eye. Roderick has a goodly share of the old Southern arrogance; he has the aristocratic temperament. He'll have nothing to do with the small towns-people; he says they're 'ignoble.' He cannot endure his mother's friends — the old ladies and the ministers and the tea-party people; they bore him to death. So he comes and lounges here and rails at everything and every one."

This graceful young scoffer reappeared a couple of evenings later, and confirmed the friendly feeling he had provoked on Rowland's part. He was in an easier mood than before, he chattered less extravagantly, and asked Rowland a number of rather naïf questions about the condition of the fine arts in New York and Boston. Cecilia, when he had gone, said that this was the wholesome effect of Rowland's praise of his statuette. Roderick was acutely sensitive, and Rowland's tranquil commendation had stilled his restless pulses. He was ruminating the full-flavored verdict of culture. Rowland felt an irresistible kindness for him, a mingled sense of his personal charm and his artistic capacity. He had an indefinable attraction — the something divine of unspotted, exuberant, confident youth. The next day was Sunday, and Rowland proposed that they should take a long walk and that Roderick should show him the country. The young man assented gleefully, and in the morning, as Rowland at the garden gate was giving his hostess Godspeed on her way to church, he came striding along the grassy margin of the road and out-whistling the music of the church bells. It was one of those lovely days of August when you feel the complete exuberance of summer just warned and checked by autumn. "Remember the day, and take care you rob no orchards," said Cecilia, as they separated.

The young men walked away at a steady pace, over hill and dale, through woods and fields, and at last found themselves on a grassy elevation studded with mossy rocks and red cedars. Just beneath them, in a great shining curve, flowed the goodly Connecticut. They flung themselves on the grass and tossed stones into the river; they talked like old friends. Rowland lit a cigar, and Roderick refused one with a grimace of extravagant disgust. He thought them vile things; he didn't see how decent people could tolerate them. Rowland was amused, and wondered what it was that made this ill-mannered speech seem perfectly inoffensive on Roderick's lips. He belonged to the race of mortals, to be pitied or envied according as we view the matter, who are not held to a strict account for their aggressions. Looking at him as he lay stretched in the shade, Rowland vaguely likened him to some beautiful, supple, restless, bright-eyed animal, whose motions should have no deeper warrant than the tremulous delicacy of its structure, and be graceful even when they were most inconvenient. Rowland watched the shadows on Mount Holyoke, listened to the gurgle of the river, and sniffed the balsam of the pines. A gentle breeze had begun to tickle their summits, and brought the smell of the mown grass across from the elm-dotted river meadows. He sat up beside his companion and looked away at the far-spreading view. It seemed to him beautiful, and suddenly a strange feeling of prospective regret took possession of him. Something seemed to tell him that later, in a foreign land, he would remember it lovingly and penitently.

"It's a wretched business," he said, "this practical quarrel of ours with our own country, this everlasting impatience to get out of it. Is one's only safety then in flight? This is an American day, an American landscape, an American atmosphere. It certainly has its merits, and some day when I am shivering with ague in classic Italy, I shall accuse myself of having slighted them."

Roderick kindled with a sympathetic glow, and declared that America was good enough for him, and that he had always thought it the duty of an honest citizen to stand by his own country and help it along. He had evidently thought nothing whatever about it, and was launching his doctrine on the inspiration of the moment. The doctrine expanded with the occasion, and he declared that he was above all an advocate for American art. He didn't see why we shouldn't produce the greatest works in the world. We were the biggest people and we ought to have the biggest conceptions. The biggest conceptions of course would bring forth in time the biggest performances. We had only to be true to ourselves, to pitch in and not be afraid, to fling Imitation overboard and fix our eyes upon our National Originality. "I declare," he cried, "there's a career for a man, and I've twenty minds to decide, on the spot, to embrace it — to be the consummate, typical, original, national American artist! It's inspiring!"

Rowland burst out laughing and told him that he liked his practice better than his theory, and that a saner impulse than that had inspired his little Water-drinker. Roderick took no offense, and three minutes afterwards was talking volubly of some humbler theme, but half heeded by his companion, who had returned to his cogitations. At last Rowland delivered himself of the upshot of these. "How would you like," he suddenly demanded, "to go to Rome?"

Hudson stared, and, with a hungry laugh which speedily consigned our National Originality to perdition, responded that he would like it reasonably well. "And I should like, by the same token," he added, "to go to Athens, to Constantinople, to Damascus, to the holy city of Benares, where there is a golden statue of Brahma twenty feet tall."

"Nay," said Rowland soberly, "if you were to go to Rome, you should settle down and work. Athens might help you, but for the present I shouldn't recommend Benares."

"It will be time to arrange details when I pack my trunk," said Hudson.

"If you mean to turn sculptor, the sooner you pack your trunk the better."

"Oh, but I'm a practical man! What is the smallest sum per annum, on which one can keep alive the sacred fire in Rome?"

"What is the largest sum at your disposal?"

Roderick stroked his light mustache, gave it a twist, and then announced with mock pomposity: "Three hundred dollars!"

"The money question could be arranged," said Rowland. "There are ways of raising money."

"I should like to know a few! I never yet discovered one."

"One consists," said Rowland, "in having a friend with a good deal more than he wants, and not being too proud to accept a part of it."

Roderick stared a moment and his face flushed. "Do you mean — do you mean" . . . he stammered. He was greatly excited.

Rowland got up, blushing a little, and Roderick sprang to his feet. "In three words, if you are to be a sculptor, you ought to go to Rome and study the antique. To go to Rome you need money. I'm fond of fine statues, but unfortunately I can't make them myself. I have to order them. I order a dozen from you, to be executed at your convenience. To help you, I pay you in advance."

Roderick pushed off his hat and wiped his forehead, still gazing at his companion. "You believe in me!" he cried at last.

"Allow me to explain," said Rowland. "I believe in you, if you are prepared to work and to wait, and to struggle, and to exercise a great many virtues. And then, I'm afraid to say it, lest I should disturb you more than I should help you. You must decide for yourself. I simply offer you an opportunity."

Hudson stood for some time, profoundly meditative. "You have not seen my other things," he said suddenly. "Come and look at them."

"Now?"

"Yes, we'll walk home. We'll settle the question."

He passed his hand through Rowland's arm and they retraced their steps. They reached the town and made their way along a broad country street, dusky with the shade of magnificent elms. Rowland felt his companion's arm trembling in his own. They stopped at a large white house, flanked with melancholy hemlocks, and passed through a little front garden, paved with moss-coated bricks and ornamented with parterres bordered with high box hedges. The mansion had an air of antiquated dignity, but it had seen its best days, and evidently sheltered a shrunken household. Mrs. Hudson, Rowland was sure, might be seen in the garden of a morning, in a white apron and a pair of old gloves, engaged in frugal horticulture. Roderick's studio was behind, in the basement; a large, empty room, with the paper peeling off the walls. This represented, in the fashion of fifty years ago, a series of small fantastic landscapes of a hideous pattern, and the young sculptor had presumably torn it away in great scraps, in moments of aesthetic exasperation. On a board in a corner was a heap of clay, and on the floor against the wall stood some dozen medallions, busts, and figures, in various stages of completion. To exhibit them Roderick had to place them one by one on the end of a long packing-box, which served as a pedestal. He did so silently, making no explanations, and looking at them himself with a strange air of quickened curiosity. Most of the things were portraits; and the three at which he looked longest were finished busts. One was a colossal head of a negro, tossed back, defiant, with distended nostrils; one was the portrait of a young man whom Rowland immediately perceived, by the resemblance, to be his deceased brother; the last represented a gentleman with a pointed nose, a long, shaved upper lip, and a tuft on the end of his chin. This was a face peculiarly unadapted to sculpture; but as a piece of modeling it was the best, and it was admirable. It reminded Rowland in its homely veracity, its artless artfulness, of the works of the early Italian Renaissance. On the pedestal was cut the name — Barnaby Striker, Esq. Rowland remembered that this was the cognomen of the legal luminary from whom his companion had undertaken to borrow a reflected ray, and although, in the bust, there was naught flagrantly set down in malice, it betrayed, comically to one who could relish the secret, that the features of the original had often been scanned with an irritated eye. Besides these there were several rough studies of the nude, and two or three figures of a fanciful kind. The most noticeable (and it had singular beauty) was a small modeled design for a sepulchral monument; that, evidently, of Stephen Hudson. The young soldier lay sleeping eternally, with his hand on his sword, like an old crusader in a Gothic cathedral.

Rowland made no haste to pronounce; too much depended on his judgment. "Upon my word," cried Hudson at last, "they seem to me very good."

And in truth, as Rowland looked, he saw they were good. They were youthful, awkward, and ignorant; the effort, often, was more apparent than the success. But the effort was signally powerful and intelligent; is seemed to Rowland that it needed only to let itself go to compass great things. Here and there, too, success, when grasped, had something masterly. Rowland turned to his companion, who stood with his hands in his pockets and his hair very much crumpled, looking at him askance. The light of admiration was in Rowland's eyes, and it speedily kindled a wonderful illumination on Hudson's handsome brow. Rowland said at last, gravely, "You have only to work!"

It was the artist's opinion that there is no essential difference between beauty and ugliness; that they overlap and intermingle in a quite inextricable manner; that there is no saying where one begins and the other ends; that hideousness grimaces at you suddenly from out of the very bosom of loveliness, and beauty blooms before your eyes in the lap of vileness; that it is a waste of wit to nurse metaphysical distinctions, and a sadly meagre entertainment to caress imaginary lines; that the thing to aim at is the expressive, and the way to reach it is by ingenuity; that for this purpose everything may serve, and that a consummate work is a sort of hotch-potch of the pure and the impure, the graceful and the grotesque.

WILSON McDONALD

Senate Testimony on the Arts and Art Education in the United States

In this excerpt from his testimony to the U.S. Senate on October 1, 1883, sculptor Wilson McDonald argues in favor of government-sponsored or subsidized art education in the United States. McDonald describes the kind of emphasis that other nations place on art and then argues that in order to be considered one of the great "civilized" nations of the world, the United States must understand the importance of art, not as a luxury meant for the very wealthy, but as an element "necessary to the continuation of civilization." For a discussion of the 1883 Senate Committee on Education and Labor, see page 97.

The following excerpt is taken from *Report of the Committee of the Senate upon the Relations between Labor and Capital, and Testimony Taken by the Committee,* vol. 2 (Washington, D.C.: Government and Printing Office, 1885).

NEW YORK, *Monday, October* 1, 1883.
WILSON McDONALD examined.

By the CHAIRMAN:

Question. Please state your residence and occupation. — Answer. My residence is No. 221 West Forty-second street, New York City; I am by profession a sculptor.

Q. State, if you will, to the committee some of the works of art which you have produced, for the purpose of explaining to us your knowledge of the subject that you are about to present. — A. I did not know that that was exactly my business here.

The CHAIRMAN. It is not; but, as I have asked the question, and it is a proper one, you may as well give us the answer.

The WITNESS. My public works are: A colossal bust of Washington Irving, in Prospect Park, Brooklyn; a colossal statue of Fitz-Greene Halleck, in Central Park; a colossal statue of Edward Bates, in Saint Louis, and a colossal statue of General Custer, at the Military Academy, West Point. I have also executed a large number of individual busts of distinguished, notorious, and other men in this country.

Q. Will you then proceed and give us your views, in your own way, and at such length as you choose. — A. For the last ten or twelve years England has been improving her means for art-industrial education; that is, the education of her young mechanics and apprentices of both sexes. Hundreds of schools have been established by the Government of Great Britain, the principal one being the National Art Training School, at South Kensington. . . . There are now over four hundred of these art-industrial schools in France supported almost entirely by the Government.

The decorations of our public buildings and dwelling-houses, the carpets, chandeliers, wall paper, articles of vertu, furniture, tapestries, &c., are nearly all copied from the designs of the skilled designers and workmen who have been educated in the art-industrial schools of France. . . .

America is doing little or nothing in comparison with other governments.

We have a few schools in Massachusetts, one in New York, and one or two in Connecticut, and one in Cincinnati, and it may be, some others.

Even the apprentice system in our country seems to have been abandoned.

Notwithstanding the plain facts that good plasterers, bricklayers, carpenters, tailors, cabinet-makers, and other mechanics earn from $70 to $100 per month, the fathers and mothers of to-day appear to think that their sons should all become professional men, or perhaps clerks or salesmen, at $50 or $60 per month, and the facts and conditions now are, that the country is overstocked with briefless lawyers, bad doctors, worse preachers, half-educated engineers, untrained business men, speculators; and the large crop of the new specimen of the *genus homo*, the "Dude," the out-put of our rich society families, is becoming alarmingly prevalent. . . .

With three hundred or four hundred industrial schools in the great manufacturing centers of our country we would in less than one generation take our place in the front rank of the art and manufacturing nations of the earth. This, in my judgment, humble as it may be, is the biggest political, moral, and wealth-producing idea now before the American people. It looks to the success of our country and the perpetuity of republican institutions. . . .

In the State of Massachusetts they have a number of art-industrial schools, and the boys and girls, especially boys, are taken and are taught the rudiments of the various trades or professions they intend to undertake, and they are taught more especially the use of the pencil and modeling tools. They draw from designs of all kinds, from the simplest up to the human form. This educates the eye and the taste; and, instead of having a common box-maker or an ordinary half-soler of shoes, or a man who can simply shove a plane, and who would get probably from $1 to $1.50 a day, they propose to make skilled mechanics, who would get from $3 to $4 a day. And in this way, by the establishment of these schools in the various manufacturing centers of our country, it is contended that thousands of young men and young women could learn to draw, carve, engrave, and model with good taste, and, by this means of art education, be more fully prepared to learn and practice their trade. . . .

Q. Is there any other matter or any other branch of this subject that you would like to allude to?

A. Well, I would like to say, in a general way, that art and art education is the basis of all successful mechanism in any country, and that the combined fine arts is the surest standard by which to judge the status of any nation in the scale of civilization.

Q. You mean the masses of the people at large? — A. The tastes of the people at large. It is said that the fine arts are luxuries. I contend that they are a necessity as well, and that they are necessary to the continuation of civilization; and without fine arts no country can expect to continue its civilization. In other words, I cannot see how a nation can exist as a civilized people without poetry, painting, sculpture, drama, architecture, and, last and greatest, music.

Q. Do you look upon the fine arts as the cause or as the consequence of civilization? — A. I think they go hand in hand with the advance guard of civilization, and assist in civilization. They have done more to civilize mankind and more to continue civilization than anything else.

Q. In what really does civilization exist, unless it may be proficiency in these arts? — A. Civilization, as I understand it, consists in the morality and intellect of a people — their proficiency in art, science, mechanics, and agriculture.

Q. Would you mean by that to suggest that you think Government ought to patronize the fine arts in their higher aspects?

A. I do.

The tough experience of our early artists, many of whom I could name, would form a very interesting and instructive history. While the artists of the Old World have had galleries, schools, and teachers from their babyhood — and often a palette and brush have been placed in the hands of a boy in Europe at four or five years of age, before he could reach up to the easel — many of our distinguished artists of to-day were plowing in the fields or digging potatoes or hoeing corn in Ohio or Kentucky, or cradling wheat in Massachusetts or New York. These other young gentlemen across the ocean had the best teachers that they could possibly have, while our struggling young artists had no advantages at all. Now, if you will take the productions of many of our older artists and compare them with European educated artists, and take advantages and disadvantages, you will find that we have shown enough ability to induce the Government to recognize the fine arts, which it has never done. Every other civilized Government in the world has recognized the fine arts and their importance as a factor, but no branch of our Government has yet done so. I think that it is time that some action should be taken in the direction of the cultivation of the fine arts in America. In music we are going forward very fast. We import the best artists and singers in the world, and we pay them higher prices than they can get in any other country. The taste of our people in music is equal to that of almost any other country — the few, not the many. I do not see why the intelligence of this country should not be capable of judging of art and the productions of artists as well as the people of any other country.

FLORENCE ELIZABETH CORY

Senate Testimony on Industrial Art Schools for Women

In this excerpt, designer Florence Elizabeth Cory touches on several issues relevant to *Life in the Iron-Mills:* she discusses the lack of art education in the United States, emphasizes the connection between art and industry, and stresses women's unique qualifications for the work of the design industry. Rather than describing the emotional or moral benefits of art, Cory emphasizes the practical skills her women students need. Note that Cory's gender per se seems to equip her for the job of carpet designer in a capitalist marketplace. As one manufacturer tells her, "As women bought carpets he thought it was a very good thing for women to design them, as they would know better what women would like."

The following excerpt is taken from *Report of the Committee of the Senate upon the Relations between Labor and Capital, and Testimony Taken by the Committee,* vol. 2 (Washington, D.C.: Government and Printing Office, 1885).

Q. State your employment? — A. I am the principal of the School of Industrial Art for Women, and I am a designer.

Q. State to the committee, in your own way, the subject-matter you have in your mind in reference to your pursuit and the school which you have established, its efficiency, and its present and prospective usefulness in the way of furnishing occupation and culture to women? — A. Perhaps it would do as well to tell a little of my own experience first. Seven years ago I wished to become a designer for carpets, having made up my mind to that effect by seeing a very ugly carpet and wondering why more beautiful ones were not made, and I could find no one who could tell me where I could learn anything of the kind, or even where carpets were made. I looked in the encyclopœdia and found very unsatisfactory instruction there, telling me merely that carpets were made in the United States, but not telling me where they were made or how. Finally, during the centennial year, I was looking through a pile of papers, Harper's Illustrated Weekly, and they were filled with illustrations of the centennial exhibits. Among others was one of the carpet department at the Philadelphia exhibition. This design was made with divisions, and over each division was the name "Yonkers," "Hartford," "Lowell," &c. I took the first name I came to, which happened to be Hartford, and wrote a letter to the Hartford Carpet Company asking them if designs were in demand, how much they were paid for, how they were made, whether one was restricted in color, and where I could procure the paper from which to make these designs, if they were made on paper. I waited two weeks and received an answer, stating that designs were in great demand, that they could not possibly fill the demand in this country for designs for carpets. This happened to be for carpets alone, not for any other industrial branch. They were very much pleased with the idea of a woman thinking of designing, as I seemed to be the first one who had ever thought of anything of the kind, and Mr. Martin, the agent of the Hartford company, who wrote to me, said that as women bought carpets he thought it was a very good thing for women to design them, as they would know better what women would like. He sent me as full instructions as he could by letter, five designs to look at and several sheets of paper. I made three or four designs and sent them to him, having had no instruction in drawing or painting, or anything of the kind. Of course they were returned to me as being very imperfect, but he thought with instruction I might be able to please them, and advised my going to the Cooper Institute,[1] in this city. I gained admission to the Cooper Institute, and came here and found that they knew less about it than I did myself, because in the three months that intervened I had been finding out as much as I could about it. In the Cooper Institute, in the women's art department, there is a normal class, in which they profess to teach designing. They do teach the elements and principles of designing, and teach them well, but they do not teach practical designing; they do not teach it as applied to any one practical purpose, neither do they teach it in any other school in the country that I know of. The Institute of Technology in Boston comes the nearest to it. For instance, at Cooper Institute they might teach a young lady, as they would say, to make a wall-paper design; set her down with paper and brushes and colors, and it might be a very beautiful design that she would make, but she would not know, and neither would the teachers, whether that design could be printed by the machinery or not. She would not know how many colors she should use, how the colors should fill the size, the dimensions of the drawings, or anything of the kind, because the teachers do not know. I was very much disappointed in that way at not learning anything really practical.

I visited all the carpet departments in all the principal stores here in New York, and studied carpets. I finally found in one of the carpet departments in A. T. Stewart's, a book called the "Carpet Trade Review," which gave me the information I wanted to know — that is, where carpets were made, and whom they were made by. I found that a number of the agents were here in New York City, most of them in Worth street. I went to Worth street, and almost the first

---

[1] *Cooper Institute:* Also called Cooper Union, this tuition-free undergraduate college in New York City was endowed in 1859 by wealthy merchant and philanthropist Peter Cooper.

person I called on was Mr. William B. Kendall, who was president of the carpet association of the United States, and agent of the Bigelow Carpet Company. He was very much pleased with my idea, and sent one of his designers up to give me a lesson. It was the second lesson really, because old Mr. Barber, of Albany, just before his death, gave me my first lesson in carpets. Then Mr. Kendall sent me with a note to the head designer at the carpet factory in the city. There is only one factory in this city, and that is Mr. E. S. Higgins', at the foot of West Forty-third street. He sent me there, and the head designer very kindly offered to give me six weeks instruction, which he did. I learned a great deal there. At that time I was still a pupil at Cooper Union, but by the end of the time I had taken this practical instruction they thought me competent to teach a class at Cooper Union, and I taught a class of seventeen girls and women, which was the first class of the kind that had ever been taught in this country, and probably in the world anywhere; at least they told me so at that time. Then, three years ago, I taught a class at the Ladies' Art Association rooms on Fourteenth Street, a very small class, however. At that time I was not a teacher, and did not profess or intend to be. I was a designer, and earned my living in that way; but there seemed to be such a demand, so many women wanted to know, so many were trying to learn at Cooper Union and the other schools, and had met with the same difficulty I had encountered, that is, that the instruction was not practical, and many of them hearing of me, came to me and asked me to help them. I presume I helped hundreds of women in three or four years, by giving them instruction, giving them hints, and telling them as well as I could, until there began to come so many of them that I could not attend to my business and them too, and I decided to start a school, which I did two years ago, classifying them, of course, and confining them to regular hours, so that I had leisure for my other business and to teach besides. I think that answers your question.

Q. Is there any other school like yours in the world that you know of? — A. There was no other school when I established mine.

Q. Either in this country or any other? — A. Not that I know of, exclusively for women. There are other schools of design; there are very fine schools of design in Paris; there is a very good school at South Kensington, in England, connected with the South Kensington Museum; and there are schools of design all over Europe, but none that are exclusively for women that I know of.

Q. Yours is meant to teach women what they teach men? — A. — Yes; to teach women what they teach men, and in the Lowell Institute they teach men and women both, as far as they go. They teach designing for prints and they teach designing, I think, for some wall papers practically, but they do not teach all kinds of industrial training practically.

Q. Give us some idea of the opening that seems to you to exist in this direction for employment for women. — A. I think it is one of the best openings for women labor in the country. It is remunerative; it is easy work; it is just as easy as for a lady to sit down to paint anything for her own amusement. There is a great demand for patterns which cannot be filled by the designers already in this country. There is not a manufacturer of any extent in the country but that sends abroad for hundreds and some for thousands of dollars' worth of patterns yearly. . . . These designs could be made just as well in our own country and by women. Women will be just as competent, after they are trained, to do it as men, and some of them are as competent and more so than some of the men now. Of course it takes time.

Q. For what purposes are patterns and designs needed? You mentioned prints, wall paper, and carpeting. In what other industries are they wanted? — A. In this country carpets of all grades, wall papers of all grades, silk for dresses and handkerchiefs and ribbons — everything of that kind. There is very little lace manufactured in this country and I think no lace curtains, though they are talking of establishing a factory now for that purpose, but there are embroideries of all kinds, those made by machine, and the Hamburg edgings are made in this country. Furniture chintz, which I did not include in calico, tile, all kinds of reponssé work in silver and gold and brass, carpets, designs for furniture, gas-fixtures, almost anything you look at that is ornamented is made in this country and there is a demand for designs. Of course some factories require more than others.

Q. State a little more fully as to the competency of women to do this kind of work, to receive the necessary training, and what aptitude do they develop for actually doing this work as well as men do it. — A. They learn very readily. I would not hesitate to take any young girl or lady of average intelligence, and I am quite sure I could teach her to become a designer in two school years. Of course a girl having natural taste and regular genius for this kind of work would do much better than one who had not, but any one with any intelligence at all can learn to design, although some will do better than

others; but if they can understand the machinery and the requirements of it, and I see no reason why they should not, they can learn
to design and to make designs to meet the requirements of the machinery. . . .

Q. How many have you instructed these two years, and between
what ages? — A. Two years ago I opened school with 2 pupils; at the
end of the third week I had 5 pupils, and at the end of the school year
I had 41 pupils. The second year I opened the school with 38 pupils
and closed with 75 pupils. Then I presume in the two years I have
had 20 or 30 private pupils who were not regular pupils at the
school. . . .

Q. How old are these pupils? — A. Last year the youngest pupil I
had was fourteen years old, and the oldest one was sixty-two or
sixty-three, I would not venture to say. I have a number of pupils
with gray hair and glasses. The first year of the school all but four
were older than myself. . . . I begin at the beginning, and any pupil
that is graduated from my school understands thoroughly all the
technicalities for all the fabrics. For instance, if she enters the carpet
class for all fabrics, she learns the technicalities of all, which is more
than many male designers in this city can say, even the best. . . .

Q. Can you answer from your observation this question, Whether
women appear to possess as much natural aptitude for this work as
men? — A. Yes, sir; I think they do and more. I think they have a
greater taste. It comes more natural to them.

Q. You think that here is a field of industry specially open to
women? — A. I do most decidedly.

Figure 18. *Interior of [Hiram] Powers's Studio,* from *Harper's Weekly,* October 4, 1873. The busts and full-figure sculptures in Powers's studio indicate his high productivity as an artist who frequently worked for special-order commissions. The open studio doors invite visitors to tour the workplace and showroom and perhaps to place an order.

Figure 19. *William Randolph Rogers Modeling His Colossal Statue of America at Rome*, from *Harper's Weekly*, August 22, 1868. Illustration by J.O'B. Inman. The sculptor puts finishing touches on a statue whose "colossal" size bespeaks nationalistic pride.

Figure 20. *Undine,* by Chauncy B. Ives, ca. 1855. Marble, 61 inches high. Yale University Art Gallery. Gift of Mrs. Alice A. Allen, in memory of her father Simon Sterne. A female water spirit, the Undine of classical mythology received a soul only when she married a mortal. Ives's sculpture attempts to present the classical ideal, though the draping of the figure suggests Rebecca Harding Davis's intention to lift veils of concealment.

Figure 21. *Carthaginian Girl,* by Richard Saltonstall Greenough, 1863. Marble. Boston Athenaeum. Carthage, founded in the ninth century B.C., and located in the center of the northern coast of Africa, became a major commercial site dealing in gold, ivory, grain, textiles, and slaves. Greenough may have wished to evoke exotic associations to Carthaginian religious practices, which included human sacrifice, and to elicit pathos for the Carthaginian maiden.

Figure 22. *Nydia*, by Randolph Rogers, 1859. Marble. The Metropolitan Museum of Art, Gift of James Douglas, 1899. (99.7.2) Sometimes referred to as *Nydia, the Blind Girl of Pompeii*, this sculpture depicts the pathos of the sightless maiden trying to flee the ancient city in southwest Italy that was buried when Mount Vesuvius erupted in 79 A.D.

Figure 23. *Mrs. Bloomfield Moore's Hall,* from *Artistic Houses* (1883).
Classical sculpture in a sumptuous hall was intended to validate educated
taste and the appropriate wealth with which to express it. Notice that Clara
Jessup Moore's (Mrs. Bloomfield Moore's) collection features Rogers's
Nydia (far right).

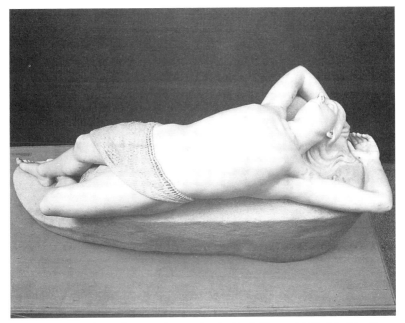

Figure 24. *Dead Pearl Diver*, by Benjamin Paul Akers, 1858. Marble. Portland Museum of Art, Maine. Akers's sculpture of a diver presumably
drowned while seeking valuable pearls can be viewed as an aestheticized version of the body of Rebecca Harding Davis's iron worker, Hugh Wolfe.

Figure 25. *Torso,* by William Rimmer, 1877. Plaster. Bequest of Caroline Hunt Rimmer. Courtesy, Museum of Fine Arts, Boston. Rimmer's representations of the human body — craggy, sinewy, tortuous — stand in distinct contrast to the smoothly modeled contours of the sculpture of artists like Powers, Rogers, Greenough, and Akers. The korl woman in *Life in the Iron-Mills* may be most akin to the sculptural work shown here in Rimmer's *Torso.*

Figure 26. *Seated Youth (Despair)*, by William Rimmer, ca. 1830. Soap-stone. Gift of Mrs. Henry Simonds. Courtesy, Museum of Fine Arts, Boston. Rimmer's display of human anatomy rejects concealment or veiling of the human form and evokes feelings of dejection comparable to those exploited by Davis.

Figure 27. *Mrs. A.T. Stewart's Picture-Gallery,* from *Artistic Houses* (1883). The private art collection of a nineteenth-century patron of the arts included sculpture and paintings exhibited in close proximity. As the wife of a New York department store magnate (A.T. Stewart), Cornelia M. Stewart developed a gallery, open only to friends and social acquaintances, which exhibited the family's wealth and desired social position via its art collection.

Figure 28. *Opening of the American Art Galleries, Madison Square, New York*, from *Harper's Weekly*, November 15, 1884. Drawing by William St. John Harper. The American art patrons James F. Sutton and Thomas E. Kirby opened several galleries for American artists in order to promote the exhibition and sale of American art, which was suffering in its competition with European art. Admission was charged to ensure that only serious patrons would be in attendance.

SCHOOL OF DESIGN FOR FEMALES, COOPER INSTITUTE.

SCHOOL OF DESIGN FOR MALES, COOPER INSTITUTE.

ANTIQUE SCHOOL, NATIONAL ACADEMY OF DESIGN.

Figure 29. *Art Schools of New York,* from *Harper's Weekly,* February 8, 1868. Scenes of drawing and drafting show the education of young artists and designers of both sexes, though classes were segregated by sex.

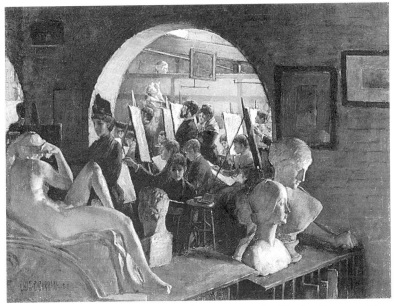

Figure 30. *An Alcove in the Art Students' League,* by Charles Courtney Curran, American, 1861–1942. Oil on canvas, 1888, 8.5 inches × 11.5 inches. Bequest of Kate L. Brewster, 1950.1514. Photograph © 1996, The Art Institute of Chicago. All Rights Reserved. The Art Students' League began in New York in 1875.

4

Women and Writing:
The Public Platform

Toward the end of *Life in the Iron-Mills*, the narrator remarks that "the deep of the night is passing while I write." This line is significant because it draws attention to the narrator's identity as a professional writer, a figure associated with the commitment of thought to written form, with art and intellect, with publication, and with readers and financial compensation. Though the narrator's gender is not specified, readers are likely to assume that the narrator-writer, like Rebecca Harding Davis herself, is female.

The reader might also recall that early in the novella the narrator describes Hugh Wolfe as a feminine figure with a "woman's face" and the nickname of "Molly Wolfe." The proto-artist is thus feminized, suggesting possible similarities between Davis's working-class sculptor and nineteenth-century American women writers who struggled

Figure 31 (opposite). *Portrait of Anna Vaughan Hyatt,* by Marion Boyd Allen, 1915. Oil on canvas. Maier Museum of Art, Randolph-Macon Woman's College, Lynchburg, Virginia. Though painted in the opening years of the twentieth century, Allen's portrait addresses the difficulties of women artists and writers of Rebecca Harding Davis's time. The viewer sees a creative woman seriously engaged in work, but the subject of Hyatt's sculpture is the male realm of soldiers and warfare, from which she is excluded and of which she has no direct experience. Allen's portrait raises the issues of women's artistic and intellectual validation, identity, territoriality, and social status — all matters crucial to nineteenth-century American women writers.

against great odds to produce their art. The woman writer was "chipping and moulding" words, paragraphs, and stanzas just as Hugh chipped and molded korl blocks.

The documents in this chapter include nineteenth-century American women writers' representations of their struggles to voice ideas, observations, and insights in forms ranging from narrative to polemic. While Davis exploits both her narrator and her protagonist to suggest the obstacles to and complexities of literary production, her female contemporaries engage in similar acts of disclosure. Their revelations are often desultory, embedded briefly in subplots, episodic asides, and short essays inset as digressions in stories, novels, essays, and memoirs. Mainly, the struggles of these women appear over and against a masculine literary world that is largely hostile to their bid for an equal share of power in the marketplace of literary art and thought.

A backward glance shows that there had been American women writers of note since the colonial period. The New Englander Anne Bradstreet (1612–1672) wrote lyric poetry, as did the onetime African slave Phillis Wheatley (ca. 1753–1784). The tradition of the American Western novel originated with the best-selling, seventeenth-century captivity narrative of Mary Rowlandson, and Sarah Kemble Knight contributed to the genre of travel writing by keeping a journal of her round-trip journey from Boston to New Haven in the opening years of the eighteenth century. From the New Englander Abigail Adams we have voluminous correspondence not only with her husband and other family members but with Thomas Jefferson as well. In addition, in South Carolina, the letterbook of Eliza Lucas Pinckney demonstrates an aptitude for worldly social critique. Tabitha Tenney was an early author of a cookbook (*Domestic Cookery*, 1808), and Mercy Otis Warren wrote a three-volume history of the American Revolution. The American novel, moreover, was in large part launched by two women writers, Susanna Rowson (*Charlotte Temple*, 1791) and Hannah Foster (*The Coquette*, 1797), who critiqued a social system in which women's sexual transgressions were punished by ostracism, abandonment, and even death.

Given this background, one would expect that nineteenth-century American women writers encountered little resistance on the grounds of their gender, but this was not the case. In the seventeenth century, Anne Bradstreet had recorded the hostility against women who presumed to write. "I am obnoxious to each carping tongue / Who says my hand a needle better fits," wrote Bradstreet in "The Prologue"

(1650) of the ire roused when she swapped the sewing needle for the pen. Meanwhile, the magistrate of Bradstreet's own Massachusetts colony, Governor John Winthrop, wrote in his journal of 1645 of another Anne — Anne Hopkins — whose insanity was caused, Winthrop felt, "by occasion of her giving herself wholly to reading and writing." (2: 225).

In the nineteenth century, the role of women as producers and consumers in the growing literary marketplace for fiction became an object of concern, and socially authoritative men therefore kept up a drumbeat of condemnation. In 1818, just thirteen years before Rebecca Harding Davis's birth, Thomas Jefferson wrote of women's education that "a great obstacle . . . is the inordinate passion prevalent for novels, and the time lost in that reading which should be instructively employed." Jefferson advocated women's instruction in "dancing, drawing, and music," which he termed the "ornaments" and "amusements" of life, and he went on to characterize the effects of fiction as pathologic: "When this poison infects the mind, . . . it destroys its tone and revolts it against wholesome reading." The result is "a bloated imagination, sickly judgment, and disgust toward all the real businesses of life" (15: 166–67).

Even as late as the 1880s, after Davis and such cohorts as Harriet Beecher Stowe, Louisa May Alcott, and Elizabeth Stuart Phelps had enjoyed great success as authors, the prominent novelist and editor William Dean Howells inveighed against the pernicious effects of the sentimental novel, the "books that go for our heartstrings." It was, perhaps, not coincidental that the sentimental novels written by women such as Stowe had achieved sales figures measuring in the hundreds of thousands. Howells satirized such novels as *"slop, silly slop"* and condemned them as "noxious," "immoral," and "ruinous" (*Silas Lapham* 161). Given such continuous antipathy, it is not surprising that at mid-century Nathaniel Hawthorne took his turn in the chorus of male critics who showed a jealous anger toward the "d —— d mob of scribbling women" (see p. 364).

The sentimentalist "mob" were not the only American women writers to be castigated. Intellectual women such as Margaret Fuller were referred to as "bluestockings," so named for the coterie of mid-eighteenth-century English women intellectuals who gathered at the London home of Mrs. Montague to discuss literature rather than pass the hours playing cards. The name "bluestocking," a term of opprobrium, crossed the ocean to America and lingered through the nineteenth century.

While the "scribbling women" were criticized for their indulgence in sentiment, the bluestockings drew fire for their cerebral excesses. In Augusta Evans Wilson's *St. Elmo*, the orphan protagonist, Edna Earl, asks her minister and tutor, Mr. Hammond, to define the term. He replies, "A 'blue-stocking,' my dear, is generally supposed to be a lady, neither young, pleasant, nor pretty (and in most instances, unmarried), who is unamiable, ungraceful, and untidy, ignorant of all domestic accomplishments and truly feminine acquirements . . . who holds house-keeping in detestation, and talks loudly about politics, science, and philosophy; who is ugly, and learned, and cross" (see p. 374).

This profile presents the female intellectual as unwomanly in rejecting marriage and the domestic sphere and disreputable in the neglect of personal grooming (her "hair is never smooth," the ruffles of her dresses "never fluted"). She is reduced to a boorish caricature of her socially admired male counterpart, the learned man. This sort of characterization moved author Mary Abigail Dodge (Gail Hamilton) to retort, "They make a great mistake, who think a strong, brave, self-poised woman is unwomanly. The stronger she is, the truer she is to her womanly instincts." It is perhaps significant that in *Life in the Iron-Mills*, Davis's narrator writes in the library, a room in the household framed by literary authority. Indeed, the references in the text to such landmark figures of Western civilization as Francis Bacon, J. W. Goethe, and Oliver Cromwell, together with the numerous interspersed phrases in Latin and French, suggest that the narrator, if female, identifies with the so-called bluestockings as well as with those committed to the exploration of the complexities of sentiment.

Despite the attacks on "scribbling women" and bluestockings, nineteenth-century American women writers proved irrepressible. Relegated to a female sphere of domesticity that was separate from the male public arena, women developed authority through their management of the home and their perceived role as agents of middle-class morality. Such "domestic" authority undergirded their writings as they turned their attention, in Susan Warner's term, to the "wide, wide world." George W. Curtis, editor at *Harper's Monthly Magazine* in the 1850s, wrote that "every woman in modern society who has strong character, great intelligence, a fine and fastidious taste, a nature which demands unusual scope, and a [capable] heart . . . feels the want of a career. They try to find it in a hundred ways." Writing, whether poems or tracts, textbooks or fiction, proved to be an important career path for women.

Nineteenth-century women writers, however, acknowledged the personal and emotional costs of their efforts to write, to negotiate the labyrinth of skeptical, tyrannical and meddlesome editors, and to win public attention. Indeed, their texts frequently register such painful moments of discouragement. Fanny Fern's Ruth Hall, the title character of the novel, receives a letter of rejection couched as advice from her brother, an influential editor, who advises her to forget about writing and instead seek "*unobtrusive* employment." In spite of such advice, Ruth defiantly determines to move ahead, knowing there will be "a desperate struggle first," including "scant meals, and sleepless nights, and weary days, and a throbbing brow, and an aching heart," together with "the chilling tone, the rude repulse" (see p. 395). Louisa May Alcott portrays such a "rude repulse" in *Little Women* when Jo submits her story to the editor of the "Weekly Volcano" only to have him axe its meaningful messages and blithely advise her to "make it short and spicy, and never mind the moral" (see p. 415).

Such tones of spunky irreverence or morally uplifting determination ought not to mask the difficulty that women writers encountered in running this painful gauntlet. Their determination is all the more remarkable when one considers the prevalence of what has been termed the "cult of female invalidism" in nineteenth-century British and American culture. Upper-class and upper-middle-class women were encouraged to identify themselves as weak, frail, prone to illness, afflicted, and in need of constant nursing and medical attention for a variety of vaguely defined "conditions." In 1895, Dr. Mary Putnam Jacobi wrote that it was "considered natural and almost laudable to break down under almost all conceivable varieties of strain — a winter dissipation, a houseful of servants, a quarrel with a female friend, not to speak of more legitimate reasons." Jacobi understood the ways in which her culture fostered a psychogenic invalidism: "Constantly considering their nerves, urged to consider them by well-intentioned but short-sighted advisors, [women] pretty soon became nothing but a bundle of nerves" (qtd. in Gilbert and Gubar 55). Those who were determined to avoid the sisterhood of sickness (including some who, like Alcott, actually suffered from debilitating illness) rejected powerful cultural messages that equated the identity of the genteel lady with debilitation.

The texts included in this chapter contain numerous reflections by nineteenth-century women writers on the conditions and status of their writing. In an era in which women forfeited their "respectability" by speaking in public, Margaret Fuller worries about how learned and expressive women "could get a platform on which to stand." Fuller's use of the term "platform" refers both to the actual dais from which such orators and speakers as ministers, politicians, and reformers addressed listeners — and to the secured position, held by right, which enables one to assume the authoritative position of public speaker. Fuller's own "platform" constituted not just the speaker's stage but also books, magazines, and journals.

Women writers were also recording their daily efforts to pursue their craft within households occupied by spouses, parents, children, siblings, long-term guests, visitors, and servants. When writing, Alcott's Jo dons her "scribbling suit," a black wool pinafore "on which she could wipe her pen at will." Jo's cap secures her hair (which otherwise could dip into an open inkwell) and also functions as a do-not-disturb sign to the members of her household. Infants and children, however, are shown to clamor unbounded for the attention of the mother-writer in Annie Fields's record of an incident in which Harriet Beecher Stowe's bustling kitchen becomes the scene of the writing of a serialized, torrid romance episode produced for a magazine deadline.

Davis, too, often wrote under duress — to earn money for seaside family vacations after she married and had children, or to supplement the family income when her editor-husband was poorly paid or between newspaper jobs. Financial remuneration was a major consideration, but so was a sense of social duty. "Who will do the work of redressing social inequalities?" asks Lucie True Ames Mead in 1899, and then answers her own question in terms directly relevant to Davis's novella — "chiefly those who have the time; those whose energies are not mainly given to iron and coal and wood." Davis's colleague Elizabeth Stuart Phelps called life a "moral responsibility" and reflected in 1910 on the impact that *Life in the Iron-Mills* had made upon her, situating the novella "at the point where the intellect and moral nature meet." This was the very point occupied by most nineteenth-century, U.S. women's writing.

NATHANIEL HAWTHORNE

Letter to George D. Ticknor

Nathaniel Hawthorne (1804–1864), though now one of America's most respected authors of novels and short stories, was not a best-selling author in his lifetime. Much to his chagrin, his writing never provided him with a comfortable income, and he was therefore forced to work in government jobs. Hawthorne wrote this letter, which is preoccupied with official duties and private finances, while serving as U.S. Consul at Liverpool, England (1853–1857). It contains his now-notorious denunciation of women writers, whose work was selling many more copies in the United States than his own.

The text is from *The Letters, 1853–1856,* in *The Centenary Edition of the* Works *of Nathaniel Hawthorne,* vol. XVII (Columbus: Ohio State UP, 1987), 303–05.

Liverpool, Jany 19th 1855

Dear Ticknor,

I am sorry to have given a false alarm; but as it turns out, I shall have no occasion to draw on you at present — having a good portion of the requisite amount on hand, and supplying the rest by drafts on the State Department for advances made. I shall lose nothing by this investment; and as to your advice not to lend any more money, I acknowledge it to be good, and shall follow it so far as I can and ought. But when the friend of half my lifetime asks me to assist him, and when I have perfect confidence in his honor, what is to be done?[1] Shall I prove myself to be one of those persons who have every quality desirable in friendship, except that they invariably fail you at the pinch? I don't think I can do that; but, luckily, I have fewer friends than most men, and there are not a great many who can claim anything of me on that score. As regards such cases as those of Rogers and Gibson,[2] my official position makes it necessary that I should

---

[1] *the friend . . . done:* John Lewis O'Sullivan (1813–1895), editor of *The Democratic Review,* published many of Hawthorne's writings and was a close friend of the Hawthorne family, who affectionately referred to him as "the Count." Hawthorne had borrowed money to buy real estate in New York for O'Sullivan.

[2] *Rogers and Gibson:* Henry A. Rogers was a traveler to whom Hawthorne, in his official capacity as U.S. consul, loaned money, noting in an earlier letter, "I think there can be no doubt of Mr. Rogers being an honest and honorable fellow." Walter Murray Gibson (1823–1888) was an American adventurer to whom Hawthorne also loaned money.

sometimes risk money in that way; but I can assure you I exercise a great deal of discretion in the responsibilities which I assume. I have not been a year and a half in this office, without learning to say "No" as peremptorily as most men.

I enclose a letter to Rogers, which you will please to send to his direction, unless he has already deposited funds for your draft and that of Mr. Cunard.[3] I also transmit the latter, which has been returned by Cunard, and paid by me. If Mr. Rogers neglects to refund, he is the meanest scoundrel that ever pretended to be a gentleman; for without my interference and assistance, he could have had no resource but starvation, or possibly a Liverpool workhouse. If he refuses to pay, himself, the fact of my aiding him, and of his extreme necessity at the time, should be stated to his brother or nearest relative, who, in the merest decency, cannot but pay the amount. But I still believe that he has a sense of honor in him.

It seems to be a general opinion that the Consular bill will not pass. If it should, I shall (according to your statement) be at least a good deal better off than when I took the office. Reckoning O'Sullivan's three thousand dollars, I shall have bagged about $15000; and I shall estimate the Concord place and my copyrights together at $5000 more; — so that you see I have the twenty thousand, after all! I shall spend a year on the Continent, and then decide whether to go back to the Way Side, or to stay abroad and write books. But I had rather hold this office two years longer; for I have not seen half enough of England, and there is the germ of a new Romance[4] in my mind, which will be all the better for ripening slowly. Besides, America is now wholly given over to a d —— d mob of scribbling women, and I should have no chance of success while the public taste is occupied with their trash — and should be ashamed of myself if I did succeed. What is the mystery of these innumerable editions of the Lamplighter,[5] and other books neither better nor worse? — worse they could not be, and better they need not be, when they sell by the 100.000.

---

[3] *Mr. Cunard:* In 1839, Sir Samuel Cunard (1787–1865) founded the Royal Mail Steam Packet Company.

[4] *new Romance:* "The Ancestral Footstep"(1861).

[5] *the Lamplighter:* (1854) The first novel of Maria Susanna Cummins (1827–1866), which sold 40,000 copies in two months and 70,000 during the first year.

A gentleman here wishes for the Unitarian newspaper (the Enquirer I think it is called) published by Mr. Bellows in New York.[6]
You can subscribe for it in my name, pay in advance, and send the
numbers in your regular package.

The children are delighted with the books you sent them.

I meant to write to Fields by this steamer, but fear I shall not have
time. Please to convey to him my thanks for his slice of cake, and
warmest congratulations on his marriage.

Your friend,
Nath[l] Hawthorne.

[6] *Mr. Bellows in New York:* Henry Whitney Bellows (1814–1882) was minister of
the Church of All Souls in New York and, since 1847, editor of the *Christian Inquirer.*

MARGARET FULLER

From "The Great Lawsuit"[1]

Margaret Fuller (1810–1850) was one of the early nineteenth century's most important activists for women's rights. She held a prominent
role in the community of transcendentalist authors and thinkers, which
included Ralph Waldo Emerson, Orestes Brownson, Jones Very, Lydia
Maria Child, and Bronson Alcott. "The Great Lawsuit: Man versus
Men: Woman versus Women," published in the transcendentalist journal
The Dial in 1843, argues passionately for women's independence and for
the interdependence of men and women. In this selection, Fuller calls for
women's right to speak, for equality in marriage and other male-female
relations, and for the education of women to prepare them to embark on
independent investigations of the truth. Fuller revised and expanded this
essay into the book *Woman in the Nineteenth Century* (1845), which
has become a classic of American feminism.

[1] *"The Great Lawsuit":* In 1844 Fuller expanded this essay under the title *Woman
in the Nineteenth Century;* in this later edition she explains her earlier title as follows:
"I meant . . . to intimate the fact that, while it is the destiny of Man, in the course of
the ages, to ascertain and fulfill the law of his being, so that his life shall be seen, as a
whole, to be that of an angel or messenger, the action of prejudices and passions which
attend, in the day, the growth of the individual, is continually obstructing the holy
work that is to make earth a part of heaven. By Men I mean both man and woman;
these are the two halves of one thought. I lay no especial stress on the welfare of either.
I believe that the development of the one cannot be effected without that of the other.
My highest wish is that this truth should be distinctly and rationally apprehended, and
the conditions of life and freedom recognized as the same for the daughters and sons of
time; twin exponents of a divine thought."

Female authors, even learned women, if not insufferably ugly and slovenly, from the Italian professor's daughter, who taught behind the curtain, down to Mrs. Carter[2] and Madame Dacier,[3] are sure of an admiring audience, if they can once get a platform on which to stand.

But how to get this platform, or how to make it of reasonably easy access is the difficulty. Plants of great vigor will almost always struggle into blossom, despite impediments. But there should be encouragement, and a free, genial atmosphere for those of more timid sort, fair play for each in its own kind. Some are like the little, delicate flowers, which love to hide in the dripping mosses by the sides of mountain torrents, or in the shade of tall trees. But others require an open field, a rich and loosened soil, or they never show their proper hues.

It may be said man does not have his fair play either; his energies are repressed and distorted by the interposition of artificial obstacles. Aye, but he himself has put them there; they have grown out of his own imperfections. If there *is* a misfortune in woman's lot, it is in obstacles being interposed by men, which do *not* mark her state, and if they express her past ignorance, do not her present needs. As every man is of woman born, she has slow but sure means of redress, yet the sooner a general justness of thought makes smooth the path, the better. . . .

Civilized Europe is still in a transition state about marriage, not only in practice, but in thought. A great majority of societies and individuals are still doubtful whether earthly marriage is to be a union of souls, or merely a contract of convenience and utility. Were woman established in the rights of an immortal being, this could not be. She would not in some countries be given away by her father, with scarcely more respect for her own feelings than is shown by the Indian chief, who sells his daughter for a horse, and beats her if she runs away from her new home. Nor, in societies where her choice is left free, would she be perverted, by the current of opinion that seizes her, into the belief that she must marry, if it be only to find a protector, and a home of her own.

---

[2] *Mrs. Carter:* Elizabeth Carter (1717–1806), English poet and translator of classical literature.

[3] *Madame Dacier:* Anne LaFebvre Dacier (1654–1720), French scholar and translator of classical literature.

Neither would man, if he thought that the connection was of permanent importance, enter upon it so lightly. He would not deem it a trifle, that he was to enter into the closest relations with another soul, which, if not eternal in themselves, must eternally affect his growth.

Neither, did he believe woman capable of friendship, would he, by rash haste, lose the chance of finding a friend in the person who might, probably, live half a century by his side. Did love to his mind partake of infinity, he would not miss his chance of its revelations, that he might the sooner rest from his weariness by a bright fireside, and have a sweet and graceful attendant, "devoted to him alone." Were he a step higher, he would not carelessly enter into a relation, where he might not be able to do the duty of a friend, as well as a protector from external ill, to the other party, and have a being in his power pining for sympathy, intelligence, and aid, that he could not give.

Where the thought of equality has become pervasive, it shows itself in four kinds.

The household partnership. In our country the woman looks for a "smart but kind" husband, the man for a "capable, sweet-tempered" wife.

The man furnishes the house, the woman regulates it. Their relation is one of mutual esteem, mutual dependence. Their talk is of business, their affection shows itself by practical kindness. They know that life goes more smoothly and cheerfully to each for the other's aid; they are grateful and content. The wife praises her husband as a "good provider," the husband in return compliments her as a "capital housekeeper." This relation is good as far as it goes.

Next comes a closer tie which takes the two forms, either of intellectual companionship, or mutual idolatry. The last, we suppose, is to no one a pleasing subject of contemplation. The parties weaken and narrow one another; they lock the gate against all the glories of the universe that they may live in a cell together. To themselves they seem the only wise, to all others steeped in infatuation, the gods smile as they look forward to the crisis of cure, to men the woman seems an unlovely syren, to women the man an effeminate boy.

The other form, of intellectual companionship, has become more and more frequent. Men engaged in public life, literary men, and artists have often found in their wives companions and confidants in thought no less than in feeling. And, as in the course of things the intellectual development of woman has spread wider and risen higher, they have, not unfrequently, shared the same employment. As in the case of Roland and his wife,[4] who were friends in the household and the nation's councils, read together, regulated home affairs, or prepared public documents together indifferently.

It is very pleasant, in letters begun by Roland and finished by his wife, to see the harmony of mind and the difference of nature, one thought, but various ways of treating it.

This is one of the best instances of a marriage of friendship. It was only friendship, whose basis was esteem; probably neither party knew love, except by name.

Roland was a good man, worthy to esteem and be esteemed, his wife as deserving of admiration as able to do without it. Madame Roland is the fairest specimen we have yet of her class, as clear to discern her aim, as valiant to pursue it, as Spenser's Britomart,[5] austerely set apart from all that did not belong to her, whether as woman or as mind. She is an antetype of a class to which the coming time will afford a field, the Spartan matron, brought by the culture of a book-furnishing age to intellectual consciousness and expansion.

Self-sufficing strength and clear-sightedness were in her combined with a power of deep and calm affection. The page of her life is one of unsullied dignity.

Her appeal to posterity is one against the injustice of those who committed such crimes in the name of liberty. She makes it in behalf of herself and her husband. I would put beside it on the shelf a little volume, containing a similar appeal from the verdict of contemporaries to that of mankind, that of Godwin in behalf of his wife, the celebrated, the by most men detested Mary Wolstonecraft.[6] In his view it was an appeal from the injustice of those who did such wrong in the name of virtue.

Were this little book interesting for no other cause, it would be so for the generous affection evinced under the peculiar circumstances. This man had courage to love and honor this woman in the face of the world's verdict, and of all that was repulsive in her own past history. He believed he saw of what soul she was, and that the thoughts

---

[4] *Roland and his wife:* Jean Mari Roland de la Platière (1734–1793), French statesman and enemy to the Jacobins; his wife, Marie Jean Phlipon (1754–1793) was very influential with the Girondists and wrote her memoirs while imprisoned by the Jacobins.

[5] *Spenser's Britomart:* A character in Spenser's *The Faerie Queene* (1590–1596) representing chastity; Spenser (ca. 1552–1599) was an English poet.

[6] *Godwin . . . Wolstonecraft:* William Godwin (1756–1836) was married to Mary Wollstonecraft (1759–1797) and wrote *Memoirs of the Author of "A Vindication of the Rights of Woman"* in 1798, shortly after Wollstonecraft died in childbirth.

she had struggled to act out were noble. He loved her and he defended her for the meaning and intensity of her inner life. It was a good fact.

Mary Wolstonecraft, like Madame Dudevant (commonly known as George Sand[7]) in our day, was a woman whose existence better proved the need of some new interpretation of woman's rights, than anything she wrote. Such women as these, rich in genius, of most tender sympathies, and capable of high virtue and a chastened harmony, ought not to find themselves by birth in a place so narrow, that in breaking bonds they become outlaws. Were there as much room in the world for such, as in Spenser's poem for Britomart, they would not run their heads so wildly against its laws. They find their way at last to purer air, but the world will not take off the brand it has set upon them. The champion of the rights of woman found in Godwin one who plead her own cause like a brother. George Sand smokes, wears male attire, wishes to be addressed as Mon frère;[8] perhaps, if she found those who were as brothers indeed, she would not care whether she were brother or sister. . . .

Women like Sand will speak now, and cannot be silenced; their characters and their eloquence alike foretell an era when such as they shall easier learn to lead true lives. . . .

Another sign of the time is furnished by the triumphs of female authorship. These have been great and constantly increasing. They have taken possession of so many provinces for which men had pronounced them unfit, that though these still declare there are some inaccessible to them, it is difficult to say just *where* they must stop.

The shining names of famous women have cast light upon the path of the sex, and many obstructions have been removed. When a Montague[9] could learn better than her brother, and use her lore to such purpose afterwards as an observer, it seemed amiss to hinder women from preparing themselves to see, or from seeing all they could when prepared. Since Somerville[10] has achieved so much, will any young girl be prevented from attaining a knowledge of the physical sciences, if she wishes it? De Stael's[11] name was not so clear of offence; she

---

[7] *Madame Dudevant . . . Sand:* Amandine Aurore Lucile Dupin, baronne Dudevant (1804–1876), who wrote under the name George Sand, was a French Romantic novelist known for her work for women's liberation.

[8] *Mon frère:* "My brother" or "old friend" (French).

[9] *Montague:* Lady Mary Wortley Montague (1689–1762), renowned letter writer.

[10] *Somerville:* Mary Somerville (1780–1872), British scientific writer.

[11] *De Stael:* Madame Anne-Louise-Germaine de Staël (1766–1817), French writer with a famous literary-political salon.

could not forget the woman in the thought; while she was instructing you as a mind, she wished to be admired as a woman. Sentimental tears often dimmed the eagle glance. Her intellect, too, with all its splendor, trained in a drawing room, fed on flattery, was tainted and flawed; yet its beams make the obscurest school house in New England warmer and lighter to the little rugged girls, who are gathered together on its wooden bench. They may never through life hear her name, but she is not the less their benefactress.

This influence has been such that the aim certainly is, how, in arranging school instruction for girls, to give them as fair a field as boys. These arrangements are made as yet with little judgment or intelligence, just as the tutors of Jane Grey,[12] and the other famous women of her time, taught them Latin and Greek, because they knew nothing else themselves, so now the improvement in the education of girls is made by giving them gentlemen as teachers, who only teach what has been taught themselves at college, while methods and topics need revision for those new cases, which could better be made by those who had experienced the same wants. Women are often at the head of these institutions, but they have as yet seldom been thinking women, capable to organize a new whole for the wants of the time, and choose persons to officiate in the departments. And when some portion of education is got of a good sort from the school, the tone of society, the much larger proportion received from the world, contradicts its purport. Yet books have not been furnished, and a little elementary instruction been given in vain. Women are better aware how large and rich the universe is, not so easily blinded by the narrowness and partial views of a home circle.

Whether much or little has or will be done, whether women will add to the talent of narration, the power of systematizing, whether they will carve marble as well as draw, is not important. But that it should be acknowledged that they have intellect which needs developing, that they should not be considered complete, if beings of affection and habit alone, is important.

Yet even this acknowledgment, rather obtained by woman than proffered by man, has been sullied by the usual selfishness. So much is said of women being better educated that they may be better com-

---

[12] *Jane Grey:* Lady Jane Grey (1537–1554) was crowned queen of England on July 10, 1553, after the death of Henry VIII's son, Edward VI, and reigned for nine days. She was imprisoned and ultimately executed when the people rallied to the cause of Mary I.

panions and mothers *of men!* They should be fit for such companionship, and we have mentioned with satisfaction instances where it has been established. Earth knows no fairer, holier relation than that of a mother. But a being of infinite scope must not be treated with an exclusive view to any one relation. Give the soul free course, let the organization be freely developed, and the being will be fit for any and every relation to which it may be called. The intellect, no more than the sense of hearing, is to be cultivated, that she may be a more valuable companion to man, but because the Power who gave a power by its mere existence signifies that it must be brought out towards perfection. . . .

Women here are much better situated than men. Good books are allowed with more time to read them. They are not so early forced into the bustle of life, nor so weighed down by demands for outward success. The perpetual changes, incident to our society, make the blood circulate freely through the body politic, and, if not favorable at present to the grace and bloom of life, they are so to activity, resource, and would be to reflection but for a low materialist tendency, from which the women are generally exempt.

They have time to think, and no traditions chain them, and few conventionalities compared with what must be met in other nations. There is no reason why the fact of a constant revelation should be hid from them, and when the mind once is awakened by that, it will not be restrained by the past, but fly to seek the seeds of a heavenly future. . . .

Every relation, every gradation of nature, is incalculably precious, but only to the soul which is poised upon itself, and to whom no loss, no change, can bring dull discord, for it is in harmony with the central soul.

If any individual live too much in relations, so that he becomes a stranger to the resources of his own nature, he falls after a while into a distraction, or imbecility, from which he can only be cured by a time of isolation, which gives the renovating fountains time to rise up. With a society it is the same. Many minds, deprived of the traditionary or instinctive means of passing a cheerful existence, must find help in self-impulse or perish. It is therefore that while any elevation, in the view of union, is to be hailed with joy, we shall not decline celibacy as the great fact of the time. It is one from which no vow, no arrangement, can at present save a thinking mind. For now the rowers are pausing on their oars, they wait a change before they can pull together. All tends to illustrate the thought of a wise contemporary.

Union is only possible to those who are units. To be fit for relations in time, souls, whether of man or woman, must be able to do without them in the spirit.

It is therefore that I would have woman lay aside all thought, such as she habitually cherishes, of being taught and led by men. I would have her, like the Indian girl, dedicate herself to the Sun, the Sun of Truth, and go no where if his beams did not make clear the path. I would have her free from compromise, from complaisance, from helplessness, because I would have her good enough and strong enough to love one and all beings, from the fullness, not the poverty of being.

Men, as at present instructed, will not help this work, because they also are under the slavery of habit. I have seen with delight their poetic impulses. A sister is the fairest ideal, and how nobly Wordsworth, and even Byron, have written of a sister.[13] . . .

But men do *not* look at both sides, and women must leave off asking them and being influenced by them, but retire within themselves, and explore the groundwork of being till they find their peculiar secret. Then when they come forth again, renovated and baptized, they will know how to turn all dross to gold, and will be rich and free though they live in a hut, tranquil, if in a crowd. Then their sweet singing shall not be from passionate impulse, but the lyrical overflow of a divine rapture, and a new music shall be elucidated from this many-chorded world.

[13] *have written of a sister:* William Wordsworth paid literary tribute to his sister Dorothy, and Lord Byron did the same for his half-sister Augusta Leigh.

AUGUSTA EVANS WILSON

From St. Elmo

Augusta Jane Evans Wilson (1835–1909) was a Southern novelist, a well-educated woman, and an ardent supporter of the Confederacy. *St. Elmo,* her best known novel, was published in 1866 and achieved immediate popularity. The novel was adapted for the stage, repeatedly produced, and then made into a silent movie in 1923. The following selections describe the stigma attached to educated women in the nineteenth century and the difficulties women faced if they wanted to learn or to write. Edna Earl, the novel's heroine, is an orphan under the guardianship of Mrs. Murray, a wealthy Southern woman. Mrs. Murray arranges Edna's education with Mr. Hammond, her minister. In the following passages, Edna argues in favor of women's right to be educated and to write, but she is careful to temper her arguments, explaining that women must not encroach on the rights of men.

The text is from *The Works of Augusta Evans Wilson* (New York: Co-operative Publication Society, 1896).

"I think the child is as inveterate a book-worm as I ever knew; but for heaven's sake, Mr. Hammond, do not make her a blue-stocking."

"Ellen, did you ever see a genuine blue-stocking?"

"I am happy to be able to say that I was never so unfortunate!"

"You consider yourself lucky then, in not having known De Staël, Hannah More, Charlotte Brontë, and Mrs. Browning?"[1]

"To be consistent of course I must answer yes; but you know we women are never supposed to understand that term, much less possess the jewel itself; and beside, sir, you take undue advantage of me, for the women you mention were truly great geniuses. I was not objecting to genius in women."

"Without these auxiliaries and adjuncts which you deprecate so earnestly, would their native genius ever have distinguished them, or charmed and benefitted the world? Brilliant success makes blue-stockings autocratic, and the world flatters and crowns them; but unsuccessful aspirants are strangled with an offensive *sobriquet,* than which it were better that they had millstones tied about their necks. After all, Ellen, it is rather ludicrous, and seems very unfair that the whole class of literary ladies should be sneered at on account of the colour of Stillingfleet's[2] stockings eighty years ago."

"If you please, sir, I should like to know the meaning of 'blue-stocking'?" said Edna.

[1] *De Staël . . . Mrs. Browning:* Madame Anne-Louise-Germaine de Staël (1766–1817), French writer with a famous literary-political salon; Hannah More (1745–1833), English playwright and religious writer known for being a bluestocking; Charlotte Brontë (1816–1855), English novelist, author of *Jane Eyre, Shirley,* and *Villette;* Elizabeth Barrett Browning (1806–1861), English poet and wife of poet Robert Browning.

[2] *Stillingfleet:* Benjamin Stillingfleet (1702–1771), English author and botanist.

"You are in a fair way to understand it if you study Greek," answered Mrs. Murray, laughing at the puzzled expression of the child's countenance.

Mr. Hammond smiled, and replied:

"A 'blue-stocking,' my dear, is generally supposed to be a lady, neither young, pleasant, nor pretty (and in most instances, unmarried), who is unamiable, ungraceful, and untidy, ignorant of all domestic accomplishments and truly feminine acquirements, and ambitious of appearing very learned; a woman whose fingers are more frequently adorned with ink-spots than thimble; who holds housekeeping in detestation, and talks loudly about politics, science, and philosophy; who is ugly, and learned, and cross; whose hair is never smooth and whose ruffles are never fluted. Is that a correct likeness, Ellen?"

"As good as one of Brady's photographs.[3] Take warning, Edna."

"The title of 'blue-stocking,'" continued the pastor, "originated in a jest, many, many years ago, when a circle of very brilliant, witty, and elegant ladies in London, met at the house of Mrs. Vesey, to listen to and take part in the conversation of some of the most gifted and learned men England has ever produced. One of those gentlemen, Stillingfleet, who always wore blue stockings, was so exceedingly agreeable and instructive, that when he chanced to be absent, the company declared the party was a failure without: 'the blue stockings,' as he was familiarly called. A Frenchman, who heard of the circumstance, gave to these conversational gatherings the name of '*bas bleu*,' which means blue stockings; and hence, you see, that in popular acceptation, I mean in public opinion, the humorous title, which was given in compliment to a very charming gentleman, is now supposed to belong to tiresome, pedantic, and disagreeable ladies. Do you understand the matter now?"

"I do not quite understand why ladies have not as good a right to be learned and wise as gentlemen."

"To satisfy you on that point would involve more historical discussion than we have time for this morning; some day we will look into the past and find a solution of the question. Meanwhile, you may study as hard as you please, and remember, my dear, that where one woman is considered a blue-stocking, and tiresomely learned, twenty are more tiresome still because they know nothing. I will

---

[3] *Brady's photographs:* Mathew Brady (1823–1896), American photographer who oversaw extensive photographic documentation of the Civil War.

obtain all the books you need, and hereafter you must come to me every morning at nine o'clock. When the weather is good you can easily walk over from Mrs. Murray's."

As they rode homeward Edna asked:

"Has Mr. Hammond a family?"

"No; he lost his family years ago. But why do you ask that question?"

"I saw no lady, and I wondered who kept the house in such nice order."

"He has a very faithful servant who attends to his household affairs. In your intercourse with Mr. Hammond be careful not to allude to his domestic afflictions."

Mrs. Murray looked earnestly, searchingly at the girl, as if striving to fathom her thoughts; then throwing her head back, with the haughty air which Edna had remarked in St. Elmo, she compressed her lips, lowered her veil, and remained silent and abstracted until they reached home.

The comprehensive and very thorough curriculum of studies now eagerly commenced by Edna, and along which she was gently and skilfully guided by the kind hand of the teacher, furnished the mental aliment for which she hungered, gave constant and judicious exercise to her active intellect, and induced her to visit the quiet parsonage library as assiduously as did Horace, Valgius, and Virgil[4] the gardens on the Esquiline where Mæcenas[5] held his literary assize. Instead of skimming a few text-books that cram the brain with unwieldy scientific technicalities and pompous philosophic terminology, her range of thought and study gradually stretched out into a broader, grander cycle, embracing, as she grew older, the application of those great principles that underlie modern science and crop out in ever-varying phenomena and empirical classifications. Edna's tutor seemed impressed with the fallacy of the popular system of acquiring one branch of learning at a time, locking it away as in drawers of rubbish, never to be opened, where it moulders in shapeless confusion till swept out ultimately to make room for more recent scientific invoices. Thus in lieu of the educational plan of "finishing natural philosophy and chemistry this session, and geology and astronomy next

---

[4] *Horace . . . Virgil:* Horace (65–8 B.C.), Roman poet and satirist; Valgius, Roman poet and critic of the Augustan age, mentioned by Horace; Virgil (70–19 B.C.), Roman poet, author of the *Aeneid*, considered by many to be the best Latin poet.

[5] *Mæcenas:* (d. 8 B.C.) Roman statesman, counselor of Augustus; his name has come to refer to anyone who is a patron of letters.

term, and taking up moral science and criticism the year we graduate," Mr. Hammond allowed his pupil to finish and lay aside none of her studies; but sought to impress upon her the great value of Blackstone's[6] aphorism: "For sciences are of a sociable disposition, and flourish best in the neighbourhood of each other; nor is there any branch of learning but may be helped and improved by assistance drawn from other arts."

Finding that her imagination was remarkably fertile, he required her, as she advanced in years, to compose essays, letters, dialogues, and sometimes orations, all of which were not only written and handed in for correction, but he frequently directed her to recite them from memory, and invited her to assist him, while he dissected and criticised either her diction, line of argument, choice of metaphors, or intonation of voice. In these compositions he encouraged her to seek illustration from every department of letters, and convert her theme into a focus, upon which to pour all the concentrated light which research could reflect, assuring her that what is often denominated "far-fetchedness" in metaphors, furnishes not only evidence of the laborious industry of the writer, but is an implied compliment to the cultured taste and general knowledge of those for whose entertainment or edification they are employed — provided always said metaphors and similes really illustrate, elucidate, and adorn the theme discussed.

His favourite plea in such instances was, "If Humboldt and Cuvier, and Linnæus, and Ehrenberg[7] have made mankind their debtors by scouring the physical cosmos for scientific *data,* which every living *savant* devours, assimilates, and reproduces in dynamic, physiologic, or entomologic theories, is it not equally laudable in scholars, orators, and authors — nay, is it not obligatory on them, to subsidize the vast cosmos of literature, to circumnavigate the world of *belles-lettres,* in search of new hemispheres of thought, and spice islands of illustrations; bringing their rich gleanings to the great public mart, where men barter their intellectual merchandise? Wide as the universe, and free as its winds, should be the range of the human mind." . . .

---

[6] *Blackstone:* Sir William Blackstone (1723–1780), English jurist, author of *Commentaries on the Laws of England,* the most influential book on English law.

[7] *Humboldt . . . Ehrenberg:* Alexander, Baron Von Humboldt (1769–1859), German naturalist and traveler; Georges Cuvier (1769–1832), French anatomist, considered the father of comparative anatomy and paleontology; Carolus Linnaeus (1707–1778), Swedish naturalist and physician, considered the founder of the modern scientific nomenclature for plants and animals; Christian Gottfried Ehrenberg (1795–1876), German naturalist.

The daring scheme of authorship had seized upon Edna's mind with a tenacity that conquered and expelled all other purposes, and though timidity and a haunting dread of the failure of the experiment prompted her to conceal the matter, even from her beloved pastor, she pondered it in secret, and bent every faculty to its successful accomplishment. Her veneration for books — the great elemosynary granaries of human knowledge to which the world resorts — extended to those who created them; and her imagination invested authors with peculiar sanctity, as the real hierophants[8] anointed with the chrism[9] of truth. The glittering pinnacle of consecrated and successful authorship seemed to her longing gaze as sublime, and wellnigh as inaccessible, as the everlasting and untrodden Himalayan solitudes appear to some curious child of Thibet or Nepaul; who, gamboling among pheasants and rhododendrons, shades her dazzled eyes with her hands, and looks up awe-stricken and wondering at the ice-domes and snow-minarets of lonely Deodunga, earth's loftiest and purest altar, nimbused with the dawning and the dying light of the day. There were times when the thought of presenting herself as a candidate for admission into the band of literary exoterics seemed to Edna unpardonably presumptuous, almost sacrilegious, and she shrank back, humbled and abashed; for writers were teachers, interpreters, expounders, discoverers, or creators — and what could she, just stumbling through the alphabet of science and art, hope to donate to her race that would ennoble human motives or elevate aspirations? Was she, an unknown and inexperienced girl, worthy to be girded with the ephod[10] that draped so royally the Levites[11] of literature? Had God's own hand set the Urim and Thummim[12] of Genius in her soul? Above all, was she mitred with the plate of pure gold — "Holiness unto the Lord?"[13]

Solemnly and prayerfully she weighed the subject, and having finally resolved to make one attempt, she looked trustingly to heaven for aid, and went vigorously to work.

---

[8] *hierophants:* Chief priests of Eleusinian or Orphic mysteries of ancient Greece.

[9] *chrism:* Mixture of oil and balm used in sacramental annointing in the Greek and Roman Catholic Churches; has come to refer to anything used for annointing.

[10] *ephod:* Priestly linen vestment that Aaron wears to speak before the Pharaoh. See Exodus 28:31.

[11] *Levites:* Biblical tribe descended from Levi, son of Jacob.

[12] *Urim and Thummim:* Two objects used to determine the will of the Hebrew God; God commands them to be in Aaron's heart when he goes to speak before the Pharaoh. See Exodus 28:30.

[13] *"Holiness unto the Lord":* An insignia for Aaron to wear when he goes before the Pharoah. See Exodus 28:36.

To write *currente calamo*[14] for the mere pastime of author and readers, without aiming to inculcate some regenerative principle, or to photograph some valuable phase of protean truth, was in her estimation ignoble; for her high standard demanded that all books should be to a certain extent didactic, wandering like evangels among the people, and making some man, woman, or child happier or wiser, or better — more patient or more hopeful — by their utterances. Believing that every earnest author's mind should prove a mint, where all valuable ores are collected from the rich veins of a universe — are cautiously coined, and thence munificently circulated — she applied herself diligently to the task of gathering from various sources the *data* required for her projected work: a vindication of the unity of mythologies. The vastness of the cosmic field she was now compelled to traverse, the innumerable ramifications of polytheistic and monotheistic creeds, necessitated unwearied research, as she rent asunder the superstitious veils which various nations and successive epochs had woven before the shining features of truth. To-day peering into the golden Gardens of the Sun at Cuzo[15]; to-morrow clambering over Thibet glaciers, to find the mystic lake of Yamuna[16]; now delighted to recognize in Teoyamiqui (the wife of the Aztec God of War) the unmistakable features of Scandinavian Valkyrias[17]; and now surprised to discover the Greek Fates[18] sitting under the Norse tree Ygdrasil,[19] deciding the destinies of mortals, and calling themselves Nornas[20]; she spent her days in pilgrimages to mouldering shrines, and midnight often found her groping in the classic dust of extinct systems. Having once grappled with her theme, she wrestled as obstinately as Jacob[21] for the blessing of a successful solution, and in order to popularize a subject bristling with rocondite archaisms and philologic problems, she cast it in the mould of fiction. The information and pleasure which she had derived from the perusal of Vaughan's delightful Hours with the Mystics,[22] suggested the idea of adopting a

[14] *currente calamo:* "A free style" or "a facile pen" (Latin).

[15] *Cuzo:* (Cuzco) capital of Peru during the Inca civilization, ca. 1200.

[16] *Yamuna:* Hindu river goddess.

[17] *Valkyrias:* In Norse mythology, three daughters of Odin, the chief of the gods; they choose those who will fall in battle.

[18] *Fates:* Three Greek goddesses who control human and divine destinies.

[19] *Ygdrasil:* In Norse mythology, the great cosmic ash tree or the world tree.

[20] *Nornas:* The Fates of Norse mythology, three women who live near Ygdrasil.

[21] *Jacob:* Jacob wrestles with an angel and wins a blessing, the name Israel. See Genesis 32:24–30.

[22] *Hours with the Mystics:* Robert Alfred Vaughan's (1823–1857) *Hours with the Mystics* went through several editions in the mid-1800s.

similar plan for her own book, and investing it with the additional interest of a complicated plot and more numerous characters. To avoid anachronisms, she endeavoured to treat the religions of the world in their chronologic sequence, and resorted to the expedient of introducing pagan personages. A fair young priestess of the temple of Neith, in the sacred city of Sais[23] — where people of all climes collected to witness the festival of lamps — becoming skeptical of the miraculous attributes of the statues she had been trained to serve and worship, and impelled by an earnest love of truth to seek a faith that would satisfy her reason and purify her heart, is induced to question minutely the religious tenets of travellers who visited the temple, and thus familiarized herself with all existing creeds and hierarchies. The lore so carefully garnered is finally analyzed, classified, and inscribed on papyrus. The delineation of scenes and sanctuaries in different latitudes, from Lhasa to Copan, gave full exercise to Edna's descriptive power, but imposed much labour in the departments of physical geography and architecture.

Verily! an ambitious literary programme for a girl over whose head scarcely eighteen years had hung their dripping, drab, wintry skies, and pearly summer clouds. . . .

[Edna has sent her manuscript to a famous writer-publisher in New York. Here, the manuscript is returned. Mr. Manning urges Edna to redirect her writing toward domestic subjects and thus to curb her larger ambitions.]

On her lap lay the package and letter, which she no longer felt any desire to open, and her hands drooped listlessly at her side. The fact that her MS. was returned rung a knell for all her sanguine hopes; for such was her confidence in the critical acumen of Mr. Manning, that she deemed it utterly useless to appeal to any other tribunal. A higher one she knew not; a lower she scorned to consult.

She felt like Alice Lisle[24] on that day of doom, when Jeffreys pronounced the fatal sentence; and after a time, when she summoned courage to open the letter, her cheeks were wan and her lips compressed so firmly that their curves of beauty were no longer traceable.

---

[23] *temple of Neith . . . Sais: Neith* was the goddess of weaving and the creative arts who was thought to have woven the world. *Sais* was Egypt's capital during the Twenty-Sixth Dynasty.

[24] *Alice Lisle:* Alice or Alicia Lisle (ca. 1614–1685) was an English parliamentarian who was beheaded by order of Judge Jeffreys for sheltering two of Monmouth's rebels.

"MISS EARL: I return your MS., not because it is devoid of merit, but from the conviction that, were I to accept it, the day would inevitably come when you would regret its premature publication. While it contains irrefragable evidence of extraordinary ability, and abounds in descriptions of great beauty, your style is characterized by more strength than polish, and is marred by crudities which a dainty public would never tolerate. The subject you have undertaken is beyond your capacity — no woman could successfully handle it — and the sooner you realize your over-estimate of your powers, the sooner your aspirations find their proper level, the sooner you will succeed in your treatment of some theme better suited to your feminine ability.

"Burn the enclosed MS., whose erudition and archaisms would fatally nauseate the intellectual dyspeptics who read my 'Maga,' and write sketches of home-life — descriptions of places and things that you understand better than recondite analogies of ethical creeds and mythologic systems, or the subtle lore of Coptic priests. Remember that women never write histories nor epics; never compose oratorios that go sounding down the centuries; never paint 'Last Suppers'[25] and 'Judgment Days;'[26] though now and then one gives to the world a pretty ballad that sounds sweet and soothing when sung over a cradle, or another paints a pleasant little *genre* sketch which will hang appropriately in some quiet corner, and rest and refresh eyes that are weary with gazing at the sublime spiritualism of Fra Bartolomeo[27] or the gloomy grandeur of Salvator Rosa.[28] If you have any short articles which you desire to see in print, you may forward them, and I will select any for publication which I think you will not blush to acknowledge in future years.

"Very respectfully,   Your obedient servant,

DOUGLAS G. MANNING."

Unwrapping the MS., she laid it with its death-warrant in a drawer, then sat down, crossed her arms on the top of her desk, and rested her head upon them. The face was not concealed, and as the light shone on it, an experienced physiognomist would have read there profound disappointment, a patient weariness, but unbending resolution and no vestige of bitterness. The large, thoughtful eyes were sad

---

[25] '*Last Suppers*': *The Last Supper* (1495–1498), Leonardo da Vinci's famous fresco painting of Christ's last supper with his disciples.

[26] '*Judgment Days*': Manning may be referring to Michelangelo's *Last Judgment* (1534–1541) fresco on the wall of the Sistine Chapel.

[27] *Fra Bartolomeo*: Originally named Baccio della Porta (1475–1517), Fra Bartolomeo was an Italian painter and one of the leading artists of the High Renaissance.

[28] *Salvator Rosa*: (1615–1673) Italian painter and poet known for his wild, savage landscapes.

but dry, and none who looked into them could have imagined for an instant that she would follow the advice she had so eagerly sought. During her long reverie, she wondered whether all women were browbeaten for aspiring to literary honours; whether the poignant pain and mortification gnawing at her heart was the inexorable initiation fee for entrance upon that arena, where fame adjudges laurel crowns, and reluctantly and sullenly drops one now and then on female brows. To possess herself of the golden apple[29] of immortality, was a purpose from which she had never swerved; but how to baffle the dragon critics who jealously guarded it was a problem whose solution puzzled her.

To abandon her right to erudition formed no part of the programme which she was mentally arranging, as she sat there watching a moth singe its filmy, spotted wings in the gas-flame; for she was obstinately wedded to the unpardonable heresy, that, in the nineteenth century, it was a woman's privilege to be as learned as Cuvier, or Sir William Hamilton,[30] or Humboldt, provided the learning was accurate, and gave out no hollow, counterfeit ring under the merciless hammering of the dragons. If women chose to blister their fair, tender hands in turning the windlass of that fabled well where truth is hidden, and bruised their pretty, white feet in groping finally on the rocky bottom, was the treasure which they ultimately discovered and dragged to light any the less truth because stentorian, manly voices were not the first to shout Eureka?

She could not understand why, in the vineyard of letters, the labourer was not equally worthy of hire, whether the work was successfully accomplished in the *toga virilis*,[31] or the gay kirtle of *contadina*.[32]

Gradually the expression of pain passed from the girl's countenance, and, lifting her head, she took from her desk several small MSS., which she had carefully written from time to time, as her reading suggested the ideas imbodied in the articles. Among the number were two, upon which she had bestowed much thought, and which she determined to send to Mr. Manning. . . .

---

[29] *golden apple:* In Greek mythology, golden apples grew in the Garden of Hesperides as a wedding gift from Gaia to Zeus and Hera and were guarded by a dragon; Heracles stole them as one of his labors.

[30] *Sir William Hamilton:* (1805–1865) Irish mathematician.

[31] *toga virilis:* A gown worn by young men upon coming of age in ancient Rome.

[32] *contadina:* A country woman.

[Edna informs her benefactress, Mrs. Murray, that she is moving to New York to earn her living as a writer. Mrs. Murray disapproves but cannot dissuade Edna. The minister, Mr. Hammond, also disapproves, but in the following speech, he focuses on Edna's ambition to be a writer rather than on her decision to move away. He feels that this ambition will lead Edna to unhappiness.]

"My child, your ambition is your besetting sin. It is Satan pointing to the tree of knowledge, tempting you to eat and become 'as gods.' Search your heart, and I fear you will find that while you believe you are dedicating your talent entirely to the service of God, there is a spring of selfishness underlying all. You are too proud, too ambitious of distinction, too eager to climb to some lofty niche in the temple of fame, where your name, now unknown, shall shine in the annals of literature and serve as a beacon to encourage others equally as anxious for celebrity. I was not surprised to see you in print; for long, long ago, before you realized the extent of your mental dowry, I saw the kindling of that ambitious spark whose flame generally consumes the women in whose heart it burns. The history of literary females is not calculated to allay the apprehension that oppresses me, as I watch you just setting out on a career so fraught with trials of which you have never dreamed. As a class, they are martyrs, uncrowned and uncanonized; jeered at by the masses, sincerely pitied by a few earnest souls and wept over by the relatives who really love them. Thousands of women have toiled over books that proved millstones and drowned them in the sea of letters. How many of the hundreds of female writers scattered through the world in this century will be remembered six months after the coffin closes over their weary, haggard faces? You may answer, 'They made their bread.' Ah child! it would have been sweeter if earned at the wash-tub, or in the dairy, or by their needles. It is the rough handling, the jars, the tension of her heart-strings that sap the foundations of a woman's life, and consign her to an early grave; and a Cherokee rose-hedge is not more thickly set with thorns than a literary career with grievous, vexatious, tormenting disappointments. If you succeed after years of labour and anxiety and harassing fears, you will become a target for envy and malice, and, possibly for slander. Your own sex will be jealous of your eminence, considering your superiority as an insult to their mediocrity; and mine will either ridicule or barely tolerate you; for men detest female competitors in the Olympian game of literature. If you fail, you will be sneered down till you become embittered, soured, misanthropic; a curse to yourself, a burden to the friends who sympathize with your blasted hopes. Edna, you have talent, you write well, you are conscientious; but you are not De Staël, or Hannah More, or Charlotte Brontë, or Elizabeth Browning; and I shudder when I think of the disappoint[ment] that may overtake all your eager aspirations. . . .

[Here, Edna explains her belief that women should be educated as long as they remain properly womanly in so doing. According to Edna, women have no right to usurp rights, roles, and privileges of men (such as voting).]

I never hear that much abused word 'equality' without a shudder. . . . I have no aristocratic prejudices, for my grandfather was a blacksmith, and my father a carpenter; but I do not believe that 'all men are born free and equal;' and think that two-thirds of the Athenians were only fit to tie Socrates'[33] shoes, and not one-half of Rome worthy to play valet and clasp the toga of Cato or Cicero.[34] Neither do I claim nor admit the equality of the sexes, whom God created with distinctive intellectual characteristics, which never can be merged or destroyed without outraging the decrees of nature, and sapping the foundations of all domestic harmony. Allow me to say, sir, in answer to your remark concerning learned women, that it seems to me great misapprehension exists relative to the question of raising the curriculum of female education. Erudition and effrontery have no inherent connection, and a woman has an unquestionable right to improve her mind, *ad infinitum,* provided she does not barter womanly delicacy and refinement for mere knowledge; and in her anxiety to parade what she has gleaned, forget the decorum and modesty, without which she is monstrous and repulsive. Does it not appear reasonable that a truly refined woman, whose heart is properly governed, should increase her usefulness to her family and her race, by increasing her knowledge? A female pedant who is coarse and boisterous, or ambitious of going to Congress, or making stump-speeches, would be quite as unwomanly and unlovely in character if she were utterly illiterate. I am afraid it is not their superior learning or ability which afflicts the nineteenth century with those unfortunate, abnormal developments, familiarly known as 'strong-minded women;' but that it is the misdirection of their energies, the one-sided

[33] *Socrates:* (469–399 B.C.) Greek philosopher.
[34] *Cato or Cicero:* Roman orators, statesmen, and men of letters ca. 70 B.C.

nature of their education. A woman who cannot be contented and happy in the bosom of her home, busied with ordinary womanly work, but fancies it is her mission to practise law or medicine, or go out lecturing, would be a troublesome, disagreeable personage under all circumstances; and would probably stir up quite as much mischief, while using ungrammatical language, as if she were a perfect philologist. Whom did Socrates find most amiable and feminine, learned Diotima, or unlearned Xantippe?[35] I think even mankind would consent to see women as erudite as Damo,[36] or Isotta Nogarola,[37] provided they were also as exemplary in their domestic relations, as irreproachable and devoted wives and daughters.

[35] *Xantippe:* Socrates' shrewish wife, according to Plato.

[36] *Damo:* Daughter of Pythagoras who guarded her father's secret writings.

[37] *Isotta Nogarola:* (1418–1466) Italian scholar of Latin and Greek who translated and wrote poetry; she never married so that nothing would interfere with her scholarship.

CAROLINE KIRKLAND

"Literary Women"

This essay, published in 1853 in *A Book for the Home Circle,* shows Caroline Kirkland's wit, humor, and dedication to the rights of women. Kirkland (1801–1864) came from a family interested in literature. Although her literary career began with the publication of her humorous frontier novel, *A New Home, Who'll Follow?* (1839), she began writing full-time in order to support her family after the 1846 death of her husband. Her essay "Literary Women" dates from this period of her writing. In it she critiques nineteenth-century popular opinion which held that women interested in reading and writing were inadequate mothers and wives.

Text from *A New Home, Who'll Follow?,* ed. Sandra A. Zagarell (New Brunswick, NJ: Rutgers UP, 1990).

Let it not be for a moment supposed that we are about to attempt a crusade in defence of blue-stockings! Better undertake, single-handed, to lay a Trail to the Pacific, tunnelling the Rocky Mountains.

Whether the prejudice entertained against this class — is it numerous enough to claim the title of a class? — be just or not, it is most potent; and, like the deaf adder, it stoppeth its ears. We hardly know of one more obstinate, unless it be that against old maids, — or that other, perhaps worse one, against stepmothers. . . .

How many literary women has any one person ever seen? How many has the world seen? How would the list compare in length with that of the pretty triflers who never in the whole course of their mortal lives took up a book with the least intention of obtaining any information from it? The spite which is generally nourished against these unhappy ladies implies great respect; for their numbers are too insignificant to attract notice, if the individuals were not of consequence. And it may be noticed here, as being particularly curious, that the man who declaims loudest against the idea of a writing woman, is sure to be the most vain-glorious of the smallest literary performance on the part of his wife or daughter. The gift of a place does not sooner silence a vehement patriot, than the first essay or magazine story produced by a lady of his family does the indignant definer of 'woman's sphere,' with a pudding and a shirt for its two poles.

But as to the comparative scarcity of literary ladies. It seems strange to a simple looker-on that they should not be prized, at least on the principle of the Queen Anne's farthing, which, valueless in itself, became precious because there were but four struck. There is not even yet a 'mob of gentle [*women*] that write with ease.' Women are said to be peculiarly favoured in the possession of the quality called 'passive courage,' (fortitude?) one of the benevolent provisions of nature for need — but they have always, as a body, shown a good deal of cowardice in this matter. The risks are too fearful. So that really the number is kept down as low as prudence can desire. It would require no Briareus[1] to count on his fingers all that have dabbled in ink during the last century. No fear of usurpation; no danger that the pen will be snatched from strong hands and wielded in defiance, or even in self-defence. A handful of chimney swallows might as well be suspected of erecting their quills against the eagles — or owls. Swallows! literary ladies are hardly more abundant than dodos.

---

[1] *Briareus:* In Greek mythology, a monster with one hundred arms, son of Uranus and Ge.

Now let us ask what is the distinguishing mark of the literary woman of our day. Is it inky fingers — corrugated brows — unkempt locks — unrighteous stockings — towering talk — disdain of dinner — aspirations after garments symbolical of authority — any or all of these? Who pretends anything of the kind? One could almost wish there were some startling peculiarities, even though exhibited by only a few individuals, to break up the uniformity of society. What a treat it would be to see a blue enter a party with the suitable airs, and cross the awful space of carpet which sometimes intervenes between the door and the hostess, with gown pinned up from the mud, or one black slipper and one white one, the unconscious head all the while nodding graciously on either side, secure of the due effect of the *entrée!* But alas! no literary lady, since Mrs. Anne Royall,[2] has borne about with her the least outward token of the dreaded power within. Curls, ribbons, bracelets, bouquets, fans — not an item lacking; all correct, to the very shoe-tie. Here surely is a title to respect — a claim to the feminine character, though a loss to society. Lady Mary Wortley Montagu[3] did better when she received her English visitors at Venice in a mask and domino, as a reproof to their curiosity.

And as in dress, so in other matters. Whether from the increased facilities of life, or because the world has grown older, and so more cunning and commonplace, there is no telling a bookish woman any more, even in her housekeeping. There are no more cobwebs in literary parlours than elsewhere. The presence of 'books that are books' does not necessarily now imply the absence of books which are principally covers and 'illustrations.' All sorts of unmanageable and worse than useless bindings may be found intermixed with plain, serviceable duodecimos, and the blue, and yellow, and gray paper of the Reviews and Magazines. Even an inkstand does not take the place of nick-nacks and pretty lumber, though these generally drive the more suspicious article into a by-corner.

'There is a general notion,' says Sydney Smith,[4] 'that if you once suffer women to eat of the tree of knowledge, the rest of the family will soon be reduced to the same aerial and unsatisfactory diet.' But the children of literary mammas seem to be nearly as well cared for,

[2] *Mrs. Anne Royall:* (1769–1854) American writer who began writing to earn money after her inheritance from her husband was threatened; in 1824, Royall went to Washington in rags to lobby Congress to grant her an income because of her husband's service in the military.

[3] *Lady Mary Wortley Montagu:* (1689–1762) English writer who settled in Venice.

[4] *Sydney Smith:* (1721–1771) Scottish satirist and essayist.

as if their mothers did not, or could not read — which is probably in some minds the criterion of a thoroughly admirable wife and mother. They are even found in some cases to entertain the profoundest and most tender affection for her whom society agrees to consider a deluded female. This would seem as if a love of books did not quite extinguish the affections, or the qualities which inspire affection. 'Would a mother desert her infant for a quadratic equation?' says the satirist just quoted. And it remains to be proved that there is greater complaint of missing buttons, or more neglect of the 'stitch in time,' in consequence of some use of the pen as well as the thimble, than in houses where the only amusement is dressing, and the only serious employment scolding the servants.

With regard to domestic government, the point on which the sensitive wisdom of the world is most alarmed — fearing lest the staff of authority should be wrested from the grasp of the legal ruler by hands that were long ago decided to be too weak to wield it, even if peaceably accorded — does it not seem as if the want of interest in home affairs, which is charged as a natural fault in the literary lady, should set at rest any dread of her usurping too large a share of direction in home arrangements? Is it the absent-minded, absorbed, woolgathering, star-gazing dame that will quarrel to have the bacon fried instead of boiled? Will she recall the eyes ever 'in fine frenzy rolling,' to the dull earth long enough or with interest enough to insist upon new carpets? It seems as if one fear or the other must be unfounded. Either literary women care about domestic matters or they do not. If they do, their employments cannot be objected against as interfering with exclusively feminine duties; if not, surely their husbands need not fear improper interference.

But we have hitherto neglected to inquire what it is that entitles a woman to the appellation of literary; or perhaps we should express the matter better, if we should say, what fastens upon her that imputation. Must she have written a book? Phœbus Apollo! how few then have claims upon a *tabouret*[5] at thy court! And must the size of the book be taken into account? Then those who dilate most unscrupulously will sit highest. Or will the number of volumes settle precedence? There will, in that case, be little room for any but Mrs. Ellis, Mrs. Gore,[6] and their immediate sisterhood. But to the point. If not a

---

[5] *tabouret:* Low stool without a back or arms.

[6] *Mrs. Ellis, Mrs. Gore:* Sarah Stickney Ellis (1812–1872), prolific British writer of advice books for women; Catherine Grace Frances Gore (1799–1861), British writer who wrote seventy novels between 1824 and 1862 and whom Thackeray parodied.

book, will a poem be sufficient? or an essay? or a magazine article? Then more of us are included in the glory or odium of female authorship. Or does writing letters make one literary? In these Californian days it is to be hoped not, lest some of our fair friends should be tempted to neglect their absent brothers rather than be liable to misconstruction, in so important a particular. Writing letters sometimes ends in writing books, as more than Madame de Sévigné[7] can testify. How is it with keeping a journal? Does that come within the canon? Might it not be maliciously interpreted into writing a book in disguise?

Does the toleration for which a female writer may hope depend in any degree upon the class of subjects which may engage her pen? We have an idea that some gentlemen would award a palm (no pun, positively,) to her who writes a Cook's Oracle, where a rod or a fool's cap would be the doom of a lady who should presume to touch political economy. Next to a family receipt-book, one would suppose books of instruction for children would be most popular in female hands; but there is no doubt that some men think Mrs. Barbauld[8] wore, or should have worn, a beard, and would be surprised to see a picture of Mrs. Trimmer[9] in petticoats. The novel of fashionable life, provided it have no suspicion of a moral, and make no pretension to teach anything whatever, may pass as feminine, without detracting from the fame of its author; but a novel with the least bit of bone in it is 'mannish' — a very different term from 'manly.' Poetry, provided it be of the sigh-away, die-away cast, does not injure a lady's reputation; acrostic-making is considered quite an accomplishment, and so are watch-paper verses; but poetry which some unthinking, out-of-the-world critics praise as 'masculine' for vigour and freshness, is insufferable. If we could show to some objectors the delicate Elizabeth Barrett Browning[10] — the minutest, most fragile, most ethereal creature the sun ever shone upon, with a voice like a ring-dove's, we might swear in vain to her identity as the author of some of the strongest and bravest poetry that has appeared in our day; so obsti-

[7] *Madame de Sévigné:* Marie de Rabutin-Chantal, Marquise de Sévigné (1626–1696) gained her reputation from her life-long correspondence with her daughter, which was published in 1725.

[8] *Mrs. Barbauld:* Anna Laetitia Barbauld (1743–1824), British writer who wrote several books of children's prose with her brother John Aikin.

[9] *Mrs. Trimmer:* Sarah Trimmer (1741–1810), British writer of children's books and textbooks.

[10] *Elizabeth Barrett Browning:* (1806–1861) British poet who was known for being frail.

nate a conviction exists in some minds of the close connexion between mental power and masculine coarseness.

It seems a little inconsistent that anybody should venture in our day to put such dangerous weapons as the *ologies* into the hands of a sex to whose peculiar charms too much mind is known to be so fatal. Why not leave a girl in the hands of the nurse until she is fit to be transferred to those of the seamstress, the pastry-cook, the dancing-master, the teacher of music, in succession? Why occupy precious hours and risk fine eyes over even French and Italian, which could be learned in colloquy with these artists? Why not adapt means to ends? Is it certain that school-knowledge will pass in at one ear and out at the other? If not, how far safer not to impart it! Considering the advantage that may be taken of it, the unsexing and unsphering that may ensue upon an indiscreet use of it, surely it were best to send Grammar and History, Philosophy and Mathematics, to the limbo of forgotten things, as far as females are concerned. If Madame de Staël[11] had been brought up only to sing and dance, regulate household affairs, and tend children, would she have written the books which provoked Napoleon to banish her from Paris? If Mrs. Somerville[12] had spent years sitting with her feet in the stocks and her arms pinioned in a back-board to make her genteel, while her eyes were employed in counting bead-work, or devising stitches in crochet, could she ever have lowered herself by writing about the geography of the heavens? Prevention is certainly better than cure. Choke the fountain rather than have to dam the river (no pun will be suspected here). Shut up our schools for young ladies; bid the teachers 'go spin!' Use the copy-books for recipes or papillottes; the learned treatises popularized 'for the use of schools' to kindle fires less to be dreaded than those of literary ambition: and if our daughters should not thereafter be 'like polished stones at the corners of the temple,' they will at least make kitchen-hearths, which we all know to be a far more obviously useful part of the social edifice.

One great duty of woman, if not the greatest, is to be agreeable. Now, if teaching her to think for herself, and so putting her upon the temptation of expressing her thoughts, imperil in the least degree this

[11] *Madame de Staël*: Anne-Louise-Germaine de Staël (1766–1817), French writer with a famous literary-political salon; her book *D' l'Allemagne* (1810) opened French literature to the influence of German literature.

[12] *Mrs. Somerville*: Mary Somerville (1780–1872), British mathematician and scientific writer.

her high avocation, we vote for the instant abandonment of female cultivation, and would advocate a heavier fine on selling to a female under forty, unaccompanied by parent or guardian, a card of Joseph Gillott's pens,[13] than for allowing a paper of poison to go from the shop unlabelled. We would be the very Jack Cade[14] of legislators for such offenders. To be sure there may be question as to the universality of the feeling on which our zeal is predicated. Some men openly profess to like intelligent women, and there are doubtless others who in secret do not altogether reprobate the use of the pen in female hands, although they may for harmony's sake refrain from the avowal of such liberality, except, as we have hinted, the case fall within the limits of their own family circle, when they usually go beyond mere toleration. It is very desirable that unanimity be obtained in this matter. The natural desire to be agreeable will be quite strong enough to set things right after they are fully understood. To stand well with all men will far outweigh the penurious and timid praise of a few. So true is this that Madame de Staël herself confessed that she would gladly give her intellect and her fame for beauty!

But is beauty always the alternative? Ah, there is an important question. Many scandals have been uttered against the outward charms of literary ladies. 'Ugly!' said a celebrated poet in our own hearing, on this very topic; 'ugly, yes — they *all* are!' Which must mean that lines of thought are disadvantages to the peculiar charm of the female face — an equivocal compliment, rather. But waiving this delicate point, is the face which has no lines of thought, on that account beautiful? If not, how fearful the risk of leaving the head unfurnished! If the face may be vacant, yet not lovely — if we may neglect the brain without securing the beauty, how difficult becomes the decision of the parent. In old times — happy times! — when fairies attended at the birth of daughters, and offered choice of gifts, the balance between beauty and good sense was easily struck. It was understood that to select the one, precluded all chance of obtaining the other without a new and more compulsive spell. Now, without any great insight into futurity, and with only a little fat beginning of a face, with a button nose and twinkling eyes to guide our estimate of probabilities of comeliness, while on the other hand frowns the fear lest furnishing the brain may, by giving a superabundance of meaning

---

[13] *Joseph Gillott:* (1799–1873) British pen manufacturer.
[14] *Jack Cade:* Leader of a rebellion in 1450 against English royal forces; in *2 Henry VI*, Shakespeare presented him as reckless, vicious, and crude.

to the face, mar the promise of beauty, how anxious must be the deliberation! A critical survey of society might lead one to suppose that with some parents a decision proves impossible, the poor child being left to grow up without either beauty or brains.

Our own convictions on this subject were rendered unalterable some years since, in the course of a lecture by a young gentleman before a debating society, at whose sitting we were so happy as to assist. The question was one not unfrequently discussed on those occasions — the comparative education of the sexes. Our friend was warm against sharing the sciences with women. His picture of the ideal blue-stocking, a hideous man-woman, with high-crowned cap and spectacles, hoarse voice and masculine stride, still haunts our imagination, and has ever proved an effectual scare-crow in that field. On the other hand, his fancy's sketch of a charming young person, was such as to leave in one's mind a somewhat confused mass of roses, lilies, smiles, blushes, pearls, snow, raven's wings, and Aurora's[15] fingers, very fascinating, though suggestive of despair to most of the sex. But what made the most distinct impression on our memory was the question, repeated in various forms as different branches of knowledge were examined with reference to their fitness for female use — 'Will it render her more *alluring?*' Here lay the key — far more potent than Blue Beard's, which locked up only women literally headless — to the whole popular philosophy of female claims on the score of intellect. This hint as to the object of woman's being, solved a world of doubts. Here was a touchstone by which to try any pursuit — a test to determine the value of any talent. Whatever does not conduce to the grand aim must be, if not noxious, at best indifferent. Whoever contends that an education regulated by this principle would leave woman insignificant and unhappy, shows only his ignorance of the world; for do we not see every day splendid people who avow it, consciously or unconsciously? and can splendid people be unhappy or insignificant?

There is one potent argument against allowing women in habits of literary employment — the injury that would arise to the great cause of public amusements. Our theatres would be worse filled even than they are at present, and the opera would cease its languishing existence at once, if the fair eyes that now are fain to let down their "fringed curtains" as a veil against the intensity of floods of gas-light,

---

[15] *Aurora:* Roman goddess of the dawn, portrayed by poets as rising out of the ocean in a chariot, her rosy fingers dripping dew.

should learn to prefer the shaded study-lamp at home, and the singing of the quiet fire to the louder efforts of the cantatrice. Dancing, except in horrible sobriety, after the piano, would become obsolete; waltzing might be studied in the abstract, or as an illustration of the revolution of the heavenly bodies; but 'certain stars' would no longer 'shoot madly from their spheres,' to join the giddy round in person. Parties would break up at eleven; for eyes and nerves would so rise in value if put to serious use, that any wilful expenditure of their powers would soon be voted *mauvais ton*;[16] and if that should ever happen, adieu to suppers and champagne! There is really no end to the overturn that might result from an innovation of this sort. Imagination pictures the splendid fabric of Fashion tottering to its fall — undermined by that seemingly impotent instrument, the pen, wielded by female hands. We shrink from our own picture of so mournful a reversal of the present happy state of things. It is one of the perversities of the imagination to torment itself with delineations of what can never by any possibility occur; and this is truly a case in point.

The truth being conceded that no women but those who are ugly and unattractive should or do write, a thought suggests itself with respect to the limited duration of the beauty which is so justly considered the most desirable of female possessions, and the most natural and proper bar to any extensive cultivation of the mind. As none but the very robust beauty lasts beyond forty, would it not be advisable to establish schools, specially fitted for that age, in which the remains of a lovely woman might have an opportunity of some education suited to the thirty years which may be supposed still to lie before her? It would be irksome to pass so long a period in silence, and mortifying to continue to talk nonsense without rosy lips to set it off. Here a certain amount of knowledge might be communicated by those whom inexorable plainness of person had condemned to intellectual exercises in early life; and the circumstance might prove mutually beneficial, since the husbands of the once beautiful would undoubtedly be willing to pay liberally for having some ideas infused into their minds, as provision for the conversation of old age. The face could no longer be injured, while the head, and perhaps the heart too, might gain materially.

> 'Teeth for the toothless, ringlets for the bald,
> And roses for the cheeks of faded age — '

---

[16] *mauvais ton*: "Bad fashion" (French).

would be valueless, compared with this more potent elixir of life. The practice of the old surgeons, who sometimes filled the shrunken veins of decreptitude with the rich blood of bounding youth, might be considered a precedent for such efforts as we propose. Scruples were sometimes entertained as to the lawfulness of that mode of repairing the decay of Nature; but to the attempt to make education the substitute for beauty, we are sure society will not object, even though the result should be that 'dim horror' — a literary woman.

FANNY FERN

From Ruth Hall

Sara Payson Willis Parton (1811–1872), who identified herself as Fanny Fern in her newspaper columns and books, began writing after the death of her first husband and her divorce from her second. Writing was first and foremost a means of financial support for Parton and her children, and she was quite successful at it. *Ruth Hall* (1855), Fern's first novel, created a minor literary scandal because of its negative portrayal of her relatives. In the following excerpt, Ruth Hall encounters the kind of opposition to her writing that Kirkland describes in "Literary Women," and that Wilson's protagonist experiences in *St. Elmo.*

The text is from *Ruth Hall and Other Writings,* ed. Joyce W. Warren (New Brunswick, NJ: Rutgers UP, 1986).

It was a sultry morning in July. Ruth had risen early, for her cough seemed more troublesome in a reclining posture. "I wonder what that noise can be?" said she to herself; whir — whir — whir, it went, all day long in the attic overhead. She knew that Mrs. Waters had one other lodger beside herself, an elderly gentleman by the name of Bond, who cooked his own food, and whom she often met on the stairs, coming up with a pitcher of water, or a few eggs in a paper bag, or a pie that he had bought of Mr. Flake, at the little black grocery-shop at the corner. On these occasions he always stepped aside, and with a deferential bow waited for Ruth to pass. He was a thin, spare man, slightly bent; his hair and whiskers curiously striped like a zebra, one lock being jet black, while the neighboring one was as distinct a white. His dress was plain, but very neat and tidy. He never seemed to have any business out-doors, as he stayed in his room all day, never leaving it at all till dark, when he paced up and down, with his hands behind him, before the house. "Whir — whir — whir." It was early sunrise; but Ruth had heard that odd noise for two hours at least. What *could* it mean? Just then a carrier passed on the other side of the street with the morning papers, and slipped one under the crack of the house door opposite.

A thought! why could not Ruth write for the papers? How very odd it had never occurred to her before? Yes, write for the papers — why not? She remembered that while at boarding-school, an editor of a paper in the same town used often to come in and take down her compositions in short-hand as she read them aloud, and transfer them to the columns of his paper. She certainly *ought* to write better now than she did when an inexperienced girl. She would begin that very night; but where to make a beginning? who would publish her articles? how much would they pay her? to whom should she apply first? There was her brother Hyacinth, now the prosperous editor of the Irving Magazine; oh, if he would only employ her? Ruth was quite sure she could write as well as some of his correspondents, whom he had praised with no niggardly pen. She would prepare samples to send immediately, announcing her intention, and offering them for his acceptance. This means of support would be so congenial, so absorbing. At the needle one's mind could still be brooding over sorrowful thoughts.

Ruth counted the days and hours impatiently, as she waited for an answer. Hyacinth surely would not refuse *her* when in almost every number of his magazine he was announcing some new contributor; or, if *he* could not employ her *himself,* he surely would be brotherly enough to point out to her some one of the many avenues so accessible to a man of extensive newspaperial and literary acquaintance. She would so gladly support herself, so cheerfully toil day and night, if need be, could she only win an independence; and Ruth recalled with a sigh Katy's last visit to her father, and then she rose and walked the floor in her impatience; and then, her restless spirit urging her on to her fate, she went again to the post office to see if there were no letter. How long the clerk made her wait! Yes, there *was* a letter for her, and in her brother's hand-writing too. Oh, how long since she had seen it!

Ruth heeded neither the jostling of office-boys, porters, or draymen, as she held out her eager hand for the letter. Thrusting it hastily in her pocket, she hurried in breathless haste back to her lodgings. The contents were as follows:

"I have looked over the pieces you sent me, Ruth. It is very evident that writing never can be *your* forte; you have no talent that way. You may possibly be employed by some inferior newspapers, but be assured your articles never will be heard of out of your own little provincial city. For myself I have plenty of contributors, nor do I know of any of my literary acquaintances who would employ you. I would advise you, therefore, to seek some *unobtrusive* employment. Your brother,
                    "HYACINTH ELLET."

A bitter smile struggled with the hot tear that fell upon Ruth's cheek. "I have tried the unobtrusive employment," said Ruth: "the wages are six cents a day, Hyacinth;" and again the bitter smile disfigured her gentle lip.

"No talent!"

"At another tribunal than his will I appeal."

"Never be heard of out of my own little provincial city!" The cold, contemptuous tone stung her.

"But they shall be heard of;" and Ruth leaped to her feet. "Sooner than he dreams of, too. I *can* do it, I *feel* it, I *will* do it," and she closed her lips firmly; "but there will be a desperate struggle first," and she clasped her hands over her heart as if it had already commenced; "there will be scant meals, and sleepless nights, and weary days, and a throbbing brow, and an aching heart; there will be the chilling tone, the rude repulse; there will be ten backward steps to one forward. *Pride* must sleep! but — " and Ruth glanced at her children — "it shall be *done*. They shall be proud of their mother. *Hyacinth shall yet be proud to claim his sister.*"

"What is it, mamma?" asked Katy, looking wonderingly at the strange expression of her mother's face.

"What is it, my darling?" and Ruth caught up the child with convulsive energy; "what is it? only that when you are a woman you shall remember this day, my little pet;" and as she kissed Katy's upturned brow a bright spot burned on her cheek, and her eye glowed like a star.

LUCY LARCOM

From A New England Girlhood

Because the death of her father impoverished her family, Lucy Larcom (1824–1893) spent her childhood as a Lowell mill girl, a time which she treats in her short fiction as well as in *A New England Girlhood* (Boston: Houghton, 1889). She received an excellent education before and after her time at the Lowell mill, and publishing in *The Lowell Offering* and other mill publications helped her begin her literary career. Although Larcom was popular during her lifetime as a poet, her autobiographical *A New England Girlhood* is her best-known work today. Covering her life up to 1852, the work addresses young women and portrays early nineteenth-century small-town life. In the following selection, Larcom discusses the difficulties of life as a "working-girl" and examines her own process of identity formation, especially her development as an author.

Most of my mother's boarders were from New Hampshire and Vermont, and there was a fresh, breezy sociability about them which made them seem almost like a different race of beings from any we children had hitherto known.

We helped a little about the housework, before and after school, making beds, trimming lamps, and washing dishes. The heaviest work was done by a strong Irish girl, my mother always attending to the cooking herself. She was, however, a better caterer than the circumstances required or permitted. She liked to make nice things for the table, and, having been accustomed to an abundant supply, could never learn to economize. At a dollar and a quarter a week for board, (the price allowed for mill-girls by the corporations) great care in expenditure was necessary. It was not in my mother's nature closely to calculate costs, and in this way there came to be a continually increasing leak in the family purse. The older members of the family did everything they could, but it was not enough. I heard it said one day, in a distressed tone, "The children will have to leave school and go into the mill."

There were many pros and cons between my mother and sisters before this was positively decided. The mill-agent did not want to take us two little girls, but consented on condition we should be sure to attend school the full number of months prescribed each year. I, the younger one, was then between eleven and twelve years old. . . .

I went to my first day's work in the mill with a light heart. The novelty of it made it seem easy, and it really was not hard, just to change the bobbins on the spinning-frames every three quarters of an hour or so, with half a dozen other little girls who were doing the same thing. When I came back at night, the family began to pity me for my long, tiresome day's work, but I laughed and said, —

"Why, it is nothing but fun. It is just like play."

And for a little while it was only a new amusement; I liked it better than going to school and "making believe" I was learning when I was not. And there was a great deal of play mixed with it. We were not occupied more than half the time. The intervals were spent frolicking around among the spinning-frames, teasing and talking to the older girls, or entertaining ourselves with games and stories in a corner, or exploring, with the overseer's permission, the mysteries of the carding-room, the dressing-room, and the weaving-room.

I never cared much for machinery. The buzzing and hissing and whizzing of pulleys and rollers and spindles and flyers around me often grew tiresome. I could not see into their complications, or feel interested in them. But in a room below us we were sometimes allowed to peer in through a sort of blind door at the great waterwheel that carried the works of the whole mill. It was so huge that we could only watch a few of its spokes at a time, and part of its dripping rim, moving with a slow, measured strength through the darkness that shut it in. It impressed me with something of the awe which comes to us in thinking of the great Power which keeps the mechanism of the universe in motion. Even now, the remembrance of its large, mysterious movement, in which every little motion of every noisy little wheel was involved, brings back to me a verse from one of my favorite hymns: —

> "Our lives through various scenes are drawn,
> And vexed by trifling cares,
> While Thine eternal thought moves on
> Thy undisturbed affairs."

There were compensations for being shut in to daily toil so early. The mill itself had its lessons for us. But it was not, and could not be, the right sort of life for a child, and we were happy in the knowledge that, at the longest, our employment was only to be temporary.

When I took my next three months at the grammar school, everything there was changed, and I too was changed. The teachers were kind, and thorough in their instruction; and my mind seemed to have been ploughed up during that year of work, so that knowledge took root in it easily. It was a great delight to me to study, and at the end of the three months the master told me that I was prepared for the high school.

But alas! I could not go. The little money I could earn — one dollar a week, besides the price of my board — was needed in the family, and I must return to the mill. It was a severe disappointment to me. . . .

I began to reflect upon life rather seriously for a girl of twelve or thirteen. What was I here for? What could I make of myself? Must I submit to be carried along with the current, and do just what everybody else did? No: I knew I should not do that, for there was a certain Myself who was always starting up with her own original plan or aspiration before me, and who was quite indifferent as to what people generally thought.

Well, I would find out what this Myself was good for, and that she should be. . . .

I seldom thought seriously of becoming an author, although it seemed to me that anybody who had written a book would have a right to feel very proud. But I believed that a person must be exceedingly wise, before presuming to attempt it: although now and then I thought I could feel ideas growing in my mind that it might be worth while to put into a book — if I lived and studied until I was forty or fifty years old.

I wrote my little verses, to be sure, but that was nothing; they just grew. They were the same as breathing or singing. I could not help writing them, and I thought and dreamed a great many that never were put on paper. They seemed to fly into my mind and away again, like birds going with a carol through the air. It seemed strange to me that people should notice them, or should think my writing verses anything peculiar; for I supposed that they were in everybody's mind, just as they were in mine, and that anybody could write them who chose.

One day I heard a relative say to my mother, —

"Keep what she writes till she grows up, and perhaps she will get money for it. I have heard of somebody who earned a thousand dollars by writing poetry."

It sounded so absurd to me. Money for writing verses! One dollar would be as ridiculous as a thousand. I should as soon have thought of being paid for thinking! My mother, fortunately, was sensible enough never to flatter me or let me be flattered about my scribbling. It never was allowed to hinder any work I had to do. I crept away into a corner to write what came into my head, just as I ran away to play; and I looked upon it only as my most agreeable amusement, never thinking of preserving anything which did not of itself stay in my memory. This too was well, for the time did not come when I could afford to look upon verse-writing as an occupation. Through my life, it has only been permitted to me as an aside from other more pressing employments. Whether I should have written better verses had circumstances left me free to do what I chose, it is impossible now to know.

All my thoughts about my future sent me back to Aunt Hannah and my first infantile idea of being a teacher. I foresaw that I should be that before I could be or do anything else. It had been impressed upon me that I must make myself useful in the world, and certainly one could be useful who could "keep school" as Aunt Hannah did. I did not see anything else for a girl to do who wanted to use her brains as well as her hands. So the plan of preparing myself to be a teacher gradually and almost unconsciously shaped itself in my mind as the only practicable one. I could earn my living in that way, — an all-important consideration.

I liked the thought of self-support, but I would have chosen some artistic or beautiful work if I could. I had no especial aptitude for teaching, and no absorbing wish to be a teacher, but it seemed to me that I might succeed if I tried. What I did like about it was that one must know something first. I must acquire knowledge before I could impart it, and that was just what I wanted. I could be a student, wherever I was and whatever else I had to be or do, and I would!

I knew I should write; I could not help doing that, for my hand seemed instinctively to move towards pen and paper in moments of leisure. But to write anything worth while, I must have mental cultivation; so, in preparing myself to teach, I could also be preparing myself to write.

This was the plan that indefinitely shaped itself in my mind as I returned to my work in the spinning-room, and which I followed out, not without many breaks and hindrances and neglects, during the next six or seven years, — to learn all I could, so that I should be fit to teach or to write, as the way opened. And it turned out that fifteen or twenty of my best years were given to teaching. . . .

My sister . . . was really our teacher, although she never assumed that position. Certainly I learned more from her about my own capabilities, and how I might put them to use, than I could have done at any school we knew of, had it been possible for me to attend one.

I think she was determined that we should not be mentally de-frauded by the circumstances which had made it necessary for us to begin so early to win our daily bread. This remark applies especially to me, as my older sisters (only two or three of them had come to Lowell) soon drifted away from us into their own new homes or oc-cupations, and she and I were left together amid the whir of spindles and wheels.

One thing she planned for us, her younger housemates, — a dozen or so of cousins, friends, and sisters, some attending school, and some at work in the mill, — was a little fortnightly paper, to be filled with our original contributions, she herself acting as editor.

I do not know where she got the idea, unless it was from Mrs. Lydia Maria Child's[1] "Juvenile Miscellany," which had found its way to us some years before, — a most delightful guest, and, I think, the first magazine prepared for American children, who have had so many since then. (I have always been glad that I knew that sweet woman with the child's heart and the poet's soul, in her later years, and could tell her how happy she had helped to make my childhood.) Our little sheet was called "The Diving Bell," probably from the sea-associations of the name. We kept our secrets of authorship very close from everybody except the editor, who had to decipher the handwriting and copy the pieces. It was, indeed, an important part of the fun to guess who wrote particular pieces. After a little while, however, our mannerisms betrayed us. One of my cousins was known to be the chief story-teller, and I was recognized as the leading rhymer among the younger contributors; the editor-sister excelling in her versifying, as she did in almost everything.

It was a cluster of very conscious-looking little girls that assembled one evening in the attic room, chosen on account of its remoteness from intruders (for we did not admit even the family as a public; the writers themselves were the only audience); to listen to the reading of our first paper. We took Saturday evening, because that was longer than the other work-day evenings, the mills being closed earlier. Such guessing and wondering and admiring as we had! But nobody would acknowledge her own work, for that would have spoiled the plea-sure. Only there were certain wise hints and maxims that we knew never came from any juvenile head among us, and those we set down as "editorials."

---

[1] *Mrs. Lydia Maria Child:* (1802–1880) American writer, woman's rights advo-cate, and abolitionist.

Some of the stories contained rather remarkable incidents. One, written to illustrate a little girl's habit of carelessness about her own special belongings, told of her rising one morning, and after hunting around for her shoes half an hour or so, finding them *in the book-case,* where she had *accidentally locked them up* the night before!

To convince myself that I could write something besides rhymes, I had attempted an essay of half a column on a very extensive subject, "MIND." It began loftily: —

"What a noble and beautiful thing is mind!" and it went on in the same high-flown strain to no particular end. But the editor praised it, after having declined the verdict of the audience that she was its author; and I felt sufficiently flattered by both judgments.

I wrote more rhymes than anything else, because they came more easily. But I always felt that the ability to write good prose was far more desirable, and it seems so to me still. I will give my little girl readers a single specimen of my twelve-year-old "Diving Bell" verses, though I feel as if I ought to apologize even for that. It is on a common subject, "Life like a Rose": —

> Childhood's like a tender bud
>   That's scarce been formed an hour,
> But which erelong will doubtless be
>   A bright and lovely flower.
>
> And youth is like a full-blown rose
>   Which has not known decay;
> But which must soon, alas! too soon!
>   Wither and fade away.
>
> And age is like a withered rose,
>   That bends beneath the blast;
> But though its beauty all is gone,
>   Its fragrance yet may last.

This, and other verses that I wrote then, serve to illustrate the child's usual inclination to look forward meditatively, rather than to think and write of the simple things that belong to children. . . .

I do not know whether it was fortunate or unfortunate for me that I had not, by nature, what is called literary ambition. I knew that I had a knack at rhyming, and I knew that I enjoyed nothing better than to try to put thoughts and words together, in any way. But I did it for the pleasure of rhyming and writing, indifferent as to what might come of it. For any one who could take hold of every-day, practical work, and carry it on successfully, I had a profound respect.

To be what is called "capable" seemed to me better worth while than merely to have a taste or talent for writing, perhaps because I was conscious of my deficiencies in the former respect. But certainly the world needs deeds more than it needs words. I should never have been willing to be *only* a writer, without using my hands to some good purpose besides.

My sister, however, told me that here was a talent which I had no right to neglect, and which I ought to make the most of. I believed in her; I thought she understood me better than I understood myself; and it was a comfort to be assured that my scribbling was not wholly a waste of time. So I used pencil and paper in every spare minute I could find.

Our little home-journal went bravely on through twelve numbers. Its yellow manuscript pages occasionally meet my eyes when I am rummaging among my old papers, with the half-conscious look of a waif that knows it has no right to its escape from the waters of oblivion.

While it was in progress my sister Emilie became acquainted with a family of bright girls, near neighbors of ours, who proposed that we should join with them, and form a little society for writing and discussion, to meet fortnightly at their house. We met, — I think I was the youngest of the group, — prepared a Constitution and By-Laws, and named ourselves "The Improvement Circle." If I remember rightly, my sister was our first president. The older ones talked and wrote on many subjects quite above me. I was shrinkingly bashful, as half-grown girls usually are, but I wrote my little essays and read them, and listened to the rest, and enjoyed it all exceedingly. Out of this little "Improvement Circle" grew the larger one whence issued the "Lowell Offering,"[2] a year or two later.

At this time I had learned to do a spinner's work, and I obtained permission to tend some frames that stood directly in front of the river-windows, with only them and the wall behind me, extending half the length of the mill, — and one young woman beside me, at the farther end of the row. She was a sober, mature person, who scarcely thought it worth her while to speak often to a child like me; and I was, when with strangers, rather a reserved girl; so I kept myself

---

[2] *"Lowell Offering"*: Rev. Abel C. Thomas began publishing *The Lowell Offering* in 1840 to highlight the writing that the mill women were doing in their literary clubs. The magazine achieved instant fame and helped to promote the mill. Its publication ended in 1845.

occupied with the river, my work, and my thoughts. And the river and my thoughts flowed on together, the happiest of companions. Like a loitering pilgrim, it sparkled up to me in recognition as it glided along, and bore away my little frets and fatigues on its bosom. When the work "went well," I sat in the window-seat, and let my fancies fly whither they would, — downward to the sea, or upward to the hills that hid the mountain-cradle of the Merrimack.

The printed regulations forbade us to bring books into the mill, so I made my window-seat into a small library of poetry, pasting its side all over with newspaper clippings. In those days we had only weekly papers, and they had always a "poet's corner," where standard writers were well represented, with anonymous ones, also. I was not, of course, much of a critic. I chose my verses for their sentiment, and because I wanted to commit them to memory; sometimes it was a long poem, sometimes a hymn, sometimes only a stray verse. . . .

Some of the girls could not believe that the Bible was meant to be counted among forbidden books. We all thought that the Scriptures had a right to go wherever we went, and that if we needed them anywhere, it was at our work. I evaded the law by carrying some leaves from a torn Testament in my pocket.

The overseer, caring more for law than gospel, confiscated all he found. He had his desk full of Bibles. It sounded oddly to hear him say to the most religious girl in the room, when he took hers away, "I did think you had more conscience than to bring that book here." But we had some close ethical questions to settle in those days. It was a rigid code of morality under which we lived. Nobody complained of it, however, and we were doubtless better off for its strictness, in the end.

The last window in the row behind me was filled with flourishing house-plants — fragrant-leaved geraniums, the overseer's pets. They gave that corner a bowery look; the perfume and freshness tempted me there often. Standing before that window, I could look across the room and see girls moving backwards and forwards among the spinning-frames, sometimes stooping, sometimes reaching up their arms, as their work required, with easy and not ungraceful movements. On the whole, it was far from being a disagreeable place to stay in. The girls were bright-looking and neat, and everything was kept clean and shining. The effect of the whole was rather attractive to strangers. . . .

We did not forget that we were working-girls, wearing coarse aprons suitable to our work, and that there was some danger of our becoming drudges. I know that sometimes the confinement of the mill became very wearisome to me. In the sweet June weather I would lean far out of the window, and try not to hear the unceasing clash of sound inside. Looking away to the hills, my whole stifled being would cry out.

> "Oh, that I had wings!"

Still I was there from choice, and

> "The prison unto which we doom ourselves,
> No prison is."

And I was every day making discoveries about life, and about myself. I had naturally some elements of the recluse, and would never, of my own choice, have lived in a crowd. I loved quietness. The noise of machinery was particularly distasteful to me. But I found that the crowd was made up of single human lives, not one of them wholly uninteresting, when separately known. I learned also that there are many things which belong to the whole world of us together, that no one of us, nor any few of us, can claim or enjoy for ourselves alone. I discovered, too, that I could so accustom myself to the noise that it became like a silence to me. And I defied the machinery to make me its slave. Its incessant discords could not drown the music of my thoughts if I would let them fly high enough. Even the long hours, the early rising, and the regularity enforced by the clangor of the bell were good discipline for one who was naturally inclined to dally and to dream, and who loved her own personal liberty with a willful rebellion against control. Perhaps I could have brought myself into the limitations of order and method in no other way. . . .

On account of our belonging there [to the First Congregational Church], our contributions were given to the "Operatives' Magazine," the first periodical for which I ever wrote, issued by the literary society of which our minister took charge. He met us on regular evenings, read aloud our poems and sketches, and made such critical suggestions as he thought desirable. This magazine was edited by two young women, both of whom had been employed in the mills, although at that time they were teachers in the public schools — a change which was often made by mill-girls after a few months' residence at Lowell. A great many of them were district-school teachers at their homes in the summer, spending only the winters at their work.

The two magazines [*The Operatives Magazine* and *The Lowell Offering*] went on side by side for a year or two, and then were united in the "Lowell Offering," which had made the first experiment of the kind by publishing a trial number or two at irregular intervals. My sister had sent some verses of mine, on request, to be published in one of those specimen numbers. But we were not acquainted with the editor of the "Offering," and we knew only a few of its contributors. The Universalist Church, in the vestry of which they met, was in a distant part of the city. Socially, the place where we worshiped was the place where we naturally came together in other ways. The churches were all filled to overflowing, so that the grouping together of the girls by their denominational preferences was almost unavoidable. It was in some such way as this that two magazines were started instead of one. If the girls who enjoyed writing had not been so many and so scattered, they might have made the better arrangement of joining their forces from the beginning.

I was too young a contributor to be at first of much value to either periodical. They began their regular issues, I think, while I was the nursemaid of my little nephews at Beverly. When I returned to Lowell, at about sixteen, I found my sister Emilie interested in the "Operatives' Magazine," and we both contributed to it regularly, until it was merged in the "Lowell Offering," to which we then transferred our writing-efforts. It did not occur to us to call these efforts "literary." I know that I wrote just as I did for our little "Diving Bell," — as a sort of pastime, and because my daily toil was mechanical, and furnished no occupation for my thoughts. Perhaps the fact that most of us wrote in this way accounted for the rather sketchy and fragmentary character of our "Magazine." It gave evidence that we thought, and that we thought upon solid and serious matters; but the criticism of one of our superintendents upon it, very kindly given, was undoubtedly just: "It has plenty of pith, but it lacks point." . . .

In looking over the bound volume of this magazine [*The Operatives' Magazine*], I am amused at the grown-up style of thought assumed by myself, probably its very youngest contributor. I wrote a dissertation on "Fame," quoting from Pollok, Cowper, and Milton,[3] and ending with Diedrich Knickerbocker's[4] definition of immortal fame, — "Half a page of dirty paper." For other titles I had "Thoughts on Beauty;" "Gentility;" "Sympathy," etc. And in one

---

[3] *Pollok, Cowper, and Milton:* Robert Pollok (1798–1827), English writer; William Cowper (1731–1800), English poet; John Milton (1608–1674), one of the great English writers of poetry, drama, and the epic.

[4] *Diedrich Knickerbocker:* Fictional character created by the American author Washington Irving (1783–1859).

longish poem, entitled "My Childhood" (written when I was about fifteen), I find verses like these, which would seem to have come out of a mature experience: —

> My childhood! O those pleasant days, when everything seemed free,
> And in the broad and verdant fields I frolicked merrily;
> When joy came to my bounding heart with every wild bird's song,
> And Nature's music in my ears was ringing all day long!
> And yet I would not call them back, those blessed times of yore,
> For riper years are fraught with joys I dreamed not of before.
> The labyrinth of Science opes with wonders every day;
> And friendship hath full many a flower to cheer life's dreary way.

And glancing through the pages of the "Lowell Offering" a year or two later, I see that I continued to dismalize myself at times, quite unnecessarily. The title of one string of morbid verses is "The Complaint of a Nobody," in which I compare myself to a weed growing up in a garden. . . .

What we wrote was not remarkable, — perhaps no more so than the usual school compositions of intelligent girls. It would hardly be worth while to refer to it particularly, had not the Lowell girls and their magazines been so frequently spoken of as something phenomenal. But it was a perfectly natural outgrowth of those girls' previous life. For what were we? Girls who were working in a factory for the time, to be sure; but none of us had the least idea of continuing at that kind of work permanently. Our composite photograph, had it been taken, would have been the representative New England girlhood of those days. We had all been fairly educated at public or private schools, and many of us were resolutely bent upon obtaining a better education. Very few were among us without some distinct plan for bettering the condition of themselves and those they loved. For the first time, our young women had come forth from their home retirement in a throng, each with her own individual purpose. For twenty years or so, Lowell might have been looked upon as a rather select industrial school for young people. The girls there were just such girls as are knocking at the doors of young women's colleges today. They had come to work with their hands, but they could not hinder the working of their minds also. Their mental activity was overflowing at every possible outlet. . . .

That they should write was no more strange than that they should study, or read, or think. And yet there were those to whom it seemed incredible that a girl could, in the pauses of her work, put together words with her pen that it would do to print; and after a while the assertion was circulated, through some distant newspaper, that our magazine was not written by ourselves at all, but by "Lowell lawyers." This seemed almost too foolish a suggestion to contradict, but the editor of the "Offering" thought it best to give the name and occupation of some of the writers by way of refutation. It was for this reason (much against my own wish) that my real name was first attached to anything I wrote. I was then book-keeper in the cloth-room of the Lawrence Mills. We had all used any fanciful signature we chose, varying it as we pleased. After I began to read and love Wordsworth, my favorite *nom de plume* was "Rotha."[5] In the later numbers of the magazine, the editor more frequently made use of my initials. One day I was surprised by seeing my name in full in Griswold's "Female Poets;"[6] — no great distinction, however, since there were a hundred names or so, besides.

It has seemed necessary to give these gossip items about myself; but the real interest of every separate life-story is involved in the larger life-history which is going on around it. We do not know ourselves without our companions and surroundings. I cannot narrate my workmates' separate experiences, but I know that because of having lived among them, and because of having felt the beauty and power of their lives, I am different from what I should otherwise have been, and it is my own fault if I am not better for my life with them.

In recalling those years of my girlhood at Lowell, I often think that I knew then what real society is better perhaps than ever since. For in that large gathering together of young womanhood there were many choice natures — some of the choicest in all our excellent New England, and there were no false social standards to hold them apart. It is the best society when people meet sincerely, on the ground of their deepest sympathies and highest aspirations, without conventionality or cliques or affectation; and it was in that way that these young girls met and became acquainted with each other, almost of necessity.

There were all varieties of woman-nature among them, all degrees of refinement and cultivation, and, of course, many sharp contrasts of agreeable and disagreeable. It was not always the most cultivated, however, who were the most companionable. There were gentle, un-

---

[5] *Rotha:* William Wordsworth (1770–1850) wrote "To Rotha Q — " to the daughter of his son-in-law, Mr. Quillinan.

[6] *Griswold's "Female Poets":* Probably refers to *The Female Poets of America* (Philadelphia: Carey, 1849), edited by Rufus Wilmot Griswold (1815–1857).

taught girls, as fresh and simple as wild flowers, whose unpretending goodness of heart was better to have than bookishness; girls who loved everybody, and were loved by everybody. Those are the girls that I remember best, and their memory is sweet as a breeze from the clover fields.

As I recall the throngs of unknown girlish forms that used to pass and repass me on the familiar road to the mill-gates, and also the few that I knew so well, those with whom I worked, thought, read, wrote, studied, and worshiped, my thoughts send a heartfelt greeting to them all, wherever in God's beautiful, busy universe they may now be scattered: —

LOUISA MAY ALCOTT

From Little Women

Louisa May Alcott (1832–1888) was the second of four daughters of the famous transcendentalist philosopher Amos Bronson Alcott. Her writing, like that of many other nineteenth-century women authors, was often a means of support for her family. *Little Women, or Meg, Jo, Beth, and Amy* (Boston: Little, 1868), a novel loosely based on Alcott's family life, was and is her best-known work. The autobiographical Jo is especially memorable because of her strong will, her imperfections, and her status as a sympathetic character. In the following two chapters, Jo revels in her ability to make money with her writing and negotiates the demands of publishers over and against her own artistic integrity.

Literary Lessons

Fortune suddenly smiled upon Jo, and dropped a good-luck penny in her path. Not a golden penny, exactly, but I doubt if half a million would have given more real happiness than did the little sum that came to her in this wise.

Every few weeks she would shut herself up in her room, put on her scribbling suit, and "fall into a vortex," as she expressed it, writing away at her novel with all her heart and soul, for till that was finished she could find no peace. Her "scribbling suit" consisted of a black woollen pinafore on which she could wipe her pen at will, and a cap of the same material, adorned with a cheerful red bow, into which she bundled her hair when the decks were cleared for action. This cap was a beacon to the inquiring eyes of her family, who during these periods kept their distance, merely popping in their heads semi-occasionally, to ask, with interest, "Does genius burn, Jo?" They did not always venture even to ask this question, but took an observation of the cap, and judged accordingly. If this expressive article of dress was drawn low upon the forehead, it was a sign that hard work was going on; in exciting moments it was pushed rakishly askew; and when despair seized the author it was plucked wholly off, and cast upon the floor. At such times the intruder silently withdrew; and not until the red bow was seen gayly erect upon the gifted brow, did any one dare address Jo.

She did not think herself a genius by any means; but when the writing fit came on, she gave herself up to it with entire abandon, and led a blissful life, unconscious of want, care, or bad weather, while she sat safe and happy in an imaginary world, full of friends almost as real and dear to her as any in the flesh. Sleep forsook her eyes, meals stood untasted, day and night were all too short to enjoy the happiness which blessed her only at such times, and made these hours worth living, even if they bore no other fruit. The divine afflatus usually lasted a week or two, and then she emerged from her "vortex," hungry, sleepy, cross, or despondent.

She was just recovering from one of these attacks when she was prevailed upon to escort Miss Crocker to a lecture, and in return for her virtue was rewarded with a new idea. It was a People's Course, the lecture on the Pyramids, and Jo rather wondered at the choice of such a subject for such an audience, but took it for granted that some great social evil would be remedied or some great want supplied by unfolding the glories of the Pharaohs to an audience whose thoughts were busy with the price of coal and flour, and whose lives were spent in trying to solve harder riddles than that of the Sphinx.

They were early; and while Miss Crocker set the heel of her stocking, Jo amused herself by examining the faces of the people who occupied the seat with them. On her left were two matrons, with massive foreheads, and bonnets to match, discussing Woman's Rights and making tatting. Beyond sat a pair of humble lovers, artlessly holding each other by the hand, a sombre spinster eating peppermints out of a paper bag, and an old gentleman taking his preparatory nap behind a yellow bandanna. On her right, her only neighbor was a studious-looking lad absorbed in a newspaper.

It was a pictorial sheet, and Jo examined the work of art nearest her, idly wondering what unfortuitous concatenation of circumstances needed the melodramatic illustration of an Indian in full war costume, tumbling over a precipice with a wolf at his throat, while two infuriated young gentlemen, with unnaturally small feet and big eyes, were stabbing each other close by, and a dishevelled female was flying away in the background with her mouth wide open. Pausing to turn a page, the lad saw her looking, and, with boyish good-nature, offered half his paper, saying bluntly, "Want to read it? That's a first-rate story."

Jo accepted it with a smile, for she had never outgrown her liking for lads, and soon found herself involved in the usual labyrinth of love, mystery, and murder, for the story belonged to that class of light literature in which the passions have a holiday, and when the author's invention fails, a grand catastrophe clears the stage of one half the *dramatis personæ,* leaving the other half to exult over their downfall.

"Prime, isn't it?" asked the boy, as her eye went down to the last paragraph of her portion.

"I think you and I could do as well as that if we tried," returned Jo, amused at his admiration of the trash.

"I should think I was a pretty lucky chap if I could. She makes a good living out of such stories, they say;" and he pointed to the name of Mrs. s.l.a.n.g. Northbury, under the title of the tale.

"Do you know her?" asked Jo, with sudden interest.

"No; but I read all her pieces, and I know a fellow who works in the office where this paper is printed."

"Do you say she makes a good living out of stories like this?" and Jo looked more respectfully at the agitated group and thickly-sprinkled exclamation-points that adorned the page.

"Guess she does! She knows just what folks like, and gets paid well for writing it."

Here the lecture began, but Jo heard very little of it, for while Prof. Sands was prosing away about Belzoni, Cheops, scarabei, and hieroglyphics, she was covertly taking down the address of the paper, and boldly resolving to try for the hundred-dollar prize offered in its columns for a sensational story. By the time the lecture ended and the audience awoke, she had built up a splendid fortune for herself (not the first founded upon paper), and was already deep in the concoction of her story, being unable to decide whether the duel should come before the elopement or after the murder.

She said nothing of her plan at home, but fell to work next day, much to the disquiet of her mother, who always looked a little anxious when "genius took to burning." Jo had never tried this style before, contenting herself with very mild romances for the "Spread Eagle." Her theatrical experience and miscellaneous reading were of service now, for they gave her some idea of dramatic effect, and supplied plot, language, and costumes. Her story was as full of desperation and despair as her limited acquaintance with those uncomfortable emotions enabled her to make it, and, having located it in Lisbon, she wound up with an earthquake, as a striking and appropriate *dénouement*. The manuscript was privately despatched, accompanied by a note, modestly saying that if the tale didn't get the prize, which the writer hardly dared expect, she would be very glad to receive any sum it might be considered worth.

Six weeks is a long time to wait, and a still longer time for a girl to keep a secret; but Jo did both, and was just beginning to give up all hope of ever seeing her manuscript again, when a letter arrived which almost took her breath away; for on opening it, a check for a hundred dollars fell into her lap. For a minute she stared at it as if it had been a snake, then she read her letter and began to cry. If the amiable gentleman who wrote that kindly note could have known what intense happiness he was giving a fellow-creature, I think he would devote his leisure hours, if he has any, to that amusement; for Jo valued the letter more than the money, because it was encouraging; and after years of effort it was *so* pleasant to find that she had learned to do something, though it was only to write a sensation story.

A prouder young woman was seldom seen than she, when, having composed herself, she electrified the family by appearing before them with the letter in one hand, the check in the other, announcing that she had won the prize. Of course there was a great jubilee, and when the story came every one read and praised it; though after her father had told her that the language was good, the romance fresh and hearty, and the tragedy quite thrilling, he shook his head, and said in his unworldly way, —

"You can do better than this, Jo. Aim at the highest, and never mind the money."

"*I* think the money is the best part of it. What *will* you do with such a fortune?" asked Amy, regarding the magic slip of paper with a reverential eye.

"Send Beth and mother to the seaside for a month or two," answered Jo promptly.

"Oh, how splendid! No, I can't do it, dear, it would be so selfish," cried Beth, who had clapped her thin hands, and taken a long breath, as if pining for fresh ocean-breezes; then stopped herself, and motioned away the check which her sister waved before her.

"Ah, but you shall go, I've set my heart on it; that's what I tried for, and that's why I succeeded. I never get on when I think of myself alone, so it will help me to work for you, don't you see? Besides, Marmee needs the change, and she won't leave you, so you *must* go. Won't it be fun to see you come home plump and rosy again? Hurrah for Dr. Jo, who always cures her patients!"

To the sea side they went, after much discussion; and though Beth didn't come home as plump and rosy as could be desired, she was much better, while Mrs. March declared she felt ten years younger; so Jo was satisfied with the investment of her prize money, and fell to work with a cheery spirit, bent on earning more of those delightful checks. She did earn several that year, and began to feel herself a power in the house; for by the magic of a pen, her "rubbish" turned into comforts for them all. "The Duke's Daughter" paid the butcher's bill, "A Phantom Hand" put down a new carpet, and the "Curse of the Coventrys" proved the blessing of the Marches in the way of groceries and gowns. . . .

[Jo moves to New York City, where she lives in a boarding house while writing and attempting to sell her new "sensation stories."]

A Friend

Though very happy in the social atmosphere about her, and very busy with the daily work that earned her bread, and made it sweeter for the effort, Jo still found time for literary labors. The purpose which now took possession of her was a natural one to a poor and ambitious girl; but the means she took to gain her end were not the best. She saw that money conferred power: money and power, therefore, she resolved to have; not to be used for herself alone, but for those whom she loved more than self.

The dream of filling home with comforts, giving Beth everything she wanted, from strawberries in winter to an organ in her bedroom; going abroad herself, and always having *more* than enough, so that she might indulge in the luxury of charity, had been for years Jo's most cherished castle in the air.

The prize-story experience had seemed to open a way which might, after long travelling and much up-hill work lead to this delightful *château en Espagne*.[1] But the novel disaster quenched her courage for a time, for public opinion is a giant which has frightened stouter-hearted Jacks on bigger bean-stalks than hers. Like that immortal hero, she reposed awhile after the first attempt, which resulted in a tumble, and the least lovely of the giant's treasures, if I remember rightly. But the "up again and take another" spirit was as strong in Jo as in Jack; so she scrambled up, on the shady side this time, and got more booty, but nearly left behind her what was far more precious than the money-bags.

She took to writing sensation stories; for in those dark ages, even all-perfect America read rubbish. She told no one, but concocted a "thrilling tale," and boldly carried it herself to Mr. Dashwood, editor of the "Weekly Volcano." She had never read "Sartor Resartus,"[2] but she had a womanly instinct that clothes possess an influence more powerful over many than the worth of character or the magic of manners. So she dressed herself in her best, and, trying to persuade herself that she was neither excited nor nervous, bravely climbed two pairs of dark and dirty stairs to find herself in a disorderly room, a cloud of cigar-smoke, and the presence of three gentlemen, sitting with their heels rather higher than their hats, which articles of dress none of them took the trouble to remove on her appearance. Somewhat daunted by this reception, Jo hesitated on the threshold, murmuring in much embarrassment, —

"Excuse me, I was looking for the 'Weekly Volcano' office; I wished to see Mr. Dashwood."

Down went the highest pair of heels, up rose the smokiest gentleman, and, carefully cherishing his cigar between his fingers, he advanced, with a nod, and a countenance expressive of nothing but sleep. Feeling that she must get through the matter somehow, Jo produced her manuscript, and blushing redder and redder with each sentence, blundered out fragments of the little speech carefully prepared for the occasion.

[1] *château en Espagne:* Castle in Spain.
[2] *"Sartor Resartus":* A work by English author Thomas Carlyle (1795–1881), the title of which means, literally, "The Tailor Re-Tailored." The work claims to be an account of a Professor Teufelsdröck's ("devil's dung"'s) "Clothes Philosophy." Carlyle uses the clothes metaphor to suggest that individuals and society cannot hide their moral and spiritual nakedness behind bankrupt systems and beliefs.

"A friend of mine desired me to offer — a story — just as an experiment — would like your opinion — be glad to write more if this suits."

While she blushed and blundered, Mr. Dashwood had taken the manuscript, and was turning over the leaves with a pair of rather dirty fingers, and casting critical glances up and down the neat pages.

"Not a first attempt, I take it?" observing that the pages were numbered, covered only on one side, and not tied up with a ribbon, — sure sign of a novice.

"No, sir; she has had some experience, and got a prize for a tale in the 'Blarneystone Banner.'"

"Oh, did she?" and Mr. Dashwood gave Jo a quick look, which seemed to take note of everything she had on, from the bow in her bonnet to the buttons on her boots. "Well, you can leave it, if you like. We've more of this sort of thing on hand than we know what to do with at present; but I'll run my eye over it, and give you an answer next week."

No, Jo did *not* like to leave it, for Mr. Dashwood didn't suit her at all; but, under the circumstances, there was nothing for her to do but bow and walk away, looking particularly tall and dignified, as she was apt to do when nettled or abashed. Just then she was both; for it was perfectly evident, from the knowing glances exchanged among the gentlemen, that her little fiction of "my friend" was considered a good joke; and a laugh, produced by some inaudible remark of the editor, as he closed the door, completed her discomfiture. Half resolving never to return, she went home, and worked off her irritation by stitching pinafores vigorously; and in an hour or two was cool enough to laugh over the scene, and long for next week.

When she went again, Mr. Dashwood was alone, whereat she rejoiced; Mr. Dashwood was much wider awake than before, which was agreeable; and Mr. Dashwood was not too deeply absorbed in a cigar to remember his manners: so the second interview was much more comfortable than the first.

"We'll take this" (editors never say I), "if you don't object to a few alterations. It's too long, but omitting the passages I've marked will make it just the right length," he said, in a business-like tone.

Jo hardly knew her own MS. again, so crumpled and underscored were its pages and paragraphs; but, feeling as a tender parent might on being asked to cut off her baby's legs in order that it might fit into a new cradle, she looked at the marked passages, and was surprised to find that all the moral reflections — which she had carefully put in as ballast for much romance — had been stricken out.

"But, sir, I thought every story should have some sort of a moral, so I took care to have a few of my sinners repent."

Mr. Dashwood's editorial gravity relaxed into a smile, for Jo had forgotten her "friend," and spoken as only an author could.

"People want to be amused, not preached at, you know. Morals don't sell nowadays;" which was not quite a correct statement, by the way.

"You think it would do with these alterations, then?"

"Yes; it's a new plot, and pretty well worked up — language good, and so on," was Mr. Dashwood's affable reply.

"What do you — that is, what compensation — " began Jo, not exactly knowing how to express herself.

"Oh, yes, well, we give from twenty-five to thirty for things of this sort. Pay when it comes out," returned Mr. Dashwood, as if that point had escaped him; such trifles often do escape the editorial mind, it is said.

"Very well; you can have it," said Jo, handing back the story, with a satisfied air; for, after the dollar-a-column work, even twenty-five seemed good pay.

"Shall I tell my friend you will take another if she has one better than this?" asked Jo, unconscious of her little slip of the tongue, and emboldened by her success.

"Well, we'll look at it; can't promise to take it. Tell her to make it short and spicy, and never mind the moral. What name would your friend like to put to it?" in a careless tone.

"None at all, if you please; she doesn't wish her name to appear, and has no *nom de plume*," said Jo, blushing in spite of herself.

"Just as she likes, of course. The tale will be out next week; will you call for the money, or shall I send it?" asked Mr. Dashwood, who felt a natural desire to know who his new contributor might be.

"I'll call. Good morning, sir."

As she departed, Mr. Dashwood put up his feet, with the graceful remark, "Poor and proud, as usual, but she'll do."

Following Mr. Dashwood's directions, and making Mrs. Northbury her model, Jo rashly took a plunge into the frothy sea of sensational literature; but, thanks to the life-preserver thrown her by a friend, she came up again, not much the worse for her ducking.

Like most young scribblers, she went abroad for her characters and scenery; and banditti, counts, gypsies, nuns, and duchesses appeared upon her stage, and played their parts with as much accuracy and spirit as could be expected. Her readers were not particular about such trifles as grammar, punctuation, and probability, and Mr. Dashwood graciously permitted her to fill his columns at the lowest prices, not thinking it necessary to tell her that the real cause of his hospitality was the fact that one of his hacks, on being offered higher wages, had basely left him in the lurch.

She soon became interested in her work, for her emaciated purse grew stout, and the little hoard she was making to take Beth to the mountains next summer grew slowly but surely as the weeks passed. One thing disturbed her satisfaction, and that was that she did not tell them at home. She had a feeling that father and mother would not approve, and preferred to have her own way first, and beg pardon afterward. It was easy to keep her secret, for no name appeared with her stories; Mr. Dashwood had, of course, found it out very soon, but promised to be dumb; and, for a wonder, kept his word.

She thought it would do her no harm, for she sincerely meant to write nothing of which she should be ashamed, and quieted all pricks of conscience by anticipations of the happy minute when she should show her earnings and laugh over her well-kept secret.

But Mr. Dashwood rejected any but thrilling tales; and, as thrills could not be produced except by harrowing up the souls of the readers, history and romance, land and sea, science and art, police records and lunatic asylums, had to be ransacked for the purpose. Jo soon found that her innocent experience had given her but few glimpses of the tragic world which underlies society; so, regarding it in a business light, she set about supplying her deficiencies with characteristic energy. Eager to find material for stories, and bent on making them original in plot, if not masterly in execution, she searched newspapers for accidents, incidents, and crimes; she excited the suspicions of public librarians by asking for works on poisons; she studied faces in the street, and characters, good, bad, and indifferent, all about her; she delved in the dust of ancient times for facts or fictions so old that they were as good as new, and introduced herself to folly, sin, and misery, as well as her limited opportunities allowed. She thought she was prospering finely; but, unconsciously, she was beginning to desecrate some of the womanliest attributes of a woman's character. She was living in bad society; and, imaginary though it was, its influence affected her, for she was feeding heart and fancy on dangerous and unsubstantial food, and was fast brushing the innocent bloom from her nature by a premature acquaintance with the darker side of life, which comes soon enough to all of us.

She was beginning to feel rather than see this, for much describing of other people's passions and feelings set her to studying and speculating about her own, — a morbid amusement, in which healthy young minds do not voluntarily indulge. Wrong-doing always brings its own punishment; and, when Jo most needed hers, she got it.

I don't know whether the study of Shakespeare helped her to read character, or the natural instinct of a woman for what was honest, brave, and strong; but while endowing her imaginary heroes with every perfection under the sun, Jo was discovering a live hero, who interested her in spite of many human imperfections. Mr. Bhaer, in one of their conversations, had advised her to study simple, true, and lovely characters, wherever she found them, as good training for a writer. Jo took him at his word, for she coolly turned round and studied him, — a proceeding which would have much surprised him, had he known it, for the worthy Professor was very humble in his own conceit.

Why everybody liked him was what puzzled Jo, at first. He was neither rich nor great, young nor handsome; in no respect what is called fascinating, imposing, or brilliant; and yet he was as attractive as a genial fire, and people seemed to gather about him as naturally as about a warm hearth. He was poor, yet always appeared to be giving something away; a stranger, yet every one was his friend; no longer young, but as happy-hearted as a boy; plain and peculiar, yet his face looked beautiful to many, and his oddities were freely forgiven for his sake. Jo often watched him, trying to discover the charm, and, at last, decided that it was benevolence which worked the miracle. If he had any sorrow, "it sat with its head under its wing," and he turned only his sunny side to the world. There were lines upon his forehead, but Time seemed to have touched him gently, remembering how kind he was to others. The pleasant curves about his mouth were the memorials of many friendly words and cheery laughs; his eyes were never cold or hard, and his big hand had a warm, strong grasp that was more expressive than words.

His very clothes seemed to partake of the hospitable nature of the wearer. They looked as if they were at ease, and liked to make him comfortable; his capacious waistcoat was suggestive of a large heart underneath; his rusty coat had a social air, and the baggy pockets plainly proved that little hands often went in empty and came out full; his very boots were benevolent, and his collars never stiff and raspy like other people's.

"That's it!" said Jo to herself, when she at length discovered that genuine good-will towards one's fellow-men could beautify and dignify even a stout German teacher, who shovelled in his dinner, darned his own socks, and was burdened with the name of Bhaer.

Jo valued goodness highly, but she also possessed a most feminine respect for intellect, and a little discovery which she made about the Professor added much to her regard for him. He never spoke of himself, and no one ever knew that in his native city he had been a man much honored and esteemed for learning and integrity, till a countryman came to see him, and, in conversation with Miss Norton, divulged the pleasing fact. From her Jo learned it, and liked it all the better because Mr. Bhaer had never told it. She felt proud to know that he was an honored Professor in Berlin, though only a poor language-master in America; and his homely, hard-working life was much beautified by the spice of romance which this discovery gave it.

Another and a better gift than intellect was shown her in a most unexpected manner. Miss Norton had the *entrée* into literary society, which Jo would have had no chance of seeing but for her. The solitary woman felt an interest in the ambitious girl, and kindly conferred many favors of this sort both on Jo and the Professor. She took them with her, one night, to a select symposium, held in honor of several celebrities.

Jo went prepared to bow down and adore the mighty ones whom she had worshipped with youthful enthusiasm afar off. But her reverence for genius received a severe shock that night, and it took her some time to recover from the discovery that the great creatures were only men and women after all. Imagine her dismay, on stealing a glance of timid admiration at the poet whose lines suggested an ethereal being fed on "spirit, fire, and dew," to behold him devouring his supper with an ardor which flushed his intellectual countenance. Turning as from a fallen idol, she made other discoveries which rapidly dispelled her romantic illusions. The great novelist vibrated between two decanters with the regularity of a pendulum; the famous divine flirted openly with one of the Madame de Staëls[3] of the age, who looked daggers at another Corinne,[4] who was amiably satirizing her, after out-manœuvring her in efforts to absorb the profound

---

[3] *Madame de Staël:* Anne-Louise-Germaine de Staël (1766–1817), French writer with a famous literary-political salon.

[4] *Corinne:* Celebrated Greek lyric poet who lived around 500 B.C.

philosopher, who imbibed tea Johnsonianly[5] and appeared to slumber, the loquacity of the lady rendering speech impossible. The scientific celebrities, forgetting their mollusks and glacial periods, gossiped about art, while devoting themselves to oysters and ices with characteristic energy; the young musician, who was charming the city like a second Orpheus,[6] talked horses; and the specimen of the British nobility present happened to be the most ordinary man of the party.

Before the evening was half over, Jo felt so completely *désillusionnée*, that she sat down in a corner to recover herself. Mr. Bhaer soon joined her, looking rather out of his element, and presently several of the philosophers, each mounted on his hobby, came ambling up to hold an intellectual tournament in the recess. The conversation was miles beyond Jo's comprehension, but she enjoyed it, though Kant and Hegel[7] were unknown gods, the Subjective and Objective unintelligible terms; and the only thing "evolved from her inner consciousness," was a bad headache after it was all over. It dawned upon her gradually that the world was being picked to pieces, and put together on new, and, according to the talkers, on infinitely better principles than before; that religion was in a fair way to be reasoned into nothingness, and intellect was to be the only God. Jo knew nothing about philosophy or metaphysics of any sort, but a curious excitement, half pleasurable, half painful, came over her, as she listened with a sense of being turned adrift into time and space, like a young balloon out on a holiday.

She looked round to see how the Professor liked it, and found him looking at her with the grimmest expression she had ever seen him wear. He shook his head, and beckoned her to come away; but she was fascinated, just then, by the freedom of Speculative Philosophy, and kept her seat, trying to find out what the wise gentlemen intended to rely upon after they had annihilated all the old beliefs.

Now, Mr. Bhaer was a diffident man, and slow to offer his own opinions, not because they were unsettled, but too sincere and earnest to be lightly spoken. As he glanced from Jo to several other young people, attracted by the brilliancy of the philosophic pyrotechnics, he knit his brows, and longed to speak, fearing that some inflammable

---

[5] *Johnsonianly:* Reference to Samuel Johnson (1709–1784), English author celebrated for his wit, brilliant conversation, and literary criticism.

[6] *Orpheus:* In Greek mythology, a poet, musician, and inventor, he enchanted animals with the music from his lyre.

[7] *Kant and Hegel:* Immanuel Kant (1724–1804) and Georg Wilhelm Friedrich Hegel (1770–1831), great German philosophers.

young soul would be led astray by the rockets, to find, when the display was over, that they had only an empty stick or a scorched hand.

He bore it as long as he could; but when he was appealed to for an opinion, he blazed up with honest indignation, and defended religion with all the eloquence of truth, — an eloquence which made his broken English musical, and his plain face beautiful. He had a hard fight, for the wise men argued well; but he didn't know when he was beaten, and stood to his colors like a man. Somehow, as he talked, the world got right again to Jo; the old beliefs, that had lasted so long, seemed better than the new; God was not a blind force, and immortality was not a pretty fable, but a blessed fact. She felt as if she had solid ground under her feet again; and when Mr. Bhaer paused, out-talked, but not one whit convinced, Jo wanted to clap her hands and thank him.

She did neither; but she remembered this scene, and gave the Professor her heartiest respect, for she knew it cost him an effort to speak out then and there, because his conscience would not let him be silent. She began to see that character is a better possession than money, rank, intellect, or beauty; and to feel that if greatness is what a wise man has defined it to be, "truth, reverence, and good-will," then her friend Friedrich Bhaer was not only good, but great.

This belief strengthened daily. She valued his esteem, she coveted his respect, she wanted to be worthy of his friendship; and, just when the wish was sincerest, she came near losing everything. It all grew out of a cocked hat; for one evening the Professor came in to give Jo her lesson, with a paper soldier-cap on his head, which Tina had put there, and he had forgotten to take off.

"It's evident he doesn't look in his glass before coming down," thought Jo, with a smile, as he said "Goot efening," and sat soberly down, quite unconscious of the ludicrous contrast between his subject and his head-gear, for he was going to read her the "Death of Wallenstein."[8]

She said nothing at first, for she liked to hear him laugh out his big, hearty laugh, when anything funny happened, so she left him to discover it for himself, and presently forgot all about it; for to hear a German read Schiller is rather an absorbing occupation. After the reading came the lesson, which was a lively one, for Jo was in a gay

---

[8]*"Death of Wallenstein"*: Poetic drama by the German writer Johann Christoph Friedrich von Schiller (1759–1805).

mood that night, and the cocked-hat kept her eyes dancing with merriment. The Professor didn't know what to make of her, and stopped at last, to ask, with an air of mild surprise that was irresistible, —

"Mees Marsch, for what do you laugh in your master's face? Haf you no respect for me, that you go on so bad?"

"How can I be respectful, sir, when you forget to take your hat off?" said Jo.

Lifting his hand to his head, the absent-minded Professor gravely felt and removed the little cocked-hat, looked at it a minute, and then threw back his head, and laughed like a merry bass-viol.

"Ah! I see him now; it is that imp Tina who makes me a fool with my cap. Well, it is nothing; but you see, if this lesson goes not well, you too shall wear him."

But the lesson did not go at all for a few minutes, because Mr. Bhaer caught sight of a picture on the hat, and, unfolding it, said, with an air of great disgust, —

"I wish these papers did not come in the house; they are not for children to see, nor young people to read. It is not well, and I haf no patience with those who make this harm."

Jo glanced at the sheet, and saw a pleasing illustration composed of a lunatic, a corpse, a villain, and a viper. She did not like it; but the impulse that made her turn it over was not one of displeasure, but fear, because, for a minute, she fancied the paper was the "Volcano." It was not, however, and her panic subsided as she remembered that, even if it had been, and one of her own tales in it, there would have been no name to betray her. She had betrayed herself, however, by a look and a blush; for, though an absent man, the Professor saw a good deal more than people fancied. He knew that Jo wrote, and had met her down among the newspaper offices more than once; but as she never spoke of it, he asked no questions, in spite of a strong desire to see her work. Now it occurred to him that she was doing what she was ashamed to own, and it troubled him. He did not say to himself, "It is none of my business; I've no right to say anything," as many people would have done; he only remembered that she was young and poor, a girl far away from mother's love and father's care; and he was moved to help her with an impulse as quick and natural as that which would prompt him to put out his hand to save a baby from a puddle. All this flashed through his mind in a minute, but not a trace of it appeared in his face; and by the time the paper was turned, and Jo's needle threaded, he was ready to say quite naturally, but very gravely, —

"Yes, you are right to put it from you. I do not like to think that good young girls should see such things. They are made pleasant to some, but I would more rather give my boys gunpowder to play with than this bad trash."

"All may not be bad, only silly, you know; and if there is a demand for it, I don't see any harm in supplying it. Many very respectable people make an honest living out of what are called sensation stories," said Jo, scratching gathers so energetically that a row of little slits followed her pin.

"There is a demand for whiskey, but I think you and I do not care to sell it. If the respectable people knew what harm they did, they would not feel that the living *was* honest. They haf no right to put poison in the sugar-plum, and let the small ones eat it. No; they should think a little, and sweep mud in the street before they do this thing."

Mr. Bhaer spoke warmly, and walked to the fire, crumpling the paper in his hands. Jo sat still, looking as if the fire had come to her; for her cheeks burned long after the cocked hat had turned to smoke, and gone harmlessly up the chimney.

"I should like much to send all the rest after him," muttered the Professor, coming back with a relieved air.

Jo thought what a blaze her pile of papers upstairs would make, and her hard-earned money lay rather heavily on her conscience at that minute. Then she thought consolingly to herself, "Mine are not like that; they are only silly, never bad, so I won't be worried;" and taking up her book, she said, with a studious face, —

"Shall we go on, sir? I'll be very good and proper now."

"I shall hope so," was all he said, but he meant more than she imagined; and the grave, kind look he gave her made her feel as if the words "Weekly Volcano" were printed in large type on her forehead.

As soon as she went to her room, she got out her papers, and carefully re-read every one of her stories. Being a little short-sighted, Mr. Bhaer sometimes used eye-glasses, and Jo had tried them once, smiling to see how they magnified the fine print of her book; now she seemed to have got on the Professor's mental or moral spectacles also, for the faults of these poor stories glared at her dreadfully, and filled her with dismay.

"They *are* trash, and will soon be worse than trash if I go on; for each is more sensational than the last. I've gone blindly on, hurting myself and other people, for the sake of money; I know it's so, for I can't read this stuff in sober earnest without being horribly ashamed of it; and what *should* I do if they were seen at home, or Mr. Bhaer got hold of them?"

Jo turned hot at the bare idea, and stuffed the whole bundle into her stove, nearly setting the chimney afire with the blaze.

"Yes, that's the best place for such inflammable nonsense; I'd better burn the house down, I suppose, than let other people blow themselves up with my gunpowder," she thought, as she watched the "Demon of the Jura" whisk away, a little black cinder with fiery eyes.

But when nothing remained of all her three months' work except a heap of ashes, and the money in her lap, Jo looked sober, as she sat on the floor, wondering what she ought to do about her wages.

"I think I haven't done much harm *yet*, and may keep this to pay for my time," she said, after a long meditation, adding impatiently, "I almost wish I hadn't any conscience, it's so inconvenient. If I didn't care about doing right, and didn't feel uncomfortable when doing wrong, I should get on capitally. I can't help wishing sometimes, that father and mother hadn't been so particular about such things."

Ah, Jo, instead of wishing that, thank God that "father and mother *were* particular," and pity from your heart those who have no such guardians to hedge them round with principles which may seem like prison-walls to impatient youth, but which will prove sure foundations to build character upon in womanhood.

Jo wrote no more sensational stories, deciding that the money did not pay for her share of the sensation; but, going to the other extreme, as is the way with people of her stamp, she took a course of Mrs. Sherwood, Miss Edgeworth, and Hannah More;[9] and then produced a tale which might have been more properly called an essay or a sermon, so intensely moral was it. She had her doubts about it from the beginning; for her lively fancy and girlish romance felt as ill at ease in the new style as she would have done masquerading in the stiff and cumbrous costume of the last century. She sent this didactic gem to several markets, but it found no purchaser; and she was inclined to agree with Mr. Dashwood, that morals didn't sell.

Then she tried a child's story, which she could easily have disposed of if she had not been mercenary enough to demand filthy lucre for it. The only person who offered enough to make it worth her while to try

---

[9] *Mrs. Sherwood . . . Hannah More:* Mary Martha Sherwood (1775–1851), English author of children's books; Maria Edgeworth (1767–1849), Irish novelist; Hannah More (1745–1833), English playwright and religious writer, known for being a bluestocking.

juvenile literature was a worthy gentleman who felt it his mission to convert all the world to his particular belief. But much as she liked to write for children, Jo could not consent to depict all her naughty boys as being eaten by bears or tossed by mad bulls, because they did not go to a particular Sabbath-school, nor all the good infants, who did go, as rewarded by every kind of bliss, from gilded gingerbread to escorts of angels, when they departed this life with psalms or sermons on their lisping tongues. So nothing came of these trials; and Jo corked up her inkstand, and said, in a fit of very wholesome humility, —

"I don't know anything; I'll wait till I do before I try again, and, meantime, 'sweep mud in the street,' if I can't do better; that's honest, at least;" which decision proved that her second tumble down the bean-stalk had done her some good.

While these internal revolutions were going on, her external life had been as busy and uneventful as usual; and if she sometimes looked serious or a little sad no one observed it but Professor Bhaer. He did it so quietly that Jo never knew he was watching to see if she would accept and profit by his reproof; but she stood the test, and he was satisfied; for, though no words passed between them, he knew that she had given up writing. Not only did he guess it by the fact that the second finger of her right hand was no long inky, but she spent her evenings downstairs now, was met no more among newspaper offices, and studied with a dogged patience, which assured him that she was bent on occupying her mind with something useful, if not pleasant. . . .

ANNIE FIELDS

From Life and Letters of Harriet Beecher Stowe

Annie Fields (1834–1915) was thrown into the New England literary community by way of her husband, James Thomas Fields, a partner in the publishing house of Ticknor and Fields and editor of the *Atlantic*. James Fields was one of the most powerful publishers in the United States in the mid-nineteenth century, and Annie became the center of a kind of literary salon in New England, conversing with virtually all the major and minor writers of the day. These literary friendships became the basis of her best-known works, her books of literary reminiscence. Among these is *Life and Letters of Harriet Beecher Stowe* (Boston: Houghton, 1897). In the following passage, Fields highlights the difficulties Stowe faced as a professional writer attempting to support her family while attending to the never-ending domestic duties required of a nineteenth-century middle-class woman.

One of her friends at this time was anxious to get her to finish a story she had partly written, and for the conclusion of which the editor was waiting. This friend's account of difficulties is amusing, because both the ladies chose to be amused, and carried the matter off in such a humorous vein; but it easily has another side, when we consider Mrs. Stowe's health, and the work which lay before her.

"'Come, Harriet,' said I," wrote her friend, "as I found her tending one baby and watching two others just able to walk, 'where is that piece for the "Souvenir" which I promised the editor I would get from you and send on next week? You have only this one day left to finish it, and have it I must.'

"'And how will you get it, friend of mine?' said Harriet. 'You will at least have to wait till I get house-cleaning over and baby's teeth through.'

"'As to house-cleaning, you can defer it one day longer; and as to baby's teeth, there is to be no end to them, as I can see. No, no; to-day that story must be ended. There Frederick has been sitting by Ellen and saying all those pretty things for more than a month now, and she has been turning and blushing till I am sure it is time to go to her relief. Come, it would not take you three hours at the rate you can write to finish the courtship, marriage, catastrophe, éclaircissement, and all; and this three hours' labor of your brains will earn enough to pay for all the sewing your fingers could do for a year to come. Two dollars a page, my dear, and you can write a page in fifteen minutes! Come, then, my lady housekeeper, economy is a cardinal virtue; consider the economy of the thing.'

"'But, my dear, here is a baby in my arms and two little pussies by my side, and there is a great baking down in the kitchen, and there is a "new girl" for "help," besides preparations to be made for house-cleaning next week. It is really out of the question, you see.'

"'I see no such thing. I do not know what genius is given for, if it is not to help a woman out of a scrape. Come, set your wits to work, let me have my way, and you shall have all the work done and finish the story, too.'

"'Well, but kitchen affairs?'

"'We can manage them, too. You know you can write anywhere and anyhow. Just take your seat at the kitchen table with your writing weapons, and while you superintend Mina, fill up the odd snatches of time with the labors of your pen.'

"I carried my point. In ten minutes she was seated; a table with flour, rolling-pin, ginger, and lard on one side, a dresser with eggs, pork, and beans, and various cooking utensils on the other, near her an oven heating, and beside her a dark-skinned nymph, waiting orders.

"'Here, Harriet,' said I, 'you can write on this atlas in your lap; no matter how the writing looks, I will copy it.'

"'Well, well,' said she, with a resigned sort of amused look. 'Mina, you may do what I told you, while I write a few minutes, till it is time to mould up the bread. Where is the inkstand?'

"'Here it is, close by, on the top of the tea-kettle,' said I.

"At this Mina giggled, and we both laughed to see her merriment at our literary proceedings.

"I began to overhaul the portfolio to find the right sheet.

"'Here it is,' said I. 'Here is Frederick sitting by Ellen, glancing at her brilliant face, and saying something about "guardian angel," and all that — you remember?'

"'Yes, yes,' said she, falling into a muse, as she attempted to recover the thread of her story.

"'Ma'am, shall I put the pork on the top of the beans?' asked Mina.

"'Come, come,' said Harriet, laughing. 'You see how it is. Mina is a new hand and cannot do anything without me to direct her. We must give up the writing for to-day.'

"'No, no; let us have another trial. You can dictate as easily as you can write. Come, I can set the baby in this clothes-basket and give him some mischief or other to keep him quiet; you shall dictate and I will write. Now, this is the place where you left off: you were describing the scene between Ellen and her lover; the last sentence was, "Borne down by the tide of agony, she leaned her head on her hands, the tears streamed through her fingers, and her whole frame shook with convulsive sobs." What shall I write next?'

"'Mina, pour a little milk into this pearlash,'[1] said Harriet.

.   .   .   .

"'Here,' said I, 'let me direct Mina about these matters, and write a while yourself.'

---

[1] *pearlash:* A refined potash, calcium carbonate.

"Harriet took the pen and patiently set herself to the work. For a while my culinary knowledge and skill were proof to all Mina's investigating inquiries, and they did not fail till I saw two pages completed.

"'You have done bravely,' said I, as I read over the manuscript; 'now you must direct Mina a while. Meanwhile dictate and I will write.'

"Never was there a more docile literary lady than my friend. Without a word of objection she followed my request.

"'I am ready to write,' said I. 'The last sentence was: "What is this life to one who has suffered as I have?" What next?'

"'Shall I put in the brown or the white bread first?' said Mina.

"'The brown first,' said Harriet.

"'What is this life to one who has suffered as I have?'" said I.

"Harriet brushed the flour off her apron and sat down for a moment in a muse. Then she dictated as follows: —

"'"Under the breaking of my heart I have borne up. I have borne up under all that tries a woman, — but this thought, — oh, Henry!"'

"'Ma'am, shall I put ginger into this pumpkin?' queried Mina.

"'No, you may let that alone just now,' replied Harriet. She then proceeded: —

"'"I know my duty to my children. I see the hour must come. You must take them, Henry; they are my last earthly comfort."'

"'Ma'am, what shall I do with these egg-shells and all this truck here?' interrupted Mina.

"'Put them in the pail by you,' answered Harriet.

"'"They are my last earthly comfort,'" said I. 'What next?'

"She continued to dictate: —

"'"You must take them away. It may be — perhaps it *must* be — that I shall soon follow, but the breaking heart of a wife still pleads, 'a little longer, a little longer.'"'

"'How much longer must the gingerbread stay in?' inquired Mina.

"'Five minutes,' said Harriet.

"'"A little longer, a little longer,'" I repeated in a dolorous tone, and we burst into a laugh.

"Thus we went on, cooking, writing, nursing, and laughing, till I finally accomplished my object. The piece was finished, copied, and the next day sent to the editor."

Bibliography

This bibliography is divided into two parts, "Works Cited" and "Suggestions for Further Reading." The first part contains all primary and secondary works quoted or discussed in the general or chapter introductions. The second part is a selective list of materials that will be useful to students who want to know more about Rebecca Harding Davis's life and culture or are interested in reading some of the major critical studies of her work. In addition to biographical and critical works, this list includes suggestions for further reading in the four areas covered by the historical documents in Part Two: work and class, social reform, art and artists, and women and writing. With one or two exceptions, a book or article that appears in "Works Cited" is not recorded again under "Suggestions for Further Reading." Thus, both lists should be consulted.

WORKS CITED

Davis, Rebecca Harding. *Bits of Gossip*. Boston: Houghton, 1904.
Franklin, Benjamin. *Writings*. Ed. J.A. Leo Lemay. New York: Library of America, 1987.
Gilbert, Sandra M., and Susan Gubar. *The Madwoman in the Attic: The Woman Writer and the Nineteenth-Century Literary Imagination*. New Haven: Yale UP, 1979.

Grimké, Angelina E. "Appeal to the Christian Women of the South." *The Anti-Slavery Examiner* 1.2 (1836): 1–36.

Howells, William Dean. *Criticism and Fiction and Other Essays.* Ed. Clara M. Kirk and Rudolf Kirk. New York: New York UP, 1959.

———. *The Rise of Silas Lapham.* Boston: Houghton, 1957.

Jefferson, Thomas. *The Writings of Thomas Jefferson.* Ed. Andrew A. Lipscomb. Vol. 15. Washington, D.C.: Thomas Jefferson Memorial Association, 1904.

Johnson, Edward. *Johnson's Wonder-Working Providence.* Ed. J. Franklin Jameson. New York: Scribner's, 1910.

Kaplan, Amy. *Social Construction of American Realism.* Chicago: U of Chicago P, 1988.

Mather, Cotton. *Bonifacius: An Essay Upon the Good.* Ed. David Levin. Cambridge: Belknap, 1966.

Mintz, Steven. *Moralists and Modernizers: America's Pre-Civil War Reformers.* Baltimore: Johns Hopkins UP, 1995.

Pattee, Fred Lewis. *The Feminine Fifties.* New York: Appleton, 1940.

Riis, Jacob. *How the Other Half Lives.* New York: Dover, 1971.

Spiller, Robert, ed. *Literary History of the United States.* Vol. 2. New York: Macmillan, 1948.

Thoreau, Henry David. "Paradise (To Be) Regained." *The United States Magazine and Democratic Review.* Nov. 1843. n. pag.

———. *The Portable Thoreau.* Ed. Carl Bode. Rev. ed. New York: Viking, 1975.

Winthrop, John. *Winthrop's Journal: "History of New England,"* *1630–1649.* Vol. 2. Ed. James Kendall Hosmer. New York: Scribner's, 1908.

Zinn, Howard. *A People's History of the United States.* New York: Harper, 1990.

SUGGESTIONS FOR FURTHER READING

Bibliographies on Rebecca Harding Davis

Harris, Sharon M. "Rebecca Harding Davis (1831–1910): A Bibliography of Secondary Criticism, 1958–1986." *Bulletin of Bibliography* 45 (1988): 233–46.

Rose, Jane Atteridge. "A Bibliography of Fiction and Non-Fiction by Rebecca Harding Davis." *American Literary Realism* 22.3 (1990): 67–86.

Biographies

Beer, Thomas. *The Mauve Decade: American Life at the End of the Nineteenth Century*. New York: Knopf, 1926.

Downey, Fairfax. "Portrait of a Pioneer." *Colophon* 12 (1932): n. pag.

Langford, Gerald. *The Richard Harding Davis Years: A Biography of a Mother and Son*. New York: Holt, 1961.

Olsen, Tillie. "A Biographical Interpretation." *Life in the Iron Mills*. By Rebecca Harding Davis. New York: Feminist, 1972. 69–174.

Pfaelzer, Jean. "Legacy Profile: Rebecca Harding Davis (1831–1910)." *Legacy: A Journal of American Women Writers* 7.2 (1990): 39–45.

Rose, Jane Atteridge. *Rebecca Harding Davis*. New York: Twayne, 1993.

Critical Studies

Austin, James. "Success and Failure of Rebecca Harding Davis." *Midcontinent American Studies Journal* 3 (1962): 44–46.

Boudreau, Kristin. "'The Woman's Flesh of Me': Rebecca Harding Davis's Response to Self-Reliance." *American Transcendental Quarterly* 6.2 (1992): 132–40.

Buckley, J. F. "Living in the Iron Mills: A Tempering of Nineteenth-Century America's Orphic Poet." *Journal of American Culture* 16.1 (1993): 67–72.

Cohn, Jan. "The Negro Character in Northern Magazine Fiction of the 1860s." *New England Quarterly* 43 (1970): 572–92.

Conron, John. "Assailant Landscapes and the Man of Feeling: Rebecca Harding Davis's *Life in the Iron Mills*." *Journal of American Culture* 3 (1980): 487–500.

Culley, Margaret M. "Van Dreams: The Dream Convention in Some Nineteenth-Century American Women's Fiction." *Frontiers: A Journal of Women's Studies* 1.3 (1976): 94–102.

Duus, Louise. "Neither Saint nor Sinner: Women in Late Nineteenth-Century Fiction." *American Literary Realism* 7 (1974): 276–78.

Goodman, Charlotte. "Portraits of the Artiste Manqué by Three Women Novelists." *Frontiers: A Journal of Women Studies* 5.3 (1980): 57–59.

Harris, Sharon M. *Rebecca Harding Davis and American Realism*. Philadelphia: U of Pennsylvania P, 1991.

———. "Rebecca Harding Davis: A Continuing Misattribution." *Legacy: A Journal of American Women Writers* 5.1 (1988): 33–34.

———. "Rebecca Harding Davis: From Romanticism to Realism." *American Literary Realism* 21.2 (1989): 4–20.

———. "Redefining the Feminine: Women and Work in Rebecca Harding Davis's 'In the Market.'" *Legacy: A Journal of American Women Writers* 8.2 (1992): 118–32.

Hesford, Walter. "Literary Contexts of 'Life in the Iron-Mills.'" *American Literature* 49 (1977–78): 70–85.

Hood, Richard A. "Framing a 'Life in the Iron Mills.'" *Studies in American Fiction* 23 (1995): 73–84.

Lang, Amy Schrager. "Class and the Strategies of Sympathy." *The Culture of Sentiment: Race, Gender, and Sentimentality in Nineteenth-Century America.* Ed. Shirley Samuels. New York: Oxford UP, 1992. 128–49.

Lasseter, Janice Milner. "'Boston in the Sixties': Rebecca Harding Davis's View of Boston and Concord during the Civil War." *The Concord Saunterer* 3 (1995): 64–86.

Malpezzi, Frances M. "Sisters in Protest: Rebecca Harding Davis and Tillie Olsen." *RE: Artes Liberales* 12.2 (1986): 1–9.

Molyneaux, Maribel W. "Sculpture in the Iron Mills: Rebecca Harding Davis's Korl Woman." *Women's Studies* 17 (1990): 157–77.

Pattee, Fred Lewis. *Development of the American Short Story: An Historical Overview.* 1923. New York: Biblio, 1996.

Pfaelzer, Jean. "Domesticity and the Discourse of Slavery: 'John Lamar' and 'Blind Tom' by Rebecca Harding Davis." *ESQ: A Journal of the American Renaissance* 38.1 (1992): 31–56.

———. "Rebecca Harding Davis: Domesticity, Social Order, and the Industrial Novel." *International Journal of Women's Studies* 4 (1981): 234–44.

———. "The Sentimental Promise and the Utopian Myth: Rebecca Harding Davis's 'The Harmonists' and Louisa May Alcott's 'Transcendental Wild Oats.'" *American Transcendental Quarterly* 3 (1989): 85–99.

———. "Subjectivity as Feminist Utopia." *Utopian and Science Fiction by Women: Worlds of Difference.* Eds. Jane L. Donawerth and Carol A. Kolmerten. Syracuse: Syracuse UP, 1994. 93–106.

Quinn, Arthur Hobson. *American Fiction: An Historical Survey.* New York: Appleton, 1936.

Rose, Jane Atteridge. "The Artist Manqué in the Fiction of Rebecca Harding Davis." *Writing the Woman Artist: Essays on Poetics, Politics, and Portraiture.* Ed. Suzanne W. Jones. Philadelphia: U of Pennsylvania P, 1991. 155–74.

————. "Images of Self: The Example of Rebecca Harding Davis and Charlotte Perkins Gilman." *English Language Notes* 29.4 (1992): 70–78.

————. "Reading 'Life in the Iron-Mills' Contextually: A Key to Rebecca Harding Davis's Fiction." *Conversations: Contemporary Critical Theory and the Teaching of Literature.* Eds. Charles Moran and Elizabeth F. Penfield. Urbana: National Council of Teachers of English, 1990. 187–99.

Scheiber, Andrew J. "An Unknown Infrastructure: Gender, Production, and Aesthetic Exchange in Rebecca Harding Davis's 'Life in the Iron-Mills.'" *Legacy: A Journal of American Women Writers* 11.2 (1994): 101–17.

Seltzer, Mark. "The Still Life." *American Literary History* 3 (1991): 455–86.

Shurr, William H. "'Life in the Iron-Mills': A Nineteenth-Century Conversion Narrative." *American Transcendental Quarterly* 5 (1991): 245–57.

Tichi, Cecelia. *New World, New Earth: Environmental Reform in American Literature from the Puritans through Whitman.* New Haven: Yale UP, 1979.

Yellin, Jean Fagan. "The 'Feminization' of Rebecca Harding Davis." *American Literary History* 2 (1990): 203–19.

On Work and Class

Blumin, Stuart M. *The Emergence of the Middle Class: Social Experience in the American City, 1760–1900.* New York: Cambridge UP, 1989.

Bromell, Nicholas K. *By the Sweat of the Brow: Literature and Labor in Antebellum America.* Chicago: U of Chicago P, 1993.

Burke, Martin J. *The Conundrum of Class: Public Discourse on the Social Order in America.* Chicago: U of Chicago P, 1995.

Curtis, Susan. *A Consuming Faith: The Social Gospel and Modern American Culture.* Baltimore: Johns Hopkins UP, 1991.

Dimock, Wai Chee, and Michael T. Gilmore. *Rethinking Class: Literary Studies and Social Formations.* New York: Columbia UP, 1994.

Gutman, Herbert G. et al., eds. *Who Built America: Working People and the Nation's Economy, Politics, Culture, and Society.* 2 vols. New York: Pantheon, 1989.

Hawke, David Freeman. *Nuts and Bolts: A History of American Technology, 1776–1860.* New York: Harper, 1988.

Horsman, Reginald. *Race and Manifest Destiny: The Origins of American Racial Anglo-Saxonism.* Cambridge and London: Harvard UP, 1981.

"Industries, Extraction and Processing." *The New Encyclopedia Britannica: Macropaedia.* Vol. 21. 385–528.

Kasson, John. *Civilizing the Machine: Technology and Republican Values in America.* New York: Penguin, 1977.

Keir, Malcom. *The Epic of Industry.* New Haven: Yale UP, 1926.

Marcus, Alan I., and Howard Segal. *Technology in America: A Brief History.* San Diego: Harcourt, 1989.

Rodgers, Daniel T. *The Work Ethic in Industrial America.* Chicago: U of Chicago P, 1974.

Roediger, David. *The Wages of Whiteness: Race and the Making of the American Working Class.* New York: Verso, 1991.

Samuels, Shirley, ed. *The Culture of Sentiment: Race, Gender, and Sentimentality in Nineteenth-Century America.* New York: Oxford UP, 1992.

Wilentz, Sean. *Chants Democratic: New York City and the Rise of the American Working Class, 1788–1850.* New York: Oxford UP, 1984.

Zinn, Howard. *A People's History of the United States, 1492–Present.* Rev. Ed. New York: Harper, 1995.

On Social Reform

Abzug, Robert H. *Cosmos Crumbling: American Reform and the Religious Imagination.* New York: Oxford UP, 1994.

Davis, David Brion, ed. *Antebellum Reform.* New York: Harper, 1967.

Freedman, Estelle B. *Their Sisters' Keepers: Women's Prison Reform in America, 1830–1930.* Ann Arbor: U of Michigan P, 1981.

Kasson, John F. *Rudeness and Civility.* New York: Hill, 1990.

Mintz, Steven. *Moralists and Modernizers: America's Pre-Civil War Reformers.* Baltimore: Johns Hopkins UP, 1995.

Tichi, Cecelia. *New World, New Earth: Environmental Reform in American Literature from the Puritans to Whitman.* New Haven: Yale UP, 1979.

Walters, Ronald G. *American Reformers, 1815–1860.* New York: Hill, 1978.

On Art and Artists

Craven, Wayne. *Sculpture in America.* New York: Crowell, 1968.

Fryd, Vivien Green. *Art and Empire: The Politics of Ethnicity in the United States Capitol, 1815–1860.* New Haven and London: Yale UP, 1992.

Kasson, Joy S. *Marble Queens and Captives: Women in Nineteenth-Century American Sculpture.* New Haven and London: Yale UP, 1990.

Vance, William L. *America's Rome*. Vol. 1. New Haven and London: Yale UP, 1989.

On Women and Writing

Baym, Nina. *Feminism and American Literary History*. New Brunswick: Rutgers UP, 1992.

Conrad, Susan Phinney. *Perish the Thought: Intellectual Women in Romantic America, 1830–1860*. New York: Oxford UP, 1976.

Davidson, Cathy N., and Linda Wagner-Martin, eds. *The Oxford Companion to Women's Writing in the United States*. New York: Oxford UP, 1995.

Gilbert, Sandra M., and Susan Gubar. *The Madwoman in the Attic: The Woman Writer and the Nineteenth-Century Literary Imagination*. New Haven: Yale UP, 1979.

Hedrick, Joan D. *Harriet Beecher Stowe*. New York: Oxford UP, 1994.

Kelley, Mary. *Private Woman, Public Stage: Literary Domesticity in Nineteenth-Century America*. New York: Oxford UP, 1984.

Pattee, Fred Lewis. *The Feminine Fifties*. New York: Appleton, 1940.

Tomkins, Jane. *Sensational Designs: The Cultural Work of American Fiction*. New York: Oxford UP, 1985.

Acknowledgments

Andrew Carnegie, excerpts from *The Gospel of Wealth and Other Timely Essays,* edited by Edward C. Kirkland (1962), reprinted by permission of Harvard University Press.

James Jackson Jarves, excerpts from *The Art-Idea,* edited by Benjamin Rowland, Jr. (1960), reprinted by permission of Harvard University Press.

Material from *The Letters, 1853–1856,* volume 17 of the Centenary Edition of *The Works of Nathaniel Hawthorne,* is reprinted by permission. Copyright 1987 by the Ohio State University Press. All rights reserved.

Reese E. Lewis, "March of the Rolling-Mill Men"; Felix O'Hare, "The Shoofly"; and Anonymous, "In Soho on Saturday Night" are reprinted from *Pennsylvania Songs and Legends,* edited by George Korson. Copyright 1949. Pp. 380–82, 432–33, and 447–48. Reprinted by permission of the Johns Hopkins University Press.

Excerpts from Herman Melville, *The Piazza Tales and Other Prose Pieces, 1839–1860.* Edited by Harrison Hayford, Alma A. MacDougall, and G. Thomas Tanselle. Evanston and Chicago: Northwestern UP and the Newberry Library, 1987. Vol. 9 of *The Writings of Herman Melville.* Harrison Hayford, Hershel Parker, G. Thomas Tanselle, gen. eds. 15 vols. 1968–1989.